Holding Her Hand

Sylvia Mintz

SYLVIA MINTZ

ARCHWAY
PUBLISHING

Archway Publishing books may be ordered through booksellers or by contacting:

Archway Publishing
1663 Liberty Drive
Bloomington, IN 47403
www.archwaypublishing.com
1-(888)-242-5904

ISBN: 978-1-4808-1171-3 (sc)
ISBN: 978-1-4808-1169-0 (hc)
ISBN: 978-1-4808-1170-6 (e)

Library of Congress Control Number: 2014918643

Printed in the United States of America.

Archway Publishing rev. date: 10/27/2014

Contents

Chapter One
LABOR DAY, 1961

5:30 A.M.

*V*ALERIE SAT LOOKING straight ahead, one hand on her enormous belly and the other braced on the dash of the truck. Although she wasn't complaining and was trying not to show any signs of discomfort, it was obvious she was in pain.

Val, as Daniel like to call her, let out a slow breath as the contraction eased off and then asked the question she had been asking for months—one last time. "So what have you decided for the boy's name?"

When Daniel didn't answer right away, it was more than Val could take. "Daniel, you promised! I picked out a girl's name. You're responsible for the boy's name. Davis will be the middle name after my side of the family. All you had to do was pick out his first name. We even narrowed it down to a biblical name. How much more help do you need? What if it's a boy? Should I just say his father needs more time? 'We'll get back to you'?"

When another contraction hit, Val pressed harder on the dash. A bead of sweat trickled down the side of her face. She knew Daniel's body was probably tightening up right along with hers. As they rounded the Appleton courthouse, two blocks from the clinic, Daniel said, "Kind of funny you going into to labor on Labor Day, huh?"

Val sensed the nervousness in his voice. "Yeah, first day of dove hunting season too. I wonder what kind of omen that is."

Daniel pulled up to the curb of the Appleton clinic. The building itself was rundown, but they would take good care of her. Daniel got out of the truck, grabbing her bag out of the back, and walked her to the bottom of the steps leading to the main entrance. "Are you sure you don't want me to go in with you?"

"No, I'll be fine. Your mom called and told them I was coming. Someone should be coming out to get me. She'll be here herself, after she drops Will off at your sister's house."

A nurse came out the front door and looked their way. "Are you Mrs. Branch?"

Val nodded. "Yes, that's me." Turning back to Daniel, Val placed a tender hand to the side of his face. She knew he was worried. "I'll be fine."

Daniel kissed her on the cheek and then turned back to the truck. Val watched him hesitate before climbing in. "Nimrod," he said.

Val returned his stare, puzzled.

"Nimrod might get him picked on a bit so, I figured we would just name him Rod. We'll know where the name came from." He opened the door, and as he settled behind the wheel, he said, "Genesis 10:8–9. Look it up." And with that, he winked and drove off.

Val stood there holding onto the rail with one hand and the other placed over her belly. She watched the truck until it turned down a side street and out of sight. Then, with the nurse by her side, she bent over and let out the gut-wrenching scream she'd been holding for Daniel's sake for the last hour.

"That's okay, Mrs. Branch. You just let it all out." Nurse Ann waited for the contraction to pass, and then she gently supported her elbow.

Next, she grabbed Val's bag and slowly helped her up the steps. When inside, she quickly got her into a wheelchair and they made their way down the hall to the reception area. "You still doing okay, Mrs. Branch?"

Val grabbed her arm. "I need a Bible right away!"

Ann patted her hand. "There will be one in the bedside table. I know at times like these it sure does a body good to call upon the Lord. You're going to do just fine though. I'll say a prayer for you myself."

In a matter of minutes, Val was changed into a hospital gown and in her bed. As soon as she was alone, she took the Bible from the nightstand and turned to Genesis 10:8.

She read, "And Cush begat Nimrod: he began to be a mighty one in the earth. He was a mighty hunter before the Lord: wherefore it is said, Even as Nimrod the mighty hunter before the Lord."

Val smiled and whispered to herself, as she closed the book, "He wants a mighty hunter, huh?" Her smile was soon wiped away as another contraction hit.

Daniel and his father sat quietly on stumps, guns lying across their laps at the edge of the cornfield. The hunters had only two birds by their side.

"I guess ya ain't much got ya mind on hunting today, do ya, son?" Edgar nodded and shifted his legs. "Yeah, neither do I." After another long pause, he continued. "Don't tell any of the men folk, but I'm kinda pulling for a little girl this time. Always did like to imagine myself with a little granddaughter hugging my neck and crawling up in my lap, calling me Grandpa."

Daniel smiled at the thought. "That's fine with me. I just want to bring 'em both home safe and healthy." He stared out over the field, still deep in thought. "Val's been after me to give up farming. She likes the idea of a regular paycheck, maybe taking that job at Sears department store." He smiled. "You know how she is, needs everything to be planned out." Daniel glanced back at his dad. "What do you think?"

"I think that's a big decision to make on a day when you're not all worried about other things." Edgar got up and gently patted Daniel on the shoulder. "What'd ya say? Let's give up on hunting for today and head back to the house for a cup of coffee. Just don't tell your ma I drunk a cup this late in the day. She'll tan my hide. Can't enjoy anything around that old woman!"

Daniel nodded and bent down to pick up their birds. "Well, we only got two. Not much of a meal or bragging rights, but I got 'em both with one shot."

Little did he know that at the exact moment of Daniel's monumental, two-bird kill, Val gave birth to twins. Rod Davis, the great and mighty hunter, one with the earth, had arrived. His sister, Carla Marie, came a few minutes later. The doctor joked that she seemed to be allowing enough time for Rod to be taken care of first, before making her appearance.

Chapter Two

TWEETY BIRDS

*W*ILL AND ROD sat side-by-side on the back door steps, BB guns in hand, with a coffee can full of extra ammo between them. They had been shooting at tin cans all morning and other random targets at will. They were surprisingly responsible for their age and never shot at any object not approved by Daniel first. He had been strict on the ground rules when he presented them with their first real guns last Christmas. Val, of course, worried about it but accepted it as a boy's rite of passage into manhood.

Annie Mae came out the door, cup of coffee in hand. "Will, honey, go take this to ya daddy. It ain't but half-full, but you be mindful not to spill it." Will carefully leaned his gun up against the house and gingerly took the cup from Annie Mae. Enough cream had been added to the coffee to give it a smooth mocha color that matched Annie Mae's dark skin.

Daniel and Leroy had been tinkering on the Massey Ferguson all morning and welcomed the break when Will walked up. "Here, Daddy, Annie Mae sent ya some coffee."

Daniel wiped his hands on a greasy rag hanging out his back pocket and accepted the cup.

Leroy looked down at Will. "I reckon she didn't send nothing out here for ole Leroy, did she?"

Will just shrugged his shoulders and climbed up on the wheel of the tractor to check out the engine they were repairing.

Daniel smiled. "You and Annie Mae quarrelling again?"

Leroy shrugged. "You know how it is … Every Monday she got it in for me, and by Wednesday, she got it out of her system."

"I don't think Monday mornings are your problem. I think it's your Saturday nights that's the problem. I know ole Bess here would appreciate it if *somebody* didn't take her for a spin down the highway grinding her gears out once a week, driving like he just rode the Tilt-a-Whirl too many times."

Leroy shook his head. "Naw, naw. If it won't dat, it would be something else I done that gets her riled up." He leaned back with one hand on the small of his back. "Well, I think we done all we can to patch her up, Daniel. New set of spark plugs and she ought to run pretty good."

Daniel knew he was trying to change the subject, so he smiled and ruffled the top of Will's head. "What do ya say 'bout riding up to Millsville with me and Leroy to buy some spark plugs, and maybe a zero bar?" Will nodded and jumped down off the tractor. "Well, run. Take this cup back to Annie Mae and let her know where we're going."

Will took off inside the house and Daniel yelled for Rod. When Rod peeped around the corner of the house, he still had his BB gun in hand. "Ya want to ride up to Millsville with us?"

Rod scrunched up his face and then shook his head. "Nah, I'm gonna stay here and keep practicing my shooting." Cocking his head sideways, he looked at Daniel and asked, "Daddy, is it okay if I shoot the tweety birds in dem pine trees?"

Daniel laughed and gave Leroy a quick wink before he yelled back, "Yeah, son! Shoot all the birds ya want!"

"Why'd you tell him that, Daniel?"

Daniel smiled as he climbed in the truck behind the wheel. "I haven't heard him hit a single tin can since Will stopped shooting. I doubt he can hit a moving target if he can't even hit one sitting still. Won't hurt him to think he could though."

Just then, Will ran out of the house. Annie Mae was close behind, shouting out a list of things to be picked up at the store. Daniel nodded but knew they would forget them. They had a way of getting sidetracked at the store, talking with the other men, sometimes even forgetting to bring home the very thing they went there to buy.

An hour and half later, the men arrived back, Zero bars and spark plugs in hand. Rod jumped up as soon as they rounded the corner of the house. "Daddy! Daddy! Look how many I got!" Daniel looked down beside the step at a pile of at least a dozen birds, including a cardinal and a blue jay.

Rod's smile soon faded. "What's wrong, Daddy? You said it was okay." Daniel didn't reply. Rod's bottom lip began to quiver and a tear slid down the side of his face. Leroy let out slow whistle and shook his head. Will bent down and started examining the pile of feathered creatures, whistling as if in awe.

Almost on cue, Carla appeared at Rod's side from inside the house, just like she always did anytime Rod was upset. Val had told Daniel it was a connection that twins had, but it still amazed them every time it happened. She reached for Rod's hand but was silent. Daniel got down on one knee and looked at the pile of birds, picked up the cardinal, and let out a sigh. "It's okay, Rod. It's not your fault. I should've explained myself better. Ya see, there are some birds that we're not supposed to kill. Like this cardinal and this blue jay. We don't eat those birds. The cardinal is our state bird, which makes it sort of special. You're not supposed to shoot those."

The tears were flowing freely now down Rod's face "I'm s-sorry, D-daddy." He stretched out his arm, still holding the gun, to Daniel. But Daniel held up his hand and waved, shaking his head. "No, son, you go ahead and keep your gun. This was my fault." He ran a hand through his hair and sighed. "You just go back to shooting targets until I can sit with you and explain what you can and can't shoot. Got it?"

Rod sniffed and wiped his nose on the back of his hand that Carla still held.

Carla looked up and asked, "Daddy, can we bury the birds over there beside where we buried Smokey last spring?" She pointed to the edge of the woods, where a single cross made of sticks stood to mark the spot where they buried the family dog.

"Yes, sweetie. You and Rod go get the shovel." Pulling Rod along, they headed off, hand-in-hand, toward the shed.

Daniel stood, shaking his head, and turned to Leroy, who was standing with his hands on his hips, clicking his tongue. "How in the world did he kill all those birds when he couldn't even hit a tin can?"

Will, who was still investigating the mighty kill, looked up at his dad and said, "Oh, Rod wasn't shooting at the cans, Daddy. I was. He was shooting at the labels." Will pointed beyond the lined-up tin cans to where small pieces of paper hung from the tree limbs.

Daniel and Leroy walked over to find that the boys had tied several fishing lines from the tree branches. On each string, they had taken fishing hooks and attached tiny strips of the can labels. The strips of paper fluttered in the breeze. When Daniel examined one, he could see the paper was riddled with BB holes. Rod had been hitting moving targets all morning long. Daniel looked up at Leroy and glanced back to where Rod and Carla were dragging the shovel across the drive toward the house. He shook his head.

Rod, the great and mighty hunter, was indeed, already, an excellent shot—at only five years old.

Chapter Three

OUTHOUSE BLUES

VAL LIFTED THE large metal tub from its hook on the wall. She was glad it was warm enough again to bathe the kids out on the porch. It was not yet warm enough to take the plastic down from the screens, but soon it would be. She enjoyed their screened-in porch, which served as the main entrance to their home. It was large enough for the washing machine, a sink, and an old church pew.

There was everything from shoes, fishing poles, and toys crammed under the pew to randomly scattered nails along open wall space for jackets and other hanging items. Val used the sink to wash everything from summer vegetables and fish the boys brought home from the stream out back to muddy shoes. Their new house would have a proper front porch, which was not as cozy, but Val would have two bathrooms and a utility room. Now that they had settled on a house plan, she could not wait to break ground.

Val was putting the last bucket full of warm water into the tub when Carla bounced onto the porch. She immediately started taking off her clothes, preparing to get into the tub for her nightly bath. Val grabbed the soap and a washcloth she had laid on the pew, handing them to her when she was seated comfortably in the warm water. "Boy, it's a good thing we'll be moving soon, cause you kids are getting way too big to bathe in this tub."

"Mama, we're already too big. I can't even stretch my legs out anymore. I can't wait to take a bath standing up in the rain!"

Val smiled. "It's called a shower," she corrected for the hundredth time. "I hope your brothers are even half as excited. Maybe then I won't have to struggle every night to get them to take a bath."

Val gathered Carla's clothes up off the cement floor and placed them in the washing machine. It would be full by the time everyone else had their bath tonight. Luckily, Annie Mae would do the washing for her the next afternoon while the woman watched Val's kids after school. She was a godsend around the house. Val had asked her a dozen times, making sure she could keep the kids again this summer during the day while they were out of school.

Since she had no family in the area, she really didn't have anyone else to turn to for help. The kids would drive Daniel's mother crazy for more than an hour at a time, even though his dad would love having them. Val didn't take it personally; Daniel had jokingly said she hadn't particularly cared for her own kids when they were this age. Patience was not her virtue, but Daniel's dad had enough for the whole community.

Carla was soaping up with her bar of Dial when she interrupted Val's thoughts. "Mama, what ya thinking about?"

Val looked down at her and smiled, ruffling her curly hair. "Oh, just about everything, I guess. It's been a long day. Do you want me to wash your hair tonight, or do you want to?"

"I can do it, Mama." Carla hesitated and then said, "Do you know what I've been thinking about?"

"Okay, I give up. What's on your mind?"

Carla dipped the rag into the water and then wrung it out over different body parts to rinse off the soap. She looked up and simply said, "Darlene Baker."

Val straightened and raised her eyebrows "Really? Darlene Baker, huh? Now let me see. She's the pretty, blonde girl in your class, right?"

"Mama, she's the prettiest girl in the whole first grade. She lives in Appleton, in a big white house, like the president. She never scribble-scrabbles when we color either. She takes her time and stays in the lines, no matter if she's the last one to finish her picture. I bet she's worn fifteen different dresses so far this year to school, and she has a pair of pants and shorts in every color there is. *Everybody* likes her, Mama."

"She sounds like a very special girl, but why are you thinking about her?"

"Well, she spent the night with another girl last month, Sandra Wells, and now they're best friends at lunch. She still sits at our table, but all they talk about is stuff they did at her house, and I was just wondering if maybe she could come spend the night with me sometime."

Val had turned her down twice now, so she knew that was why Carla didn't wait for a reply but went straight to pleading.

"Mama, she's never been on a school bus because her mama brings her to school, and she's been dying to ride one. She could ride the bus home with me to spend the night and then ride the bus back to school the next day. We don't even have to take her home." Carla's veins stretched tightly in her neck as she pleaded. Her hair, now wet, was clinging to her face and shoulders, giving her the appearance of a wet duck. Val sighed, and instead of saying no, she told Carla she would talk to her dad about it and see what he thought.

Carla jumped up, sloshing water everywhere, including all over Val. She did a quick shake and grabbed the towel Val had been holding in her lap. "Oh thank you, Mama. I can't wait. I know all kinds of fun stuff we can do. She's going to have s-o-o-o much fun." After wrapping the towel around her body, she took off inside the house. As she hit the kitchen door, Val heard her yell, "I'm out of the tub! One of y'all has to go next! Mama's waiting."

Val could hear grumbling coming from both Will and Rod, who were rolling matchbox cars back and forth on the floor by the wood stove. Carla disappeared to her room.

Later that night, when Val crawled into bed, Daniel put his arm around her waist and spooned up against her. "So has Carla already asked you about Darlene Baker coming over to spend the night?" Daniel smiled and told her that she had and that he had told her yes, but only if she agreed.

"Daniel, I just don't know. I am sure she's a fine girl, but I've seen her mama a time or two and she seems a little too ... proper."

Daniel smiled. "Well, that was a nice way to put it. Her husband's all right. Friendly, but in a salesman kind of way. You're right about the mom though. She's a snob, and there ain't no nice way to put it."

Daniel kissed the back of Val's neck. Val responded by pulling Daniel's arm closer. She let out a sigh. "I guess I had to eventually say yes. I just wish she would hold off until we get in the new house. I have a feeling there will be nothing to little Miss Darlene's liking around here, and the boys will definitely have to be on their best behavior for the evening."

Daniel threw his head back like he was offended. "Now what's wrong with how the boys behave?"

Val rolled over to face Daniel. "Nothing's wrong with the boys. I'm just worried about *everything*, I guess. I don't want Carla to get her feelings hurt. She's looking forward to this. It's a big deal."

Daniel began giving Val small kisses on her face and shoulder. "You worry too much. Let the kids be kids and let them grow up and figure out what's what on their own." He pulled Val closer and gave her a deep kiss. The conversation was over for the night.

Carla and Darlene had giggled all day. The teacher had quieted them several times, and when the bell rang at the end of the day, the girls were the first ones to their cubbies, grabbing their jackets along with Darlene's suitcase. It was a pink triangle-shaped case trimmed in black, with a fuzzy, white poodle in the middle. It was the prettiest thing Carla had ever seen. It looked just like something her Barbie doll would have.

After getting their things and giggling even more, they headed for the bus. Carla led the way and Darlene followed. Carla climbed the steps up into the bus and turned around to grab Darlene's suitcase. It seemed Darlene was used to being taken care of and allowed her friend to take the bag.

Once inside, Carla picked out a seat on the right side of the bus, about three rows back, a perfect location in her mind. They settled down in their seat and the other kids piled in one-by-one. When Will and Rod appeared, Carla stood up and grabbed them by the arm. "Will, this is Darlene. She's coming home with me."

Will appeared distracted when he looked at Darlene. "Oh yeah. Hey," he said as he went on his way.

Expecting more from Rod, Carla practically stood in front of him in the aisle and again pointed to Darlene. "Rod, this is Darlene. She's coming home with us." Rod smiled, looking bashfully, and cocked his head a little to one side. "Hey," he said as he nudged past. Carla was more than a little disappointed in their lack of enthusiasm.

Rod's sweet smile seemed to be enough for Darlene though, because as soon as Carla sat back down, she leaned over and whispered, "They're cute, especially Rod."

Carla, relieved that she had passed the first test, sighed. "Yeah, I guess. Rod's in the other first grade class: Ms. Poindexter's. We're twins, but not the look-alike kind."

Darlene's eyes got wide, as though hearing a huge secret. "Wow, I never knew anybody that was a twin that didn't look alike, and y'all are not even both girls."

The rest of the ride home was filled with more laughter, as Carla pointed out different points of interest along the way. Darlene had traveled down Highway 46 many times with her family; going to Raleigh to shop or visit her dad at work, but she said she had never really paid much attention to the scenery. They made several stops along the way, letting off different children. Darlene stretched her neck to watch each one depart. When they passed Millsville Store, Darlene remarked that she had stopped there several times with her family to get gas and a Pepsi or snack. The girls laughed at the possibility of them both being in the store at the same time. Right after they passed Millsville, Carla pointed at the long dirt drive where her grandparents lived. "Right behind their house is where we're going to build our new house. They're almost ready to start."

After only a few miles, they were home. Carla led the way, helping Darlene with her suitcase. Rod and Will were close behind, and as soon as their feet hit the driveway, they barreled past, leaving nothing but a trail of dust. The girls took their time, and when Darlene got her first look at the rented blockhouse the Branch family called home, her only comment was "It is small, but cute."

Carla exhaled, lugging her book satchel and Darlene's suitcase. "Yeah, the house we're building is like three times bigger."

When the girls stepped onto the porch, Annie Mae met them at the kitchen door. "You girls get on in here and wash ya hands before these two hungry boys eat all the pound cake." Remembering her manners, Carla turned to Darlene, holding her palm out to Annie Mae, and said, "Darlene, this is Annie Mae. Annie Mae, this is Darlene Baker."

Annie Mae looked her over with her hands still on her hips and with only a nod said, "Nice to meet ya, Ms. Darlene. Now if you want some pound cake, I suggest you wash up on the porch sink there." The girls laid their bags and books down on the pew and turned to the sink to wash up as instructed.

When Annie Mae was safely back inside the kitchen, Darlene looked over at Carla and whispered, "My mom has help too, but she doesn't go to work like your mom. She says you have to stay home to watch over the help or they'll rob you blind."

Carla raised her eyebrows. "Annie Mae would never steal nothing from nobody, especially us. Her daddy's a Baptist preacher, and my momma likes going to her job. She reads everybody's death certificates. She could probably tell ya a million ways to die." Carla frowned. "My daddy doesn't like that part. He says it makes her scared of too many things."

After washing up, the girls sat down and enjoyed a slice of chocolate pound cake and a glass of milk. The boys had wolfed their cake down and were already outside. Annie Mae cleaned up the boys' plates and headed to the porch to start on the laundry already in the machine. When the girls finished, Carla grabbed Darlene's bag and led her through the house.

Next to the kitchen was the small den. To the left of the den was a doorway that led to her parents' bedroom, and at the back of the den was another doorway that led to two small bedrooms for the boys and Carla. Walking through the den, Carla pointed out her parents' room and headed to her own. Darlene seemed to take it all in but gave no indications of approval or distain.

In her bedroom, Carla started bringing out all her dolls for the girls to choose from. They had already decided to play school and needed to put the dolls in place for the classroom set-up.

Darlene looked the room over and plopped down on the end of the bed. "Before we start playing, I need to go to the bathroom. Where is it, please?" With a puzzled look she said, "I don't see it."

"Oh," Carla piped in. "Come on. I'll show ya." Carla headed out the bedroom door and Darlene slid off the bed and followed.

Once outside, Carla continued to chatter on about playing school and headed down a worn path to a very small wood shed at the edge of the backyard, practically in the forest. Darlene followed behind quietly until Carla stopped in front of the shed. She grabbed Carla's arm, turning her around just before she opened the door. "Carla, I really need to pee. Let's go back to the house so I can go to the bathroom!" Then her eyes widened and she pinched her nose. "Oh my gosh! What's that terrible smell?"

Carla tilted her head toward the door. "I guess it's the outhouse. It's actually not that bad today. It's worse on hot days." Darlene began to look a little frightened, so Carla continued. "But if you go really fast and hold your nose, it's not a big deal at all, really." Darlene still looked unsure, so Carla said, "Here, I'll go first and make sure there are no spiders or anything in there, and then you can go."

Carla disappeared inside for no more than thirty to forty seconds and then swung the door open for Darlene. "Come on. I checked. It's okay. I can stay in here with you if you want me to. I can even hold your nose for ya."

Darlene stepped up into the small room, holding to the doorframe with white knuckles and the other free hand still pinching her nose. She looked all around the small shed—floor to ceiling—then leaned over just far enough to get a peek down the hole in the bench. "Oh my gosh. It's, it's moving!"

Carla could see the disgust in her friend's face and didn't quite know how to respond. "That's just worms. They won't hurt you."

Darlene backed out the door and instantly turned white. She started running back toward the house. She didn't go very far, however, before she bent over and threw up her pound cake. Carla secretly wished then that she had requested plain pound cake instead of chocolate.

When the retching stopped, she looked up at Carla, who was by her side, and weakly said, "I have to call my daddy to come get me. I- I- I'm sick. I can't stay. I need to call him right now before he leaves work. I have to go home *now*."

Back at the house, Carla stood on the porch while Darlene whispered into the phone receiver placed on a kitchen chair by Annie Mae. When she had finished, Annie Mae took the phone and placed it back on the small table where it normally sat and looked down at Darlene. "Go on now and lay down on the couch until your daddy comes. You plum look as white as new lard." Annie Mae shook her head and mumbled something under her breath as she headed on back to the washing machine.

Darlene did as she was told and crawled up on the couch, curling up on her side into the fetal position. Carla sat down beside her on the floor and looked up at her. "I'm sorry you got sick. Maybe you come can back another day." She quickly looked the other way though. She knew why Darlene had gotten sick and that she would never be coming back to visit. "Well, at least you got to ride the school bus."

Carla glanced back up at Darlene, who nodded and seemed to attempt a smile. "Yeah, that was fun." Then she rolled over to her other side, facing the back of the couch. Carla sat in silence beside her, until Darlene's father came to pick her up.

Will, Rod, and Daniel were standing by the back door, working on a fishing pole propped up against the house, when Mr. Baker pulled up in his shiny, red Ford. Mr. Baker rolled down his window and Daniel headed toward the car, both boys at his side.

"Wow! That's a nice car," Will said, running his hands over the fender. Daniel, who looked a little annoyed, told Will to go in the house and let Darlene know her daddy was here.

Daniel nodded in greeting and announced Darlene would be right out. Rod leaned his head inside the car. "Hey! It's cold inside your car."

Mr. Baker, looking rather smug, said, "That would be my air-conditioner. This baby has all the extras. Just bought it last week."

"What's an air-conditioner?" Rod asked.

Mr. Baker opened his mouth to answer, but Darlene came barreling out of the house. When she opened the car door, Mr. Baker looked over at her sympathetically. "Hey, sweetie. Sorry you got sick. Hopefully, it's not that nasty stomach bug that's been going around. Maybe it's just one of those twenty-four-hour viruses."

Daniel crossed his arms over his chest and said, "I imagine she'll be just fine by the time you get home."

Mr. Baker nodded good-bye to Daniel and the boys and backed up. Rolling his window up, he grunted. "I hate dirt roads. I'll have to rinse the car off as soon as I get home, not to mention wipe down the dash."

As he grumbled on about the dust on his new vehicle, Darlene relieved herself on his new front seat. She evidently had held it in as long as she could.

Chapter Four

FORT SUMMER

VAL WAS STANDING at the kitchen counter, fixing a sandwich to take to work, when Annie Mae arrived. She was out of breath from the walk from her house. It was a good half mile down the old, dirt drive they shared off Highway 46. Marcus barreled in behind her and looked at Val. "They are already down at the fort, Marcus," Val said with a smile. He flew back out, slamming the screen door behind him.

"It amazes me how when they don't have to go to school, the kids are up and gone before I even leave for work. Then when school rolls around, I have to drag them out of bed."

Annie Mae plopped down in a chair at the table, chuckling. "Dat fort they working on keeps 'em boys busy all live-long day. That's for sure. They come running when I ring the lunch bell though. Eat like they plum starving." She shook her head and continued. "Marcus would sure drive Leroy crazy if he was home with him all day. That boy asks a million questions, and after five kids, Leroy just ain't got the patience for it no more. The Lord sho nough almost waited too late to send us that one."

Val laughed, remembering how surprised Annie Mae had been to find out she was pregnant. She thought those days were long gone. Her first child already had a child of his own, so she was a new mama and new grandma. Leroy, of course, strutted around, proud of this major manly accomplishment in his old age. Marcus was a good kid, and being the only child within walking distance, he was a constant in the Branch home.

Val finished bagging her lunch and grabbed her purse to leave. "Sarah will be here soon with Jimmy. She told me yesterday she'd be running late today."

Annie Mae nodded and got up to see Val to the screen door on the porch. She stood there watching until the car made its way down the dusty drive and pulled out on the highway.

Annie Mae started humming and half-singing her favorite gospel tune as she loaded up the old wringer washing machine with clothes. She had pulled a wagon behind her today that held a basket of her own laundry. She was at the Branch house more than her own during the summer, so she just brought her laundry with her and washed it there.

Annie Mae was hanging her clothes out on the line by the time Sarah showed up with Jimmy. When she pulled up, Jimmy hopped out of the car, struggling to hold a large paper bag. He had to shut the car door by leaning against it with his shoulder. He turned around to give his mom his award-winning smile and a good-bye wave, and then he headed straight toward the woods, where he knew the other kids were already working on the fort. He paused long enough when he passed Annie Mae to say good-morning. Sarah waved out the car window to Annie Mae and then backed up, turning her car around. She headed back down the drive.

"Whatcha got in dat bag, Jimmy?" He looked up and said it was stuff for the fort. Marcus had come home digging around in the barn and his room for items as well. Will had told all the kids to find stuff to donate. He was the ringleader of the bunch, but it wasn't because he was the oldest. He was a planner and a thinker by nature. His mind was always working on details for one thing or another. It wouldn't have surprised Annie Mae if he wound up being some big businessman or politician, the way he got kids following orders.

Annie Mae paused and watched Jimmy run until he disappeared in the woods. Jimmy was the only child Sarah and Herman had been given. Sarah had complications with Jimmy and could not have another child. Jimmy was a sweet child but a little slow, and he even slumped forward when he walked. The kids at school picked on him, but the Branch kids never did. Jimmy, being their only cousin, was family and was accepted just like he was because they loved him.

Marcus had made the mistake of ribbing Jimmy about something, or laughing at him when he said something not too bright. Will or Rod had quickly put him in his place. Not that it ever actually bothered Jimmy. He had a forgiving nature and tended to ignore when people made fun of him. Or it could be that he didn't realize they were being cruel.

The fort was nestled in an open area of the woods beside the Branches' rental house. The woods, being mature, kept enough fallen leaves and pine straw on the ground to discourage a lot of weeds. This kept the forest open enough for the kids to run and play. A stream trickled down just a few yards from where their fort was located. The kids often fished there for crawfish and, if they were lucky, an occasional fish. Will explained that it was the perfect location. The stream provided a food and water source for when the enemy attacked and they were barricaded in.

The fort itself was actually four large trees that were almost in a perfect square. A tobacco tarp tied to the lower limbs served as the roof. Dead logs had been laid out and tied to the tree trunks. Although they were only a couple of feet high, they served as boundaries for their pretend structure.

The kids brought junk from home to use for one thing or another. They had a pile of things that Will had yet to decide what their purpose would be, but he assured them everything would eventually be used. A plank hung from low branches at the entrance of the fort, serving as the top of a pretend doorframe that simply said, "FORT."

When Jimmy arrived, Carla was raking leaves away from the front of the fort to make a clearing. She was piling the leaves up around the outside walls. Will, Marcus, and Rod were toting rocks up from the stream and placing them in the clearing to form a circle for a campfire site. Jimmy put his bag down and waited for Will to inform him of today's duties.

Will and Marcus came up from the stream at the same time, bringing rocks with them. Will nodded over to Jimmy and told him to help Marcus roll over two or three logs to put around the fire pit to sit on. "It's almost time for our morning meeting. I want to have it by the fire pit today since it's almost done."

Marcus dropped his rock down next to Rod's then went to help roll the logs. Rod brought his final rock and dropped it down to complete the circle. Will gathered a few small branches to stack in the circle for their first fire, while Rod used a shovel to snap off stray roots sticking up out of the ground. They wouldn't be able to actually build a fire unless Daniel was around, but they wanted to have everything ready.

After the wood was stacked and Marcus and Jimmy had three good-sized logs rolled by the fire pit, Rod called for the morning meeting. Carla and Rod shared one log. Will, being in charge, had a log to himself, and Jimmy and Marcus plopped down on the last log. Will began by saying that now that the fire pit was complete, he would talk to Daniel about having a fire that weekend. "We need to make some sticks to use for roasting marshmallows and hotdogs, so we'll do that this afternoon."

Will kept talking about things they needed to complete on the fort and how they all needed to keep contributing things from home. While he was talking, the gang was enjoying a good rest from all their morning work and listening to every word he said.

The hollow log that Jimmy and Marcus had rolled over and now were sitting on had been the temporary home of a now angry copperhead. After getting its bearings back from its joy ride, it slithered out of the log through a hole on the backside. The snake kept close to the log. No one could see it from where they sat, and since the area had been raked clean of leaves and debris, it didn't make a sound as it maneuvered its way.

As Will continued his morning speech, Jimmy remembered the bag he had brought and jumped up to retrieve it. This made the log gently roll back a few inches. The movement was just enough to make the snake coil up tighter and sit ready to strike.

After fetching his bag, Jimmy plopped back down on the log, still completely unaware of the snake inches away. "I brought some stuff from home today." First, he pulled out two feet of rope, which was always in demand. Then he pulled out an old, copper pot.

Marcus looked at Jimmy and grunted. "Yippee! Another pot with a hole in it," he said as he pointed to the pile of pots Jimmy had already brought.

Will stared Marcus and sternly said, "We can use it." Will then looked over at Jimmy. "Thanks, Jimmy. Like I said before, we'll find a use for everything that's donated. You keep bringing what you can." Jimmy beamed, which made Marcus grunt again. Will's eyes darted back at Marcus, as if it was his final warning.

All Marcus's animated grunting and twitching continued to rock the log. This kept the snake constantly alert and on the move. By now, it was almost to the end of the log and directly behind Marcus.

"I'm hungry," Rod said, as though oblivious to the tiff about the pot. Tilting back slightly and looking up through the tree branches to check the position of the sun, he said, "It should be around noon. Annie Mae will be ringing the bell soon."

Marcus grunted again and reached down to grab the copper pot Jimmy had laid on the ground between them. He shook it in Jimmy's face. "Yeah, next time, why don't you bring something we can at least eat, instead of another stupid pot?"

When Marcus jerked the pot back, it connected with something in midair. Marcus raised his eyebrows and sat up straight. "Huh-Oh."

The snake had made his move, only to be conked in the head with the copper pot. As soon as Rod saw the snake, he jumped into action. "Snake!" Rod sprang the five to six feet that separated them. He still had the shovel across his lap, so with one fluid motion, like a karate expert, he raised it high and thrust it down right below the dazed snake's head. It yielded a fatal blow. He followed with two more blows.

The snake lay pinned to ground by the shovel. It kept moving slightly for several minutes, as snakes always do. Everyone gathered round to investigate the deadly animal.

"Man," Rod said, "a copperhead. A big one too."

Jimmy bent over, staring at the reptile. "How long do you think it is, Rod?"

Rod continued poking the snake with the tip of his foot, watching the snake twitch. "He's a good two and half feet."

Marcus hadn't said a word yet. He was practically in shock, having come so close to being bitten. They stood there in silence for a few seconds, and then Will smiled and looked over at Jimmy. "Well, I guess we found our first use for that copper pot, Jimmy."

Marcus perked up a little then and thrust out his chest, saying, "Yeah, how you like that copper pot, copperhead?"

Now the copper pot was not what had killed the snake. It had only kept it from striking at Marcus, but the phrase stuck. From that day forward, every time Marcus did something worth bragging about, he would puff out his chest and yell, "How you like that copper pot, copperhead?"

Carla kept her distance from the snake and only peeped at it over the boys' shoulders. "I hate snakes." She shuddered once as though to prove her disgust then announced she was going to the house to help Annie Mae get lunch on the table.

Will and Rod left for the stream to rinse off the shovel and gather the other tools they had borrowed from the barn. Will looked over his shoulder. "Y'all go throw that snake away or bury it somewhere."

Marcus and Jimmy stood there, still staring at the snake. "Man, it sure was a good thing I brought that pot, huh, Marcus?"

Marcus rolled his eyes but then nudged Jimmy and said, "Hey, you know who would love this snake?"

Jimmy turned toward Marcus with raised eyebrows "No, who Marcus?"

"Ma would. Rod hasn't killed her no squirrels in a couple of weeks now. She sure would love to fry herself up some fresh snake."

Jimmy's eyes got wider. "Really, y'all eat snakes."

Marcus nodded. "Well, uh, we haven't had it in a long, long time." Then he paused a second to think up what he could actually say without fibbing. "Awh man, our people are from Africa. We eat anything: snakes, monkeys, lizards."

"Let's take it to her then," Jimmy said.

Marcus shook his head. "Na, you take it to her, Jimmy. I mean, it was your pot and all."

Just then, they heard Annie Mae ringing the dinner bell. Rod and Will ran past. Rod, who was in the lead, yelled, "Last one's a rotten egg!"

Marcus finally stood. They had both been bent down with their hands on their knees to stare at the snake. "Well, do what you want to." And he took off toward the house, leaving Jimmy behind to be the rotten egg.

Annie Mae was still waiting at the screen door when Jimmy finally reached the house, carrying a big, metal dishpan. She held the door open for Jimmy. Annie Mae couldn't see what was in the pan because Jimmy had a towel draped over it. "Whatcha got there, Mr. Jimmy?"

Smiling, Jimmy said, "I know you haven't had any squirrel in a while, so I got ya something else to take home and fix."

Annie Mae looked at Jimmy in surprise. "You don't say? Well, now ain't that nice of ya. Well, you go on and wash your hands in the sink and just leave the pan there, so I can dress it later."

Jimmy did as he was told.

Jimmy sat down at his place at the table and Annie Mae asked who would like to say grace. As usual, nobody volunteered, so she blessed the food and they dug in. After lunch, the children were expected to help clear the table, and then they would have a short Bible lesson before Annie Mae made them lie down for a nap. The kids didn't actually go to sleep, but she felt it was important to rest their bodies and their brains for a few minutes every day while their food settled.

The boys always lay on a pallet on the family room floor, and Carla, being the only girl, would lie down on the couch. The kids were there for several minutes with their eyes closed, listening to the birds outside, while Annie Mae was puttering around the kitchen and porch doing her chores. At times, they complained about having to take naps, but in reality, they were usually tired from the morning's hard play and enjoyed the rest.

All of a sudden, Annie Mae let out a holler followed by another. The kids all bolted upright and sat frozen, staring at each other. The commotion continued from the porch as they heard scraping metal, splitting wood, and some indescribable sounds. It sounded like the porch was being ripped from the house.

Will stood and had a straight view out the kitchen window. He could see Annie Mae running up the driveway, leaving nothing but a trail of dust. "Man, look at Annie Mae run! I haven't seen her run that fast since she saw that black snake in the outhouse."

It was all Marcus could do not to burst out laughing.

Jimmy, with a look of concern, turned to Will. "Does she not like snakes?" And then they all turned and stared at Jimmy, with the realization of what he had done. They would all be in trouble. It was going to be big trouble.

Val walked out to the porch when she finished the dishes that night. She was still drying her hands on the dishtowel when she stopped beside Daniel and put her hands on her hips. Daniel had a hammer in one hand and was scratching his head with the other, staring at the big rip in the screen of their porch.

"What I can't figure out is how in the world Annie Mae jumped high enough to go out that window." Daniel nodded toward the door. "Why in the world didn't she just run out the door?"

Val sighed. "I might have done the same thing. Women hate snakes. Always have and always will." She put her hands on her hips. "I've told them kids over and over again about how they need to be careful and watch out for copperheads. They are completely camouflaged in those woods. People come upon those things every day and die. Why, last summer alone—"

Daniel rubbed his temple and mumbled. "Here we go. I knew it was coming." She swatted him with her dishrag. "Well, they do!"

They stood there a couple of more minutes before Val said, "She sat the kids down in the kitchen and preached to them for hour and half." After pausing, she added, "Ya know, it's a wonder she didn't have a heart attack. Did you know that thing was still moving?" Val shuddered. "Not to mention her jumping around like that, at her age. I mean really, Daniel. She could have gotten hurt."

When Val looked back over at Daniel, she could tell he was on the verge of laughter. One scolding look from Val and the dam broke. He began snickering. "Oh, Daniel, please." But it didn't take long for Val to get the same image in her head of Annie Mae jumping around the porch and through the screen to make them both laugh until they cried.

Chapter Five

FOOD FOR THOUGHT

*V*AL WAS WALKING down the hall at church after Sunday school when Carla ran up. "Look what I colored in class, Mama. We had a new box of crayons and they always color the best."

Val took the picture from Carla's hand and pretended to study it closely. "I do believe you did do an outstanding job." As she handed the picture back to her, Carla took off down the hall to go find Daniel or Grandpa, so she could show it off again.

Ms. Patsy, the children's Sunday school teacher, was standing by the class door and smiling when she caught Val's eye. "They are such precious kids, Valerie. Always well behaved."

"Thank you, Patsy. You do a good job with them on Sundays."

Patsy sighed, heavy shaking her head. "I need the patience of Job some days. They're not all so well behaved. Some days, Jackie talks nonstop, and the boys ... Well, some days the boys are just boys."

Val smiled and nodded in agreement.

Patsy put her hand on Val's arm. "And hey, your kids told me today they have all the books of the Bible memorized. I was so impressed that the rest of the class is going to start working on that too."

Val waved her hand and shook her head. "Oh, I can't take any credit for that. Annie Mae has worked with the kids all summer on that. Especially after the snake incident, they have had extra Bible study time every day."

Patsy put her hand to her mouth and snickered. "Yes, the kids told me all about that too."

Patsy turned to go back in the classroom but stopped short, turning back to Val. "Hey, Val, there's something in the bulletin today about the ladies working on that wallpaper in the parsonage next Saturday. Is that right?"

"Yeah. Margaret is having a fit to take that paper down. It's faded and popping up at the seams pretty bad. She doesn't trust the men to have it finished in time for the new pastor." They both smiled. When Margaret wanted something done, she wanted it done right then.

The Branch family was seated at their usual pew on the right hand side and halfway back. There was empty place at both ends, saved for Daniel and Edgar who served as ushers and would not take their place until the offering was collected. Aunt Sarah, Uncle Herman, and Jimmy always sat directly behind them.

The boys would often mix up the order and sit with Jimmy or Jimmy would come up and sit with them. However, this only took place if they kept quiet. Val and Daniel might let a snicker or two slip, but Grandma Margaret didn't abide by any show of disrespect during the service. One look from her would make the kids straighten up in a second. She had never actually spanked any of her grandchildren, but they all knew that she was capable. Daniel and Sarah had shared how they had gotten their share growing up, and it was always from Grandma, not Edgar.

Mr. Leary took his place at the podium after the choir was seated. He began by saying how glad he was to be filing in until the new pastor arrived next month and then went right into announcements. As he began going over them, Carla dropped her hymnal. She had placed it on her lap to use as a makeshift desk so she could write on her bulletin. She slipped down to the floor to retrieve all her lost objects.

Margaret pierced her lips and glared at Val, as if she could somehow control the universe and make paper not rattle or carpets absorb the sound of fallen objects.

So Margaret was rattled when she realized Mr. Leary was looking her way and had asked a question. Mr. Leary held up the note in his hand and repeated, "Do you have an announcement for the ladies concerning next Saturday?"

Trying to regain her composure and look as though she had been paying complete attention, she stood and addressed the church in her usual gruff manner. "Yes. The ladies will be stripping next Saturday at the parsonage beginning at 8:00. It will probably be an all-day affair, so bring yourself a bag lunch."

Half the congregation had not looked at the bulletin yet, so they had no idea that she was actually talking about working on the wallpaper. Snickers could be heard, but Margaret was not fazed as she continued on in a huff. "And *please,* ladies. This is no place for children. The floor is going to get pretty slippery and they will just be in the way."

More snickers could be heard, which drew a stern glance from Margaret. She was almost seated when she abruptly stood back up. "And men," she said with emphasis, "if you want to come help, that's fine, but please don't come if all you plan to do is stand around and watch." And with that, she plopped back down on the pew, oblivious to the humor in her announcement.

Mr. Leary glanced over the congregation, where he could see several people with their heads down, as though any eye contact would trigger the laughter they were suppressing. He cleared his throat, thanked Margaret, and tried to regain order.

As the service continued, Daniel took his place, standing behind his father and Mr. Roscoe, ready to take up the offering. Harold Johnson, who everybody called Punchy, took his place beside Daniel. The four stood reverent with their hands clasp behind their backs, waiting for their cue.

Punchy, who Daniel had known all his life, was always looking for a way to rib him. He leaned over toward Daniel and whispered, "You gonna let Val go to the parsonage next Saturday?"

Daniel glanced over to see the grin across Punchy's face just before they headed toward the front of the church.

After services, Mr. Leary stood at the back of the church, shaking people's hands as they left. Boys ran around the gravel parking lot in front of the church, trying to spend some of the pent-up energy from sitting for the past hour.

While walking down the front steps and holding Carla's hand, Val overheard Margaret talking to her friend, the snooty Ms. Thelma. "Oh, for goodness sake, Thelma, it was in the bulletin. I tell you the truth; I think half the people in this church are not saved sometimes!" Val just smiled to herself and waited at the bottom for Daniel to catch up. As she was standing there, she noticed Mr. Carpenter coming down the steps.

Mr. Carpenter was a man in his midfifties who had lost his wife to cancer a few months earlier. He had one son, Jesse, who was the same age as Will. He seemed to be a quiet boy in church and never smiled much. His mom had always been sick and their world had probably always revolved around helping her.

They lived above the garage Mr. Carpenter owned and operated beside Millsville General Store on Highway 46. They had owned a house at one time, but it was suspected they sold it to help pay medical bills.

She had asked them several times to come over for lunch on Sundays at Daniel's parents' house, but he never accepted. Attempting one more time, she hurried to catch up to them. Carla was in tow. "Mr. Carpenter!" He and Jesse stopped and slowly turned around to face Val.

"I guess I'm going to keep asking until you decide to join us. Won't you and Jesse please join us for lunch today at Margaret and Edgar's?" Carla curiously stared at Jesse's face.

He glanced awkwardly at her then focused on the other boys running around the parking lot. Mr. Carpenter turned his sad eyes to Val. "I appreciate you asking. I really do. But me and Jess are just going to head on home. Maybe another time. Thanks again though, Val." And with that, he simply turned around and left.

Carla stared after them. "Mama, why won't they come? I think they really are hungry."

Val looked down at Carla and said, "I think they are just sad, baby. Maybe they need some more time."

Margaret, Val, and Sarah were gathering up the lunch dishes while Herman, Daniel, and Edgar stayed seated at the table. All three boys were already outside playing, probably at a big gulley in the woods they called Up and Down Hill or the Up and Down for short.

Edgar leaned back, rubbing his belly. "Boy, I sure do hope I don't get a headache this afternoon." Carla looked up at Edgar. "Why, Grandpa?"

He winked. "Cause I done ate so much I don't even have room for an aspirin!"

Carla giggled and Margaret turned, giving Edgar a disapproving look.

"Hey, little girl. Why ain't you outside with them boys, running wild?"

Carla scrunched her face up. "I don't like playing war or shooting games all the time. Plus they never want to play what I want to play." Aunt Sarah turned around and looked at Carla. "It's hard being the only girl. Ain't it, sweetie?"

Margaret gestured toward the table. "Well, you can help get these dishes up. It's about time you started helping in the kitchen."

Val rolled her eyes at the remark but didn't make a comment.

Daniel stretched his arms up in the air and yawned. "Well, I think I'll take a ride up to the store and see what's going on."

Margaret whipped around. "That store shouldn't even be open on Sunday."

Daniel grunted as he got up. "Ah, ma, Mr. Mills ain't doing no business to speak of on Sundays. It's just a place to hang out. He's sure not doing any work."

Carla jumped up and ran to Val. "Oh, Mama, can I fix some food to take to Mr. Carpenter and Jesse? I really do think they're hungry."

Val looked at Carla and smiled. "Why, I think that's a great idea, sweetie."

The ladies excitedly began fixing plates for Carla to take to the Carpenters. Even Margaret commented on how it was good idea and that somebody at the church should be doing more for them. That, of course, was followed by her standard comment of "Why, it wouldn't surprise me if half the people in that church don't make it past St. Peter when the time comes."

With the plates loaded between them, Daniel and Carla got in the truck. Daniel started the engine and looked down at Carla. "Well, little lady, do you want to get on the highway or take the back way down the dirt road?"

She looked up smiling and said, "Let's do both. Take 46 there, so we don't bump the food around, and then coming back, we can go down the dirt road."

Daniel nodded. "Sounds like a plan." They headed out the drive.

When they arrived at the Carpenter's Garage and Millsville Store, Daniel grabbed one wrapped plate and handed the other one to Carla. They climbed the steps behind the garage and knocked on the door to the small apartment where the Carpenters lived. Jesse opened the door but didn't say a word. Daniel asked if his dad was at home, but before the boy could answer, Mr. Carpenter shuffled from around the corner. He looked somewhat surprised, but mostly, Carla thought he looked sad.

The apartment had one open area for the den, kitchen, and dining area. There was a hallway to the left, behind the door that led to two small bedrooms and one bath. Carla went right in, past Jesse and her dad, to set her plate down on the kitchen table. "We brought y'all food. If you've already had lunch, then it can be your supper."

She looked at them both expectantly. Mr. Carpenter was the first to speak. "Well, that's nice of you. We did already eat a couple of biscuits though, so maybe we'll hold off until suppertime."

Jesse looked at his dad. "The biscuits were this morning. We didn't eat no lunch."

Mr. Carpenter nodded more to himself than anybody. "So we did, Jess. I guess I just get forgetful sometimes, especially when it comes to cooking."

Daniel placed his plate down on the table, looking a little uncomfortable, and said, "Yeah, well, uh I've got to run in the store."

He looked down at Carla, but before he could say anything, she piped up. "I'm gonna stay up here a little while, Daddy. Is that okay?" Daniel nodded and told her to come on down when she was ready but not to stay long.

When Daniel left, she looked at Jesse and his dad. "Ain't y'all gonna come eat?" Jesse once again looked at his dad. Mr. Carpenter shrugged and motioned toward the table.

When both were seated and busy unwrapping their meals, Carla plopped down in the empty chair between them. Jesse and Mr. Carpenter bowed their heads while Mr. Carpenter said grace. When he finished, they both looked at her with curiosity but didn't say a word.

In fact, they couldn't, because Carla started talking first and didn't slow down. She talked about everything from the weather, church, and the new preacher coming, to how the boys play at the Up and Down. She suggested that Jesse should come over to play and then changed the subject to school. She talked about *everything*.

The boys were trapped, so they listened and ate. Before they realized it, they had eaten everything on their plates. Satisfied that her mission was accomplished, Carla collected the empty plates and Mr. Carpenter and Jesse saw her to the door. She told them good-bye and they watched her descend the steps.

After he closed the door, Mr. Carpenter looked at Jesse. "I believe that's the talkingest girl I've ever seen."

Jesse nodded in agreement. "Yeah, but that food sure was good. Wasn't it, Dad?"

Mr. Carpenter looked at his son, who was actually smiling. He smiled back with tears almost forming in his eye. "Yes, son. It sure was. Reminded me of ya mama's cooking."

They were quiet for a second and then Jesse continued. "Remembering is kind of good sometimes, ain't it?"

Mr. Carpenter patted him gently on his back. "Yes, it is, son. Yes, it is."

Who knew that all it took was a home-cooked meal and the chatter of a female voice in the Carpenter home to begin the healing of two broken hearts? They had gotten through the days by not feeling anything. Not even hunger.

Their lives were not over. It had just changed drastically, but they had to move on. Mr. Carpenter had to start being there for Jesse. He had promised his wife. Maybe Carla had been sent as his little reminder.

Chapter Six

BOYS, BOYS, BOYS

*A*NNIE MAE SAT with her eyes closed, nodding her head as the children repeated each book of the Bible. She was proud of how quickly they had memorized them in order. Her father was coming sometime soon to visit with the children and she had a mini program planned for him. She wanted the children to recite the books of the Bible and sing the two songs she'd taught them. All the children had beautiful voices and Annie Mae often bragged that they sounded better than the children on *The Sound of Music*.

"Oh, bless my soul, but you children are some kind of smart. My daddy's gonna sure be impressed." The kids smiled, showing pride in their accomplishments. "Now y'all go on and lay down for your nap. Rest them brains a little while before they done get overworked."

They scampered down from their chairs at the kitchen table and went to the den for their naps as told. The boys lay down on the blanket already on the floor, while Carla took her spot on the couch. It wasn't long before everyone was asleep.

Carla rustled in her sleep. She had been lying on her side, facing the back of the couch. When she rolled over, she lazily opened her eyes, blinking them into awareness.

Jimmy and Marcus, who were already awake, were sitting there staring at her. Will and Rod had already left the pallet. Carla sat up and looked at them curiously. She started to question why they were staring when Jimmy blurted out, "We pulled down your panties and saw your butt."

He said this matter-of-factly, as though it was an everyday occurrence. Marcus immediately popped Jimmy on the shoulder with the back of his hand. "Man, what did you tell her for? You won't suppose to say nothing!"

Carla jumped up and stood rigid, letting out a long, high-pitched scream. Jimmy just sat there, still staring at her. Marcus jumped up and shot out the kitchen door without saying a word. Annie Mae was outside getting clothes off the line when she heard all the commotion. She looked up just in time to see Marcus barreling out the screen door. She got her laundry basket and headed inside as quickly as she could.

When she reached Carla, the girl was still standing rigid, but now she had clinched her hands into fists by her side. She was blowing her breath out in big puffs like a freight train. Annie Mae put the basket down. "Goodness, chile, what's the matter with you? I heard you screaming like somebody trying to kill ya, and I finds ya standing there like *you* fixin to kill somebody else."

Annie Mae sat down on the couch beside her, took a hold of Carla's hand, and gently pulled her down on the couch beside her, trying to calm her down. She opened her mouth, about to ask again, when Jimmy volunteered the information. "Marcus and me pulled down her panties to see her butt. I won't suppose to tell her, but I forgot."

Annie Mae gasped and gave Carla a sympathetic look. She put her arm around Carla's shoulders and gave her a squeeze. "Oh, baby. I'm sorry you been done violated like that." She looked down at Jimmy and said, "Now Jimmy, I know Marcus probably put you up to this, and believe you me: that boy will be paying for it when he gets home tonight. But that was wrong what y'all done. That was a violation of Ms. Carla's privacy. Young boys ain't supposed to treat little girls like that. That's why Ms. Carla sleeps on the couch. Looks like I am gonna have to put her clean in another room if y'all can't control your curious minds."

Annie Mae knew Jimmy didn't mean anything by what happened, but he still needed to know what he did was wrong. She took a deep breath and waved her hand to shoo Jimmy out. "Now go on outside with the rest of them boys. Your mama can deal with you tonight." Jimmy got up and ran toward the door, but before he left, he turned around and looked at Carla. "I'm sorry, Carla."

Carla sniffed and nodded her head, although she didn't appear to be ready to accept his apology yet. Before Jimmy took off, he added, "I thought it was going to look different like the front, but it didn't."

Annie Mae squeezed Carla's shoulder, looked down at her again, and took a deep breath. "Now, girl. You just forget all about what them boys done. They just curious is all. Neither one of them boys is around no girls but you. Jimmy ain't got no sisters and Marcus's sisters done been long gone out of my house. Will and Rod done growed up around you and seen you since you was a baby. That's why they ain't got that curious nature." Annie Mae put her finger to her head and tapped it a couple of times as though deep in thought.

"What you need is another girl around here to play with. It ain't good for you to be romping around them woods with them boys all the time." Carla jerked her head up toward Annie Mae and gasped before the smile overtook her face.

Annie Mae patted her leg and got up to her feet. "Come on, now, and help poor Annie get these clothes in. When your mama gets home, we'll talk to her about it." Carla grinned and jumped up. The boys looking at her butt would be worth it if it helped to get a friend here for her to play for the rest of the summer.

That Sunday, as everybody was filing out of church, Val and Carla waited by the car for the boys. Mr. Carpenter and Jesse soon came by, heading toward their car as well. He nodded at Val and thanked her again for sending the plates.

"Oh, you are quite welcome, but won't you come over today and eat it while it's hot this time?" Before he could answer, Carla chirped in, "Or I could bring it to ya again."

Mr. Carpenter glanced over at Jesse, whose eyes had widened at the comment. "Maybe Jesse and me might just do that, Val. Don't want to worry Ms. Carla with hanging around us two ole men watching us eat again." A look of relief flashed across Jesse's face.

Val smiled. "Good. Y'all have time to run home and change out of your Sunday clothes if you want. That way, Jesse can play with the boys when we're done."

Val and Sarah set up a side table in Margaret and Edgar's kitchen for the boys. Carla sat with the adults at the main dinning table. Everyone chatted lightly and was enjoying their meal when Val turned to Carla. "Oh, sweetie, guess what. Somebody actually approached me this morning at church about a little girl close to your age who needs a place to stay this summer, two or three days a week."

Carla's eyes widened. "Who is it, Mama? Is it Karen?"

Val shook her head, so Carla took another guess.

"Is it Jane?" Once again, Val shook her head.

"Oh, I know. Please tell me it's Terrie."

Val shook her head and finished swallowing her mouthful. "No, it's Jackie Walker."

The boys got up and were now standing by the adult table, looking expectantly at Daniel to be excused. Will paused long enough to snicker, look at Carla, and say, "Ooooh, Wacky Jackie."

Carla and Val both shot Will a disapproving look. Will grinned and nudged Rod.

Val turned back to Carla. "She seems like a sweet girl. You like her, don't you, sweetie?"

Carla sighed and slowly said, "She's okay. She's not as much fun as the other girls though, plus she's a chatter box."

Mr. Carpenter and Jesse exchanged a quick look but didn't say a word.

Daniel excused the boys and they made a speedy exit.

"Well," Val continued, "she's coming this week to the house. I agree with Annie Mae. You need a girl you can play with instead of hanging out with the boys all the time."

When Carla didn't look completely sold on the idea, Val continued. "We'll see, sweetie. If you get along and have fun, great. If not, then she doesn't have to come back." Val nodded as if to say it was settled.

As conversations continued, Carla sat silently, wondering if having Wacky Jackie there would really be any better than playing alone or with the boys.

Chapter Seven
WACKY JACKIE

CARLA WAS STILL unsure about Jackie coming, so when she pulled up that day with her mother, Carla didn't go out to meet them. She watched from the screened porch as Annie Mae went out to greet them. They exchanged greetings and Mrs. Walker made what looked like a speedy exit, backing up quickly and spinning gravel and dust everywhere. Annie Mae covered her mouth with her apron and squinted as she waved good-bye and the car rolled down the drive.

She looked Jackie over. "Well now, Ms. Jackie, let's go see if we can find out what Ms. Carla is up to."

When they came onto the porch, Carla just stood there silently. Annie Mae put her hands on hips and, eyeing the girls, said, "Well, I got to get to work, girls. So unless you want to help me peel potatoes, I suggest you go on off and play." With that, Annie Mae headed toward the kitchen, humming and smiling to herself.

The girls stood there looking at each other for a second, then Carla blurted out, "We don't have an inside bathroom, ya know. So if you need to go, you'll have to use the outhouse."

Jackie didn't so much as flinch, which was not what Carla expected. She shrugged nonchalantly and said, "Oh, I've used one before at my grandmother's house, but she also has a pot inside." Carla, not wanting to be outdone, quickly said, "We do too, but if you use it, you'll have to go outside and dump it yourself." They stood there another few seconds, eyeing each other in silence, and then Jackie said, "So do you want to show me your room? Or would you rather go help peel potatoes?"

Carla didn't say a word but slowly started inside. Jackie followed behind, looking around with her nose in the air as they walked through the kitchen. Annie Mae glanced up from where she sat at the kitchen table, peeling potatoes as they paraded by. She kept humming but chuckled to herself when they were out of earshot.

When the girls entered Carla's small bedroom, Jackie inspected it thoroughly, walking around occasionally and picking something up for a closer look. Then she faced Carla. "I like your room. So what would you like to play?"

Carla, feeling somewhat friendlier after receiving the compliment, laughed. "How about school?" Jackie shrugged her shoulders and said, "I guess that's okay, but I want to be the teacher." So Carla proceeded to open her drawer where she kept all her paper, pencils and other school supplies, and the girls began to play with each other.

By the time Annie Mae called them for lunch, Carla was even enjoying herself. Jackie was a little bossy, but not as bad as Will, and she found herself admiring the flamboyant personality.

The girls went to the porch sink and washed for lunch before sitting down at the kitchen table. The boys filed in soon afterward, and they all took their places.

Annie Mae looked at Jackie. "Now, Ms. Jackie, I think you already know Jimmy, Will, and Rod, but this here is Marcus." Motioning toward Marcus, she continued. "This here is Ms. Jackie, Marcus. She's going to be coming over a few days this summer too, so I expect you all to get along."

Jackie looked at Marcus and asked, "So are you related to Annie Mae? I assume you're not related to the Branches."

Marcus snickered. "Yeah, she's my ma."

Jackie glanced at Annie Mae then back at Marcus. "Don't you mean grandma?"

Annie Mae grunted and interrupted by saying, "Everybody, bow your heads now for the blessing." She stared at Jackie evenly as she clasped her hands together. She took a deep breath to help shake off the insult and then went to the Lord in prayer.

The children chatted during their meal and Annie Mae quickly dismissed Jackie's earlier comment. Especially when she seemed to be enjoying the meal and asked for a second helping. Annie Mae always said that if a person asks for seconds, no compliment needs to be expressed.

When the children finished their meal and helped put the dishes in the sink, Jackie turned to Carla. "Come on. Let's go finish our pictures."

Carla looked at her. "Oh, we can't until we do our Bible studies and take a nap."

Jackie's brows went up in surprise "Bible study and a nap? I get enough of that at church, and I haven't taken a nap since I was a baby!"

Carla just looked at her like it was a fact of life that couldn't be helped, and then she sat back down at the table. The boys had already taken their seats and stared at Jackie.

Annie Mae reached on top of the cupboard and pulled down an old, beaten-up Bible, putting it on the table in front of her. "Ms. Jackie, this is our body and soul time. We do a little Bible study to heal the soul, then we's lay down for a nap to heal the body. You go on and sit down now."

Jackie slowly took her seat, seeming to accept that there was no way out.

Annie Mae began by telling Jackie that they had just finished learning about Moses and how he brought the people out of bondage in Israel, and now he was up on the mountain getting the Ten Commandments written by God's own hand.

Jackie's eyes became wide. "Oh yeah. That's when all the people were fornicating with each other."

Everybody turned and stared at Jackie, but only Jimmy spoke up. "What's fornicating?"

"Well," Jackie began, "it's when men and women sometimes—" but she was quickly interrupted by Annie Mae who slammed her hand down on the table.

Everybody quickly turned their gaze toward Annie Mae, who turned toward Jackie and said, "Now we don't have that kind of talk here. This ain't church, but we are still sharing the Word and you needs to be respectful."

Jackie didn't look fazed however and just shrugged.

Jimmy turned to Annie Mae and again asked, "But what's fornicating?"

Annie Mae sighed and turned to Jimmy. "It's sinning, and sin is sin no matter what kind of sin it is, so we'll just leave it at that." Taking a breath, she continued. "Now God was giving Moses the Ten Commandments, and if you follow these commandments full and true, you won't need to worry about being caught sinning." She continued on and Jimmy seemed to either be satisfied with her answer or had forgotten his question, so the lesson continued without further interruption.

When Annie Mae put the kids down for their naps, the boys stayed in the den on their pallet and the girls lay on Carla's bed. Annie Mae gave a warning look to the girls and told them to not be talking or giggling but to be quiet as mice so the boys wouldn't get stirred up too.

Carla nodded and rolled over on her side immediately, facing the opposite direction. Soon, she was sound asleep, breathing deeply. Jackie, however, never went to sleep and lay flat on her back the whole time with her arms behind her head, staring up at the ceiling. Annie Mae, wanting to keep an eye on her, walked by the room a couple of times, but Jackie never flinched. She just stared up at the ceiling, eyes wide open. Annie Mae just shook her head and walked off, mumbling under her breath. "Now that is one curious chile, that's for sure."

After their naps, the girls resumed their play, but after about an hour, Jackie said, "So what do the boys do all day?" Carla looked up from her paperwork. "They mostly play in the woods at the fort."

Jackie thought for a second. "Let's go see what they're doing. I'm tired of playing school and being inside."

So they got up and headed outside, telling Annie Mae where they were going on their way out.

Annie Mae stopped what she was doing and yelled at the girls as they left the kitchen. She asked them to grab the paper bag on the porch bench and take with them. The woman had brought apples from her tree at home and told them they could have a snack while they were there. Carla grabbed the bag and headed toward the woods and the fort.

When they arrived at the fort, Marcus and Jimmy were held up inside the fort, crouching behind the fort wall, looking into the woods intently. Will was outside the fort, standing behind a tree, peeping around both sides.

All three had sticks in their hands, holding them like pretend guns ready to attack the enemy. When they heard the girls coming, all three turned sharply, aiming in their direction. By the time they realized who they were, it was too late. Rod jumped from behind a stump in the opposite direction and pointed his pretend gun at each one of the boys. He yelled, *"Pow! Pow! Pow!"* You're all dead."

Smiling, he swung his pretend gun over his shoulder. Marcus got up slowly and said, "Awh, man! That's not fair. The girls came up and messed us up. We had you that time. I knew you were behind that stump. I was just waiting for you to pop up."

Jimmy looked over at him. "I thought you said he was behind that oak tree over there." He pointed in the opposite direction.

Marcus grunted a couple of times. "Well, I did at first, but then I changed my mind. I just hadn't told you yet."

Rod grinned. "Awh man, you didn't know where I was, or you wouldn't have jumped when the girls came up from the other direction."

Jackie surveyed the fort and the situation. "It didn't look like a fair fight anyway, three against one."

They all looked at her dully and Will sat disgustedly on a log by the fire pit. "It wouldn't be a fair fight if it was fifteen against one if the one was Rod."

Jackie turned and looked at Rod with newfound curiosity as he headed toward one of the other logs to sit.

Carla held out the bag and announced that Annie Mae had sent apples. The boys came up and got one then proceeded to sit and munch on their afternoon snack.

After a few seconds of silence, except for the sound of crunching, Marcus looked over at Jackie and asked, "So why do they call you Wacky Jackie?" Carla's eyes widened along with the other boys as they turned hesitantly toward Jackie to see how she would respond.

Surprisingly, Jackie didn't act the least bit offended. She just sat there quietly, took another bite of her apple, and shrugged. Marcus wouldn't let it go though and talking with his mouth full said, "Must be because you're crazy. Ain't that what wacky means?"

Jackie chewed a couple of more times purposefully and swallowed her mouthful then looked over at Marcus and said, "Or it could be that I wacked somebody."

He looked at her strangely and said, "What do you mean 'wacked somebody'?"

She kept staring at him then glanced down at her half-eaten apple, tossing it straight up in the air and catching. She said, "Like maybe I took an apple and threw it at somebody and wacked them upside the head."

Marcus leaned back, laughing. "You probably couldn't hit somebody's head if you wanted to. You're just wacky, crazy."

She stood up defiantly. "Pick a target."

Marcus, still grinning, looked around and finally settled on the prized copper pot. After the snake incident, they had tied the pot to a limb by the fort. It hung about two feet down and about six feet off the ground. It served as their warning symbol to other snakes who tried to enter their territory.

"Okay," Marcus said, pointing to the copper pot. "See if you can hit that pot." Jackie looked at the pot and simply nodded. As a matter of fact, she moved back another few feet, putting more distance between her and the chosen target.

Everyone watched her intently as she stared at the pot like a professional baseball pitcher and then took aim. She threw the apple hard and straight. It hit the pot dead center with so much force the pot swung backward then up and over the limb, wrapping around the branch before gently swinging back and forth.

The boys turned and looked at Jackie in awe. She just stood there glaring back and put her hands on her hips. She announced, "By the way, I really don't care for the nickname Wacky Jackie, so I would appreciate it if you didn't call me that." She whipped around and started walking back toward the house, calling over her shoulder, "Come on, Carla. It's boring out here."

Carla looked at her with newfound admiration. She had never done anything to impress the boys and now took pride in the fact that her new friend had done so on her first day. All of a sudden, Carla thought this summer with Jackie was, indeed, going to be an adventure. She hopped up and ran after her toward the house.

Later that day when Mrs. Walker came to pick Jackie up, she hesitantly got out of the car and approached Annie Mae, who was walking up from the edge of the yard where she had just dumped a dishpan full of apple peelings. Mrs. Walker crossed her arms. "Well, how did things go today?"

Annie Mae, with one hand on her hip and the other one still holding the dishpan, kept walking toward the house. She didn't look at Mrs. Walker as she said. "Just fine, I reckon." Mrs. Walker shuffled behind her like a little puppy dog and continued. "So I can continue to bring her by then?" She hesitated and corrected herself. "I mean two or three days a week, that is."

Annie Mae just grunted uh-hu in the affirmative and opened the screen door before yelling, "Ms. Jackie, your mama's here." She walked to the sink and began rinsing out the dishpan.

Mrs. Walker waited in the doorway and breathed a sigh of relief.

Carla and Jackie ran onto the porch from inside, and the girls said their good-byes. Jackie chattered away as they walked to the car.

Carla stood beside Annie Mae and watched as they headed down the drive. Annie Mae said more to herself than to Carla, "I think I was wrong about us needing that girl. That girl needs us. She's got a wild spirit and she needs taming."

Carla just grinned. "I like her."

Chapter Eight

SHOW AND TELL

*J*ACKIE'S MOTHER HELPED her bring in a large box. As Mrs. Walker set it down on the kitchen floor, the girls immediately started going through the articles inside. Jackie had promised to go through her things at home and bring more dress-up clothes for the girls to use while playing. Mrs. Walker exchanged a cool good-morning with Annie Mae and made a speedy exit. She always seemed a little nervous.

The truth of the matter was that Jackie was a handful, and she was afraid any day now Annie Mae would say she'd had enough and would ask not to bring Jackie back. Annie Mae would never do that, of course. She was tough enough to take whatever Jackie or any of the other kids could dish out. Plus Jackie and Carla were now best of friends.

Carla oohed and aahed over all the things Jackie had brought and decided to take them to the front porch and have a fashion show. The girls stayed busy all morning, trying on different dresses and accessories, walking back and forth across the porch on their pretend runway.

Jimmy and Marcus came across the yard at one point and stared curiously at the girls. Marcus shook his head. "I don't see what's so fun about putting on a bunch of clothes all day long."

Carla snapped back, "It's better than running around in the stupid woods all day."

Marcus stuck his tongue out and they continued walking toward the shed. They had been sent by Will to get some tools they needed. While looking around, Marcus nudged Jimmy and, talking low, said, "Let's sneak up on the girls and hide in the bushes to try and scare 'em."

Jimmy looked a little unsure. "I don't know. I don't want make 'em mad." Marcus rolled his eyes. "Ah, come on. They been prancing around that porch all morning like Miss America or something."

Neither one, unfortunately, was very good at sneaking up on anybody. The girls figured out what they were trying to do but didn't let on that they knew. They squatted down, pretending to be digging around in the box, plotting their own scheme.

That's when Carla told Jackie about the day they had pulled down her pants to see her backside. "Annie Mae says they're just curious though."

Jackie glanced back to make sure the boys were still there and said, "Hmm, is that so?"

She stood and looked down at Carla. "I have to go use the bathroom. I'll be right back." But before she left, she grabbed a pink, fluffy bathrobe from the box and headed into the house. Carla sat there thumbing through a small box of clip-on earrings until Jackie returned.

When Jackie came out the front door, she was wearing the pink bathrobe. She reached down, clipped on a pair of earrings, and slipped her feet into a pair of red high-heeled shoes. Looking at Carla, she made a pose and asked, "How do I look?"

Carl snickered. "Kind of funny in that pink, fluffy bathrobe."

Jackie tugged at the collar. "Oh, this ole thing is just my jacket. It comes off at the end of the runway." And with that, she winked and took off strutting down their pretend runway with her hands on her hips, heading right toward the end of the porch where she knew the boys were hiding behind a bush.

Just as she reached the end of the porch, Marcus and Jimmy jumped up, but before they could yell out, Jackie untied the bathrobe and let it drop to the floor. Underneath the robe, she was naked as a jaybird.

The boy's mouths dropped open and they were frozen in their tracks. Jackie, standing there wearing nothing but the red high heels and those big, gaudy clip-on earrings, smiled and, putting one hand on her hip, made the required runway model pose and turn. Then, making her return, she walked back, dragging the pink bathrobe like a true professional. When she was halfway back, she looked over her shoulder toward the boys and asked, "Still curious, boys?"

They were both still standing there frozen and so was Carla. As if on cue, Annie Mae stepped out of the other end of the house to ring the lunch bell. Jackie flipped her hair back with her hand and turned to open the front door. "Let's go eat lunch, Carla. I'm starving."

When Aunt Sarah pulled up with Jimmy, he jumped out of the car, slamming the door behind him. Carla and Annie Mae were on the porch peeling apples. Jimmy looked through the screen at Annie Mae and said, "Good morning," then waited. Annie Mae waved her hand toward the woods. "Good morning. Go on. You know where they're at, baby."

Sarah walked over to the screen, taking the time this morning to chat before heading off to work. "Aunt Sarah, me and Annie Mae are making an apple pie for her daddy. He's coming over this afternoon to visit."

"Oh, how nice," Sarah replied. "Jimmy told me he was coming today. I'm sure he'll be real proud of how well y'all can recite the books of the Bible and sing those nice songs. I hear Jimmy practicing at home when he's taking his bath."

Carla frowned. "I just wish he could have come yesterday when Jackie was here. She doesn't know all the books yet, but she could sing the songs with us." Annie Mae cleared her throat and kept peeling apples. The truth was that Annie Mae had asked her daddy to come on a day when she knew Jackie wouldn't be there. After Marcus told her about the naked runway incident she had performed, she didn't trust her to behave. It was rather selfish of her, she knew, but she wanted to impress her dad too.

Sarah then looked at Annie Mae and asked, "How long has your daddy been retired, Annie Mae?"

"Oh, he ain't ever gonna retire from the Gospel, child. He ain't got no regular church now, but he still fills in when he's asked and does a revival seems like every time I turn around. Fact is he's busier now than when he was a full-time pastor."

Sarah smiled and nodded then said her good-byes before heading off to work. Carla helped Annie Mae all morning straightening the house and preparing lunch. Annie Mae wanted to have lunch a little earlier so the children could still get their naps in before her father arrived. She wanted the kids rested and alert so they would be on their best behavior.

The boys played hard all morning and were getting hungry and thirsty when Will decided they would sneak into the garden and pick a watermelon to eat before lunch. Daniel had warned the boys that they needed a few more days to ripen up, but the boys decided it had been long enough so they were going to get one anyway.

They brought the melon back to the fort and dropped it on a rock to bust the melon open. They rinsed their hands off in the stream and dug in to pull out chunks to munch on. They had all swallowed several mouthfuls when Rod said, "I think Daddy's right. These melons are not ready yet. It don't taste good. Plus it's hot from being in the sun. We should of set it in the stream for a little while to cool it down. I can't eat it."

The other boys nodded in agreement and proceeded to throw the leftover melon carcass in the stream to wash away the evidence. They all stood there watching as the melon bits floated away, when Jimmy ran to get the bag he had brought that morning.

"I forgot I brought something again today." He dropped his bag on the rock where they had bust the melon. He smiled when he looked over at Marcus and said, "Today, it's something to eat."

"Good!" Marcus replied. "I need something to get that nasty melon taste out of my mouth." Jimmy pulled a Tupperware container out of the bag and took the lid off. "Oooh chocolate," Marcus said as he reached his hand in first to snap off a piece of the bar.

They all grabbed a chunk and then another. "This chocolate tastes funny too," Rod said.

"I think it's because that stupid watermelon messed up our taste buds," Will replied.

Just then, they heard the lunch bell, but instead of running off toward the house like they usually did, they wandered in that direction, not caring if they ate or not.

After they got to the house and washed up, they took their places at the table. Annie Mae and Carla chatted away during lunch, excited about Reverend Cooper coming to visit, but the boys hardly spoke and just played with their food. Annie Mae noticed the way the boys were acting and scolded them for not eating. They each exchanged glances, but no one mentioned the watermelon. Instead, they all tried to force themselves to eat their lunch.

When lunch was over, Annie Mae put the kids down for their nap and skipped their Bible lessons, since they would do that when her daddy came. Carla went right to sleep, obviously tired from the busy morning. The boys, however, did not seem to rest. Their stomachs churned and gurgled the whole time, and by the time Annie Mae woke them, the boys were all miserable.

Annie Mae lined the boys up on the porch pew and tried to straighten their hair. Carla was in her room getting ready by herself. She put on a different dress, combed her hair, and then decided last minute to add a touch of her mama's lipstick.

When she walked out on the porch and took her place beside the boys, Annie Mae gasped. "Gracious, child, what have you got on your face?"

Carla smiled sweetly, acting proud of how nice she looked, and said she had added some makeup so she would look especially nice for Reverend Cooper. Annie Mae didn't have the heart to tell her she looked like a Jezebel, plus it was too late; her daddy was coming down the drive.

The children sat quietly while Annie Mae went out to greet her daddy. She led the elderly man onto the porch and they sat down in the two wooden chairs Annie had placed in front of the pew.

Reverend Cooper was wearing a suit and tie, just like he was going to a real service instead of the little pretend one on the Branches' porch. He carried a large, worn Bible. Annie Mae made introductions, pointing out each child. He didn't say a word when she pointed to Carla and seemed not to notice her plastered face but simply smiled and asked if he could begin with prayer.

He closed his eyes and raised his right hand up in the air, and then he delivered a short prayer of thanksgiving to God. During the prayer, one of the boy's stomachs could be heard gurgling, so after the prayer, Reverend Cooper chuckled and said, "One of you boys sound hungry. Must not have got enough lunch. But I hear there's a promise of apple pie when we get finished." He smiled sweetly and winked at Annie Mae.

Then Reverend Cooper looked the children over and asked, "So what have you children been studying this summer in the Word?" They all stared at him blankly. The boys were beginning to squirm a little in their seats and somebody's stomach could still be heard gurgling.

Annie Mae shifted, sat up tall, and answered for them. "They know all their books of the Bible. They been working hard on that all summer now."

Reverend Cooper raised his eyebrows. "Well, now, stand up and let's hear it then."

The kids looked at Annie Mae and she nodded for them all to do as they were told. Carla hopped right up, but the boys took their time, slowly getting to their feet. Before they could begin, Jimmy looked at Annie Mae. "Annie Mae, my stomach hurts. I need to go to the bathroom."

Then Marcus chirped in, "Mine too, Ma. It hurts real bad." Annie Mae looked sternly at the boys. "Now that's just nerves. You boys straighten up and recite them books like we learned."

Slowly the children began "Genesis, Exodus, Leviticus, Numbers, Deuteronomy."

Beads of sweat could be seen running down Will's face as he interrupted with a grunt. He was holding his stomach and yelled, "I'm sorry I can't hold it" as he ran out the screen door toward the outhouse.

Reverend Cooper leaned forward in his chair, looking out just in time to see the outhouse door slam shut. Rod took off next and ran outside, disappearing in the woods since the outhouse was now occupied.

Annie Mae looked shocked. "Now where in the world is he heading off to?" Carla looked at Annie Mae and stated, "Rod really is sick, Annie Mae. I could feel it."

Marcus was still squirming as he stood there, shifting from one foot to another, looking at his mama pleadingly. Finally, he just took off toward the back bedroom where the inside pot was kept. He barely got his pants down in time to sit and let loose. His moaning could be heard all the way through the house, along with the thudding sound of his loose stool splattering the enamel pot.

Reverend Cooper stood and looked toward the outhouse then back in the direction of Marcus's moaning, then back toward Annie Mae. He was just about to speak when he heard a strange noise. They all turned to Jimmy, who now had a strained look on his face. He was pale, with beads of sweat forming on his forehead. Something brown was trickling down his legs. Then the smell hit everyone's nostrils.

Annie Mae jumped up, pushing her chair back, and said, "Have mercy!"

Carla backed away from Jimmy with a disgusted look on her face. Reverend Cooper looked at Annie Mae and asked, "Heaven's sake, Annie. What in the world have you been feeding dees children?"

Carla, still wanting to impress Reverend Cooper and now realizing it was going to be up to her, decided to try to say something to repair the situation. She knew the boys had evidently been up to no good that day and wanted to confess on their behalf, so she chose the only biblically impressive word she could think of to save the moment.

"The boys have obviously been fornicating today, Reverend Cooper. Fornicating, fornicating, fornicating. That's all they know how to do. Why they plum made Jackie Walker strip down naked on the front porch last week to satisfy their curiosity." Annie Mae fell back in her chair, mumbling, "Have mercy," over and over.

Needless to say, Reverend Cooper made a speedy exit, even though Annie Mae finally did pull herself together enough to try to get him to stay and eat a piece of apple pie. He strangely enough had lost his appetite.

"Oh, but they didn't even get to sing for ya. Dem children got soul when they sing. I tell ya the truth, they do." But Reverend Cooper drove off and Annie Mae was left standing alone in his dust.

Later that night, Uncle Herman was digging through a drawer when Aunt Sarah walked in the kitchen at their home. "Have you seen the ex-lax? I just bought a new bar last week. I can't find it anywhere."

Sarah sighed. "You're the one who keeps moving it. It's supposed to be kept in the medicine cabinet, but I find it everywhere else. One day last week, it was on the kitchen table." Giving him a scolding look, she said, "Really, Herman, you need to be more careful. Jimmy's going to think it's candy."

He shook his head. "No. I'm careful. I even put it in a Tupperware container this time." Sarah sighed and left the room with Herman standing there scratching his head.

Chapter Nine

SOULFUL NOISE

*V*AL PULLED UP to the house and was greeted by Carla, who came running out. "Mama, Rod fell out of a tree again today."

Val looked up as Annie Mae was coming out the door. "Oh my, is he okay?" she asked, looking at both Carla and Annie Mae.

Annie Mae, shaking her head, spoke up first. "Oh, he's fine, Ms. Val. He just got the breath knocked out of him. Now don't go spouting none of them statistic you got piled up in that pretty little head of yours. It wouldn't make no difference no how. You not going to keep that jackrabbit son of yours out of climbing no trees. Besides, Ms. Carla here with that sixth sense, twin sense of hers, let me know something was going on with that child near 'bout before he hit the ground."

Putting her hands on her hips and shaking her head, she smiled. "Sure wish I had a notion when my Leroy or Marcus was in harm's way." She paused before she continued. "Then again, I might not ever get a moment's rest with them two rascals."

Carla looked up at Annie Mae. "Can I go ring the bell to let Marcus know you're ready to go home?"

She patted her on the shoulder. "Why, that'd be just fine. Matter of fact, I'm going to head on down the road. He'll catch up to me before I get too far. I don't know if I'm walking slower these days or if he's running faster." Smiling, she looked at Val. "I guess it's a little of both; these child'rin are growing way to fast, Ms. Val." Val nodded in agreement. "But you should have heard them singing this afternoon. I tell you these young'ins sound like angels, I tell ya. Pure angels! Hearts full of soul, now that is for sure."

Just as Annie Mae was turning down the drive toward the dirt road leading to her house, Daniel pulled up in the yard. Carla ran over to greet him, and Daniel obliged by picking her up and giving her a big bear hug. "How's my favorite little girl today?"

Carla giggled. "Good, Daddy."

When he reached Val, he leaned down, gave her a peck on the cheek, and asked, "And how is my favorite big girl?"

Smiling, Val looked up at Daniel and answered, "Fine now. Good to be home." Carla hopped down from Daniel's arms and headed back toward the house.

Just then Marcus ran, flying by. "Hey, Mr. Daniel, Ms. Val! See y'all tomorrow!" And with that, he was halfway down the road.

Val shook her head. "I do believe Annie Mae is right. That boy runs as fast as lightning."

That night, when Val crawled into bed, she snuggled up next to Daniel and told him how Annie Mae had commented on how big the children were getting. "Ya know, Daniel, with the kids getting grown and the work now finally getting started on the house, it's about time we finally settled this birth control issue."

Daniel grunted and squirmed under the covers, not wanting to start the conversation he knew she was heading toward. "Do we have to talk about that tonight?"

"No," Val said, "but the problem is you never want to talk about it." She sighed and continued softly. "Honey, I'm done having kids. I want us to take care of things, so we don't have any surprises. If you'll remember, the last time I gave birth, they came in twos." She slid deeper under the covers, wrapping her arms around Daniel and snuggling in closer to his neck.

Daniel breathed deeply, smelling Val's hair. She always knew how to soften him up. Just where to touch, exactly what to say and how to say it, so she went on. "You know you're the one who promised to take care of things anyway. I volunteered when I gave birth to the twins, but you weren't ready yet to make things permanent, so you said you'd do it. Plus it's easier on a man than it is a woman to get things taken care of."

Daniel's head jerked back. "I don't see how it's any easier. I mean, you're talking about messing around with the family jewels. That's major renovations. It's huge!"

Val smiled and looked up at Daniel, teasing. "Well, I don't know if I would exactly say it's huge."

Daniel cut his eyes at Val, and even in the dark, he could see her eyes twinkling.

He smiled in spite of her ribbing and pulled her closer to him. She softly began to rub his chest and kiss his check. Daniel let out a sigh and gave in, saying, "Fine, I promise I'll check into it. A couple of boys at work had it done last year, so I'll see what doctor they used and see what our insurance plans will cover. Deal?"

Val smiled. "Yes." She kissed him a couple of more times and he pulled her close, kissing her back deeply.

Between more kisses, Val added, "Ya know there'll be some perks too. We'll both be a little more at ease with that burden taken off us. Might even spice things up a lot." With that, Daniel made a purring sound, threw the covers over his head, and buried his head in Val's stomach. She tried to muffle her giggles so they didn't wake the children.

Ms. Thelma poked her head into the children's Sunday school class and scanned the room. Ms. Patsy looked up at her and asked, "What is it, Thelma?"

"Oh, I was just looking to see if Susie was here. Michael isn't here to help sing today, and I was trying to find out if he was coming, but I guess since she's not here either, he won't be showing up."

She let out an exaggerated sigh and came in. "Every time I plan for these children to sing, they don't show up. I told all their parents months ago we would be singing today. Sometimes, I think they do this to me on purpose. I was hoping to have at least a dozen kids today, and so far, I only have four. They're not even my strongest singers. I wanted to have a choir, not a quartet."

Ms. Patsy smiled. "They'll be just fine. Nobody expects you to work miracles. You've practiced, but they just didn't come today. That's no reflection on you."

Thelma replied harshly, "Why, of course, it's a reflection on me! Even though it's not my fault, I'll be the one with egg on my face!" She crossed her arms. "If I could go grab some neighborhood children that could sing "John the Revelator," I'd go drag them down the aisle, then the children that didn't show up would feel bad that they missed out."

When Carla heard what song they were singing, she looked up from her paper. "We know that song. We sing it at home with Annie Mae all the time."

Ms. Thelma's eyes widened and she came all the way into the room. Bending down, she looked at all three of the Branch children and asked them again for confirmation "Do you really know all the words to that song?"

Carla nodded. "Jimmy and Jackie know it too."

Ms. Patsy shrugged. "Oh, I don't know, Thelma. They haven't practiced or anything and you don't have time now."

Thelma looked at her harshly. "I don't have any other choice right now, do I? They can sing well can't they?"

Patsy nodded. "The Branch children all have beautiful voices. So does Jackie and Jimmy, but I—"

Thelma cut her off and looked down at the children. "All right, it's settled then. I'll have my children's choir after all."

Before Thelma had time to say anything else, the bell rang to let out classes. The kids jumped up and Ms. Thelma quickly stopped the children before they tore out of the room. She looked them all in the eyes, giving them a serious look. She said, "Now listen, you go sit with your family like usual, but when you see me get up and go down front with the other children, you come down too. I will put them on the second step of the pulpit and you five can stand right in front of them on the bottom step so you can watch me." She paused and looked at them to make sure they were taking in all her instructions before letting them go. She stood up, straightening her skirt, and shot Patsy a defiant look. Patsy giggled to herself after Thelma left the room and then hurried to clean up the class. She didn't want to miss this.

As soon as Carla reached Val, who was sitting in their usual pew, she immediately told her that she and the boys were singing with the big kids during the service. Val looked surprised and replied, "Well, I didn't even know you had been practicing with Ms. Thelma."

"We haven't. She just needs some extra singers today so we get to help."

Val sounded a little unsure. "Well, I don't know. If you haven't practiced or anything, y'all need-"

Margaret cut her off. "Well, I think that's wonderful. You all have beautiful voices just like your daddy. You need to be using them in the Lord's house."

Val clamped her mouth shut turning abruptly to face the front while the pews continued to fill.

The service began, and soon it was time for the children to take their places and sing. Ms. Thelma got up and stood in front, scanning the pews and motioning for the children to come down front and take their places. While the children made their way down, Thelma addressed the congregation by saying what a pleasure it had been to work with such talented children and that she knew the church was going to be impressed, and blessed, with their song. It was all Patsy could do not to laugh out loud. She knew it was Thelma who would was going to be surprised, and she was going to love every minute of it.

The first verse went off pleasantly, and Thelma was more than pleased by the beautiful flow of the children's voices. But when they hit the second verse, the children in the first row took the song and ran with it. They revved up the volume and added soul like this little Baptist church hadn't heard before.

The older children in the back looked surprised and confused. They didn't know how to jump in, or compete with what was flowing from the newest choir members. They looked at Ms. Thelma for direction, but she looked as shocked as they were and offered nothing in the way of a clue as to how to proceed, so they just stood there.

The girls, along with Jimmy and Will, were carrying the melody while Rod, who had a surprising deep voice, was singing the backup, coming in occasionally during the chorus. The children leaned back during the higher parts as if they needed the extra room to bellow out the verses.

Occasionally, the girls would raise one of their hands and close their eyes as though really feeling the spirit, which definitely never took place during a song or any other part of worship. When they finished the song, the children just stood there smiling at Thelma, waiting for her to direct them next, but she was frozen in the pew.

Reverend Crumpler finally stood, looked down at Thelma, and said, "Thank you, children and Thelma, for that—ah—*riveting* song." He then glanced over at the choir director, who stood as well, and instructed the congregation to stand for the offertory hymn. The children made their way back to their pews, and Thelma somehow staggered back to hers.

As the offertory song drew to a close, the men took their place at the back of the church, standing reverently. Punchy leaned over toward Daniel and whispered, "Annie Mae's still taking care of your children, I take it?" Daniel just kept looking straight ahead so he wouldn't have to see the grin on Punchy's face. He said, "Yep."

Punchy grinned. "Something told me she was."

Thelma was seen leaving the church, whispering excitedly to

Margaret. Margaret, who was not whispering in return, said, "Oh, for heaven sakes! Who cares what they think? Half the people in this church wouldn't know the Holy Spirit if he came up and introduced himself." She grunted and continued on. "Besides, it's your own fault. You should have told the children how you wanted them to sing. You're the director."

Thelma looked around nervously then made a beeline across the yard toward her car.

Chapter Ten

SOLID GROUND

*E*VERYBODY WAS RELAXING after lunch when the boys announced they were heading out to the Up and Down to play. Jesse had come home from church with them, which had become the norm, and Marcus had come over to play as well. Rod looked at Carla and asked if she was coming today. "No, I'm going to walk up to look at the house with Mama and Daddy."

Margaret piped in, "It ain't a whole lot different since last Sunday, other than them digging up the yard and making a mess."

Daniel snapped his fingers and jumped up after the boys. Catching them outside, he nodded his head toward their house now under construction. "Now look, boys. Stay out of the yard there where they've been plowing. See that red flag sticking out of the ground?" The boys all turned and looked in that direction then turned back to face Daniel, nodding to let him know they had seen it. "That's where the well was for the old home place. They haven't filled it in yet proper, so it ain't safe to go messing around there. You might wind up sinking all the way down to China." He winked at the boys and they grinned back before they took off.

Will yelled back over his shoulder, "Don't worry. We'll stay away from there!"

Daniel watched them run off and then headed back inside. The women were almost finished clearing the dishes and his dad was already nodding off in his recliner.

Val walked over and asked if he was ready to walk up. He nodded. Carla had gone to change out of her Sunday dress, so they waited outside for her to come out. Daniel stood behind Val with his arms wrapped around her waist, staring up the dirt road at the construction of their home.

The property had a gradual slope up from his parents' house. There were only a few scattered trees, but it was still a pretty, open view from his parents' backyard. The outside was complete and the tedious inside work was underway but going slowly. The workers had been working outside this week, digging up old tree stumps and pushing off debris.

Carla finally came bounding out of the house and they made their way up the dirt drive. They passed the boys, who were bent over at the edge of the plowed yard where it met the woods.

The boys were gathering dirt clods. They would gingerly tote them to the Up and Down and keep them in their pretend ammo site as grenades, picking them up during battle and giving them the heave hoe. The clod would explode on impact just like a real bomb. They would come home with dirt in their ears, up their noses and all over their clothes.

She yelled over, "You boys be careful! A rock could be inside those dirt clods and you wouldn't even know it! If you throw it upside somebody's head, it could put them in a coma!"

Daniel looked down at Val "A coma? Then let me guess: medical complications and then death. Val, they're just playing with *dirt*."

"Well … it could."

Daniel just nudged her along by putting his arm around her shoulder. Under his breath he said, "Yeah, I know it already did, right?"

Daniel and Val walked through every room, looking at new accomplishments. Carla skipped from room-to-room. Carla yelled from somewhere at the other end of the house, "I just love the smell of new wood, don't y'all?"

"I sure do," Val replied. She turned and looked at Daniel. "It's amazing how good you can hear in here now. That will all change when they put up the rest of the sheetrock and flooring." She hugged herself and let out a sigh.

Daniel looked over at her and his heart melted to see her so happy. He walked over, wrapping his arms around her, and they both stood staring out one of the front windows that faced his parents' backyard. They stood a few seconds in silence, lost in their own thoughts while enjoying the view and how they felt in each other's arms.

Daniel was the first to break the silence when he gently asked, "You sure you're going to be okay practically living in my parents' backyard?"

Val gave him a sideways glance, smiling, and replied, "Daniel, you know I love your dad."

They both let out a low chuckle. "That's not what I was asking. Everybody loves my dad, but not too many people can take a daily dose of Margaret Branch." Val smiled and turned to face Daniel, still wrapped in his arms. Daniel leaned his head down and kissed Val deeply. When he forced himself free, he let his headrest against her forehead, continuing to hold her tightly. "I'd live under the same roof with Margaret Branch if that's the only way I'd get you, Daniel Jacob Branch," Val whispered.

Daniel smiled. "Don't speak too soon. The bank is letting us move in, but if we don't pay that fat mortgage every month, we won't get to stay here."

After inspecting every inch of the house with them, Carla headed off to go play with the boys for a little while. They watched her run until she disappeared into the woods. They could hear the muffled sounds of the boys yelling and running through the trees.

Instead of going straight back to his parents' house, they decided to stroll down to the pond and back by the garden to enjoy the day and each other's company. As they were walking, Daniel looked over at Val. "I forgot to tell you what I did Friday."

Val looked over at him questioningly.

"I talked to Kenneth at work and he said that he went to Dr. Weaver for his vasectomy."

Val raised her eyebrows and kept staring so he would continue.

"I called him. Seems he only does two of those kinds of appointments a week, two every Friday morning. Said since most of his patients that get that done are of working age, they have the weekend to recover and can go to work on Monday like nothing happened."

Val poked him in his side. "See? I told you there's nothing much to it."

Daniel winced and said, "I wish you would quit saying there ain't nothing much to it. It's my jewels we're talking about. *My jewels*!"

Val reached over and patted his stomach. "Sorry. I'll keep that in mind."

After a couple of seconds to collect himself, Daniel continued. "Anyway, he thinks I can get in around the middle of September. I figured that's a good time. The kids will be back in school. We should be moved into the house by then too. So what do you think?"

She stopped and placed her hand up to his cheek. Looking at him, she said, "I think I'm a lucky woman and you're a mighty brave man, Daniel Branch." She gave him a quick kiss. Then with her hand still on his cheek, she gave him a light pop. "It's about time you listened to me, ya big baby!"

Carla sat by the tree where the kids had painted a big, red cross that served as the hospital for the Up and Down battlegrounds. Jimmy sat beside her as she mended his pretend wounded arm. Soon Jesse plopped down side him. He let out a grunt and said, "Nobody is ever going to get Rod. It's just impossible, even when we took away all his dirt clods."

Jimmie nodded. "The last battle he blew my arm off before I had even got in position." Soon Marcus, Will, and Rod joined them at the hospital. Marcus fell down beside Jesse and started patting his clothes, filling the air with dust from the clods. All the boys had dirt chunks clinging to their hair and muddy streaks down their face where the dust had mixed with sweat. Everyone, that is, but Rod. He was surprisingly clean and smiling. "I think that was the quickest battle yet."

All the boys were used to losing to Rod, but it frustrated Will. He wouldn't give up on coming up with the ultimate plan to finally outwit Rod. He looked at his wounded troops and said, "I have one more plan."

Looking at Rod, he said, "You stay out of the woods until we are set, then we'll send Carla out to get you." Rod nodded and left the woods. Will squat down in front of the other three and they huddled together to go over their plan. After they mapped out their strategy, they sent Carla out to go get Rod.

When she exited the woods, Rod was lying flat on his back, chewing on long strands of dry grass and staring up at the sky. He had one arm under his head, and the other cradled his pretend stick gun. He got up when he saw Carla. She told him that this time the plan was that after he killed somebody, they could run and tag the tree at the hospital, and then reenter the battle. So, basically, Rod would have to kill all four of them twice before the battle was won.

He nodded, agreeing to the terms. Glancing back up at the sky, he said, "I better make this a quick one. It's fixing to storm."

Carla looked up and shrugged. "Maybe not."

Rod smiled as he ran into the woods but yelled back over his shoulder, "No, it's definitely going to rain."

Carla looked around after Rod disappeared, trying to decide if she wanted to head back to the house or continue manning the hospital for the boys. Just then, something shiny caught her eye. It was probably a piece of glass, but she decided to go investigate anyway. It was sticking out of the ground beside a stick with a red flag tied on the end. The breeze was picking up and the flag was fluttering harder in the wind. Rod was probably right again. It really was going to rain—and soon.

When Carla reached the area where she noticed the sparkle, the sun dipped behind a cloud and she lost sight of her treasure. She turned slowly in every direction, scanning the area intently. She didn't even notice the area closest to the flag was moist, so she was surprised when she backed into the muddy ground and sank up to her knees.

She immediately tried to pick her feet up out of the mud but only managed to sink deeper. It was as though she was in quick sand. She was now sunk up her waist and couldn't maneuver herself out of the mud. Luckily, one foot hit something hard and narrow to stop her from progressing deeper into the mud. Carla reached over and grabbed the stick to see if she could use it to pull herself out, but she didn't have a way to get any leverage, so she was trapped. And then it began to rain ...

The sky had gotten dark fast and soon the storm hit. The hard downpour brought the boys running back to the house. They were all out of breath, laughing and muddy from head to toe. Margaret started fussing and getting out towels for the boys to dry off before they could make a mess in her kitchen. Just then, they heard a horn blow outside. Marcus jerked his head up and said, "That will be my uncle Leonard. See y'all later."

He waved and ran out the door. They heard the car as it made its way back out the drive. After a few minutes of fussing over the boys passed, Val looked up and asked, "Where's Carla?"

They all glanced around at each other and finally Will said, "I thought she came back to the house; she wasn't at the last battle."

Rod looked at Val. "Last time I saw her was right before it started raining."

Daniel stood. "Where exactly was she then?"

Rod did not even reply but was the first one out the back door with Daniel right behind him. They ran blind through the downpour. The lightning flashed only once while Daniel ran toward the well, but it didn't last long enough for his eyes to adjust in the downpour to tell if she was there.

Daniel beat Rod to the site of the old well but only by a couple of steps. There Carla was, both hands white knuckles still holding the stick. She was still only stuck in the mud up to her waist, but water had begun to puddle around her, as though she was a mermaid just popping up out of the sea. Her foot was still in contact with something hard, keeping her from sinking farther into the sinkhole.

Daniel knelt down and, grabbing Carla under her arms, pulled her out of the hole and into his tight embrace. She clutched her arms around his neck and cried hard enough that it caused her to hiccup.

Daniel rocked back and forth, holding her tightly and shushing her, saying over and over again, "It's okay."

Carla, in-between sobs, said, "I t-t-tried to y-y-ell at the boys, b-b-ut they c-c-ouldn't hear me over the r-r-rain."

Rod was on his knees right behind Daniel. Tears mixed with the rain on his face. His bottom lip quivered and his eyes never left Carla's face. She never loosened her grip on Daniel's neck. Over his shoulder, she turned her head to look at Rod.

"Didn't you feel anything, Rod?"

He shook his head and his bottom lip rolled out slightly. Guilt was written in his expression.

"Not even a little something? I called your name over and over."

Rod slumped forward, shaking his head, his shoulders visibly jerking from his sobs. The twin sixth sense was Carla's alone. She could sense when Rod was even uncomfortable or nervous, but tonight when Carla needed him the most, Rod never felt a thing.

Chapter Eleven
TIME FOR CHANGE

*L*EROY AND DANIEL were packing up tools from his shed and loading them in back of his truck. The house had been cleared out and all their belongings had already been moved to their new home. Val and Annie Mae were there with the kids, trying to get everything put away.

Daniel heaved the last box in back of the truck and looked around the empty shed one last time, checking to see if he had missed anything. "Well, I believe that's it, Leroy."

"Yep," Leroy said, looking back at the house. "Me and Annie sure gonna miss y'all." Then looking back at Daniel, he said, "And Marcus too. Him the most, I expect."

Daniel nodded. "Yeah, but at least this year they'll be at the same school. Being together at school will make up for missing out during the summer. Plus you know Marcus is welcome to come over any time he wants."

Leroy rubbed the back of his neck, looking concerned. "You don't reckon there's gonna be any trouble next week at the schoolhouse, do ya?"

Daniel shook his head. "Nah, we're not in a big city. We're just country folk, Leroy. We know how to get along."

"I don't know. Some older boys at church been filling Marcus's head with talk of there being some trouble."

"These boys in high school?"

Leroy nodded in the affirmative.

"Well, you know how high school boys are, Leroy. They like a scuffle every now and then. That's about all that amounts to. Our kids don't have anything to worry about in middle school. It'll just be a normal first day at school." Grinning even bigger, he continued. "The boys especially hate going back so bad. I doubt any organized brawl is in the works."

With that, he patted him on the back and nodded toward his tractor. "What do you say? You take the Massey Ferguson one last time down Highway 46 and I'll follow you in the pickup."

Leroy put his hands on his hips. "Now you know that hain't happened in 'bout four or five years now." Shaking his head, he laughed. "If I even thought about looking at a bottle, Annie would knock me into next week, and she'd make sure I landed there on Sunday, sitting in the church house, listening to her daddy preach!"

They both laughed, then with nothing else to be said, and not wanting to get sentimental, Leroy climbed onto the tractor and Daniel followed him. Daniel stared up at the house through the truck's rearview mirror one last time.

A million memories flashed through his head.

Val rolled over in bed and was disoriented for a few seconds. She was still surprised every morning waking up in their new home. But then reality would hit her. She glanced over to the nightstand to check the time. She had fixed the time on the clock but never set the alarm. It was the first day of school and they were already running late. She pushed the covers back and nudged Daniel hard in the back. He grunted loudly and jerked. He looked up groggily as she grabbed her robe and headed down the hall.

Val went in Carla's room first and shook her gently. "Sweetie, it's time to get up." Carla opened her eyes and Val continued, smiling. "First day of school and your mama overslept, so don't dilly dally." Carla was not the child Val had to worry about however. She was excited and hopped right up. She already had her clothes and school supplies laid out in the rocking chair beside her bed.

Val went down the hall to wake the boys up next. The boys' room was already a mess with clothes, toys, and comics strung all over the place. Val sighed as she stopped at the foot of Will's bed. She reached over and grabbed his foot and shook it until he began to wiggle.

"Wake up, Will. You have to get ready for school and there's no time to play around. It's already almost 7:00." She started to walk toward Rod's bed, but there was so much on the floor, she just let out an aggravated sigh and yelled for Rod to get up. He was buried under a pile of blankets, motionless. She turned around to leave the room, and on her way out, she bumped the end of Will's bed hard with her thigh to jostle him one last time. "Get on up now and make sure Rod does too." She heard Will grumble as she headed down the hall.

Val was frantically opening cabinets when Daniel walked in the kitchen. She sighed and said over her shoulder, "I can't remember where I put the pot I use for the oatmeal." Daniel looked at her and glanced at the stove then back at her. Catching the comical look in his eyes, she glanced toward the stove herself and saw the pot sitting there ready to be used.

She closed the cabinet, grabbed the pot, and began filling it with water. "I forgot I laid it out last night so I would have it ready for this morning." Aggravated with herself, she muttered, "I would've been better off to leave it in the cabinet and set the alarm instead."

Daniel grinned and leaned back against the bar. "We've got plenty of time."

She set the pot down and turned on the eye. "Well, they definitely are going to miss the bus. One of us will have to drop them off at school. I guess I will, since I'm off today, unless you have time to do it on your way in."

Before he could answer, Carla came bounding into the kitchen, grinning. She was always excited the first day of school. "Mama, where's the box with my shoes in it? I want to wear my white sandals today instead." Val told her to look in the boxes still in the den then walked over and yelled down the hall one more time for the boys to get a move on.

Just then, they heard the back door open and Rod walked in like it was an ordinary day. Daniel straightened up and asked, "Where have you been?"

Rod nonchalantly said, "Me and Grandpa was checking our rabbit boxes." Then, grinning wide, he shouted, "We got three!"

"Well, I can see we're going to have to have a talk with Grandpa about not making you late for school," Val said. Then told Rod to run get cleaned up so he'd have time to eat breakfast before school. She teasingly popped Daniel in the belly with the back of her hand and said jokingly, "And I thought your mother was going to be the troublemaker."

Marcus got on the bus and glanced around for a familiar face. The bus was quiet and Marcus felt as though every eye was on him as he made his way down the aisle. The bus route had changed and some people that he was used to riding with had been replaced with new faces ... white faces.

He was halfway down the aisle when he found the first available seat. It was with Darnell. He was a twelfth grader, and although in the past Darnell would have never let one of the little kids share a seat with him, today he nodded to let Marcus know he could sit.

After a few minutes, Darnell looked down at Marcus. "You nervous 'bout today, little man?"

Marcus looked up at him, shaking his head. "Naw, I just don't like school."

Darnell grunted. "Well, today might be a day for the history books."

Then leaning closer to talk lower, he said, "You got to be prepared, little man. You gonna have white kids in your class. Things are going to be different." Marcus's eyes lit up. "Yeah, I know my best friend Will is going to be in my class. They're the last pickup on the bus route."

Darnell slumped in his seat and muttered, "Hmmm. That the Branch boy that just moved from in front of you?" Marcus nodded and Darnell grunted again. He turned to stare out the window.

Soon, they were at the Branch driveway, but nobody was standing there to get on the bus. Marcus stood up to look up the hill. Margaret and Edgar's house was visible, but only the roof of Val and Daniel's new home could be seen. The bus blew the horn and waited a few seconds before slowly pulling away. Marcus slumped back down in his seat, disappointed and confused.

Darnell leaned back. "See, little man, things are different now. They done moved up in the world. Got that big, nice house. Yep, things are changed. When you get to school, you'll see. That boy ain't even gonna know who you are."

Marcus listened to Darnell grumble the whole way to school, talking about "the man" and the "the government" and other things that just didn't make any sense. The only thing Marcus was worried about now was his first day at a new school. He hadn't been nervous until now. He and Will had made all kinds of playground plans for the year, but Will didn't even get on the bus. Was Darnell right? Were things really going to be different now?

The bus pulled up to the drop off area and waited its turn. Kids were walking from the buses to the front doors, as teachers stood guiding any lost kids along the way.

Darnell reached over and nudged Marcus. "Is that your buddy over there, little man?" Marcus stood slightly, leaning over Darnell to look out the window. He saw Will standing with a group of other boys, chatting and laughing.

Darnell sucked in through his front teeth. "Yeah, see? I told you. He's already grouped up with his old buddies. You're on your own, little man. You need to do what I told you and watch your back. Get your own clan together."

Marcus looked at Darnell, still not sure what he was talking about, but felt somehow sad. He was sad to see Will already laughing with strange boys, sad to be at a new school, sad because everything was changing.

Marcus was one of the last kids off the bus, and when he stepped down to the ground, he looked up to see Will pointing over at him and yelling, "That's him. Hey, Marcus!" Will ran up to meet him, almost knocking him down. Will took Marcus's hand to drag him over to the group of boys.

Will introduced the other boys to Marcus, but Marcus didn't really hear a word he said. He was so relieved that Will was just Will and that Darnel had been wrong. He glanced back at the bus as it slowly rounded the circle to head out on the highway toward the high school. He still didn't know what Darnell was trying to tell him, but somehow it didn't matter now.

He turned back toward Will, who was still talking excitedly, lining up their kickball team for recess. He glanced around at the other boys who were nodding and listening intently to everything Will was saying. They didn't seem to have any hesitations about bringing Marcus into their group. Marcus smiled and realized it was just like being at the fort. Will was in charge and set the pace that everybody followed, which is what a true leader always does.

Chapter Twelve
SNIP-SNIP

*V*AL AND DANIEL rode in silence. Val had tried to make small talk, but it was it was obvious to her that Daniel wasn't in the mood. She decided to sit back and keep quiet, especially since she was trying to make mental notes of where they were going. She hated driving in Raleigh and usually never did alone. Today, however, she wanted to be able to get back home without having to ask Daniel for directions.

When they arrived at the clinic, Val and Daniel went up to the reception desk to sign in. The receptionist handed Daniel a clipboard with forms for Daniel to fill out. He was told to have a seat and wait to be called. The waiting area was almost to capacity with mostly men and women in their later years of life.

Daniel leaned toward Val and whispered, "Should be easy to pick out the other victim in this crowd." Val smiled as Daniel exchanged a brief nod with the only other young man in the waiting area.

Daniel and Val walked across the waiting room and grabbed the last open seats side-by-side. When finished with his paperwork, Daniel picked up a magazine but seemed to just be turning pages. Then the fidgeting started. Finally, he turned to Val, who was quietly reading a magazine, and whispered, "Since the other Mr. Snip-Snip hasn't been called yet, I'm going to go to the bathroom one last time."

Daniel walk down the hall to the men's room and Val turned back to her magazine. The young man Daniel had pinned as the next victim was called next. He winced and kept his left leg out straight as his wife grabbed his elbow to help him stand. The nurse asked him what had happened and he shrugged it off as a stupid motorcycle accident. He grinned and made a comment about while he was already laid up with a bum leg, he would get this little procedure over too, killing two birds with one stone.

Humph, Val thought. She wished Daniel would be that easygoing about it. He had been acting like a big baby ever since he made the appointment last week.

As soon as Daniel sat back down, Val laid her magazine down and leaned over to tell him the other man had been called back and to give him a heads-up about his condition. She nodded toward where the man had been sitting. "Daniel, they called the other man back and as—"

But Daniel jerked in her direction, interrupting her sharply. "Yeah, yeah. I know they called him back. I'm next."

"But Daniel, I was just going to tell you that—"

Interrupting her again and shifting in his seat, he said a little too loudly, "Mercy, Val, will you quit harping on me?"

Other patients glanced in their direction but quickly looked the other way. Val had been nothing but nice to Daniel, babying him the whole time so he wouldn't change his mind, but that did it. She sat back in her chair, folded her arms, and clamped her mouth shut. She didn't have to fume long before Mr. Snip-Snip came limping out of the exam room. The nurse helped to support him as he walked out. The man's wife came over and grabbed his elbow, looking at him sympathetically. The nurse seemed to be giving them both instructions and then walked over to the hold the door open for them as they left.

Val suppressing a grin, turned to take in Daniel's response. His face was drained of color and his mouth was hanging wide open. He looked like he wanted to say something, but nothing was coming out. The man was long gone, but Daniel kept staring at the exit door.

Then the nurse called Daniel's name and looked in his direction with a blank glaze. Daniel flinched but didn't move out of his seat. Val realized he had been holding his breath because when he jumped, he took in a big gulp of air and almost choked. While Daniel coughed, Val raised her hand to confirm they had heard his name. She patted Daniel on the thigh, nudging him with her elbow.

Daniel made his way across the room, slowly turning back once to give Val one last pitiful glance, like someone heading to the electric chair. She smiled sweetly but was laughing deep down.

Pulling into the driveway, Val glanced over at Daniel and asked one more time how he felt.

"Fine," Daniel said, almost through gritted teeth.

Val had practically laughed the whole way home.

"You know you could've tried harder to fill me in on Snip-Snip number one."

She turned and looked at him sharply, but still grinning, and said, "Daniel, I tried but you didn't want to listen." Then she laughed again. "Oh, but Daniel, if you could've just seen your face!"

"Look, just don't go telling that story around anybody else. As a matter of fact, this little procedure is just between you and me, okay?"

Val was still laughing, so he looked at her harshly and demanded again. "Okay?"

She nodded.

Val pulled the car under the carport and she and Daniel were just shutting the car doors when they saw Punchy's pickup coming up the drive. Daniel gave Val a warning look and said, "Not a word."

Aggravated, she said, "Oh, for heaven's sake! I wasn't going to say anything." She returned a warning look of her own and said, "Don't encourage him to stay long. You need to rest. That medicine will wear off soon and all you can take is Ibuprofen, so you don't need to be standing around with him all afternoon."

Daniel just nodded and turned to watch Punchy jump out of his pickup.

Punchy yelled out a greeting and reached in the back of his truck to grab a chainsaw. Holding it up, he said, "Brought your chainsaw back. Thought today was your day off." He turned and nodded at Val and she smiled politely in return. Turning back to Daniel, he asked if he wanted him to go put it back in the barn, but Daniel told him he would do it later, so he just sat it down. He leaned against the car with one hand and asked where they had been. Val, a little too quickly, blurted out they had errands in town.

Punchy raised his eyebrows and looked at Daniel. "Well, if you're not doing anything right now, you want to ride up to Millsville with me and grab a soda? I got to check in at the garage. Mr. Carpenter's working on my tractor and I want to see how things are coming along. Parts should have been in yesterday."

Val blurted out before Daniel could respond. "I think Daniel better pass."

Punchy raised his eyebrows again and looked at Daniel questioningly.

Val never jumped in and answered for him. As a matter of fact, she didn't care much for Punchy, so she usually excused herself whenever he came over.

Daniel shrugged. "Sure." He then quickly looked over at Val and said, "We won't be long."

Val opened her mouth to speak, but glancing at Punchy changed her mind and walked over by Daniel. Lowering her voice, she said calmly, "But didn't you say you had a headache, dear? Maybe you really should just come inside for a while."

But Daniel just kissed her on the cheek and whispered, "I won't be long." Then turning to Punchy, he nodded and said, "Let's go."

When Daniel and Punchy got in his pickup, Punchy looked over at

Daniel. "Man, Daniel, I was beginning to worry that Val was wearing the pants in the family now instead of you."

Daniel didn't comment but was already wishing he had taken her advice and stayed home.

Four hours later, the phone rang and Val jumped up to grab it, hoping it was Daniel. It was Sarah checking in to see if Daniel had gotten back home and how he was doing. When Val told her he was still out with Punchy, Sarah told her not to worry. Daniel was a grown man and should have enough sense to take care of himself.

Val wasn't so sure though. His ego was also at stake, and that tended to cloud his common sense. "The doctor said he was supposed to take it easy all weekend, absolutely no lifting. Not even a five-pound bag of sugar."

"Humph," Sarah said. "Men! You know that just goes to show you they're all big babies. We deliver seven- to eight-pound babies, and within the hour, they're throwing them back at us to take care of, even if our babies are delivered by C-section. Men have a couple of half-inch incisions and they're told to take it easy for a whole weekend. Where's the justice in that?"

Val smiled in agreement and started to say something but heard the back door close, so she quickly said, "I think Daniel just came in. I'll call you later."

Val hung up the phone and walked into to the den in time to see Daniel gingerly easing himself into the recliner.

As she walked over, she heard him breathing deeply. His eyes were closed and he was ashen. He slowly opened his eyes and said, "I think I'm ready for another round of that Ibuprofen now." Val disappeared and returned with a glass of water and the two tablets. Daniel took them and handed back the glass.

She softly asked if he was all right. Daniel replied that he had been better, but it was his own fault. He had stood at the garage for longer than he should. Then Punchy wanted to show him some deer tracks in one of his fields, so he had been walking around plowed fields for another couple of hours. When Daniel almost passed out, he had to finally break down and tell Punchy what he had done.

Later that night, when Daniel eased himself into bed and gingerly drew up the covers, he let out a long heavy sigh. "Well, one thing's for sure. That procedure does work."

Val rose up one elbow and rolled over to face Daniel in the dark. "What makes you say that?"

"I do believe for the first time in my life that is the absolute last thing on my mind."

Val smiled and kissed him on the cheek and whispered, "I guess there really is a first time for everything."

Chapter Thirteen
FAIR JUDGMENT

M R. MILLS WAS sitting on his stool behind the counter at Millsville General Store, ringing up the occasional customer. He only had one speed and that was slow. So if it actually got hectic, Victor Sears, his only employee, took over. Victor was a good worker and kept busy all day stocking shelves, sweeping and ordering supplies.

Mr. Mills kept the store open because he enjoyed it and felt it was a cornerstone in the community—just as much as the local churches. It was the checkpoint for hunters when they killed their deer and the local gathering place for everything else. If anything happened in the community, the men would flock to the store to sit around and talk. As long as the store was stocked with soft drinks, snacks and a few fishing supplies, nobody complained.

Victor, however, took his job seriously. He needed the money and was always afraid the store was going to go belly-up. He saved every penny he could, hoping to one day have his own store, but not here. Not in Millsville. He had bigger dreams than this little, backwoods community. He was checking dates on some of the grocery items in the back coolers when he heard the door open and Mr. Mills chatting away. After hearing the door open twice more, he decided to check on things up front.

Edgar was there talking with Cleo Williams. Mr. Cleo was a widower in his mideighties who lived a few miles from the store. He had farmed all his life but now just rented out his fields to others younger than himself. His wife, Emma, had passed away years earlier and they had never been blessed with any children, so he lived alone. Victor nodded a greeting to both men but then noticed a stranger through the window. The man had finished pumping gas and was headed toward the entrance, so Victor took his place behind the register.

Edgar had been expressing his condolences about Mr. Cleo's sister passing when the gentleman walked in. As he walked toward the counter, Mr. Cleo looked up and said, "Edgar, this is Mary's son, Marty. He brought me home from the funeral." Edgar and Marty shook hands and exchanged greetings.

"Sure sorry to hear about your ma, Marty. She was a fine woman, from what I've been told."

Marty acknowledged with a nod.

"Yeah, with Mary gone, I'm the last young'in left. Marty here is the only grandchild. He's actually the only living relative I got left now." He shook his head and clicked his tongue. "I guess us Williams turned out to be a weak bunch."

Edgar puffed his chest out. "What are you talking about? You're 'bout as tough as a lighter knot."

Mr. Cleo smiled and said, "Well, I used to be anyway, huh?"

Victor hated to interrupt, but when he caught Marty's eye, he said, "If the gas will be all, it's $10.75."

Marty quickly reached for his wallet. "Oh yeah, yeah, that's all. Thank you."

He paid for his gas and then turned back to his uncle. "You ready to head on home, Uncle Cleo?"

Cleo nodded and started making his way toward the door. "Yeah, we better get a move on. I know you have that long drive back to Charlotte tonight." Turning to Edgar and Mr. Mills, he said his good-byes.

When they left, Victor started back toward the coolers but stopped when he heard a noise coming from behind one of the aisles. Then he remembered that he had heard the door open three times. He walked around the first row of shelving to see who was back there. As he did, he was making a mental note to ask Mr. Mills one more time if they could change the alignment of the shelves. They ran parallel to the register so you couldn't see what people were doing. Victor had told Mr. Mills more than once that they needed to be turned in the other direction so he could have full view of the customers.

When Victor rounded the corner, there stood Marcus and Johnnie Timms. They were facing each other, talking low, and Victor clearly saw Marcus stick something in his pocket.

Johnnie, who was facing Victor, was the first to realize they were caught and took off in the opposite direction and out the door. Marcus, however, didn't have that extra second to make a move, so Victor grabbed him by the back of his shirt, before he had a chance to take his first step.

He dragged Marcus to the counter and told him to empty his pockets. Marcus pulled out two candy bars and a couple of pieces of gum. "I was going to pay for it, Mr. Vic. You just didn't give me the chance."

"Oh yeah, Marcus? Where's your money? I'll ring it up right now."

Marcus looked around nervously and then blurted out, "Johnnie has my money, and he ran away."

Victor grunted. "Yeah, right. Just like I thought. I'm calling the sheriff."

He was reaching for the phone when Mr. Mills stood from his stool. "Now wait a minute, Vic. Let's not jump to conclusions. Marcus here might be telling the truth." Victor grabbed the receiver and stared at Mr. Mills in disbelief. "He's lying and you know it. You can't let these kids walk in here and steal whatever they want."

Mr. Mills nodded. "You're right, but he didn't actually steal anything, so I can't see as he's getting away with anything." Victor turned slightly toward Mr. Mills with his back to Marcus, holding the phone receiver to his chest and lowered his voice. "At least get Sheriff Bullard over here to scare him a bit."

Edgar stepped in and said, "Now hold on here, Vic. The sheriff has better things to do. Why don't you let me take the boy home and I'll talk to his mama? Annie Mae will straighten him out quicker than any sheriff."

Mr. Mills nodded in agreement, but Victor wasn't satisfied and slammed the receiver down and puffed up like a bullfrog.

Marcus looked at Victor. "What about Johnnie? Are you going to call his parents too?"

Victor glared back at Marcus. "I didn't see Johnnie stuff anything in his pockets. Just you." Marcus puffed up and balled his fists. He looked ready to fight, but Edgar put his hand on his back. "Now, now. Come on, boy. Let me get you on home." He turned to Mr. Mills and told him he'd see him later, then nodded to Victor and led Marcus out the door.

When they got outside, Marcus was still fuming. Edgar motioned for him to get his bike and throw it in the back of his pickup. Edgar let down the tailgate and helped Marcus lift the bike.

"Mr. Branch, that still ain't fair!"

Edgar looked over at Marcus and asked, "Fair for whom?"

Marcus let the bike drop hard in the bed of the pickup. "Me! Johnnie didn't get in trouble at all and it was all his idea. It's all his fault!"

Edgar, in his easygoing manner, let the tailgate back up and looked at Marcus as he walked toward the driver's door to get in. "Just because Johnnie didn't get what he deserved, doesn't mean you were treated unfairly. Plus a man can never blame somebody else for a decision he himself made. He may have put you up to it, but you made the decision to go along with it all on your own. Nobody can do that for you."

Marcus grunted and turned his gaze out the window muttering, "It's just like Darnell said. Mr. Vic grabbed me because I'm black." Edgar had been reaching toward the ignition but stopped and let his hand drop to his thigh.

"Hmmm, is that what you think? That ole Vic in there thinks you're the bad seed cause you're black, huh?" Pausing and rubbing his chin, he said, "Well, you could be right. I don't know 'bout the man's heart, but if that's the case, it sure is a shame you just proved him right."

Marcus jerked his head around toward Edgar and crossed his arms. He let out a heavy breath, wanting to argue, but not knowing a good defense.

"A few years ago, that Martin Luther King fellow was making a speech about a dream he had for his children. Do you know what he said?"

"Of course I do! He said he had a dream that his children would grow up and not be judged by the color of their skin!"

Edgar waited a second and said, "You didn't finish the sentence. What he said was he had a dream that his children would live in a nation where they would not be judged by the color of their skin, but by the content of their character." Looking at Marcus, he continued. "Every man, woman, and child is judged, Marcus. It's part of life and it will be part of the afterlife. If Vic judged you by your skin color, he's in the wrong, but either way, the content of your character is at stake here and that's your responsibility."

Two cars pulled into the parking lot, creating a cloud of dust. Four teenagers jumped out of each car and ran into the store laughing and carrying on. Edgar knew Vic would be on his toes and at the register.

He reached in his back pocket and pulled out his wallet. He took three dollars out and handed it Marcus. "You take this back in the store and buy the candy that you had in your pocket. You tell Vic and Mr. Mills you're sorry and you come on back outside."

Marcus's eyes grew wide and he shook his head. Edgar smiled and put the money into Marcus's hand and lightly squeezed it. He looked him straight in the eye. "If you don't go back in there now, it will just be hanging over your head. You'll feel uncomfortable every time you go back in that store, and ole Vic won't ever have a reason to change his opinion of you." Pulling his hand back, but still looking at Marcus, he continued. "You have to *prove* the content of your character."

Marcus took the money and, with dread in his eyes, slowly made his way back in the store.

Edgar dropped Marcus off at his house but didn't go inside. He also didn't tell Annie Mae or Leroy what happened. Edgar knew Marcus was a good boy. He felt he had learned a valuable lesson and left that day with a stronger desire to be who he really was inside—not how others told him to be or how others may perceive him to be. Johnnie only left with a couple of candy bars that, no doubt, were already consumed and forgotten. Johnnie, the one who desperately needed the lesson, got away free. No punishment, no lesson. He probably had also left, unchanged.

Chapter Fourteen

HOLIDAY BLESSINGS

CARLA WAS LYING on the floor on her stomach, watching the Thanksgiving Day parade on TV. She had her elbows propping her up so her chin could rest in her hands. When a commercial interrupted the parade, she went to the kitchen to get a glass of water.

Val had the oven door open and was leaning over, spooning drippings out one corner of the roasting pan and pouring them back on the turkey. "Mmmmmm. That sure smells good, Mama. I'm getting really hungry." Val smiled. "Well, it won't be too much longer now. The turkey's almost ready and everybody will be here soon."

Carla got her water and took a couple of sips, watching Val finish up with the turkey and close the oven door. "I just love Thanksgiving. It's like Christmas without the tree and presents!"

Val looked around, trying to decide what she needed to do next, and said, "Yeah, me too, sweetie." Then taking a breath, she said, "But it sure is a lot of work."

"I can help, Mama." Carla put her glass down and waited. Val knew now that she would have to assign Carla a task. She had not meant to sound defeated, but she was trying to make their first Thanksgiving in the house perfect. It was only 11 a.m. and she was exhausted. She really didn't want Carla underfoot in the kitchen, so Val told her to go straighten her room before Uncle Herman and Aunt Sarah arrived. Carla immediately headed down the hall to do just that.

The back door opened and Val heard Will and Daniel come in. They paused for a few minutes in the den to view the TV and see what was coming down the street in the parade. Then they continued into the kitchen and dining area.

They both took a deep, exaggerated breath at the same time and said, "Mmmmmm, smells good." Then, as usual, they both laid their rifles down on the dining room table.

Val looked up from what she was doing and gave them both a stern look. "I've told you about putting your guns on the table. I would think that on Thanksgiving, of all days, we wouldn't have to clear guns away before we can set the table!"

The family usually sat on the stools around the bar to eat. The dining room table, for the most part, was reserved for company. Daniel and the boys had developed a bad habit of placing their guns there, instead of where they should. Will immediately apologized and grabbed his gun as he started down the hall. Daniel stopped him to hand off his gun as well and looked over at Val apologetically.

"Everything okay, grouchy pants?" He walked over behind her and put his arms around her waist to snuggle down in the nape of her neck. She scrunched up her shoulders and shrugged him off, saying a little too gruffly, "I'm just busy. That's all. While y'all were out sitting in the woods all morning, I've been cooking, cleaning, and cooking some more."

Val looked over at Daniel and realized how terrible she sounded. She was just stressed. They had always had Thanksgiving at his parents' house. But this year, she volunteered their home. She had been excited about it. But the realization that at any minute Margaret would be there with her white glove on, looking down her nose at Val, making snide remarks about something not being perfect, was not very exciting. Oh, most days it didn't bother Val, but a person could take but so much and then …

Val took a deep breath to try to calm down and then leaned her head back, closing her eyes. When she opened them, Daniel was still standing there looking at her.

"I'm sorry, but everything looks great and smells even better. You need some help with something?" He smiled.

She gave him a slight smile in return and held up her hand saying, "I'm fine." Then she looked around to decide where to begin. Rubbing her hands on her apron, she said, "I just had a mini breakdown, but I'm fine now, really."

Just then, the front doorbell rang.

Carla came bounding down the hallway yelling, "It's Uncle Herman and Aunt Sarah! I'll get it!"

Carla let them in the front door and everybody exchanged hugs. Jimmy ran down the hall to find the boys. Sarah headed straight to the kitchen to help Val, and Daniel noticed Val's mood immediately changed gears. They were laughing and clucking like hens in seconds.

Val and Sarah got along better than most sisters and were definitely best friends, so Daniel knew she'd be just fine the rest of the day. They joined forces against his mother and he and Herman just sat back and watched. The men cut through the formal living room, which was still completely empty except for a stereo that Daniel had picked up at Sears cheap, because it had a chip on the corner. They both plopped down in the den, pretending to watch the parade, but were really just waiting for the football games to begin.

Rod came in the back door, grinning as always, gun in hand. Herman looked up and asked, "See anything today, Rod?"

Rod shook his head. "Nah, just a couple of doe."

Daniel laughed. "Well, that's better than me and Will. I don't even think I saw so much as a squirrel in the woods today." The carport door opened and in came Margaret and Edgar. They never rang the doorbell and always came in through the den instead of the front door.

Daniel got up to greet them but grabbed Rod's arm first as he walked by and said almost in a whisper, "Hey, go on and put your gun up in the closet. Don't lay it down on the table."

Rod looked at him with raised his eyebrows. "Oh, I wouldn't do that. It's Thanksgiving!" Daniel cleared his throat. "Yeah right, of course not."

When dinner was ready, the family gathered together and Edgar blessed the food. Everyone chatted and enjoyed the meal; even Margaret seemed to enjoy herself. The adults sat at the table while the kids sat in the kitchen around the bar that separated the kitchen area from the dining area. The food was lined up everywhere. They had enough to feed the whole community.

The boys finished first and disappeared outside to play. Carla hopped down from her barstool announcing that she was done and going to her room. She paused in the doorway and asked if Jackie could come over that afternoon.

Val looked up and said, "No, sweetie. She'll be with family today. We'll see about tomorrow though."

Edgar, who sat at the end of the table by the doorway, reached back and grabbed Carla's hand. "Sure hope I don't get a headache." Carla smiled and they both said in unison, "Cause I don't have enough room for an aspirin." They both laughed and she skipped down the hall to play.

Herman and Daniel retired to the den with a cup of coffee, to watch the football game. Edgar thanked Val for a wonderful meal and excused himself to go take his afternoon nap. He gave Val appreciative hug and whispered, "I'll be up later for another slice of that coconut cake."

Margaret offered to stay and help clean up the dishes, but Val and Sarah, a little too quickly, volunteered to do them alone.

All the food was covered and placed on the stove, available to anyone who got hungry later. There would not be any more cooking today. Val got the water ready and began washing the dishes, while Sarah dried.

"Val, it was a wonderful meal. The turkey looked like an advertisement for Butterball."

Val smiled. "Thanks. I'm so glad it's over though. Isn't that terrible? I hate to admit it, but, I'm worn out and this morning I completely snapped at Daniel and Will."

Sarah smiled and said, "I'm sure those two deserved it."

"I was in such a knot by the time we sat down to eat, I wasn't even hungry. I had to force myself."

Sarah smiled. "Unfortunately, holidays are stressful, especially on women. We want everything to be perfect. I blame Betty Crocker for that. Who does she think she is anyway?"

"It's not just today, Sarah. I've been tired for the last month it seems. It's all the extra work with the house, I guess. At first, I was excited and loved it. Now the new has worn off. I didn't realize how much extra work a bigger house would be. Two bathrooms! What was I thinking? I miss Annie Mae too. She did most of the laundry for me. I thought having a dryer would make things easier and it does, but I do a load of laundry every day! And Margaret! She pops in here some days as soon as I get home from work, to report to me about something Daniel needs to do around the place. I constantly feel like she's inspecting things. If she walks in and I am sitting on the couch, I feel guilty." Looking at Sarah, she handed her a plate she had been washing the entire time she was ranting. Val realized she was having another mini breakdown. "I'm sorry." Then laughing at herself, she said, "I'm sure it's close to that time of the month too. Can you tell?"

Daniel walked into the kitchen, empty coffee cup in hand, and looking at Sarah, he said, "Herman wants another slice of the pecan pie."

Sarah put her hands on her hips. "You've got to be kidding."

Val laughed and got the pie out of the oven where they had put some of the leftovers. She handed the whole thing to Sarah with a fork. "There's only one slice left. It's all his."

Sarah left to take it in to Herman.

Val turned back around to the dishes, and she and Daniel laughed to themselves as they heard Sarah getting on Herman from the other room about being a glutton.

Daniel winced. "I do believe the Margaret in her comes out

occasionally." He walked over to Val and gave her a peck on the cheek as he whispered in her ear, "Everything was perfect today. Thank you."

She looked up and saw how much he really meant it. When he turned to leave, Val was overcome with a new emotion and tears rolled uncontrollably down her cheeks. As she sniffed and tried to wipe them away before Sarah came back, she couldn't help but wonder what was wrong with her today.

The days after Thanksgiving flew by, as they always did in a whirlwind and it was soon time to put up the Christmas tree. Will and Rod had walked the woods the last couple of weeks looking for the perfect one. They placed the tree in the formal living room in front of the center window. Now there were two items in the room: the tree and the stereo.

Val played the only Christmas album they owned, by Bing Crosby. Daniel placed a whopping two strands of lights on the tree. They usually only had one, so everyone was excited at the overwhelming glow. Next, the kids took turns hanging the ornaments, and minutes later, the tree was finished. The kids lay on the floor on their backs staring up at the tree, talking about what they wanted for Christmas. Daniel and Val stood off to the side, just taking in the picture postcard scene.

Daniel put his arms around Val and softly asked her what she wanted for Christmas. She smiled. "You know I told you we wouldn't exchange gifts this year. The house is enough, plus money is t-i-g-h-t." Looking back at the kids, she continued. "Just seeing the kids get something is always enough for me. You know that."

Daniel did know that. Val was not a woman who needed to be showered with gifts. But this year more than ever, he wanted to give her something special. She had been working hard fixing up the house, and dealing with her daily dose of his mother. He could tell it was wearing on her. Most nights, she was asleep before Daniel could cut off the bedroom light and climb in bed beside her.

The next week was hectic at Sears and Daniel was working long hours. The large appliance department was backed up in making its deliveries, so Daniel would sometimes volunteer to drop off an appliance to customers on his way home. It was also a good selling point for him, if he could guarantee delivery by Christmas.

One day, Daniel tried to squeeze in a local delivery during his lunch break. The appliance was loaded, and he was getting ready to drive off, when out of the corner of his eye, he saw an elderly lady. She was hunched over, using a cane and walking slowly, but with determination, toward the store entrance.

Daniel knew it would be hard for her to pull open the heavy glass doors and maneuver through, so he jogged over to assist her. He held the door open as she made her way through. She looked at him sweetly, thanking him for his thoughtfulness. Daniel just smiled and waited patiently, but he really wanted to hurry the woman up. It was going to be hard enough as it was for him to deliver the washer and be back on the floor in his allotted lunch break. When she finally cleared the entrance, he sped away to make his delivery.

Daniel made the delivery in record time, and the family had been so appreciative that when he pulled up in the Sears parking lot, he was feeling pretty good. As he pulled on the glass door to go in, he saw the same elderly lady heading his way. This time, he held the door for her to come out, feeling a little more patient.

He even chatted as she made her way slowly through the exit. "What? No shopping bags?"

She sweetly looked over at him and shook her head. "No, I'm slower at making a decision than I am at walking. I'll have to come back with my daughter so she can help me."

Daniel laughed and watched to make sure she was getting to her car safely, and then he headed out on the floor.

He was standing there directing a customer to the shoe department when he noticed one of the store's security personnel making his way outside in a hurry. Daniel stepped out in the aisle to get a better view and could see several people out in the parking lot and a buzz of activity. It wasn't busy right now in the department, so he told Kenneth, the other salesperson, that he was going outside to check things out.

When Daniel got out to the parking lot, he noticed that the elderly lady he had helped seemed to be the center of attention. He felt a twinge of guilt, hoping nothing had happened to her. He should have walked her all the way out to her car. As he got closer though, he realized she wasn't hunched over anymore and her cane had been abandoned on the ground. Her sweet demeanor was gone as well, as she argued with the security personnel.

Daniel approached the scene and asked Jeff, another salesperson, what was going on.

Jeff with a disgusted look said, "The old lady was stealing a TV set."

Daniel looked shocked. "Her?"

Jeff nodded. "Yeah, the old lady had a harness around her neck. Hooked the end of it to the handle on top of a portable TV set and let it hang down between her legs as she waddled out." He put his hands on his hips and looked around, eyeing the parking lot. "Yeah, some idiot even held the door open for her."

Daniel felt his stomach churn and all of sudden wished he hadn't come out to investigate. Then, glancing nervously around the lot, he saw Val getting out of her car. Grateful that he had an out, he immediately excused himself and started walking toward her. As he approached the car, however, he noticed she had a strained look on her face. That's when he remembered she had a checkup that morning. She hadn't said so, but he got the impression she was worried. "What's wrong, Val? Are you okay? What did the doctor say? Why are you here?"

She didn't answer right away but leaned against the car, staring at the ground. When she did finally look up at Daniel, he didn't have any trouble reading her mood. *Uh-oh,* Daniel thought. *She's not worried but mad, very mad.*

She didn't keep him guessing long, and when she began to speak, Daniel could tell she was trying to control herself. "It seems," she said slowly, "that I'm pregnant."

Daniel just stood there dumbfounded, so she continued. "That's why I've been tired. That's why I've been moody." Then, popping him in the stomach with her pocketbook, she finished. "That's why I am going to kill you, Daniel Branch!"

Daniel started to speak, "Wha- wha-" but he didn't know what else to say. He swallowed hard then said, "I thought we couldn't. I mean, I thought I couldn't."

She glared at him with her arms crossed tightly around her waist. "Well, I asked my doctor about that and it seems you didn't pay close enough attention to what Dr. Weaver instructed you to do. You told me that you were fine after a few days. Well, you weren't!"

Letting out an exaggerated breath, she continued. "It takes longer than that for everything to be cleared out of your system, and besides that, you were supposed to take a sample back to the office to be tested, to verify things were okay. Did you do that, Daniel?" Before he could answer, she continued. "No, no, you didn't do that! You told me instead things were fine."

Daniel pushed his hair back with his hands and looked around the parking lot trying to find an escape route, but there wasn't one. He honestly didn't remember anything the doctor had told him. Every time he was in his office, he was so nervous that he really had not paid attention to anything. He hadn't heard anything except when the doctor was explaining the actual surgical procedure.

He lost all the literature the doctor had given him and hadn't thought about it since then. "Val, I honestly don't remember what he said. I'm sorry. I'll take a sample this week."

She popped him again with her purse. "This week! He doesn't need one now. It's too late!" she said as she threw her hands out and jutted her stomach toward him. "I'm already pregnant. That can't happen again for another nine months, and only then if I ever allow you to touch me again!" She popped him one last time with her purse and then got in her car, mumbling about having to get back to work since she would now have to be careful with her time off and save up for maternity leave.

Daniel watched her speed away and then turned back to the scene with the shoplifter, as the police finally began to arrive. What a day he was having. How many more things could he mess up? His mood had changed in less than fifteen minutes. So had the rest of his life.

Daniel and Val hardly spoke for days. Val immediately told Sarah about the pregnancy, but no one else. Deep down, Val knew it was a blessing, but her immediate reaction didn't reflect such. She would sometimes cry softly at night after she was in bed, thinking about how their lives would change. Things were finally in place the way she had dreamed about, and now this. She didn't want to start announcing their news until she knew she could do it with a smile on her face.

On Christmas Eve, they all gathered at Edgar and Margaret's house for hot chocolate and cookies before the kids went to bed. It was tradition that Edgar read them the Christmas story from Luke chapter 2, and then for fun "'Twas the Night before Christmas." All the kids loved the readings and so did the grownups.

The kids were getting too old for Santa stories, but they never let on and played right into all the fantasy. The kids sat on the floor listening to the stories like it was their first time hearing them. When Edgar finished, he would give the grandkids their Christmas gifts.

Margaret was not one for buying Christmas gifts so Edgar would compensate by giving the children something of his. Margaret allowed it because Edgar saved everything and it was the only time when he would give away his old junk. They loved his gifts just as much as any new toy Santa would bring. He always had a way of explaining why each gift went to each child, and it always seemed to make perfect sense.

This year, he presented Will with three old coins because he was destined to be a businessman. Rod received a fishing lure, handmade by his great grandfather. Jimmy received a notepad of drawing paper because he loved to draw, and for Carla, he pulled out a guitar that had once belonged to his father.

When he laid it in her lap, her eyes lit up. "I never learned to play it, and I always felt that was a disappointment to him, but I just never had the desire. I know it's kind of big, but you'll grow into it." He winked at Carla and continued. "Something tells me you'll be the one who'll find a use for it."

She gave him a huge bear hug and he sat back down in his seat, looking pleased with his choices. The kids were busy comparing gifts and Val looked down at them, watching and listening to her children. They really were growing up fast. She looked up to catch Daniel staring at her and knew he was thinking the same thing.

He reached over and put his arm around her, and for the first time in days, she let him. With his other hand, he reached over and took her hand, holding it gently on his thigh. Their eyes never left each other's gaze as he whispered, "It's going to be okay, ya know."

Her eyes spilled over with soft tears and she smiled. "I know, Daniel, I know." At that moment, Daniel knew with God's help and his own stupidity, he had given her a special Christmas gift after all.

Chapter Fifteen

SNOWMAN MELTDOWN

*T*HE OFFERTORY SONG played while the congregation sang out. Punchy and Daniel took their positions at the back of the church and waited.

Punchy whispered to Daniel, "You think Reverend Crumpler will try to cut it short today? It's starting to come down heavier out there. Some of the senior adults left right after Sunday school. So far, it's not sticking to the roads, but that could change any minute."

Daniel shrugged. He tried to stay reverent while waiting to go down, but Punchy couldn't stand still for five minutes without talking.

Daniel just let him talk, and looked straight ahead. As they began the last verse, and they were just about to make their move, Punchy leaned over once again and began talking even lower this time.

Daniel tensed up, having a feeling he knew what he was about to ask. "Hey, ah, Daniel, I been meaning to ask you. Um, I thought you and Val, ah, couldn't have any more children. I thought you had that taken care of."

Daniel turned and looked at Punchy, smiling wide. "Yeah, but we never did stop trying." Satisfied that he had shut Punchy up, he grinned the whole way down the aisle.

After worship service, people made their way to their cars, because of the snow, without the usual chitchat. There was now a good inch or two of freshly fallen snow. The roads were still just slush, but when the temperatures dropped that afternoon, that would no longer be the case.

Margaret held onto the handrail and gingerly descended the steps of the church.

Ms. Thelma was right behind her. "Oh my, I hope they salted these steps good. I would hate to break a hip. I told Ralph we should leave after Sunday school. It's really coming down now."

Margaret replied, "I don't know why all women over the age of fifty are so obsessed with breaking a hip!"

Val had descended the steps and waited at the bottom for Daniel. When Margaret and Thelma joined her, Thelma asked how the pregnancy was going. Val told her she felt fine, and she was not experiencing morning sickness. Thelma then turned to Margaret and asked, "Well, since they live right in your backyard, Margaret, are you going to get to babysit this grandchild?"

Margaret jerked her head back. "Why in the world would I want to do that? I raised my children. I'm way too busy to raise somebody else's now."

Val quickly responded by telling Thelma that Annie Mae had already said she would love to keep the baby for them. Val would just drop the baby off at Annie Mae's house on her way to work and pick the child up there in the evening on her way home.

The children played in the snow the whole afternoon, only coming in occasionally to warm their hands or grab something to drink. The mountains of North Carolina got their fair share of snow every winter, enough to keep the skiers happy. Millsville, however, was far enough southeast that a heavy snowfall was not guaranteed every winter. Oh, they always had a flurry or two, but any kind of accumulation was rare enough to be exciting.

The next day, the Sears Department store and Val's office closed due to poor road conditions. The snow had stopped falling sometime during the night, and by noon, there wasn't a cloud in sight. The snow was already falling and melting from tree limbs and rooftops. The kids, having grown tired of snowball fights, decided to build a snowman. The snow was now wet and stuck well, so in a manner of minutes, they had built a small snowman. After decorating their creation with sticks and pinecones, they stood back to admire their work.

"That looks mighty nice," Daniel said when he came outside.

"Yeah" Carla said, "but nobody will be able to see it. Our house is too far away from the road."

Then Will came up with a plan to build a bigger one, closer to the highway. He began forming the ball and rolling it down the drive. The snow was sticking so well it left a bare path all the way to the dirt. Soon, it took all three children pushing to keep the ball moving. Their driveway ran downhill, so gravity was also on their side. When they were two thirds of the way toward their goal, they called on Daniel to help push. He put his back up against the snowball and pushed off with his legs. The kids pushed on both sides with their hands. Once they got the ball rolling again, they didn't dare stop. If they lost their momentum, it would have to stay right where it sat. Knowing this, Daniel began to gradually shift his weight to guide the ball off the drive.

They pushed the ball all the way down the drive, parking it at the edge of the tree line. It was seated on a small mound to the left of their drive, in clear view of all passersby. It was more like a blob than a ball, but with a little whittling, they rounded out the shape to an acceptable sphere. It was over six feet tall, so they could not reach high enough to add a second ball on top. They grabbed sticks and pinecones to jab in the snow to form a huge smiley face.

It warmed up that afternoon and melted the snow enough that everyone could return to work and school the following day. The snowball, however, sat in the shade, thanks to a patch of pine trees, so it didn't seem to have melted even an inch.

Days later, when all traces of the snowfall had vanished, the snowball still stood. Daniel joked that it was hanging in there longer than his aching muscles he'd pulled in his back in making it.

Temperatures rose every day, but at night, what was left of the ball would quickly refreeze. It was exciting for the children to get off the bus and check to see if the ball had made it through another day. The ball got dirtier and smaller, but still it survived the warm weather.

"Twenty-five days and counting!" Will yelled one day as he got off the bus. Rod ran over and gave the ball a gentle tap in front, close to the ground. It gave way to his foot, leaving a deep indention in the snow.

Next, Rod stuck his finger into the ball. "Yeah, but it's pretty soft. I don't think it will make it a full month now." The kids had hoped it would hold on a full month for bragging rights. They had never experienced a cold snap long enough to keep snow hanging around more than a day or two.

Later that afternoon, a man pulled into Millsville Store to ask directions. When he walked in, Sheriff Bullard was having a soda and talking with Mr. Mills and Edgar. As the man entered, his eyes rested on the sheriff and headed straight for him. He didn't bother to excuse himself for interrupting their conversation but immediately relayed his frustration.

"I'm trying to find the house of Mr. and Mrs. Alan Crawford. I have directions," he said as he flashed a piece of paper in the air with some handwritten notes. "If you can call them that." He glanced down to read his notes. "Look for a large field by a big tree right after a small brick house. I mean honestly! There's nothing on this road but trees, fields, and brick houses."

Sheriff Bullard eyed the man and asked, "What business you got with the Crawfords?"

The man puffed up and asked, "What difference does that make? I'm not breaking the law, just doing a job."

Sheriff Bullard took another slow sip of his drink. "Third drive on the right."

Edgar smiled. "Don't get too upset, young fella. I have the same problem. We're the first drive after you leave here. Oh, if you're coming from Appleton, it's easy. You get 'em to Millsville Store, then count off the drives, but if you're coming from Raleigh, there ain't a lot of landmarks, and at night, there isn't any. I always tell people to come up the store and make a U-turn. We're the first drive after that. They might get a little upset having to go past and turn around, but you won't get 'em lost that way."

The man must have mistaken Edgar for the storeowner, since he was standing behind the counter with Mr. Mills, because he said, "I guess that doesn't hurt business either if everybody gets sent to your store first." Then he marched out of the store in a huff.

Mr. Mills laughed. "Well, he wasn't too pleasant, was he? Wonder if he's the insurance inspector coming out to look at their barn? He should've been here two weeks ago."

Soon the conversation turned back to the weather, farming, and deer hunting. About ten minutes had passed when Punchy pulled up. He ran up to the door and stuck his head in, nodding a quick greeting to Mr. Mills and Edgar. He then looked over at the sheriff and said, "There's a car in the ditch right past Edgar's. Thought you might want to go check it out. I don't think anybody's hurt, but the man looks pretty mad."

Sheriff Bullard pulled off the road to find the insurance man, who had been asking for directions. The sheriff walked up and eyed the damage to the car and, seeing that the man was okay, stated, "Well, I guess you didn't quite make it to the Crawfords. You want to tell me how this happened."

The man was agitated and started right in. "I was just driving along when a huge snowball came out of nowhere and burst on the hood of my car. It scared me half to death, not to mention that I couldn't see a thing. By the time I got my windshield wipers on, I was in the ditch." He had his hands on his hips and was pacing back and forth, surveying the damage to his vehicle. "I didn't see any children, but someone had to have thrown that snowball at me! Twenty years without an accident, all down the drain. Twenty years, and a snowball ruins it all!"

The sheriff took out a notepad. "Now tell me, mister-" Then he stopped, pen poised to get a response.

"Nelson. I'm Harry Nelson. I work for the Crawfords' insurance company."

Sheriff Bullard continued. "Now tell me, Mr. Nelson, did you hear any children running away when you exited the vehicle?"

Mr. Nelson shook his head.

"Did you hear any one talking or a vehicle taking off?"

He shook his head again.

"And you say it was a snowball?"

Mr. Nelson nodded.

Sheriff Bullard walked around to the other side of the vehicle and it looked it over closely and then examined the hood. He clicked his tongue a couple of times and rubbed his jaw. "How big was this snowball, Mr. Nelson?"

He thought for a minute and said, "It was at least as big as a basketball."

The sheriff walked back over to where Mr. Nelson stood and said, "Well, we've got a few problems, Mr. Nelson. First, it hasn't snowed here in over two weeks. Second, it's at least fifty degrees right now. Third, you didn't hear anybody leaving the scene of the crime. Fourth, a child couldn't lift a snowball that big and heave it out into the road."

Leaning down over the hood and looking around, he said, "And I don't see any snow!"

Mr. Nelson yelled, "But it melted! I'm telling you it was a snowball, and I don't' know how it got thrust into my path, but it did!"

But Sheriff Bullard was already filling out his report.

Mr. Nelson just sat on the ground, put his head in his hands, and began mumbling to himself. Sheriff Bullard called for Mr. Carpenter to come with his tow truck, and soon the wreck was cleared from the ditch.

The next morning, when the kids walked down to the road to get on the bus, they noticed their snowball was completely melted. They all agreed it must have been warmer overnight than the weatherman had predicted. Little did they know their smiley-faced snowball had a sense of humor and exited this world in its own terms, with one last laugh, at the expense of an overzealous insurance inspector.

Chapter Sixteen
EXTRA SPECIAL DELIVERY

*V*AL WAS HAVING an easy pregnancy. She had not been sick a single day, and even though she got tired quickly, everyone was chipping in to help. Carla had taken on several household duties, which made Val realize that she had been wrong not to school her on housework earlier. She was not only doing a good job, but seemed to be enjoying it. It was like she was playing house, and Val knew when the baby came, she would no doubt want to play mama as well.

Actually, her biggest complaint was her back. Sitting at her desk for eight hours every day, staring at the microfiche, made her back ache. She would get up often and take a stroll around the building to stretch it out. She was determined to work right up until the day she delivered, just like she had with her first two pregnancies.

When Val left work one day, Marshall the security guard held the door open for her to exit the building. "How much longer, Ms. Branch?"

Val smiled and rubbed her belly. "Two weeks, Marshall. But you know how babies like to stretch it into three or four."

He nodded.

"Hope my back holds out for that long. It's been giving me a fit for weeks, especially today. I didn't really have that with my other two." Val continued down the sidewalk and waved good-bye over her shoulder as Marshall watched for her to make it to her car safely.

As she headed home, she was daydreaming of curling up in the recliner. Nothing sounded better than propping her feet up and falling asleep to whatever happened to be on TV. All she had to do was get supper out of the way and she would be checking into the recliner hotel. Daniel would have to do the dishes again tonight, and laundry would just have to hold off another day. It was even starting to sprinkle and Val knew hard rain was predicted for the evening. She loved the sound of thunderstorms and rain hitting the roof. It made the thought of the recliner hotel even more inviting.

But when she flipped her turn signal to make her way into the drive, she saw Porkchop wandering up the side of Highway 46. Her daydreams stopped abruptly. Porkchop was Edgar's mama sow. The kids had named her Porkchop when she was just a piglet. She had since mothered several piglets of her own that had either been sold or truly became pork chops. Edgar had always had a pig or two in the pen, and occasionally one would wiggle its way out to freedom.

It was definitely a family affair to round up a loose pig and guide it back to the pen. However, they usually didn't make it all the way to the highway. Val dreaded having to begin the chase, but it was unavoidable. A pig on a busy road mixed with the approaching storm was bad news.

As soon as Val got inside the house, she told Carla to run down and let Edgar and Margaret know the posse had to be assembled to round up Porkchop. Daniel was not expected home for another hour, so they would have to make do without him. Val changed her shoes quickly but left her work dress on. It would just have to get wet. Will and Rod took off on their bikes on the dirt road behind their house. It came out on Highway 46 above their driveway and above where Val had seen Porkchop. Val met up with Carla, Edgar, and Margaret by the drive.

Edgar and Val snapped off branches that they could use to wave at the sow to shoo her the way they needed her to go.

When they reached the highway, it was no longer sprinkling but pouring. They looked up the road and could see that Will and Rod had already made it and were making their way toward the pig slowly, so they wouldn't startle her. Edgar and Margaret crossed the highway to keep her from crossing over to that side. Val and Carla stayed positioned at the drive to keep her from going past.

Val knew Carla had always been afraid of the pigs. She hated to be in the position where the pig would be coming toward her. She could handle being behind the pig and shooing him forward, but there was nothing to be done about it now. Val looked over at Carla and yelled so she could hear her through the downpour. "It's okay, Carla. All we have to do is keep her from going past the drive. She'll start heading up the hill toward the house, if we just hold our ground. Okay?" Carla just nodded, wide-eyed and stiff. Val was stationed closer to the highway, so she would be the main one needed to keep the pig in line.

Val rubbed her back and tried to stretch it out to relieve the tension, but she knew it was hopeless. Her feet hurt now too, and she knew she looked a sight. She was sopping wet and her dress clung tightly around her huge belly. The boys were doing a good job coaxing the sow back to the drive. Porchop never tried to get on the highway, which was a relief.

When the sow approached the drive, Val shook her branch at the pig and tapped it on the ground. The process was slow, because Porkchop was taking her time. The sow acted as though she was strolling in the park and stopped often to root her nose in the ground.

By the time the animal reached the drive, it was surrounded by the Branch family. Edgar and Margaret were making their way across the highway to close in on the pig. Porkchop, obviously not ready to head up hill to the pen, ran toward the weakest link in the semicircle. She squealed and made a beeline straight for Carla. Carla froze. With her hands glued to her side, she let out a long, high-pitched scream.

Val, arms flailing, let out some short yelps of her own and ran over toward Carla to shoo Porkchop away. Edward and Margaret were close behind. The boys already had their side secured, so Porkchop finally gave up and started a slow trot up the hill. Will had the right side now, and Rod hurried to take the left, so Margaret and Edgar took the rear.

Val grabbed Carla's hand and they slowly made their way up the drive as well. "They can take it from here, sweetie. Let's take it slow up this hill. I think that pig just broke my last straw today."

Val winced a few times as they made their way up the hill. Her pace slowed. She felt as though something pulled in her back when she jumped over to Carla's rescue, and the pain had gone into overdrive now. The closer they got to the house, the slower she moved. She felt as though she weighed a thousand pounds with the sopping wet clothes clinging to her body.

When the hunting party reached the house, they kept right along the dirt road leading to the pigpen. Carla and Val, still taking their time, went straight to the house. They stood on the carport for a few minutes, wringing water out of their clothes. Val was having trouble catching her breath because her back was hurting so badly. It was then she wondered if she was having Braxton Hicks contractions.

With her other pregnancies, her labor was all in her stomach. This pregnancy was just one surprise after another. Val could barely pull herself up the steps. Carla waited for her, holding the storm door open. When they got inside, Val told Carla they should go strip down in the utility room before the others came in, so they wouldn't track water all through the house. Carla stripped in seconds and began to run toward her room. Val yelled after her and asked her to bring her pink housecoat and a towel. Val was still in the process of stripping when Carla returned fully dressed. Val had to rest in-between each article she removed, taking deep breaths to try to ease the pain.

Carla looked at Val. "Mama, are you okay?"

Val, who was leaning over to try to get her panties off from her feet, didn't say anything until the task was complete. She braced herself on the counter and took some slow breaths. She picked up the towel and, while giving herself a quick rub to dry off, said, "I'm fine. Just having some contractions, I think. If they don't go away soon, your daddy might have to take me to the hospital and check things out. Maybe this baby wants out early." Val smiled weakly, but Carla still looked concerned.

"Do you want me to go get Grandma, so she can stay with you until Daddy gets home?"

Val quickly poked her head through the housecoat and said, "Oh no, that's okay. Your daddy should be here any minute anyway." She finished sliding the housecoat down over her body then laid her hand on Carla's back, nudging her along. "Why don't you come sit down with me for a little while and let me catch my breath?"

As Val was walking to the couch, she felt a familiar pressure down low and was forced to an exaggerated waddle. Now she knew there was no mistaking it; she was in labor. For a brief second, she was excited, but then the realization hit her. She was not only in labor, but the baby was coming very soon—too soon. She braced herself on the end table and put her hand between her legs, and it didn't feel normal. She tried to keep her face calm when she turned back to Carla, who was still watching her every move.

"Sweetie, I've changed my mind. I think I do need you to go get Grandma. Tell her I need her to come to the house, okay?"

Carla nodded and took off outside.

When Carla reached the pigpen, it was still raining, but not a downpour. Edgar and the boys were working on repairing the fence. Margaret was just standing there with her hands on her hips, watching with her usual stern look.

Carla, out of breath now, stopped at her side and grabbed her arm. "Grandma, Mama needs you at the house." Margaret looked down at the child "For heaven's sake child. We haven't finished fixing—"

But Carla cut her off. "I think the baby's coming. Mama said for you to come to the house now!"

Margaret looked up at Edgar, who had straightened when he heard the excitement in Carla's voice. Edgar returned Margaret's questioning stare and said, "Well, go on with ya."

Carla held on to Margaret's arm until she had put her body in motion. When Carla was sure Margaret was indeed coming, she ran on ahead of her. She wanted to hurry and get back to Val. She didn't want her to be alone, and she didn't want to miss anything.

When she got back to the house, Val was half-lying, half-sitting on the couch. "Grandma's coming, Mama."

Val nodded.

"Do you want me to get you something or do something, Mama?"

Val just shook her head and kept taking her deep breaths. Carla wasn't sure if she was sweating now or if rainwater was still dripping down her face.

Margaret finally came in the house, but before she could open her mouth, Val barked out an order in her direction. "I need you to call the doctor let him know I'm in labor. Tell him I'm not going to make it to the hospital." Val paused a few seconds to get through a contraction and then continued. "Tell him to get an ambulance over here or to come himself. I don't care which, but this baby is going to be here by the time either one arrives."

Margaret looked at Val as though she didn't believe her and asked, "Well, has your water broke? Nothing is going to happen as quickly as all that, if your water hasn't broke."

Val looked at Margaret and said in-between gasps, "My water must have broke when I was out in the rain." Then, with a little too much emphasis, she added, "Chasing your pig!"

Margaret in a huff replied, "Well, I was just saying that—"

Val interrupted. "Just make the call!"

Margaret left the room and headed to the kitchen to place the call. She told the doctor exactly what Val wanted her to say but made sure to add that Val had been fine an hour ago and she didn't see how it was possible to be having the baby in all that big a hurry.

"Now remember, the easiest way to find us is to just go to Millsville Store and turn around. We'll be the first dirt drive on the right."

She had taken her time placing the call and had not noticed when

Carla went flying by her, grabbing a stack of towels out of the linen closet. She did, however, notice when she walked back into the den and saw that Val was now lying on the floor, on a blanket, with her back up against the couch. Carla was by her side, eyes wide.

When Carla saw Margaret walk in, she grinned and stated that the baby was coming and she could already see the head. Margaret just stood there in shock. Then another contraction hit and Val began to lean forward slightly. Before she began to push, she started to say something, but all she could get out was Margaret's name.

Margaret just looked at Val then at Carla, but then her body took over, even though her brain had not caught up. She got down on her knees in front of Val. She kept mumbling to herself over and over, "It's okay. It's okay. Everything's okay." But this was for her benefit, not Val's.

When the next contraction hit, Val grabbed Margaret's hand and pulled back on it hard for more leverage. Margaret was unaware that she was breathing in time with Val. Carla was the perfect cheerleader, for both Margaret and Val, as she announced the baby's progression.

The back door opened and in came Rod, Will, and Edgar. They took in the scene in front of them without saying a word. They stood frozen and huddled together in the doorway. It was close enough to witness what was happening, but far enough away not to be part of the action. Carla now began to report to her new audience that had joined from the rear. "The baby's head is completely out now."

She continued to tell Val she was doing a good job. Carla seemed to be in her element. All the years of playing nurse had somehow prepared her for the real thing. Margaret also held her ground and breathed in and out with Val. She was now composed enough to have her hands in position to help guide the baby out.

Carla told Val she could see the shoulders, so Val gave one more hard push. Margaret had a firm, but careful, grip on the baby, and with Val's last efforts, she eased it out the rest of the way. Carla handed her a clean towel to put the baby in, then another one to gently wipe off its face and mouth. Margaret patted the baby a few quick times on its backside and bounced it up and down in her arms, and the baby gasped for air. It began to cry, and so did Val.

Edgar's eyes welled up as he patted Will and Rod on the back. "Well, looks like we have another member of the family." The boys just stood there, unsure about what they had just witnessed. Edgar walked over slowly.

He kneeled down beside Margaret, resting his hand on her back. When Margaret turned to look at him, he asked softly, "So what do we have here? A little boy or a little girl?"

Margaret sniffed hard and shook her head, more overcome with emotion than anyone had ever seen her before. "I don't even know."

She gently pulled back the towel to unwrap the baby enough to find out, then looked up and announced that it was a girl.

Carla clapped. "Oh, thank you. That's just what I wanted."

Edgar reached for Val's hand and asked if she was okay. She nodded as she returned his grip.

Margaret looked at Val, with tears streaming down her face, and said, "You did good, Val. You did real good." It was the first true compliment she had ever given Val.

Chapter Seventeen

GRANDMA MARGARET

*W*HEN THE BABY was two weeks old, Val brought her bundle into the church nursery for the first time. Nancy and Helen, the nursery workers, met her at the door with oohs and aahhs. A couple of other children old enough to sit up were playing on the floor with toys. Val sat down in one of the rocking chairs and Carla set the diaper bag beside her.

"Can I stay in the nursery with her, Mama?"

Val looked up at Carla and shook her head. "No, sweetie, you need to go on to your class now. Maybe you and Jackie can stay during worship service, okay?"

Carla rolled her lip out in a pout and started to object, but Val raised her eyebrows and stopped her before she could voice a complaint. "We talked about this, Carla."

Carla mumbled out a "Yes, Mama" then kissed Sadie on the head before she left to go to her class.

Val handed Sadie over to Nancy, while Helen sat on the floor with the other toddlers. She was giving her instructions about when she would need to be fed as Margaret came in the room.

"There's my little girl," Margaret said as she walked over to where Nancy stood holding Sadie. She put her face down close to the baby's and began talking baby gibberish and playfully tugging at her tiny fingers.

Nancy and Helen exchanged glances and stared at Margaret like she was an alien. They had never heard Margaret coo at a baby before or seen her smile. After a few seconds of playfulness, Margaret looked up at Nancy and in her usual gruff manner asked, "Who has the nursery today for worship service?" Nancy thought for a second, caught off guard by the change in attitude, and said, "I think it's Patsy today."

Margaret nodded. "Well, I have to go to Sunday school, but I'll be in here for worship service." She then looked over at Val and gave a quick nod of her head as if to say she didn't have to worry about the baby being taken care of properly.

Val just smiled and told her that Carla had already asked to stay too. Margaret nodded and said, "Good." She turned back to Sadie and changed back to her baby voice. "Grandma will see you in a little bit. You be a good girl."

As she turned to leave, she almost ran into Patsy, who had come in to sneak a peek at Sadie. Margaret just looked at her as though it was her fault they almost crashed into each other. "Carla and I will be in here during worship service to take care of Sadie." Then Margaret abruptly turned and left the room.

Nobody said anything for a few seconds, and then all at once, they all burst out laughing. Patsy put her hand to her cheek and looked at Val. "Who was that?"

Val shook her head. "I still have no idea. She's been like that ever since the baby was born." She hesitated and continued. "She's still her usual self with the rest of us, but with Sadie, she a completely different person. She's … She's …" Val shrugged. "She's actually *nice*."

Nancy chuckled. "Well, you did have a rather dramatic delivery, Val. I guess with her being right there and being part of the whole experience … Maybe it actually touched her sentimental side. I mean, we all do have one, even her."

Val laughed and said that Will and Rod had joked around, saying it was like the Grinch when he heard all the Whos singing in Whoville and his heart grew three sizes that day. Val looked down at Sadie and lightly touched her fingers. "Yes, this is definitely Grandma Margaret's soft spot." Then letting out a sigh, she said, "I just hate that Daniel missed the birth though. He's the only one that wasn't there and I can tell he feels left out. Although, to tell you the truth, I think it may have been a blessing. He would've been the one to pass out, so I think he was spared embarrassment."

Val kissed Sadie good-bye and left the nursery with Patsy. Patsy laughed and said, "We still need to get together someday before you have to go back to work. I want to hear every detail. Carla told me most of it last Sunday, but I want to hear it from Mama. I still can't get over it."

Val nodded. "Me either, and Carla was such a little trooper. You know, she has always said she wanted to be a nurse, and I honestly thought she would grow out of that notion. I mean, all little girls at one time or another want to either be a nurse or a teacher. But I saw it that day in her eyes and how she handled herself. For the first time, I'm beginning to feel like that really is her calling."

When they reached Patsy's classroom, she turned to go inside but hesitated, saying, "Val, wasn't that terrible about Mr. Cleo?"

Val shook her head. "What's the world coming to? He was such a sweet man and never hurt a fly. They still don't know why the person did it. They didn't take anything. Just meanness and the Devil is all it is."

Patsy nodded. "His nephew came down from Charlotte yesterday to make the arrangements. He's the only relative Mr. Cleo had left. He seems real shook up about it." They both just shook their heads. Just then, the bell rang to signal the start of class so Val said good-bye and headed down the hall.

Punchy stood beside Daniel during the offertory song and whispered, "So I hear you missed the whole birth thing, huh?"

Daniel nodded.

"Some of the boys got a new nickname for ya now."

Daniel just kept looking straight ahead and waited, knowing Punchy would elaborate. "Yeah, they're calling you Blister."

Daniel thought a minute and mumbled, "Blister?" He shrugged his shoulders, implying he didn't get the connection.

Punchy elbowed him and laughed. "Yeah, showing up after all the hard work's done."

Daniel rolled his eyes, took the hit, and waited for the song to end. Punchy had him again.

After the service, Val went back to the nursery to pick up Sadie. Margaret was holding her and a few ladies had gathered around as they always did when a new baby arrives. Margaret was beaming.

Val was still surprised every time she saw the new Margaret in action. She had to remember, however, that the old Margaret was there somewhere, so she still needed to keep up her guard. Ms. Thelma turned to Val when she walked up and gave her congratulations. Val thanked her as she reached down to get the diaper bag.

"So when do you have to go back to work? I know you must dread having to leave her."

Val nodded and said she would be home the whole summer and would go back to work about the same time the kids went back to school. Thelma smiled. "Well, at least you have a good sitter lined up. I'm sure that makes it easier. Why, Annie Mae has raised more young'ins—"

Margaret cut her off. "Oh, for heaven's sake, Thelma! Why would Val need to pay Annie Mae to keep Sadie when her own grandmother is right here and can do it for free?"

Val and Thelma both looked up at Margaret.

When they continued to stare, Margaret continued. "I've just been thinking. It just makes sense that she should be with family. I realize I wasn't able to help with the other grandchildren, but I feel that it's my Christian responsibility to make up for it now with Sadie."

Carla gasped. "Oh, Grandma! That would be great! Then when I get home from school, I can help you with her!" Margaret turned toward Val and gave her a questioning look.

Val smiled at Carla and turned to Margaret. "I do believe this is going to be the most spoiled baby in the whole world. Between you kids and Grandma, I think if I stopped nursing, I may actually never get to hold my own child!" Margaret smiled at Val as if to say thank-you, but of course, she never actually said a word.

After gathering all Sadie's things, they headed out to the car. Daniel and Edgar were standing by the vehicle, talking to Marty, Mr. Cleo's nephew. They were offering their condolences and asked if there was anything he needed.

"No, I'm fine," he said. "After the services tomorrow, I'll be heading back to Charlotte. The police won't even let me go in the house until after the investigation is over. I don't know what I'll do with the place." Edgar nodded and offered his help again then shook Marty's hand good-bye.

After Val and Daniel got everyone into the car, he watched as Marty walked away. "He looks kind of lost, doesn't he?" Daniel shook his head and glanced back to make sure the kids were not listening when he whispered, "Said the police think somebody killed him with a fire poker! Can you believe that?"

Val shuddered. "Well, I got news that's even more shocking than that!"

Daniel raised his eyebrows and looked at Val. "What could that possibly be?"

She nodded in the direction of Margaret, who giving the pastor what looked like a piece of her mind. "Your mother has volunteered to keep Sadie when I go back to work instead of Annie Mae." She turned to look at Daniel with an expression that dared him to top that.

Daniel glanced at Margaret then at Val. "What in the world?"

Then, shaking his head and glancing down at Sadie, he said, "The only other baby who could work a miracle like that was born in a stable to a virgin."

Val smiled. "Well, I almost delivered in a stable and there was one farm animal involved." They both laughed at the thought of Porkchop's role in the day's events, but Daniel secretly had a pang of regret that he had missed it all.

Chapter Eighteen
MOTORCYCLE MANIA

*D*ANIEL GOT OUT of his truck and turned back toward the door. He barely had his arms out before Sadie hopped from the truck seat into his outstretched arms. "Whoa, girl! Daddy almost didn't catch you."

Sadie just laughed as she always did. She laughed at everything. If Daniel had actually missed her, she would have found humor in falling to the ground. Daniel had to laugh back. Of all the kids, he had never once scolded Sadie. Nobody did. The family joked that she was the most spoiled child that ever lived, and of course, that made her laugh too.

Daniel plopped a kiss on her cheek and closed the truck door. He hesitated, looking at Sadie. "Okay, missy. Are we walking or riding?"

She squeezed his neck hard and yelled, "Riding!" while kicking her feet like a horse on his side. Daniel took his cue and lifted Sadie up onto his shoulders. When he reached the doorway at Millsville Store, he ducked down so Sadie would clear the doorframe. Sadie leaned down too, putting her face right up beside Daniel's. She patted his cheek and scrunched up her nose. "You're scratchy. Just like Grandpa."

Daniel acted offended. "Scratchy? That's one of the seven dwarfs, isn't it?"

Once inside the store, Daniel lifted Sadie off his shoulders and sat her down. She immediately spotted Edgar and ran straight to him, yelling, "Grandpa!" Edgar was sitting at the end of the customers counter with a couple of other men who were chatting with Mr. Mills. Mr. Mills was seated on his usual stool behind the counter.

Jackie, who was now working at the store part-time, was taking care of the occasional customers. Vick had been gone a couple of years now and Mr. Mills ran through one employee after another trying to find a replacement. They either got tired of working at the store for low wages or Mr. Mills didn't like them. The arrangement with Jackie seemed to work great. She had worked all summer and wanted as many hours as she could get when school started back. She planned to get off the bus there every day and work until closing, then work all day on Saturdays. She was a hard worker and pleasant with the customers, especially the boys. Jackie was a huge flirt and her body had blossomed early, so her flirting was always well received.

Edgar grabbed Sadie and plopped her on his lap. "There's my girl," he said, grinning big.

Mr. Perkins looked over at Sadie and asked, "Ain't you had enough of this old man today?"

Sadie just laughed and shook her head.

Edgar pretended to be offended and then looked back at Sadie. "Tell ole Mr. Perkins here what we had for lunch today."

Sadie laughed. "An ear and a foot!"

Mr. Perkins leaned toward Sadie resting one elbow on his knee and asked, "Whose ear and foot?"

Sadie laughed even louder and said, "A pig's!"

Edgar snapped his finger. "That's right, and come to think of it, we didn't get dessert. Let's go see what we can find." He headed toward the candy aisle while holding Sadie's hand.

Daniel walked over and remarked to Mr. Perkins that Sadie was going to be the youngest person with high cholesterol with the way Margaret was cooking and Edgar was buying her candy.

Mr. Perkins rocked back on the hind legs of his chair and looked at Daniel smirking. He said, "Why don't you tell Margaret to change up what she cooks?"

Nobody said anything for a few seconds, and then they all burst out laughing, including Mr. Perkins. Nobody told Margaret anything. Nobody!

While the men continued to laugh and chat, Mr. Carpenter got up to go stand by Daniel, who was leaning against a post at the end of the counter. "Say I hear from Jesse that your children have been pretty busy again this summer helping folks in their tobacco fields."

Daniel tugged at his pants in a manly expression of pride. "Yeah, that Will gets out a calendar and picks up the phone every Sunday night and plans out their whole week. Rod gets a little upset sometimes, saying he doesn't leave enough room in the week for fishing, but that boy would fish all day if you let him."

Mr. Carpenter nodded. "Yeah, Jesse has helped some here and there, but he mostly helps me at the garage. He can do twice the work I can and he's got the touch when it comes to fixing an engine. It seems to come second nature to him. He'll fix things I'd never try to tackle. Actually, that's what I wanted to talk to you about. Have you got a minute to step over to the shop?"

Daniel stood immediately. "Sure." Just then, Sadie came running over to Daniel, holding a Hershey bar. She jumped up in his arms. Daniel patted her behind and said, "Come on, missy, we're going to walk over to Mr. Carpenter's garage for a minute. He's got something to show us."

Sadie's eyes grew wide. "Oooh, a surprise?"

Mr. Carpenter winked and, turning to head toward the door, said, "Well, could be, could be."

Mr. Carpenter's shop was only a few yards from the store. The man took them around back where he kept spare parts under a lean-to and walked toward a large object covered by a blue tarp. He reached down and dragged one end of the tarp off, exposing two Kawasaki 100 motorcycles.

Daniel whistled and nodded. "Didn't even know you worked on bikes."

Mr. Carpenter shook his head. "I don't, but that Jesse picked three of them up and got 'em all to run. He's still working on one inside that he's going to keep to scoot around on, but I thought maybe them young'ins of yours would like these. Sure would beat pedaling bicycles home every day for lunch. By the time they get home most days, I'm sure they barely have time to eat a sandwich before it's back to the fields."

Daniel sat Sadie down and walked around, checking out the bikes. "I'm sure they would love 'em." He stood back up, nodding his head slowly. "Okay, you got me. How much you want for em?"

Mr. Carpenter waved his hands. "Oh no. That ain't what I meant. I ain't selling 'em. I'm giving them to ya."

Daniel started to protest, but Mr. Carpenter cut him off. "No, now Jesse and me got these in trade for some work we done. The feller couldn't pay up. I wouldn't have took 'em myself, but Jess went all crazy over 'em, said he could fix 'em up. Been working on 'em for two months. He's the one that wanted to give 'em to y'all."

Daniel shook his head. "I can't just take 'em. What if—"

Mr. Carpenter put his hand up and cut Daniel off again. "No. Now listen." Mr. Carpenter took a step toward Daniel. He hesitated, glancing down at the ground, and when he looked back up and his eyes met Daniel's, he could see how sincere he was.

"Your family has done so much for me and Jess. We eat with y'all about every Sunday, and Jess probably eats more of Valerie's cooking than you do during the week. Why, that boy's at your house more than here when we ain't got the garage open. Y'all have helped me raise that boy." Mr. Carpenter looked away and continued. "After his mama died, well, I'm the boy's daddy, but y'all have been his family. I can't thank you enough for that." Mr. Carpenter took out his handkerchief and wiped his nose. Then he stood straight and looked at Daniel. "Oh just take 'em, Daniel. Besides I'm giving to the kids, not you!"

Sadie jumped up and down and clapped her hands. "That's me too, Daddy!"

Daniel knew he was outnumbered, and soon the high-pitched sound of a Kawasaki engine running around the house was destined to be in his future.

Daniel came up the drive with the motorcycles in the back of the truck. He had borrowed Mr. Carpenter's tarp to hide the bikes so he could surprise the kids. After he parked the truck under the oak tree and lifted Sadie out, he whispered in her ear, "Now listen. This is a surprise, so don't say anything until after supper, okay?"

Sadie grinned and nodded, but Daniel wondered if she was going to be able to keep the secret.

Rod and Will were at the sink washing up when Daniel and Sadie came in the back door. Jesse was sitting on top of the chest freezer. As soon as Sadie saw him, she lunged for him, grabbing his legs.

Jesse reached down to pick her up. "How's my girlfriend today?"

Sadie grabbed his neck and hugged him tightly and said, "I love you."

Rod and Will exchanged quizzical glances, while looking over their shoulders trying to keep their muck contained to the sink.

Rod was the first to ask, "Hey, what's this? Jesse gets a hug before us?"

"Yeah," Rod chimed in. "What's with the 'I love you too'? We've been working hard all day long and this is the respect we get?"

Sadie just grinned and glanced back at Daniel, who had his index finger in front of his lips and his eyebrows raised to remind her to keep the secret.

All three boys saw the exchange. Jesse smiled. "Oh, I think I know what this is all about."

Sadie squealed and gave him another big hug.

Daniel nodded and, looking at Jesse with a newfound admiration, said, "Yeah, I bet you do." Then grabbing Sadie, he said, "Come on, Chatty Patty. Let's go get ready for supper."

Jesse hopped down off the freezer. "Sounds good to me!" He followed Daniel into the kitchen.

Carla was already putting ice in the glasses when they walked in the kitchen and Val was placing serving spoons in pots on the stove. She usually left all the food on the stove and side counter and they lined up cafeteria style to fix their plates. She could never seem to keep the dining room table completely clear. It always seemed to catch the kids' schoolbooks since it was their favorite drop-off zone. Now it was cluttered with jars of tomatoes she had canned the night before. The crowd would fix their plates. Half would sit around the bar and two or three would find a clearing on the dining room table.

Daniel gave Val a peck on the cheek and asked how her day was, but before she could answer, the boys rushed into the kitchen complaining of being starved. "All right, all right, boys. Hold up and let's say grace, then you can dig in." They got in a circle and held hands. Sadie stood on a bar stool so she could participate. Val looked around and asked, "Okay, who wants to say grace tonight?"

Sadie yelled, "I will! I will!"

Daniel was holding Sadie's hand and looked down at her questioningly. "Are you sure?"

She nodded. "Well, remember what I told you." She just giggled and nodded.

Val exchanged a questioning look at Daniel and he just shrugged his shoulders innocently.

Everybody bowed their heads and Sadie began her prayer. "Dear God, thank you for Mr. Carpenter and Jesse and ..." Daniel tugged gently on her hand. This made Sadie giggle, but then she continued by ending the prayer saying, "Oh, thank you, thank you, thank you. Amen."

Val looked straight at Daniel, but he clapped his hands together and said, "Amen. Let's eat! I'm starving too!"

The kids starting grabbing their plates and chatting about their day. Daniel didn't make eye contact with Val again during the meal. He didn't think she was going to approve of the motorcycles one bit. There was no telling how many tragic statistics she could rattle off that involved motorcycles. Sadie giggled nonstop through the whole meal and kept looking at Jesse and Daniel.

Rod and Will got up to put their plates in the sink, saying they were heading out to the barn to work on some fishing equipment.

Sadie jumped up and down and looked at Daniel. "Now, Daddy? Now?"

Val finally looked at Daniel. "Okay that's it. What's going on with you two?"

Daniel eased away from the bar and said, "Well, Sadie and I ..." Then he corrected himself. "Jesse, Sadie and I have a surprise outside. So if you'll all meet us under the oak tree, we'll show y'all what it is before Sadie explodes."

The boys took off lickety-split and everybody else followed close behind. When they were all gathered outside, Sadie stood by the truck with her arms outstretched as though she was holding everybody back so they wouldn't sneak a peek.

Daniel nodded toward Jesse. "Actually, Jesse here and Mr. Carpenter have a gift for you kids. I don't know why they feel you are so deserving, but they do."

Then he extended his hand toward Jesse and told him to do the honors. Jesse was obviously self-conscious but walked over and pulled the tarp off the truck.

Sadie clapped her hands and tried to yell, "Kawasaki," but it came out more like "Cowagoki!" The boys immediately started dragging the cycles off the truck, admiring every inch of them. Jesse was explaining different aspects of the engines and how to change the gears. He seemed to be taking pride in his work. The kids were all talking at the same time, asking questions and saying, "Cool!" and "Ahhh, man!" every other sentence. Daniel still had not ventured a look at Val, but he could feel her eyes burning into the back of his head.

Rod and Will each hopped on a bike and listened while Jesse explained how to operate the machines. They looked at Daniel next and asked if they could take them for a spin.

Daniel ventured a look toward Val. Val took a deep breath and said through almost gritted teeth, "I cannot begin to tell you how many lives are lost every year to motorcycle accidents." She was almost hyperventilating by then, so she threw her hands up, turned around, and went inside.

They all watched as she slammed the back door. Daniel let out a long, low whistle and turned back toward the boys.

Jesse looked at Daniel and slowly said, "I'm sorry, Mr. Branch. I guess I forgot how she is."

Daniel slapped him on the back. "Oh, don't worry about her. She had the same reaction when I took the training wheels off Carla's bicycle." They all laughed, and then he gave the boys the go-ahead to take them for a spin.

Carla hopped on the back with Rod and Jesse hopped on the back with Will.

Sadie protested and stuck her lip out. "What about me? I want to ride too!"

Daniel reached down to pick her up and comfort her. "Let's let the boys get the hang of it before we put you on there with them. Okay?" She crossed her arms and kept her lip out but didn't say anything else.

That night, the kids took turns riding the bikes for hours. Sadie even got a few slow laps around the yard in Will's lap while holding onto the handlebars. Val never came out of the house. Daniel thought he spied her a time or two peeping out of the window but didn't let on that he had caught her.

That night, when Daniel crawled in bed beside Val, she was on her side facing the wall, which was her usual position when she was mad. Daniel faced her, propping up on his elbow, and gently said, "Oh, come on, Val.

The kids love the bikes. They'll be careful. Think how much time it will save them going to work. All of Mr. Roscoe's fields are a good two miles from the home. They can't always catch a ride with Dad. This is going to make things easier for them. They're teenagers now. They can't keep riding their bicycles forever."

When Val didn't respond, Daniel rolled on his back and put his hands behind his head. After a few seconds, he continued. "You know, the next thing is cars and trucks. You can't stop the kids from growing up." He paused and let out a heavy sigh. "You should have seen Mr. Carpenter's face. He had tears in his eyes. I couldn't say no. Plus Sadie was there jumping up and down like a monkey." Frustrated, he rolled over and now barked, "You would have said yes too, under those conditions. Plus you know what? I'm glad I did. The kids love those things. They've worked like dogs the whole summer and that's the first real fun I've seen them have. You missed it, because you were in the house sulking!" He fluffed up his pillow and slammed his head down.

Val sniffed and softly said, "I know. I saw them."

Daniel rolled over and put his arms around Val's waist and pulled her toward him. He chuckled under his breath and whispered in her ear, "I know you did. I caught you peeping out the window." Val socked him with her elbow. Daniel laughed, nuzzled his head down in her neck, and kissed her gently.

He knew she still didn't like the bikes, but he was safe for now. He just prayed the kids didn't have any accidents. The thought was enough to make him question himself and start to worry too, but just then, Val rolled over and kissed him gently. His mind immediately changed gears, smoother than the boys on the Kawasaki, and he began thinking of other things. Well, one thing really. He pulled Val closer as he revved up his own engine.

Chapter Nineteen

FIRST CYCLES

CARLA, ROD, AND Will waited at the end of the drive for the bus. Rod stared down the highway watching like it was a death sentence. Will gave him a firm slap on the back and said, "Hey, look at it this way: ninth grade now! High school! The final frontier. Four years and you are done."

Rod gave him a sideways glance. "Yeah, easier for you to say. You're down to three years." Then he glanced over at Carla and sneered. "And I guess you're excited like usual. I just don't get it."

Carla just smiled and shrugged. "The first day is exciting—seeing everybody again, catching up on what you did over the summer, finding out who is in all your classes."

Rod interrupted her. "That's the problem—classes!" Then shaking his head, he said, "Besides, Jackie is your best friend. You see her all the time at church and the store. You know exactly what she did all summer. And you're going to actually go to college after you graduate!" Shaking his head, he laughed. "I just don't get it. There's nothing I want to learn that bad."

Carla raised her eyebrows. "Oh yeah, what if you had to go to college to be able to hunt and fish? What if that was actually a profession that required a college degree? Would you go then?"

Rod looked at her like she suddenly had sprouted horns. He rubbed his stomach, almost feeling sick at the thought. He rolled his eyes and turned away when she rattled on about her dreams of being a good nurse and wanting to learn as much as possible. That's when he saw it: big orange number 81 rolling down 46 and coming to a stop. Yep, he thought, nothing was worse than the first day of school.

When they reached Ridgewood High School, the kids filed off the bus. Rod was the last person to get off the bus, dragging his feet as though he were heading to the electric chair. Jimmy almost tripped going through the doors as other students ignored him and nudged him out of the way. Will gave a few scornful looks in their direction. He was always protective of Jimmy, especially at school.

Carla and Jackie chatted excitedly as they made their way to their homerooms, catching up with different friends they met along the way. When they reached Mrs. Poindexter's class, Carla scrolled down the list of names outside the door. "There I am. I bet you're down the hall in Mrs. Ingram's class. Too bad our last names are not closer together in the alphabet."

Jackie nodded in agreement. "Yeah, too bad homeroom is all ninth graders too. I'm sick of these immature little boys."

Carla laughed. "One or two years doesn't make that much difference. They're all immature. We're not women yet either."

"Speak for yourself, sis. Look at me and tell me I don't look like a woman."

Carla rolled her eyes.

"Besides coming from somebody who hasn't even got her first cycle yet."

Carla cut her off and looked around to make sure no one had

overheard. "Jeesh, you and my mom keep bringing that up. I'm just a late bloomer. Everybody acts like it's a bad thing or weird. I'm perfectly within normal range still. I'm in absolutely no hurry either, but every time I get so much as gas pains, my mom gets excited and gives me *the look* like this could be it."

"Yeah, well, your mom's right; you're getting boobs."

Carla started to shut her up again, but Jackie seemed suddenly distracted by a tall, cute, athletic type strutting down the hall. She made obvious eye contact with him as he walked past. The look was acknowledged and returned as the boy gave Jackie the once-over from head to toe.

Carla nudged Jackie and gave her a scolding look. "Ya know you're going to get a reputation if you keep flirting like that."

Jackie smirked. "Flirting don't give you a reputation, unless you back it up with something."

"Yeah, but Jackie, that's my point. They will expect you to back it up with something. You act like you want to back it up."

Jackie shrugged. "Maybe I do, or maybe I already have."

Carla's mouth fell open and she sucked in a huge amount of air before she breathed out. "I knew it! Jackie how could you?"

Jackie looked away nonchalantly. Carla shook her head and said, "You know, I really don't know why we're best friends. We are total opposites in almost every way, from the way we look to the way we think and act to—"

Jackie cut her off. "We love each other. *That's* why." Then winking, Jackie began walking down the hall to her own class.

Getting on the bus that afternoon, Rod threw his hands up in the air and yelled, "One down!" He walked to the back of the bus beaming and joined Jesse in his seat. Carla and Jackie sat in front of them, and soon Will hopped on the bus and sat across the aisle with Jimmy.

"Hey, I talked to Charlie and he said his dad is putting in two barns of tobacco on Friday. Y'all want to skip school and help?"

Rod immediately chimed in, "I'm in, dude! Yes!"

Carla gave them both a stern look. "Like Mom will let you do that."

Will waved her off. "It's the first week. They're not going to be throwing anything heavy at us."

Rod nodded. "Yeah, that's right."

Will smiled. "Besides, Dad will say yes. He knows this is a business opportunity."

Carla rolled her eyes. "Well, count me out. I'd rather come to school. And besides, I just got the tobacco stains off my hands. I was hoping I could go a whole week without messing them back up."

Will turned back around and said, "Suit yourself. I can't see turning down good money."

Jesse laughed and whispered to Rod. "Has he even spent one dime of the money he's made the last two summers?"

Rod shook his head. "He saves every penny. Says he has big plans."

Jesse asked Rod if he still planned to use his money to travel to Canada to go bear hunting. Rod nodded and began telling him all about his trip. Jesse had heard it all a million times, but he listened again. Rod always got animated when he talked about hunting. He kept telling people he was going to Canada to kill a bear, even if he had to wrestle one to his death.

Millsville Store was the first stop for the school bus. Jesse and Jackie stood as the bus slowed. Jackie looked at Carla. "Hey, get off and stay at the store for a little while with me. I'll buy you a Tab."

Carla shook her head. "No. I'll either have to stay until you get off or walk home." Rod looked at her. "Hey, go ahead. I'll ride the bike up in a little while and get ya. I need to pick up some fishing gear anyway."

"We're not supposed to ride the bike on the highway though, remember? Even if you come up the back road, you'll have to get on the highway to get to the store."

Rod made a face and replied, "For like fifty yards is all. Besides, the only way they'll know is if *you* tell them."

"Please," Jackie said, scrunching up her face and pouting.

"Oh fine." She always gave in to Jackie. Besides, she knew Rod would ride the bike to the store anyway. At least, if she was with him, he might not pop wheelies and drive like a mad man. He barely stirred up dust around the house, but when he got out of view, his motorcycle was wide open. He had absolutely no fear behind the handlebars, just like with everything else he did in life.

Carla and Jackie whispered and giggled in-between helping customers and stocking shelves. When Rod showed up to pick her up, she wished she had said she would stay until closing time.

Rod plundered around the fishing gear for about ten minutes then brought his tackle to the register. When Jackie gave him back his change, she looked over at Mr. Mills and told him she was going to take a break and walk out back with Carla. Rod had parked the bike behind the store, so Mr. Mills and other customers wouldn't see him pulling off the highway. Carla hopped on back after he got the engine going.

Jesse, hearing the engine start up, walked outside the garage and waved over at Rod. Rod waved back and gave him the thumbs-up. Carla crammed her books between them on the seat and Rod took off. Jackie stood there with her arms crossed, watching them climb the little hill toward the highway. When they disappeared over the top, she began walking toward Jesse to chat for a few minutes before heading back in the store.

Seeing her heading that way, he wiped his hands off on a work rag in his pocket and began walking in her direction. They had only taken a few steps when they both heard the unmistakable sound of squealing tires and metal on metal, followed by the muffled sound of tree limbs and brush. They both took off up the hill, running toward the sound.

When they reached the top of the hill, it was easy to see the direction of the accident. Skid marks on the highway led toward the woods on the left-hand side. The motorcycle had also left its trail through the tall weeds, leading to the tree line. Jackie and Jesse took off in that direction.

When they reached the scene, Rod was slowly making his way to his feet. The motorcycle was wedged in-between two small pine trees, still running. Carla was flat on her back, motionless with her books scattered on the ground and across her stomach.

Rod walked over, cut the engine, and began to try to pry the bike out from the grasp of the two trees. The trees had given way to the force of the bike, and had it not been for the handlebars, they might have made it through. Of course, Rod and Carla may have also lost a kneecap in the process. Jesse and Jackie knelt down and immediately focused their attention on Carla.

When the bike came to its abrupt stop, it sent them both sailing through the air. Carla had been holding on tightly to Rod's waist so they traveled through the air and landed as one. Carla landed flat on her back, with Rod and her books on top of her. Her arms were still holding his waist, and her knees still straddling his hips, until they hit the ground. Carla's schoolbooks dug into her flesh, knocking the wind out of her.

Jackie reached for Carla's hand and asked if she was okay, but Carla didn't reply. Jesse turned pale as he stared down at Carla, who was visibly struggling to breathe. When she finally began to move and take in small gasps of air, Jackie helped her to a sitting position, cradling her shoulders and throwing the books off of her. "Are you okay? Do you hurt anywhere?"

Jesse still looked as though he was going to throw up and didn't say a word. Rod, still trying to pry the bike loose, turned around and asked Jesse to help him pull it free.

Jesse walked over to help him get the bike loose and check it out for any damage, but kept glancing back at Carla. Jackie helped her to her feet and brushed her off.

When Carla finally got her breath, she looked at Rod and asked, "Couldn't you tell I was hurt?"

Rod looked back at Carla and shrugged his shoulders. "Sorry. No twin sense, remember?"

Carla glared at him. "I'm not talking about that, stupid! I'm talking about not even checking on your own sister lying on the ground lifeless, before you check out the damage to that stupid motorcycle. I could've been dead and you wouldn't have known it!"

Rod shrugged his shoulders again and glanced at Jesse and Jackie, who were both staring at him. "Sorry. Well, are you okay?"

Carla didn't even bother to answer him but turned to Jackie. "I don't think I'm bleeding anywhere, am I?" Jackie gave her the once-over and shook her head.

Carla rubbed her ribs gently. "I think my biology book left an impression on my rib cage." She rubbed her abdomen and hipbones, saying, "And Rod landed right on my pelvic bones so they're going to be pretty tender too. I'll be bruised for days."

Rod rushed over to her. "Carla, you're gonna have to hide any bruises you get or make something up about getting hurt in gym class. Mama can't know about this, or she'll make Daddy get rid of the bikes."

"Gee, thanks for the continued concern, Rod. Don't worry. I won't let on that you drive like a maniac."

Rod threw both hands up. "Don't blame me. It was a squirrel. The thing jumped right out in front of me!"

Jesse stared at him. "A squirrel? You wrecked because you tried to dodge a squirrel? Dude, you go squirrel hunting all the time!"

Rod grinned. "Yeah, kind of ironic, huh?"

Later that night when Jackie got off work, she called Carla to see if she was okay. Carla stretched the phone cord as far as it would go into the living room and sat on the floor as she whispered into the phone. "Jackie, I don't know what to do. I took some aspirin as soon as I got home, so I wouldn't be sore, but my stomach is starting to hurt again. I went to the bathroom after I showered and I'm bleeding a little. I don't know if I have internal injuries or if I've finally started my period."

Jackie gasped. "Oh, my gosh! What are you going to do? I mean it's probably your period ... I know. Maybe the wreck gave your body a jolt and made you start. You're the one that's all medical. What do you think? I mean, if you actually had internal injuries, would you bleed from down there?"

"I don't know. I'm not a nurse *yet,* Jackie. I guess I will just wait and see what happens." Just then, Val walked around the corner and Carla told Jackie she needed to go, so she quickly hung up.

Carla kept her word and never said anything about the wreck. She hid her bruises and Rod was especially nice to her for a while. The following month, almost to the day, Carla began to bleed, so she knew she was safe from fatal internal injuries and that Mother Nature had just decided to show up. Val cried when Carla told her she had finally got her first period, even though it was actually her second.

Chapter Twenty
HOMEWORK IS A BEAR

SARAH SAT BESIDE Jimmy as he studied his math problem. Glancing down at her watch, she realized she needed to leave now or she would be late for her meeting. "Oh goodness, I'm going to be late for church if I don't leave right now, sweetie." She patted Jimmy on the back and told him to keep working on his homework and she would be back in an hour.

As she grabbed her purse, she stopped by Herman, who was beginning to nod off in his La-Z-Boy, watching the news. "I've got to go to my meeting, so you go in there and help Jimmy finish his homework. He only has three or four more problems, but if you don't sit right beside him, his mind will wander off and he won't finish."

She put her jacket on and headed for the door, then paused to look back at Herman. He had not moved from his chair. She stood glaring until Herman looked her way. She frowned. "Go on now. I don't want him to be up late again. Go on in there and *watch* him!" She rolled her eyes as Herman slowly started to ease his feet down to the ground and stand.

As Herman made his way to the dining room, he grabbed the newspaper. Once there, he plopped down across from Jimmy at the dining room table. Jimmy was already distracted and started telling Herman about Rod's trip to Canada and how he couldn't wait until he got back home and told them all about his big adventure. "He says he's gonna kill a bear even if he has to wrestle one."

Herman got his reading glasses out of his shirt pocket and began to unfold the newspaper. "Well, he won't wrestle a bear and live to tell about it. I think that boy's too young to go traipsing off, hunting wild game that he really don't have experience with."

"But, Dad, Rod knows all about hunting, and this is his ... his ..."

Herman flipped a corner of the paper down and stared at Jimmy over the rim of his glasses. "Passion?"

Jimmy stared at his dad and slowly said, "I don't think he feels *that* way about it. He still likes girls."

Herman sighed. "No, no. Passion means a strong love of something. Rod has a strong love for hunting. So it's his passion."

Jimmy shook his head. "Oh. Well, that still don't sound right" Then his eyes lit up. "Destiny! Hunting is his destiny!" Herman nodded and fluffed his paper back into position. He gave Jimmy a stern look and told him to get back to his homework or a scolding would be in his destiny when his mother got home.

Herman began reading the paper, glancing at Jimmy occasionally, but the boy seemed to have settled down to work. Every time he looked up, Jimmy's pencil was to the paper and he had an expression of concentration on his face. He was a sweet kid, but he was a slow thinker; not dumb, just slow. He was definitely teachable, but a person had to have patience. Sarah was much better in that department than Herman.

Sarah made her apologies as she walked into the classroom where the other ladies had gathered. Ms. Thelma gave her a stern look and then continued speaking, "As I was saying, Marty Williams has moved into

Mr. Cleo's place. He told Hank that he thought the government was going to buy the whole place from him for the lake, but they only took the property across the road, so he was actually left with the house, all the barns, and a few acres. So he's moved in."

Then she placed her hand on the table and looked over her shoulder as though she didn't want anybody to hear. "Actually, he told me himself that he has just gone through a nasty divorce and he just had to move away from Charlotte and start fresh. Poor thing. She took him for everything. If he didn't have his uncle's place to fall back on, he'd be destitute!"

All the women shook their heads and clicked their tongues.

Karen Thomas spoke up. "Oh, I remember him. Gosh, Mr. Cleo's been gone for years now." Then shifting in her seat and glancing around the room, she said, "You're right, Thelma. He'd be a wonderful person to take our welcome basket to. The sooner the better, since he's already moved in." She cleared her throat. "I would be happy to deliver the basket myself." Glancing at the others, she added, "Of course, anybody that would like to come with me would be welcome. I just know how busy everybody is with their families, and I—"

Thelma cut her off and gave her another stern look. "Well, of course, somebody will have to go with you. Being a single lady, it would be very inappropriate to go alone. Besides, he told me himself he is in no hurry to meet any eligible ladies, so you can get that notion out of your head. He's severely wounded and not wishing to jump back into any kind of a relationship. Why, he told me he had loved his wife dearly and would until the day he died."

Then placing her hand back down on the table, she lowered her voice. "He even confided in me that his wife wouldn't have children, even though he had wanted them badly. His heart just breaks now, knowing he may never have any of his own. He may buy some horses or open up some kind of petting zoo right there at his house, so kids from the children's home can come for day outings."

Karen put her hand over her heart. "Oh, how nice. With the lake coming in now, all kinds of city folk will be coming out this way and might be interested in paying him for that kind of thing too!"

The ladies chatted on about other business, and an hour later, Sarah was on her way home. When she opened the front door, she could see that Jimmy was still sitting there with his head bowed, working. She let out a sigh and headed in that direction.

Herman was standing in the kitchen, pouring a glass of tea, when Sarah walked in. She gave him a questioning look and Herman whispered, "He's been working hard the whole time." She raised her eyebrows and whispered back, "Oh really, and you've been watching him and checking his work this whole time?"

Herman leaned against the bar. "I promise I've been sitting there the whole time you've been gone, and he's worked every minute." Sarah just nodded. "Uh-huh."

She walked to Jimmy and put her hand on his back. "How's it going? You almost done?"

Jimmy looked up, smiling wide, and picked up his sheet of paper, holding it up for her to see. "Look! This is Rod wrestling a bear. See how I made the bear stand up on his hind legs!"

Sarah took the paper from him and held it up so she could see it better. "That's wonderful, Jimmy, but what about your math homework?" She looked down at his notebook and found that he was in the exact same spot he had been when she left him. She kept his drawing and told him to start back on his homework. She laid the drawing down on the bar and slid it over to Herman so he could see it.

Through gritted teeth, she said, "Why don't you take your glass of tea with you while you sit *right beside* Jimmy as he finishes his homework?"

Herman threw his hands up like he was under arrest and said it wasn't his fault. Sarah just turned around and walked out of the room. Herman, with his tea in hand, started walking back toward Jimmy. He paused, looking at the detailed drawing that had occupied Jimmy for the past hour. He smiled as he studied the artwork. "Not a bad drawing though. Pretty good actually."

Later that evening, right before Sarah went to bed, she took Jimmy's drawing and placed it in a box she kept in the hall closet filled with other drawings Jimmy had created. She smiled as she thumbed through a couple and then placed the box back on the shelf.

Jimmy saw the good in everything, never the bad. That was one reason he was such an easy target for other kids' bullying. He was gullible and trusting, but that was what also made him so sweet. For that reason alone, Sarah didn't wish him to be any different.

Chapter Twenty-One
BEARLY WRESTLING

R. CRAIG, WHO ran the lodge, felt a little guilty. He had given Rod the worst location every day, because he was the youngest. He was worried the boy was too young to be out there by himself. He, of course, had been hunting at Rod's age, but he wasn't sure about the boy's upbringing. Some Americans came up there hunting on a whim, and didn't have a clue what they were doing. It was just one more thing to strike off their list of many accomplishments. But Rod had been well mannered and helpful. His wife had taken an immediate liking to the boy. He was also an excellent shot with his bow and seemed to be comfortable in the woods. By the end of the week, Mr. Craig realized there was definitely something different about him.

The men had picked on Rod pretty hard because he was the only one who hadn't gotten a shot off. They had even taken photos of him in a fake wrestling pose with the life-size stuffed bear in the lobby. Rod had played along with the men, but Mr. Craig could tell he was disappointed.

The Craigs had operated their hunting lodge for twenty-five years. His wife cooked breakfast, sent men off with a bag lunch, then prepared a huge nighttime meal. They had dormitory-style rooms with showers set up separate from their own living quarters.

Each morning, Mr. Craig drove the men out, dropping them off at different locations where he had tree stands. Each stand was miles away from any kind of civilization and the men were on their own during the day until they were picked up that evening. Mr. Craig would help them dress any game or arrange for it to be shipped back to their homes. Most men were just interested in saving the hides and would leave the meat, which the Craigs served to other lodgers.

On Rod's last morning hunt, Mr. Craig made a last-minute decision and dropped Rod off at the farthest location from the lodge. It was a good location and he felt sure he would have a much better chance at a sighting. It would be up to Rod if he was successful or not. He just hoped it was the right thing to do and that the boy would be safe.

Rod crawled out of the truck and gave Mr. Craig a smile. As he grabbed his bow from the back, Mr. Craig pointed in the direction of the tree stand, explaining it would be about a quarter of a mile deep into the woods. Mr. Craig had markers along the way, so they could find their way in and out safely, as long as they didn't stray off course.

Rod found his stand easily enough and in no time was nestled down for a day of waiting. When he got settled in the stand, Rod took a second and closed his eyes. As he opened them, looking heavenward, he whispered, "Please, let me at least see a bear, Lord." Then, feeling as though he could do nothing more, he took a deep breath and waited.

After a couple of hours, hunger pains began to make his stomach rumble. He reached in his pocket and pulled out the snack Mrs. Craig had packed. He downed the bear beef jerky and then reached for the apple. His teeth had barely pierced the skin when Rod saw it.

A bear was making its way right toward his tree. It was sniffing and pawing along the way. He seemed completely unaware of a hunter's presence. Rod gingerly pulled his teeth out of the apple and eased the fruit back into his pocket. Next, he drew his bow into position and slowly pulled the arrow back. He only had to wait a second or two before a good shot was presented. He fired the arrow! It sailed swiftly through the air and found its mark, piercing the bear's flesh between his shoulder and neck.

The bear growled and began twisting his body and flailing his arms. Scratching toward the arrow, he managed to claw it free, ripping his flesh. Rod saw blood momentarily squirt through the air.

The bear took a wobbly step forward but seemed to quickly regain composure and abruptly ran away in the direction he had come. Rod quickly made his way down the tree and debated whether to follow the bear. He knew he had injured the bear and that it would not go far, but Mr. Craig had also warned the men not to track their own kills. They could easily get lost in the unfamiliar woods and part of his fee covered game recovery. But it was still early morning. Mr. Craig would not be there for hours. Rod saw the clear trail of blood that the bear was leaving and decided he wouldn't have any trouble, so he took off after the bear.

Rod followed the blood trail and kept his bow tight in his hand, ready at all times. He slid through the forest, pausing occasionally to listen for clues his prey was close. Approaching a small clearing, Rod scanned the ground for the next droplets of blood. The trail disappeared into a heavy cluster of brush. Rod gently stuck one hand in to part the limbs. He was beginning to fear the bear had gone much farther than he had anticipated.

But then Rod heard, and more importantly *felt,* his prey as it came bounding through the brush. The bear leapt toward Rod and slammed him down to the ground. The bear's breath rushed across Rod's face. Its heavy body pinned Rod to the ground with his arms straight out on each side. His right hand still clutched the bow and arrow, but it was of no use to him now. There was nothing he could do. Rod was staring straight into the bear's black eyes as it raised its right claw high. Rod turned his head away and shut his eyes, knowing what was coming next. It happened in seconds.

Carla sat at the bar eating a bowl of cereal, still in her pajamas when Jesse and Will came in. Will opened the refrigerator, got out a plastic pitcher, and sat it on the bar. Looking at Carla, he said, "Good morning, sleepyhead. Most of us have been up for hours."

Carla just rolled her eyes and continued eating her cereal. Jesse grinned as he got two glasses out of the cabinet and set them on the bar.

Will reached for the glasses one at a time and began pouring them both a glass of tea. "Yeah, we've done worked on the Massey Ferguson and got it running, then we—" But he was stopped short at the look on Carla's face.

Carla glanced wildly back and forth from Will to Jesse, bringing her right arm up, clutching her left shoulder. She leaned over and slowly began sliding off the barstool. Her left hand still clutched the bar, trying to keep herself upright, but gravity quickly took over. Will and Jesse came around the bar, finding Carla curled on the floor, gasping for air and in the fetal position.

"She must be choking! Will, do the Heimlich maneuver."

Will fell to his knees and pulled Carla up from behind to get her to a sitting position. He wrapped his arm under her ribs and was getting ready to thrust when Carla waved him away with her arm and shook her head. She was still gasping for air when she whispered, "Rod. Something's happened to Rod."

Jesse and Will exchanged quick glances.

Carla was never wrong.

The angry bear's violent and swift blow cut through Rod's clothing like tissue paper. The tip of his claws hit flesh, leaving its mark from the top of Rod's left shoulder down toward his chest. Then, just as abruptly, the bear jumped up and retreated. As the weight lifted off of Rod, he sprang up to a sitting position as though by reflex. Without thinking, he lifted his bow and arrow, his eyes never leaving the backside of the runaway bear. He fired one quick shot that hit its mark, dead center on the bear's back. The bear immediately dropped to the ground, face first.

The arrow stood straight up toward the sky, pulsing slightly with the bear's slowing heartbeat. Rod sat still, calming his own heart, and waited for the arrow to completely stop moving before he ventured near his prey. There would be no second chance for another attack. Lessons learned the hard way are ones never forgotten.

Rod sat down by the bear and gingerly checked his own wound after checking the bear and retrieving his arrow. *The bear is not huge, but a bear's a bear,* Rod thought. Then wincing while he applied some pressure to his injured shoulder, which was now beginning to throb, Rod thought, *Yeah and claws are claws too.*

Carla's lungs returned to normal breathing and she allowed Will to help her to her feet. "So … Is he okay? Car?" Jesse finally asked.

Carla nodded. "Yeah, he's been hurt, but he didn't die." Then she hesitated. "Well, I guess he didn't. He's never died before, so I can't say for sure, but something tells me I would know that." Putting her hands on her hips, she said, "Besides, I plan on killing him myself when he gets home!"

Will smiled and gave her a questioning look. "You're not going to tell Mama, are you? I mean, she'll find out anyway."

Carla shook her head. "No way! This will be his tale to tell, not mine. He's the one that needs to battle that war."

Rod should have left the bear where it was and waited for Mr. Craig, but his male ego wouldn't let him leave the carcass in the woods, so he managed to get it to the clearing alone. Once there, Rod collapsed on the ground, using the bear as a pillow for his head. He was mentally and physically exhausted, and after a few minutes, he nodded off with his bow and arrow resting across his chest.

After a good half hour to forty-five minutes, Rod slowly began to stir. He lay there letting his sleepy eyes slowly adjust back to the sunlight. Raising himself to a sitting position, he realized that his growling stomach had woken him. He once again reached in his pocket for the apple he started earlier. Twirling the apple, he sought his original bite mark he'd last made but never got the chance to finish until now.

He bit into the apple, but just as he did, he heard a twig snap behind him. Feeling the hairs stand up on the back of his head, Rod pulled the apple out of his mouth once again and placed it on the ground. With his bow and arrow ready, he slowly turned his head.

There at the edge of the tree line stood another bear! Rod shifted, got up on his knees as quietly and quickly as possible, and pulled back the arrow. Sure of his shot, he let it go, but this time, before the arrow even found its mark, he already had another arrow in hand and was firing his second shot. Both arrows found their marks, and although the bear cried out and struggled with his arms to pull the arrows out, the bear did not run.

Rod waited a full thirty minutes before he approached the bear. He made no attempt to move the animal. It would have been futile anyway. The bear was too big for one person to move. He nudged the bear with his toe. No movement. *Good*, Rod thought. Just then, he heard movement across the clearing in the opposite direction. Rod jerked his bow and arrow back into position, only to see a bird pecking away in some dry leaves. Rod was visibly sweating this time. He let out a slow breath and lowered his bow. Bending down and resting his hands on his knees, Rod shook his head at his own jitteriness.

Raising his head heavenward, once again he prayed, "Okay, okay, that's enough for today." As he slowly started walking back toward his first kill and his pickup location, he hesitated again and looked back up again, grinning. "But, oh yeah, thank you though. For the bears and for everything else."

The men could hardly believe their eyes when Mr. Craig pulled up to get Rod that afternoon. They jumped from the truck to check out his kill and, seeing the blood on his coat, to check out his injury. They were all happy for Rod, not to mention impressed. There were plenty of high fives and backslapping. But when Rod explained that his *other* bear was at the edge of the woods and pointed in that direction, the men froze in disbelief.

Carla was sitting on the brick ledge that ran down the side of the carport when she saw the pickup coming up the drive. She was playing her guitar while Sadie twirled around the metal poles on the ledge, skipping back and forth like a gymnast.

Carla stood up and laid her guitar down, waiting for the truck to come to a stop. Sadie jumped up and down yelling, "Rod's home! Rod's home!"

As soon as Rod climbed out, Carla ran and threw her arms around his waist, squeezing him tightly. Rod, acting a little self-conscious, returned the hug.

Carla was teary-eyed when she whispered, "Was it your shoulder?" Rod nodded. Looking up at his face, she asked, "Was it the bear?"

Rod nodded again and they slowly pulled away from each other.

Rod bent down and picked up Sadie, who had been tugging at his pants and squealing. "Did you get a bear, Rod?"

He looked offended. "Well, of course, I did. As a matter of fact, I got two."

She giggled and whispered, "Did you wrestle one?"

Rod looked around and could see Daniel walking up from the barn with a welcoming grin on his face. Val was just coming out the front door. Rod whispered back, "As a matter of fact, I did." Then out of the side of his mouth, looking over at Carla, he asked, "So did you tell anybody?" Carla wiped the tears from her eyes. "Just Will and Jesse. They were with me when it happened." Smiling, she punched him in the gut. "Mom's all yours."

Rod took a deep breath. The battle wounds he now had would leave scares. Val would have to be told, and he could only imagine the lecture and statistics he would have to endure. He was destined to wrestle with another bear, this time a mama bear!

Chapter Twenty-Two
TOBACCO FIELDS FOREVER

WILL CAME IN the house right before supper and asked Val if Daniel had to work late. She looked up from the stove and said, "No. He should be home any minute, unless he's volunteered to deliver something. Which I hope he hasn't. Supper is ready and it's his favorite." She wiped her hands on a dishtowel and told Will to go see if he could round up Rod.

Rod was always hard to round up at night for supper. They never waited on him, but they always made the effort to track him down. Before Will got to the back door, it swung open and in walked Rod and Jesse, laughing.

Will gave them a disapproving look and said, "Good. I didn't want to have to go hunting you down again. Supper's ready." He then spun on his heels and left the boys exchanging questioning looks.

Jesse whispered, "What's up with him?" Rod just gave his usual grin and shrugged.

Will passed through the kitchen to the front door and found Sadie twirling around the wrought-iron railing on the front porch. He told her supper was ready, so she needed to come in and wash up. He held the door open for her to come inside. As he looked up, he saw Daniel driving up the gravel drive, so he stayed outside to go catch him before he got inside the house.

Daniel and Will walked into the house together and Val sensed something was up between them, although they didn't say a word. Daniel came over, gave Val a peck on her cheek, took a deep sniff of the air, and rubbed his stomach. "Hmmm, I do love me some Carolina treat BBQ chicken!"

Sadie giggled. "Me too!"

Everybody held hands to say grace and then lined up to fix their plates. During the meal, there was the normal chatter. Val casually mentioned that it was possible to wear one's bell-bottomed jeans too long, causing them to trip and smash a head into the sidewalk. Everyone momentarily stared at her, then shrugged and continued their conversations. Everyone except Sadie, who giggled and said, "Mama, you're silly!"

Daniel pinched her on the nose and replied, "She certainly is, Sadie."

He glanced at Val, who was giving him a sarcastic look. "I mean really, Val. You can trip on just about anything, even your own feet."

She shrugged. "I'm just saying it can happen. Nothing's wrong with making sure to be extra careful and not wear your pants too long, especially those ridiculous bell-bottoms. I mean all that extra fabric around your feet—it's just an accident waiting to happen."

Will seemed to wolf down his food. When he had finished and put his plate in the sink, he sat back down at the table. This in itself was unusual, plus he was acting antsy. The front door opened and Edgar yelled his usual greeting. As soon as Will heard him, he gave a quick look over at Daniel. Daniel took his cue, pushed his plate away, and nodded. He reached over and patted Val on her leg. "We got us some men business out in the barn." Raising her eyebrows, she started to speak, but Daniel gave her a quick kiss on the mouth and told her he'd see her in a bit.

When the men retreated, Val looked at the others and asked if they knew what that was all about. Rod and Carla shrugged but did say that Will had been moody for the last couple of days.

"Hmmm," Val said as she got up to start cleaning the dishes. "Rod, you and Jesse sneak out there and let me know what they're doing. Just don't let them see ya. Okay?"

After a few minutes, the boys came back inside and reported that they were just walking around talking and looking at stuff.

"What stuff and talking about what?"

Rod shrugged. "I couldn't hear what they were saying, but they were looking and pointing at everything: the field, the tractor, just everything."

Val clicked her tongue. "Hmmm, this can't be good."

Rod looked surprised "Why? What do you think they're doing?"

Val wiped her hands on the dishtowel and said, "I don't know. But I'm telling you it can't be good."

Val was sitting in the den, mending a rip on one of Daniel's shirts, when the men came back inside. Will gave his mom a guilty look then glanced back at Daniel, who was expressionless. Will walked quickly past Val with the excuse of having to make some calls before it got too late. Daniel came in, plopped down in his usual chair, and reached for the newspaper.

Val put her sewing down in her lap. "Okay. Let's hear it. What's going on? You may as well tell me now."

Daniel held the paper up to block Val's view and asked, "What makes you think something's going on?" Val picked up her spool of thread and threw it at Daniel. Daniel started laughing and laid down his paper. He got up and sat down beside Val on the couch, putting his arm around her shoulder. He took a deep breath and began slowly. "Well, Val, it would seem that our son Will is quite the businessman." After a second, he added, "And I guess a pretty good salesman too, because he's roped me and Dad into helping him."

Val pulled back. "Help him with what? What kind of business?"

"Well, after helping everybody else in their tobacco crops for the past three summers, he feels he's learned enough to figure out that we have all the equipment to have our own crop next year."

Daniel held his hand up to ward off any quick reactions from Val. "Now hear me out, Val. He's got a good point. We have empty fields sitting here and he's asked about renting some fields from Mr. Scott. He's found a secondhand looper that, with Jesse's help, he can get up and running along with some tobacco slides. Most everything else we have."

He paused for a second to catch his breath and to give Val a chance to respond. She didn't say a word but seemed to be trying to take it all in and not rush to judgment. Daniel still had his arm around her shoulders and with his free hand reached for hers and held them in her lap. "Val, I know what you're probably thinking, but tobacco farming is different now than when I farmed. They are actually making money at it now. Good money. The kids are going to do most of the work. They'll just need to hire a hand or two when we're barning, but everything else they'll be able to handle with our help. Why, in the first year, he'll make enough to cover any loans he takes out, plus buy a decent vehicle to drive."

Val corrected him by saying, "You mean the loans *we* take out. We take out with our *house* as collateral."

"Val, you said yourself that the boys are going to want a truck of their own. Will's already got his license and Rod will too, in a few months. If they don't get something to putter around in, they'll be on the highway with those motorcycles, and you know how dangerous that is."

She knew he was trying to use her own words to prove his point.

"You know there aren't any other jobs around here other than helping with tobacco, and that's only during barning time. This way, they'll be able to reap the benefits a little bit more and learn the business side at the same time. Carla can save up to help with her college tuition. Val, it's really a win-win situation. I promise you we're not going to lose the house. The kids will work hard to make this work. You know that."

Val sat there quietly for a minute. She realized it made sense and would be good for the kids, but just the thought of farming again almost made her nauseous. Then it hit her. Daniel loved this. He was excited, and that suddenly made her mad. "I bet he didn't have to do any convincing at all. You can't wait to get back to farming again, can you? Why look at you! You're almost foaming at the mouth!"

He stammered for a few seconds but then admitted it. "Yeah, you're right. I can't wait to get back to it. I do miss it and would love the chance to do it again while the market is right for a change." He put his hand under Val's chin, looked in her eyes, and softly said, "Aah. Come on, Val. Let us do a little farming. One summer. Give us one summer, and if we don't make out good, we'll drop it."

Val knew she was defeated when Daniel looked at her like that so she just rolled her eyes and mumbled, "Fine."

Daniel gave her a quick kiss on the lips and got up to go tell Will the good news.

As he was walking out, she had an afterthought and asked, "Hey, what do I get out of it? You didn't mention that."

Daniel turned around and paused. "I don't know. We'll come up with something." Grinning, he added, "But for right now, just the pleasure of knowing that Edgar is down there telling Margaret the same thing."

That, indeed, did bring a smile to her face.

Chapter Twenty-Three

T IS FOR TURNIPS AND TOMATOES; C IS FOR COONS

GRINNING WIDE, ROD placed the two large bags on Mr. Collins' desk. Mr. Collins was writing the day's history topic on the board but stopped to look at Rod's new delivery. Peeking into the first bag, he squealed, "Oh turnips! My wife is going to love you, Rod. She's been craving some for a month now. She's having the weirdest cravings with this pregnancy." He peeped in the second bag, gasped, and then quickly closed the bag. "Tomatoes! How did you get tomatoes this late in the season? Do you have a greenhouse?"

Rod shook his head. "I have a couple of plants right up beside the back of the house. I can almost grow tomatoes until Christmas in that spot. It's in full sun all day and the bricks on the house heat up like they've been in the oven. It's probably better than a green house."

Rod was taking his seat when Carla came up behind him. "So that's where Mama's tomatoes have been disappearing to. You know, you can't count on bribery in every class. At some point, you need to study."

"It's not bribery. I'm just a student respecting the need of some of our lowly paid teachers and doing them a good deed. If they feel grateful enough to return their appreciation in the way of leniency in my grades, then that's their prerogative."

Carla raised her eyebrows. "Wow, Rod. Two big words in one sentence: leniency and prerogative. If you can spell them too, I'll be impressed!"

As usual, Jackie came into class fashionably late. Mr. Collins gave her a scornful look but let it pass. She was wearing black Levi corduroy pants and a white, long-sleeve button-up shirt. Her shirt was unbuttoned low, exposing her ample cleavage. The boys, of course, seemed to enjoy the view, and she received a few whistles and whispered flirtatious remarks as she made her way to her seat beside Carla.

Jackie just smiled but ignored the comments, although it was obvious she enjoyed them and even expected them. Carla just shook her head. "Well, good morning, Ms. Center of Attention. Where've you been?"

"Oh, you know. Tony gave me a ride to school and we sat out in the car making plans for this evening."

Carla gave her a stern look. "What's the attraction with him, other than he's a senior and a world-class jerk?"

Jackie shrugged "He has his moments. Besides, he's just a fling. Nothing serious."

Carla replied, "Oh, I in no way thought you were serious. I actually feel sorry for him, to tell you the truth."

"Sorry for him? Humph. He's getting what he wants too, believe me!" Carla shook her head and looked seriously at Jackie. Then lowering her voice, she said, "You know, Jackie, you are really going to mess yourself up. You've already ruined your reputation, but even that can be repaired if you behave yourself. If you would—"

Jackie cut her off. "Okay, Mama Car. Don't go preaching to me again. I'm not you. Remember? You're my friend, not my mama or my preacher." She nudged Carla playfully and smiled. "You really are a good friend though. Thanks for trying. When I really mess up, I know you'll be there for me even though you'll be saying, 'I told you so.'"

Later that day, as students were piling on the buses, Rod stood on the sidewalk talking to Marcus and Jesse. "So y'all coming over around seven o'clock, right? I think we'll go down below Punchy's house tonight. He told Will on Sunday that coons have been getting his trash cans. So you know businessman Will. He's worked out a deal with Punchy to get a dollar for every one we kill back there. That's on top of what we get for the hides when we sell them to Mr. Fletcher."

They all smiled. Will was always figuring out a way to make a dollar. Money was always the last thing on Rod's mind. He could live off the land without one red cent and be perfectly content.

Marcus looked around. "Where is Will today anyway? I haven't seen him get on the bus. Is he driving today?"

Rod nodded. "Yeah, he's driving one of the elementary buses today, filling in."

Marcus laughed. "Part-time job number three for ole businessman Will!"

Later that night, Marcus and Jesse met Rod to go coon hunting. Jesse, being the only one with his driver's license, drove his dad's beat-up Ford truck and they put the dog boxes in back.

They headed over to the wooded area behind Punchy's house and let the dogs lose. They sprang from the truck and took off barking, trailing their first victim. The boys took off behind them, acting just as excited as the dogs. Rod loved coon hunting. Hunting at night had its own degree of challenges. They would sometimes get twisted ankles while stepping in invisible holes, smacked in the face with branches, and scraped from head-to-toe by briars, but that was all part of the fun.

The dogs hadn't been on the trail long before they had one treed. The boys came up on the dogs. Each was barking wildly and scrapping their front paws on a large pine tree deep in the woods. Marcus tilted the spotlight up, scanning the branches, until the two beady eyes reflected back.

Rod turned to Jesse. "You want to take the shot?"

Jesse shook his head. "Nah, go ahead. I'll get the next one."

Rod grinned and took aim, then fired. The coon fell from the tree on Rod's first shot. Marcus, using his flashlight, found the carcass and bagged their kill. Looking in the bag, he asked, "How you like that copper pot, copperhead!"

Jesse shook his head. "You've still never told me what that's supposed to even mean."

Marcus grinned. "That's top secret from our old fort days. Right, Rod?"

Rod looked at Jesse and said, "Believe me: it's not worth hearing."

All three of the boys patted the blue tick coon dogs on their heads and gave them plenty of compliments like "Good boys!" and "Good job!"

The boys bagged two more coons within the hour. On the last kill though, the dogs had gotten on the trail of another scent and took off so fast the boys couldn't keep up. They could hear the dogs occasionally, off in the distance, but the direction changed so rapidly they wound up losing the dogs all together. It happened sometimes, but it was just a part of the hunt. They finally decided to give up and head back to the truck.

Rod was the only who still had his bearings and knew where they were. He led the way and soon they were on a dirt road. "Oh, now I know where we are," Marcus said. "This road leads back behind Mr. Mills's house down toward Ralph's fields."

Rod smile and nodded, and they began the long walk back to the truck. They were a good mile and half away from where they had left it, even while taking Rod's short cut. They walked and chatted for about ten minutes until they came up on a parked car. Their flashlights had been turned off because the dirt road reflected enough moonlight to find their way, so they approached the car completely unnoticed.

Jesse whispered, "That's Tony's Mustang. What's he doing way out here?" The car's windows were fogged up and they could hear voices inside.

Marcus approached the car and banged on the hood. "Hey! Hey! What's going on in there?"

A female voice squealed and fumbling noises came from the backseat. Marcus kept taunting from the front of the car, and after a few seconds, Tony opened the back door and got out. He grinned and adjusted his pants. "Hey, what's up, man? What y'all doing out here?"

Jesse and Rod approached the car on opposite sides. Rod stood beside Marcus and said, "Just doing a little coon hunting," then held up his bag.

"Oh yeah. Did you get any?" Tony asked nonchalantly.

Marcus grunted. "Yeah, how 'bout you? You get any?" He peeked past him and at his female occupant.

Rod nudged Marcus hard with his elbow and gave him a disapproving look. Tony just laughed and walked over to check out the coons in their bag. As he talked with Marcus and Rod, Jesse walked toward the back of the car and tapped on the back window.

Jackie rolled down the window and leaned out, propping her chin on her arms. "What's up, Jess?"

Jesse gave Jackie a sad look. "Jackie, come on. What are you doing?"

She held up a hand in protest. "I already got one lecture today from Carla, so just keep yours to yourself."

But Jesse just kept staring at her with that sad look on his face. She finally opened the door, grunted, and said, "Oh, for goodness sakes!"

Marcus looked up when he heard her get out of the car. "Well, well, well, Wack-A, Jack-A." Nobody had used that nickname for Jackie in years. Jackie's expression said she still despised it. Rod nudged Marcus hard again, and Marcus rubbed his arm and looked back at Rod. "Will you please stop doing that?"

Jackie gave Tony a stern look and told him she was ready to go home. Tony nodded and turned to get back in the car. "Hey, you guys need a ride back to your truck?" They told him no and watched the car leave, taillights fading into the night.

They walked the rest of the way in silence, fatigue having finally caught up with the mighty hunters. When they got back to the truck, the dogs were still nowhere in sight. Deciding they were too tired to wait or to try to track them down, Rod took off his shirt and laid it out on the ground. The dogs would catch his scent and be waiting for him the next morning after their night of adventure.

As predicted, the next day before Rod got ready for school, Edgar drove him back out to find both dogs lying on Rod's shirt. The dogs jumped up when they saw him, and he gave them both a good welcoming rub and hug. They obediently jumped in the back of the truck. Edgar and Rod chatted on the way back. Both were early risers and that seemed to be their own special time of the day. It was simple moments like these they both would remember most.

Rod killed well over their limit in coons every year, but he didn't feel guilty about it. Raccoons were plentiful and a constant nuisance, wreaking havoc in gardens and trash cans. Will, even though he never hunted much, always received a percentage of the profits because he was the mastermind at hooking up the deals. His main buyer actually shipped the hides overseas to Iran. The fur was used there for hats and other clothing items, but when the American hostage situation happened at our embassy there in the late seventies, all trade came to a halt because of trade sanctions. Rod couldn't understand how an international event like that could actually affect his coon hunting ventures in North Carolina, but it did.

One day, Mr. Collins brought up the international crisis to the students in class for discussion. He was speechless when Rod went on a rampage about the situation, stating he didn't agree with the trade sanctions. Of course, Mr. Collins had no idea the trade sanctions had put a halt to his coon hunting ventures, and that's why he was knowledgeable about the situation. He assumed his teaching had finally reached the boy, and he felt almost giddy.

When the bell rang and class was dismissed, Rod stopped by Mr. Collins' desk on his way out. "Sorry, I was so opinionated in class, Mr. Collins."

The man waved his hand. "Oh. No, no. You've got some good points. Thank you for sharing."

Rod nodded and headed toward the door. "Oh yeah. I'll be bringing you those tomatoes plants sometime next week." He gave Mr. Collins a wink.

Mr. Collins nodded back. "Tomato plants or not, you got an A for participation today, Rod. Good job."

Rod grinned and left the room.

Mr. Collins bragged to fellow teachers in the lounge that afternoon, explaining that he had a breakthrough with a difficult student. He no longer felt guilty about all the gifts of fresh veggies he had taken from Rod over the years. Good teaching always paid off. He must be a *great* teacher to reach someone like Rod, who only cared about things like hunting, fishing, and growing delicious produce.

Because of the incident, Mr. Collins never looked at a mediocre student in the same way again. He strived every year to find true potential in every student and was honored with a long list of teacher's pets and grateful students. He never knew this life-changing event was due to a hostage situation across the seas and one boy's love for coon hunting.

Chapter Twenty-Four

THE LAKE IS COMING,
THE LAKE IS COMING

A S MR. MILLS read the latest article in the newspaper about the construction of Gordan Lake, the men sat around at the end of the counter in their usual spots. "Says here when the lake is finished, it will be over thirteen thousand acres. That's a lot of uprooting of people and their family homes. I know that."

Punchy poured a pack of peanuts into his Pepsi and grunted. "The last straw in my opinion is when they dug up the graveyard over at Bell's church. I didn't think it was even legal to be digging up dead people."

Edgar nodded. "That's the government, Punchy. They make the rules, so they can pretty much do whatever they want."

Will had walked in and overheard most of the conversation, interested as always with what was going on in the community. "I just can't believe how long it's taking to finish the thing." Will was secretly excited about the coming lake and just knew living this close to the lake would benefit him in some way. He just had to figure out how.

Jackie rang up his soda and he eased toward the men to join the conversation. He was actually there on business and needed to talk to Mr. Mills about starting a charge account at the store, so he would have credit available for different items he would need that summer. He didn't want to ask for any more money than necessary from his parents. Val had gone along with the idea better than he had expected, but he knew finances caused her to stress. He had gone through most of his own savings and they had a loan out with Farm Credit in Appleton for the bulk of what he had needed for his first year. As long as he paid the loan back in the fall, things would be fine.

As Will walked over to join in the conversation, he said, "At least you'll be getting some business out of it, Mr. Mills. Jackie says you already get a lot of construction workers in here for lunch and getting gas."

Mr. Mills nodded. "Yeah, we do at that. Got Marty working for me most days now, even when Jackie's here. I'm just getting too old to handle it by myself or enjoy it, I guess. Don't care too much about all the city folk coming out here complaining about this and that, yelling and popping wheelies in the parking lot."

Will laughed. "I don't think it will be as bad as all that. If you can put up with this crowd, I think you can handle the city folk."

Punchy took a big swig of his Pepsi and peanuts and talked while he crunched. "I don't care none too much for all these construction people in and out of here either. Mr. Taylor has some tools missing from his shed. Wouldn't surprise me if that kind of thing gets worse."

Edgar frowned. "Oh, I don't know, Punchy. We got plenty of quick hands that already live here to go blaming anything on outsiders." He let out a slow breath. "It does bother me though about the Peterson's little boy who went missing. I was hoping the little fellow had just wondered off, but when they found him, even though he was pretty much gone back into the earth, Sheriff Bullard said there was definitely something suspicious. He couldn't go into details, but it didn't sound natural. I just would hate to think that the monster that might hurt a child could live right here amongst us. I can't imagine looking somebody in the eye that does that kind of evil, and not know or sense it in some way."

Punchy looked over at Marty, who was stocking shelves. He took another swig and pointed toward Marty with his bottle. "Just like your Uncle Cleo. Never did find out who did that, did they?"

Marty shook his head.

Edgar looked up at Marty. "I'm sorry, Marty. We shouldn't be bringing up bad memories for you. Just ignore us old men. We're just trying to fix all the world's problems in one afternoon."

Marty nodded but turned back to his job, looking deep in thought.

After Will bragged to the men on progress of his first crop, he pulled Mr. Mills aside to talk. When he left the store, he seemed to have more pep in his step. Will was proud of his crop. It was like his offspring out there in the field flourishing. He took pride in checking each field's growth daily.

Leroy blew the horn before he got out of the truck. Marcus had already jumped out and run over to the driver's side where he stood waiting impatiently for his dad to get out. Leroy gave him a stern look. "Now hold yer britches, boy. Don't go getting yourself in no big hurry."

"Well, I don't know why you had to come over here anyway. I told you I already worked it out with Will."

Leroy nodded. "Well, that may be so, but I'm going to make sure we do things proper."

By the time Leroy made his way to the carport, Daniel had already come out the door. Sadie followed close behind and ran up to greet Marcus. Marcus picked her up and asked, "So how's Ms. Sadie today?"

Sadie giggled. "Fine."

Leroy looked over at Sadie and just shook his head. "I declare, it seems like it was just yesterday that I was picking up Carla like that."

Daniel nodded. Sadie wiggled free, ran to the carport ledge, and began her ballerina twirling and prancing.

Daniel crossed his arms. "What can I do ya for, Leroy?"

"Well, tell ya the truth, it's Marcus who has business here. He says he has talked with Will about helping y'all work dem fields this summer, and I told him we better come on out here and check with the boss man first."

Daniel winked at Marcus. "Well, I appreciate that, Leroy, but Marcus here is right. Will's the boss. This here is his crop. I'm helping him, of course, but I'm pretty much letting him hire his own help. If he gets himself some sorry help, then he'll just have to work harder." He looked over at Marcus and grinned. "I don't think he'll have that problem with you though. I hear you're a hard worker, just like your daddy."

Marcus blushed and nodded. "Yes, sir, I am." Then he added, "And you don't have to worry about me coming over here on Saturday night and taking off with your tractor neither."

Leroy popped Marcus on the back of the head. "Now what did you have to go and say that for?"

Daniel burst out laughing. "Now that seems like it was just yesterday too!"

Leroy threw his hands up in protest but soon joined in the laughter.

They turned to look when they heard Val coming up the drive and stepped to the side so she could park her car under the carport.

As she was getting out, Leroy leaned over and whispered to Daniel, "She still working that government job doing the statistics thing?"

Daniel grimaced and nodded.

Leroy clicked his tongue. "Have mercy. I bet you have done heard it all these many years." He grunted again, but when Val caught his eye, he straightened up and smiled back. "Hello there, Val."

She walked over to hug Leroy, returning his greeting, and asked about Annie Mae. "She's doing good, Ms. Val. As long as that Rod keeps her in supply of fresh crappie, rabbit, and deer meat, she ain't got a worry in the world." He tilted his head toward Marcus. "Sep this young'in here still keeps trying to get the best of her."

Val smiled and gave Marcus a hug. When Val pulled back, she looked at his face. "You do look like your mama."

Val went inside the house to start supper and told Sadie that she had to come in when Daniel did. Sadie looked as though she was going to argue, but Daniel told her he wouldn't be going in anytime soon, which seemed to appease her. He had noticed Val had been even more overprotective of Sadie since the Peterson's little boy had disappeared.

Daniel chatted with Leroy and Marcus for a few more minutes, and then the men headed home. Daniel loved seeing Leroy again, and it stirred up more old memories, making him even more excited about the tobacco crop. He was enjoying working with Will and Rod and hanging out at the store, talking farm talk again. He felt ten years younger, and the boys were acting ten years older.

That night after supper, Will and Daniel walked down to one of the tobacco fields behind their pond. Daniel inspected the plants and told Will they looked good and strong. His plant beds had done well, and after planting all his fields and replacing any plants that had not survived, he was actually able to sell some plants to a farmer in another county who was in need. It wasn't much, but Will was excited over making his first bit of money.

"They'll need another quick plow and fertilizing in a week or so."

Will nodded. "I'm still a little worried about that back field I'm renting though. If we don't get rain just right, that field can turn dry quick. There won't be any way to run irrigation pipes back there."

Daniel rubbed his chin. "Well, now, remember what we said about that Will. Mr. Thomas ain't gonna charge ya no rent this year on that field, unless it puts out good for ya. He knows it's risky. You don't have much invested in that field so you won't lose much if it goes bad. If it does well, then you've got yourself a bonus."

Will rubbed his hand through his hair "I know. I know. I just want everything to go well. I've already got plans for my next investment."

Daniel raised his hand. "Whoa. Whoa. Now what's this about a next investment? You'd better not let your mama hear you talk that way when you haven't even got this investment to the market yet."

Will put his hands in pockets and realized he shouldn't have let his thought slip out, but his mind was racing twenty-four/seven and he had to be able to talk to somebody about it. Somebody who wouldn't think he was crazy.

"You don't understand, Dad. Looking to my next venture doesn't make me slack off on the present business deal. It pushes me harder. It's like a game of chess to me. I always have to be thinking three or four moves ahead or I'll lose the game. I don't want to farm my whole life. It's just a way to help me get started. You know that."

Daniel nodded. "Yeah, I know, son." Then letting out a deep breath and putting his arm around Will's shoulder, he said, "Let's head on back to the house, and on the way there, you can fill me in on your big idea. We'll keep it our little secret."

Will's eyes lit up as he began to tell Daniel his big idea. "Well, you know the lake is coming and it's going to bring a lot of people to this community. I was at the store today talking over some business with Mr. Mills …"

Daniel just listened as Will rattled on. They took their time making their way back to the house. By the time they got there, it was dark.

When he crawled into bed that night, Daniel was deep in thought. Will was thinking and talking like a man tonight. When had that happened? How had he missed it?

Val crawled in the bed beside him and nuzzled close. Daniel pulled her body tightly against his. Val was just as pretty as the day he married her, and Daniel knew he would never grow tired of that familiar softness next to his. It gave him comfort knowing there were still some things would never change.

Chapter Twenty-Five

SADIE'S HANDS

SADIE LOOKED PRETTY in her pink Sunday dress. Val thought she was looking more like Carla as she grew older. She smiled and reached down to grab her hand before they walked up the church steps but paused when she felt something strange. Bending down to take a closer look at Sadie's hands, Val frowned. "Ooooh, Sadie, sweetie, you have plum worn calluses on the palms of your hands."

It took Val only a second to realize how it happened. "Honey, these came from swinging around that pole playing." She looked at Sadie. "Honey, you might need to play somewhere else. Little girls shouldn't have big ole calluses like this. Your hands should be soft like the rest of you. Do they hurt, honey?"

Sadie hung her head. "No. They don't hurt, Mama, and I don't like playing anywhere else. It's my most favorite place."

Val realized Sadie was about to cry, so she decided to talk about it later.

Val dropped Sadie off in Ms. Karen's classroom and noticed that Marty was in there helping again. Val gave Karen a knowing wink as she helped Sadie take off her sweater. When she was leaving the room, Sadie ran over and jumped in Marty's lap, who was perched in one of the pint-sized chairs for the children. She almost made him topple over, so he let out an exaggerated grunt and told Sadie she must weigh at least ten pounds heavier since last Sunday.

Karen walked to the door with Val. "So I see Marty is helping you with the class again. Are you two officially dating or what, Karen?" Karen beamed and glanced back at Marty. "Shhhh, I don't want to scare him off. We're not *officially* dating, but we seem to be running into each other an awful lot."

Karen stole another glance back at him as he played with the kids and whispered, "He's already signed up to help me with the VBS class this summer too, which is perfect. He gets all nervous when we are alone, but he's not as shy when we have the kids around us as a distraction."

Val smiled. "Well, he must like you to volunteer to help with Vacation Bible School. Most men have to be dragged out here to help that week."

Karen shook her head and frowned. "That wife he had must've hurt him bad, and it's a pity she didn't want kids. He's so good with them. All the kids love him."

Val clicked her tongue. "Uh huh. It's the kids who are crazy about him, huh?"

Karen gave her a scolding look and then giggled as she shooed Val away.

Sadie found Grandma Margaret after class and sat with her in the pew. Val had started singing in the choir occasionally, so Sadie sat with Margaret, which of course Margaret loved. Sadie could get away with whispering, rattling paper, and all kinds of things that the other Branch children would have been scolded for doing. Margaret would even reprimand others if they attempted to scold Sadie, so of course no one ever did. Soon, it was time for the offertory hymn, and as the first few notes were played on the piano, Sadie gasped. She tugged at Margaret's dress and told her she had to go stand beside Rod. "They're playing our song, Grandma" was all she said as she wedged by Edgar and the others to get to the end of the pew where Rod always sat.

He reached down and picked her up, so she could stand on the pew beside him. "I was wondering what was taking you so long, Sadie Lou. They're playing our song."

By this time, the first stanza of "It Is Well with My Soul" was underway and the chorus was about to be sung. Rod had a deep, base voice and Sadie loved to stand beside him during certain songs. There were only a handful of men in the church who could sing the backup chorus, but none of them had the deeper base that flowed effortlessly from Rod.

Sadie would always try to sing along deep with Rod, and he loved to hear her try. She would sometimes even put her hand on his Adam's apple so she could feel it vibrate as he bellowed out. When the song was over, Sadie made her way back down to the other end of the pew to resume her usual spot so that *all would be well* with Margaret too.

When church was over and everyone was making their way out, Ms. Patsy walked up to Will and Rod. "Will, I just want to tell you how much I enjoyed your talk last Sunday at the graduation service. You sound like a born preacher."

Rod nudged him with his elbow. "More like a politician."

Will took the ribbing and thanked Ms. Patsy.

Meanwhile, Margaret was having another one of her little chats with the pastor. She had cornered him on the church steps. He had a pained expression on his face as she rattled off about how the church still hadn't met offering goals for the year.

"Why, I tell you I see people wearing new Sunday outfits in here week after week and we're not meeting offering goals. Something's wrong with that picture. I don't believe half the people in this church know what true giving is all about, pastor!"

In his mild and easy tone, Pastor White nodded as he listened. "Well, now, Margaret. It's not for us to judge the heart of others, and you and I both know the temptations the Devil uses with the all-mighty dollar. Let's continue in prayer for our congregation and our offering goals."

Edgar, seeing that Margaret was occupied, picked up Sadie and headed to the car. "I do believe you're almost getting too big to carry."

Sadie giggled. "I *am* getting too big. Mr. Marty told me I weighed ten pounds more than last Sunday!"

"Listen, I got a special request. I want you to tell Grandma you'd like to have one of her peach cobblers this week." Sadie looked at Edgar with curiosity and asked, "Why don't you ever ask Grandma to cook stuff."

Edgar stammered a moment. "Well, I would. I would, but I … Well, she already knows how much I love her cooking. I've been telling her for years. This way, she knows how much you love it too. It makes Grandma feel good. So we're doing this for her, ya see?"

Sadie nodded as though she understood. "Oh, okay."

Edgar had been using Sadie for months to put a bug in Margaret's ear. Margaret would drop what she was doing and fix anything Sadie requested. So this way, Edgar got what he wanted without asking.

Punchy was talking to Daniel when Jackie and Carla walked toward the car. Punchy nodded toward the girls. "I hear Ridgewood's girls' softball team did well this year. They say with Jackie pitching and Carla playing shortstop, nothing got past 'em."

"Yeah, Jackie has a knockout pitch and Carla takes after her old man I guess," Daniel said as he patted his chest.

Punchy grinned. "Yeah, I was thinking the exact same thing. You always did play like a girl."

Daniel knew he was kidding but felt the need to defend his manhood. "I wish Will had taken the time to play more with the school. He always loved playing football, but his last two years, practice always interfered with driving his bus or working the fields. That boy has a million things going on in his head at one time. All business, no play. It makes me dizzy sometimes, just listening to all his wild ideas. Rod, on the other hand, will play anything that gets him out of a class or two. One more year and I guarantee you that boy will never crack the door of a schoolhouse again. I just hope he cracks the door of some kind of a job. Got to be something outside or he'll never make it."

Punchy nodded and then said his good-byes as Val and the others made their way to the car.

The rest of the day was a typical lazy Sunday. Carla either read or played her guitar. Sadie tried to play without swinging around the pole but finally gave in to her desires and swung away most of the afternoon. The boys were off fishing or training their bird dogs while the adult men gathered at the store, keeping up with community events.

That night after a late supper that consisted of lunch leftovers, Val told Sadie it was time for bed. After a mock protest, she went around giving everyone a good-night hug. Margaret and Edgar were still there and each took their turn.

When Sadie hugged Margaret, she pulled back and said, "Oh Grandma, there's something I wanted to ask you, but I forgot what it is." She wrinkled up her face trying to remember what it was and then noticed Edgar from the corner of her eye, bringing his hand up to his mouth as though pretending to eat something.

Sadie's face lit up and she exclaimed, "Now I remember! I would sure love to have some peach cobbler this week." She grinned proud of herself for remembering and because she thought it was making Margaret happy. Edgar gave Sadie a wink.

Sadie had been in bed for almost half an hour but was still not asleep when Rod came down the hall. She sat up and whispered his name as he walked by. He went in and sat on the side of her bed. "Why ain't you asleep, Sadie Lou? Little girls need lots of sleep for getting pretty."

She rolled her lip out and said, "I'm not sleepy yet. Tell me a hunting story."

Rod grinned. "I believe I done told you about every trip I've been on about a million times. Which one can you possibly still want to hear?"

Sadie thought about it. "I know! The one about the wolves!"

So Rod began the tale. "Well, one of Mr. Craig's guests shot 'em a bear late one day and it ran off. Mr. Craig and a couple of us men went with him to go track the bear. It got dark on us, but several of the men had 'em some big ole flashlights. I was at the back of the line following the others, gun ready if any trouble happened. It was a funny sight seeing those flashlights bobbing up and down in the dark. They looked like lightning bugs."

Sadie giggled, imagining the scene. Knowing the story well, she jumped ahead and yelled, "Then you heard the wolf!" Rod nodded "That's right! We were going along pretty good, and off in the distance, we heard this lone wolf let out a howl."

Sadie jumped in again and said, "And you hollered right back and sounded just like the wolf, didn't you, Rod!"

Rod frowned. "Hey, who's telling this story: me or you?"

Sadie grinned and closed her mouth tightly.

"As I was saying, this wolf howled off in the distance to our right. I let out a howl back, mocking the wolf. The men kind of chuckled at how good I sounded."

Rod gave a prideful expression then continued. "So then the wolf howled again, just like it was talking to me, except this time it sounded a bit closer. So I howled back with a deep aaaaaahhhoooooooo. The wolf howled back at me, and then we heard another wolf from the left side howling. I turned and howled toward the left, not wanting that wolf to feel slighted, ya know. So now we have a wolf on our right howling with me and a wolf on the left howling at me, and it sounds like they're getting closer. And I'm thinking to myself, *Wow I don't know what I'm saying, but I do believe I'm talking to these wolves.*"

When Sadie couldn't hold it in any longer, she interrupted again and yelled, "Then another wolf howls, don't it, Rod?"

"That's right!" Rod exclaimed as though Sadie had just solved a puzzle. "Just then, another wolf from far away could be heard howling dead-straight ahead where we were tracking the bear!"

Sadie was visibly getting more excited. "Then what did Mr. Craig do, Rod?"

Rod paused and scratched his head. "Well, Mr. Craig wasn't none too happy with me. He was at the head of the line and all of a sudden, I saw the first flashlight stop, turn around, and start bobbing back toward me. It was Mr. Craig. He looked me straight in the eye, with that heavy Canadian accent of his, and said, 'I tell you one ting, Rod. If you howl one more time and bring dees wolves any closer; I will take dis here gun and turn it on you!'"

Sadie giggled. "You had them wolves coming right toward you, didn't you, Rod?"

"Yeah, I guess I did, Sadie Lou."

"You can sound just like any animal can't you, Rod? Do some for me."

"Oh no, not that. You're going to get me in trouble again. Last time we went through near 'bout every animal on the ark and I got in trouble for keeping you up late." He stood up to go, even though Sadie put on her best pout face. He leaned down and kissed her cheek and told her good-night. She reached up and grabbed his neck, giving him a good-night hug and singing low in his ear, "It is well."

Rod sang back, "With my soul."

As Sadie pulled her hands back, her palms dragged across Rod's neck. A strange look came over Rod's face and he took Sadie's hands, turning the palms up.

Sadie looked down and acted as though she was going to cry. Rod groaned, "Aah, Sadie, do your hands hurt?"

She shook her head. "No. They don't hurt at all, but Mama said I shouldn't swing around the pole anymore."

He examined her hands closely as though he was a doctor. "I tell ya what I think, but don't tell Mama. Okay?" He raised his eyebrows in a warning, until Sadie nodded in agreement. "I think these didn't come from swinging around the pole."

Sadie gasped with excitement. "Really!" But then a little concerned, she asked, "How did I get 'em then?"

"These come from working. That's how you always get 'em. Here, look at my hands." Rod extended his palms for Sadie to examine.

Sadie looked at his hands closely and ran her fingertips across his thick palms.

"You do plenty of work around here. Why, I believe we might be working you too hard. Now don't tell Mama though. It will be just between you and me. I'll try to keep an eye out for ya and make sure we don't overdo it on the chores."

He gave Sadie a wink. Sadie was so relieved she piped right up, "Oh, I don't mind chores, and my hands don't hurt at all, Rod. Honest!"

Rod patted her arm. "That's my girl!" He leaned over, gave her another kiss good-night, and got up to leave.

When he reached the door, Sadie said, "I love you, Rod."

Rod whispered back, "I love you too, Sadie Lou. Good-night." Rod walked down the hallway softly singing "It Is Well" with a peaceful expression to match the lyrics.

Chapter Twenty-Six

ALEX

*A*LEX MAXWELL AND his uncle Steve pulled into the Carpenters' garage. Alex was leaning against the window, looking disgusted. Steve put the car in park and slapped him on the shoulder. "Cheer up, man. Look at it this way: you'll be the new kid in town. Everybody always loves the new kid in town, especially the chicks!"

Alex gave Steve a sideways glance and smirked. "Girls already love me at my old school. I've never had a problem in that department!"

That was the truth. Alex was a good-looking kid with a muscular build, dark eyes, dark hair, and knockout smile. The boy knew how to put on the charm too.

"I just don't see why we had to move out here to the sticks and why all of a sudden I have to get a job. It's not like we need the money. Dad's just got a cob up his—"

Steve cut him off. "Hey! Watch your mouth. That's the kind of thing that's got you into trouble as it is. Your dad's just trying to teach you a lesson. One that you'd be well advised to learn. You've been a spoiled brat your whole life kid, and this past year you've acted like you've got a chip on your shoulder." When Alex didn't say anything, Steve let out a sigh and gave him a sympathetic look. "Come on now. Let's see if these good ole boys around here can give this ole Chevy a tune-up. Maybe you can even check and see if they're hiring here."

Steve got out of the car and started walking toward the shop. Alex reluctantly followed.

Jesse talked to Steve and went out to drive his car into the shop. Alex unenthusiastically asked Mr. Carpenter about the chances of getting a job. Alex was relieved when he told him he didn't have anything at the garage and didn't know of anything other than a little farming help that might be needed.

Great, Alex thought, *farming*. Things were looking gloomier by the minute.

While the car was being worked on, Steve talked Alex into walking over to the store to grab a soda and check for a job. As they were making their way across the lot toward the store, Carla came barreling up in the pickup. She hopped out of the truck and into a swirl of dust she had created. She was wearing a tank top and cut-off blue jeans that had seen better days. Her long, curly, brown hair was in a ponytail, sticking out of the back of her softball cap, blowing wild in the wind.

Steve nodded toward her, nudging Alex. "See, that's what I'm talking about. A good ole country girl! Tan from head to toe, short shorts, driving a pickup, and I bet she's got one of those cute little country accents too!"

Alex couldn't help but to give Carla an admiring once-over. Carla never glanced up from pumping her gas when the two passed by and entered the store.

Inside the store, Jackie saw Carla pull up and told Mr. Mills she was headed out to take a break. He nodded and slowly made his way over to take her place behind the register.

Jackie was walking out as Steve and Alex were making their way in. Steve stepped back and held the door open for her to pass. He gave her an approving look from head to toe, which Jackie responded in like, giving Steve her own once-over.

She smiled. "Why, thank you, boys. I do love men with manners." Making her way over to where Carla pumped gas, Steve continued to watch her as she walked away.

Carla looked up and smiled at Jackie, then seeing Steve gawking, she just shook her head. "He's too old for you and you know it."

Jackie glanced back at the door, smiling. "Just harmless flirting, Car. You need to try it."

Carla laughed. "There is absolutely nothing harmless about you, Jackie." Carla let down the tailgate and they both plopped down. They let their feet swing back and forth while they both tilted their faces toward the sun.

Jackie breathed in deeply. "It's good to be outside for a few minutes. That store gets so stuffy. You're lucky you get to work outside, and I would kill for your tan."

Carla sighed. "Yeah, I'll admit I'd rather be outside any day, but just remember I'll look eighty before I turn forty."

Jackie laughed. "I'm never going to look eighty if I have anything to do with it. I'll hook up with a plastic surgeon in a minute."

They both sat there silently for a minute, enjoying the sun. Then Jackie said, "You know we do need to change up a few things before school starts back this year. This will be our senior year. We've got to go in with both guns blasting. You need to get a boyfriend; we need to win the state championship this year in softball, and—"

Carla cut her off. "You've got big goals. But we just got out. I don't want to think about school yet." Carla took a deep breath. "I do want a boyfriend, but I honestly can't think of any guy at our school I'm even interested in, and now the options are even slimmer. I don't want to date somebody younger, so that just leaves the boys in our class." Pausing, she said, "Maybe a summer fling. That's what I need. A summer fling like on Grease with John Travolta and Olivia Newton John."

Jackie sat up straight. "Well then, if you want a summer fling, you've got to get busy. You need to start loosening up and putting on the charm."

Carla puffed. "Yeah, right." Jackie nudged her with her elbow and whispered, "Lesson number one coming up."

As she slid off the truck, Carla noticed that Steve was coming out of the store carrying a Pepsi in one hand and a small brown bag in the other. He was already smiling and heading toward Jackie. Carla got up and busied herself turning the gas pump off, and then she put the cap back on the tank. She did have to admit; however, she also loved to watch Jackie in action.

Steve took a swig of his drink and nodded. "Well, hello again, ladies." Jackie leaned back against the truck, never breaking eye contact with Steve. "Well, hello, yourself. You and your friend just passing through?"

Steve replied, "Oh, I'm just here for a day or two. My nephew Alex is actually moving in down the road with his parents."

"Why, you don't look old enough to be anybody's uncle."

Steve also never broke eye contact. "Well, I'm the baby in the family." He closed the gap between them by walking over to lean against the gas pump right in front of Jackie. There were only inches separating them now.

Carla rolled her eyes. Jackie was so brazen.

Steve shook his head while Jackie curled a chunk of her blonde hair around her fingers. "I do like that Southern accent of yours. It ain't fake, is it? Just putting on for us city slickers?"

Jackie looked offended and in her best British accent replied, "Fake, my accent fake! It bloody well is not!"

Carla had to smile at her then. She was such the actress. Carla admired her for that. She had a response to everything.

Steve laughed. Jackie shrugged. "Well, I'm glad you like it. It's one of those things you either love or you hate, I guess. I see a little of both."

Steve replied, "Oh, I definitely like it. I actually think it's very sexy."

Jackie shifted, putting her elbow against the truck and leaning her head on it. She rested her other hand on her hip, which she now had thrown out toward Steve. She gave the impression that every move was thought through with sultry precision. "Hmmm, sexy, huh? How odd."

Steve looked a little confused. "Odd, how so?"

Jackie smiled. "Well, truth is, during that particular activity, I don't do a lot of talking. Most times, it's all I can do to catch my breath."

Carla gasped and shot a quick elbow to Jackie's side. "Jackie!"

Steve laughed again and shook his head. Jackie just smiled and gave Carla a quick glance. Then she turned back to Steve. "You'll have to excuse my goody-two-shoes friend here. She doesn't realize we're just ribbing each other."

Steve pulled on his shirt collar and let out a slow whistle. "Well, if you two lovely ladies will excuse me, I think I'll go in and see what's keeping my nephew. I'm afraid I might get myself into real trouble out here." He gave a slight bow and winked at Jackie before he headed back into the store.

Jackie turned to Carla. "Okay. Your turn. I hope you took notes. When his nephew comes out, he's all yours."

Carla stared at Jackie. "You're crazy, among other things, Jackie. There's no way I would ever put on the way you do."

Jackie shrugged. "Yeah, I know; it's a gift, really." Then she turned to Carla and laughed. "I'm just kidding. You do it your way, but do *something*."

Just then, Steve and Alex came out of the store. Carla tried to steal a quick glance at Alex, but she was unprepared for how gorgeous he was. She froze and her quick glance turned to gawking. Plus he was walking straight toward her!

"So are you Carla Branch?"

Carla couldn't talk, so she just nodded.

Alex tilted his head toward the store. "I asked the man inside if he knew of anybody around here hiring summer help and he mentioned that I should ask you. He said most people around here have all their farm help lined up but that your brother might be looking more help, since he's just starting out this year."

Carla just stood there and didn't say a word. She wasn't even sure she was breathing. When she didn't respond, Alex slowly asked again, "Sooooo, what do you think?"

Carla finally pulled herself together and mumbled. "I don't know. He might be. You can ask him I guess."

Jackie piped in, "They're the next drive on the right. Will is the one you want to talk to."

Alex stole a quick look toward Jackie and nodded. He looked back at Carla again and grinned. "Thanks. Maybe I'll be seeing ya." He and Steve turned to walk away and Alex turned back around but continued walking, taking a few steps backward. He yelled in Carla's direction, "Carla, right?" She nodded and he continued. "I'm Alex." And with that, he walked away.

Jackie stared at Carla and laughed. "Somebody is smitten, I do believe."

Carla eased back against the truck. "Oh my gosh! Could I have been more spastic?" Then stealing another glance toward the garage as they disappeared into the shop, she put her hand to her heart. "Was he not the most gorgeous thing you have ever seen?"

Jackie sighed. "Yeah, he's definitely a looker. Got that boy-next-door, *GQ* look; not my type, but perfect for you. The only thing is I get the vibe he knows it."

"Well, it would be hard to be that gorgeous and not know it. It's like you looking in the mirror and not seeing Marilyn Monroe staring back at you."

Carla's head was still reeling when Rod drove up on the motorcycle, spraying them with gravel as he spun around. Talking loud enough to be heard over the engine, he told Carla that he needed to trade the bike for the truck. He didn't wait for any protest but ran and hopped in the truck and drove off.

Jackie told Carla she needed to go back inside anyway and said she would put down the gas on Will's account. Left by herself, Carla straddled the bike and looked up to see Jesse standing outside the garage and talking to Steve and Alex. She debated about making up some excuse to ride over and talk to Jesse so she could have a second chance with Alex. But afraid she would act like a fool again, so she decided against it and drove off.

She didn't see him, but Alex turned in her direction when she sped off on the motorcycle. He stared until she was completely out of sight.

A few days later, Carla was weeding the flowerbed in front of the house while Sadie played on the carport ledge and swung around the pole. She had been daydreaming about Alex when she got an uncomfortable feeling in the pit of her stomach. At first, she thought it must be time for her menstrual cycle, but when counting off the days in her head, she knew it wasn't time. Then it hit her that silly Rod must be in need of something. She told Sadie she had to run out to the field to check on the boys, so Sadie needed to run down and stay with Grandma.

Carla watched until Sadie had disappeared inside the screened porch before she took off. She started the Farmal tractor parked by the barn and began to make her way to the far end of the field behind the house. She could see the dirt cloud following Will down the rows of tobacco as he plowed and fertilized. Rod was perched on the back of the truck where they had the bags of fertilizer stacked. As Carla got closer, she could tell Rod was indeed fidgety.

She pulled up by the truck and cut off the tractor. Rod immediately hopped off the truck and gave her an appreciative look. "I knew you'd get my ESP. I've got to go to the bathroom in a bad way."

Carla grunted. "The bathroom! Why don't you just go in the woods? You do it all the time."

As he nudged her off the tractor, he replied, "I said I have to go in a bad way. I need to sit for a few minutes with maybe a magazine or two."

Carla rolled her eyes as she jumped down off the tractor. Rod cranked the tractor and while backing up yelled over the engine, "I've got you half a dozen bags laid out that are only half-full! That should be plenty to last until I get back. Thanks!" Then he headed toward the house, leaving Carla with no choice but to take his spot.

She was glad he at least thought ahead and left some bags so she could actually lift. A full bag weighed a hundred pounds, and there was no way she could raise one up high enough to pour into the tractor hopper. Will would have to stop and get down every time he needed a refill, and that would waste time. Rod knew Will was all about saving time and money.

Rod had a small radio sitting on the top of the truck cab, blaring away on a rock-and-roll station, so Carla decided to plop down on the bags of fertilizer and sun for a few minutes and enjoy a little rest. She had been busy all morning with mostly inside chores, like the never-ending laundry. She would much rather be outside on a gorgeous day like today. Then thinking about Mr. Gorgeousness, she quickly resumed her daydreams.

Soon, she was on the last bag Rod had left for her. As she emptied the bag into the hopper, she heard the sound of Rod coming back on the other tracker. Will headed back down the row and Carla turned around, starting to speak to Rod, but stopped when she realized he wasn't alone. Gorgeous Alex was with him. He had hitched a ride with Rod, standing on the trailer hitch of the tractor.

He looked up at Carla and gave her his movie-star smile. "Hello again, Carla." She mumbled hello in return as Rod hopped up beside her on the back of the truck.

"Alex said he met you up at the store last week. He's going to ask Will about helping us barn tobacco this summer."

Carla nodded and wanted to say something, but she couldn't think of a single intelligent thing. Rod, however, who had never met a stranger, rattled away with a million questions. Where were they living? What did his parents do? It was all things Carla wanted to know too, so she sat back and listened, not in a hurry to head back to the house. She tried to act nonchalant about the conversation, but when she found out Alex was also going to be a senior at Ridgewood this coming year, she almost jumped for joy.

When Will pulled up for his next refill, noticing Alex, he cut the engine and hopped down off the tractor. He grabbed a drink out of the cooler and leaned against the pile of fertilizer bags. As he talked to Alex about possibly hiring him, Will initially acted as though he didn't think he needed any help, but when he got wind that his dad was some big real estate tycoon, his whole attitude changed.

Carla knew how his mind worked and he wasn't hiring farm help; he was making a business connection. Carla didn't care what the reason was—if it meant Alex would be hanging around this summer.

They chatted for a few minutes, and the whole time, Carla remained silent. Will finally ended the conversation by shaking Alex's hand and got back on the tractor. Rod tore open one of the bags of fertilizer and motioned for Alex to pour it in the hopper as he jumped down to grab an empty bag that was blowing away.

Alex heaved the bag up to fill the hopper. When he finished and Will took off down the row, he looked over at Carla. "How in the world did you lift these heavy bags up like that?"

She started to open her mouth to explain, but comedian Rod held up her arm like a boxing champion. "She comes from good stock. She's tough as a lighter knot!"

Carla pulled her arm away and started to scold him, but Alex's appreciative laugh made her forget her anger.

Alex got off the back of the truck, thanked Rod, and said he was going to head on home. Carla got off the truck as well, and actually found her voice. "You want me to give you a ride back to the house?"

"Sure!" he said as he resumed his former spot perched on the back of the tractor. But before Carla started the engine, Alex asked, "Is there anything you can't drive?"

She smiled and Rod yelled, "Oh, she can drive about anything forward. It's when she backing up that you need to get out of the way."

Carla threw him a warning look, but he was right. She grinned sheepishly and said, "Yeah, I don't do backward very well."

Alex seemed to think that was extremely funny. Maybe it was the way she said it, but when he laughed, Carla melted.

When they got back to the house, Alex got in his car, saying his good-byes. Carla watched him disappear down the drive. She stood there until every particle of dust settled back to the driveway, thinking to herself that this was going to be her best summer ever. As she headed down to Margaret and Edgar's house to retrieve Sadie, she was singing "Summer Loving" from the *Grease* soundtrack.

Chapter Twenty-Seven
GIRL RULES

*W*ILL DROVE INTO the gravel lot at Millsville, parking on the side. Carla sat up front while Marcus, Rod, and Jimmy rode in the back. It was almost 6:00 p.m. and they had been working since 6:00 that morning topping tobacco. Will got out and told everybody they could go in and get a soda and put it on his tab. The boys jumped down off the truck with a yelp, running toward the door.

Carla yelled to Rod to please bring her a Tab. He scrunched up his nose. "Yuk, I still don't see how you can drink that stuff." Will had business over at the garage, where Jesse was helping him with some touch-up welding to his tobacco trailers.

Jackie came out to talk to Carla. "Man, y'all have had a long day of it, huh?"

Carla slowly got out of the truck. "Yeah, penny-pinching Will didn't even give us a lunch break today. He threw a pack of nabs at us and kept cracking the whip." Carla looked down at her hands with disapproval. "Look at my poor hands. They'll never be the same. The blisters I got from chopping were about gone. Now I have new blisters from topping the tobacco out. On top of that, I have beautiful brown tobacco stains to go along with it."

Jackie gave her a sympathetic look and leaned against the truck with her.

Jimmy was the first one out of the store. Handing Carla her Tab, he said, "Hey, Jackie, guess what." But before she could venture a guess, he burst out, "I finally got my driver's license."

Jackie smiled and punched him softly on his arm. "Good job, Jimmy. I knew you would kill the driving part after you got the book test out of the way."

Jimmy was eighteen and could've taken the test earlier, but he was too nervous about the written test, so he kept putting it off. Sarah and Herman were in no hurry for him to get behind the wheel either. He could drive just fine, but he had a way of getting distracted, just like he did with everything else.

Jimmy replied, "Yeah, I just don't like tests. If you need a ride to work one day or something, let me know. Me and Jesse are fixing up an old car my uncle had, so I'll have something to drive to school too."

Just then, a red Camaro pulled into the lot. Darlene Baker and her sidekick, Sandra Wells, got out of the car and made their way to the front door. They adjusted their clothes and fluffed their hair on the way. But, of course, nothing was out of place. As they walked by, they paused to acknowledge the trio's presence. Carla casually slid one hand behind her back. She also tried to hold her soda by her side, so her hands couldn't be seen.

Darlene was the first to speak. "Hello, Carla, Jackie." She gave them the once-over with a disapproving eye. She turned to Jimmy, but before she could speak, he blurted out, "Hey, Darlene, guess what. I got my driver's license! I might drive to school some this year too!"

Sandra smirked. "I thought you were a senior last year, Jimmy."

Jimmy hung his head. "I was, but I didn't pass my English class so I have to go back."

Jackie sarcastically asked, "So what brings you two out in boonies? Nothing to do in town tonight, girls?"

Darlene flipped her hair over her shoulder nonchalantly and replied, "We're actually going into Raleigh for the evening, if you must know."

Jackie returned her glare and didn't reply.

Sandra turned to Carla. "Looks like you have yourself a great tan, Carla. Have you joined a pool or gone to the beach?" Before Carla could respond, Darlene answered for her. "Oh, that's what you call a farmer's tan, Sandra. She's been working in the *fields.*"

Marcus and Rod came out of the store and gave the girls a whistle. Marcus said, "Looking good, ladies!"

They said thank-you and laughed flirtingly as they made their way to the front doors. Sandra went in first, but Darlene gave one last condescending glance in Carla's direction.

Jackie grunted. "Thank goodness, Marty is in the store, so I don't have to go in and wait on those two."

Rod nodded. "Yeah, I noticed he don't work much anymore. Got too much going on at his place, I guess, with his horses and stuff, huh?"

Jackie shrugged and turned toward Carla, who was still staring toward the store. Jackie nudged her. "Why do you let those two get to you so bad?"

Carla didn't reply.

Will came jogging across the lot and told everybody to saddle up, because he was ready to roll. Carla was more than happy to oblige. They climbed in and headed home, where Val had supper ready for the hungry crowd. They asked Marcus to stay and eat, but he said Annie Mae was fixing his favorite tonight so he sped home.

Supper was wolfed down by the hungry bunch in a matter of minutes. Before the first dish was even cleared from the table, Will said, "Hey, how 'bout we go top a few rounds in the field behind the house before it gets dark? I think if we do, I might be able to make do without hiring Marcus tomorrow, and that would save a few bucks."

Carla and Rod both rolled their eyes, but Daniel chirped up that he thought that was a good idea. He was always willing to get out in the field after being cooped up in the store all day. Val even volunteered to go help, since Sadie wanted to go play in the field too. Val turned to Carla. "Why don't you stay here and do the dishes and put on a load of laundry. I'll take your spot."

Will started to protest, but Daniel gave him a warning glance. "Remember the rules, Will. Other work needs to be done too, including the ladies' housework. We promised we wouldn't ignore everything else for your tobacco. This is still a family, not a business."

Carla frowned. "Yeah, I'd rather be in the field anyway. It's not like I'm getting out of anything." She was tired of him ignoring all the things she did around the house while they were outside. It was as though nothing done inside the house counted as work to him. Will didn't even think mowing the grass was critical to a household. He just saw it as cosmetic.

While out in the field, everybody took their row, and the snapping sound of topping out the tobacco began. Will took the row beside Daniel and they talked shop while they worked. Val took the row beside the tractor row so Sadie would have enough room to play.

Sadie picked a discarded bloom off the ground and sniffed the trumpet blooms. "These don't smell pretty like your flowers, Mama."

Val smiled. "No, they don't, sweetie."

Val snapped another bloom off and examined it. "I guess they're pretty in their own way, but tobacco plants are not planted for pretty flowers, just for their ugly leaves to make ugly cigarettes." She looked over to where Daniel and Will were to see if they had heard her ugly comments, but they were engrossed in their own conversation. Jimmy and Rod were far enough ahead on their rows, she knew they had not heard her.

Sadie squealed, "Oooh, Mama! Look at that big fly!" She pointed toward a bloom just ahead of Val. "It's pretty!"

Val realized she was pointing at a humming bird that was getting nectar from the flowers. "That's not a fly. That's actually a bird. It's just a very tiny bird. Come here and let me show you."

She reached down and picked Sadie up, and then they both stood very still so they could look at the bird as it buzzed around. "Mama, look at its wings! It's moving so fast."

Val nodded. "See its long skinny beak? That's what it's using to suck up the juice from the flowers, just like a bee does."

Sadie looked at Val quizzically. "Are you sure it's a bird then?"

Val laughed and nodded. "Tell you what, when we get home, I'll show you some pictures of some humming birds your dad has in one of his books."

That satisfied Sadie, so Val put her back down to resume her play and she went back to work.

Soon it was too dark to see and they quit for the night. Daniel was off the next day and promised to help all day so they could finish what they had left undone. Before Val could tuck Sadie in bed that night, she had to find the promised bird book. She dug it out of the cabinet in the den and sat down on Sadie's bed to search for the birds. There were several photos of different humming birds and Sadie ooh and aahed over their pretty colors. When they done looking, Val pulled the covers up and gave Sadie a good-night kiss. As she was leaving the room, Sadie, as she usually did, had one last thought to extend the good-night process.

"Mama?"

Val sighed. "Yes, Sadie."

With a sleepy voice, Sadie said, "If I were a humming bird, I wouldn't fly around so fast. I would sit still more so people could see all my colors." Val laughed softly and whispered good-night as she turned out the light.

The next morning, the gang hit the field at 6:00, ready to do a full day's work. Will had told Marcus and Jimmy they wouldn't be needed today, since Daniel was filling in. If they worked hard and fast, they could finish all the topping out that day. Will revved up, anxious to get at it. Carla felt sluggish right from the get-go and dreaded another day in the scorching heat, smelling the tobacco. Something about the smell of the tobacco in the hot field was sickening and miserable.

Carla realized close to lunchtime that she must be starting her cycle. She was cramping bad and felt sick. Luckily, since Daniel was there, Will couldn't get away with throwing a pack of nabs at them for lunch. Daniel would want something a little more substantial. When they got home, everybody made a tomato sandwich, which they practically lived off of during the summers, and sat at the bar to wolf them down.

Carla took care of her feminine issues and grabbed some Tylenol. She grabbed a little something to eat and then lay down on the couch. She didn't always have bad cramps, but when she did, they were horrible, and today was one of those days. She knew the Tylenol would only take the edge off and she would just have to endure it.

When the boys finished, and it was time to head back to the field, she moved slowly. That afternoon, she was the last one to finish out her row every time. Will finally said something sarcastic to her about lollygagging. Normally, Carla would have jumped all over Will and told him off, but she didn't have it in her.

At the end of one round, when once again they helped Carla finish out her row, they stopped to get a quick drink of water. Because Will was too cheap to invest in a water cooler, they would freeze water in milk jugs the night before. The water would melt gradually during the day to provide cool water as they needed it. They would get a new jug at lunch, and as long as it was kept in the shade, it served its purpose, although many days, the last round they would wind up with warm water.

Daniel asked Carla if she was okay when he saw her leaning over to take a breather. Carla told him that the heat was getting to her a little more than usual.

Will wiped the sweat from his forehead. "Yeah, it's a hot one today, but we're making great progress." He then slapped her on the back. "Just try to pick up the pace a bit, and maybe we'll finish early today."

Carla frowned and asked what time it was. Glancing at his watch, Daniel reported it was 3:30.

To Carla it seemed like an eternity before they would be able to stop for the day, but at least she could now take a couple of more Tylenol. She pulled out the two she had stashed in her pocket and popped them in her mouth, along with a shot of water.

Daniel asked her again if she was all right. She shrugged and said she was fine but was wondering if she could go to the house and start supper or something instead of staying in the field. Daniel told her that they would be eating with Margaret and Edgar that night. So Carla just mumbled something under her breath, and walked toward her assigned row and started back to work.

That evening, around 5:30 when they finally finished their work for the day, they made their way back to the house. Carla made a beeline straight for home, while the men took their time walking back. Will commented on how all of a sudden Carla had a little more pep in her step, now that the work was done, which made all three men chuckle.

When Carla came in the back door, she stopped to wash the tobacco gum off her hands in the utility room sink. Val was there folding clothes.

Carla looked like she was about to cry as she stood there halfheartedly scrubbing her hands. "Oh, Mama, I have had such terrible cramps today, and working in this one-hundred-degree heat just made me feel sick. I want to take a bath and go to bed." She turned and looked pleadingly at Val. "Please tell me I don't have to go down to Grandma's tonight for supper. I'm really not hungry anyway."

Val patted her gently. "Of course not. You stay here. I'll bring you a plate."

Then Val noticed out the window that the boys were almost to the house. She looked back at Carla, who was now drying off her hands on the towel, and asked, "So did you tell the boys you didn't feel well, honey? They would have let you come back to the house."

Carla grunted. "Yeah, sure they would. I asked if I could come back to the house and work and they said no, so I doubt very seriously I could have come home and lay down."

Carla left to go take her shower and Val went out to meet the boys. As she walked down the back steps, all three were smiling and chatting away. Val stood on the bottom step with her hands folded and casually asked how their day had been.

Will beamed. "Great! We got this back field done and" But he stopped when he saw the look on Val's face. He swallowed and slowly asked, "What's wrong?"

Daniel rubbed the back of his neck with his hand and grimaced.

She started in on them, by asking how Carla did today. Did they notice that she wasn't feeling well? Had she, by any chance, asked to come back to the house?

Nobody responded, until Will finally said, "Yeah, she was sort of sluggish today, I guess."

Val turned to him. "Really? Is that so?" Then she whipped her glare toward Daniel. "How about you, Daniel? Notice anything to signal she may not be feeling well?"

Daniel looked afraid to answer, but evidently more afraid to not answer at all. "Well, she did take some Tylenol this afternoon, but she just said the heat was getting to her a little is all."

Val stepped down off the bottom step so she was eye level with Daniel. "Is that so, Daniel? Just happened to have some extra Tylenol stashed away in the field, did she?"

Daniel opened his mouth to speak, but nothing came out.

Rod was the only one who actually sounded concerned when he asked, "What's wrong, Ma? Was she sick? She didn't say anything."

Once again, Val asked, "Is that so? She never asked to be excused to come back to the house?"

Daniel, in defense, said, "Well, yeah, Val, but she didn't say she was sick; she just asked to come back and get supper ready and I told her we were eating at Ma's tonight. I would've let her come back to the house if she had *said* she was sick."

That's when Val went off. "When has Carla ever asked to come back to the house? When has she ever been sluggish in the field? When has she ever not pulled her own weight right beside the boys and complained? Didn't anybody notice she was pale?"

The details of the next few minutes were sort of fuzzy, but Val gave the boys and Daniel a lesson on the differences between girls and boys. She explained that special time of the month and how a man could never understand what it felt like, but how they had better learn to try. Will got the brunt of the anger, since it was his crop they were working and he was in charge, but Daniel would be getting his own personal recap later.

After ten minutes of ranting, Val finally threw her hands in the air and told the boys to wash up and go down for supper. Abruptly, she turned around and stormed off toward Margaret and Edgar's house. The men watched her pound her way down the drive.

Daniel sucked some air in through his teeth and put his hands on his hips. "That, boys, will be your first lesson. First of many, I might add, on 'rules for girls.' Don't let their sweet faces fool ya. They *all* mean business." Then he headed up the steps.

Will and Rod exchanged confused and *scared* glances before they followed.

Chapter Twenty-Eight
ONE RED CUP

*I*T WAS FINALLY time to harvest the tobacco. Farther east people called this the act of cropping. Around the Piedmont area, or at least around Millsville, they called it priming.

On their first morning, Will and Rod were outside getting the trailers hitched and moving the tobacco looper to the barn, while Carla was inside getting the water jugs out and making sure everything was handy for a quick lunch. Val was in the kitchen straightening up from breakfast before she headed off to work.

Carla grabbed the bag of plastic cups from the top shelf of the pantry and turned to Val. "Uh oh, we only have one cup left."

Val turned around and replied, "Oh, I bought a new bag yesterday. Keep looking."

After shuffling items around, Carla found the new bag. "Oh, they're blue; I was looking for red. We always use red." Carla grabbed her red cup along with a few new blue ones and stuffed them in a cardboard box lined with a plastic bag along with the ice jugs.

She hurried outside with her cheap redneck water station and threw it in the back of the pickup. Sadie was already outside playing on her ledge while the men were going in and out of the barn moving things around like carpenter ants. Carla took in a deep breath and thought that it was a great morning. It was going to be another scorcher, but right now, it was bearable.

Marcus drove up first with Jimmy, who he promised to pick up every morning. After a few minutes, Mr. Gorgeous himself drove up. Carla stayed put and let Rod walk over to welcome him. She had run into him a couple of times at the store and actually rattled off a few complete sentences around him. Today, they would be working side-by-side.

The boys chatted for a couple of minutes before Will climbed up on the tractor seat and gave word for everybody to get on. The sides of the trailers stayed down, so they could all sit and ride to the field until they began putting tobacco inside.

Will glanced at Alex. "Rod, run in and grab Alex a shirt!"

Rod looked at Alex and nodded. "Right."

Alex looked confused.

Will shrugged. "Need to wear long sleeves, man. Sorry, I should've told you that. I forgot you haven't worked in tobacco before."

Rod ran out to the house holding a long-sleeved flannel shirt, which he handed to Alex. Alex put the shirt on but was still wondering why they all wore long-sleeved shirts. He didn't want to appear stupid, so he didn't ask anything. When they got to the field, Will reminded everyone to get the bottom leaves off right at the base of the stalk, and what constituted as a ripe leaf. Everyone seemed to be ignoring him. Alex was the only one who needed the information.

He instructed Alex how to, while bending over, grab the leaves with one hand and throw them up under the other arm. "When your arm is full, go throw it in the trailer with all the butts pointed the same way. Just watch how everyone else does it, and you'll figure it out." Alex nodded and Will watched him do the first few stalks. Priming tobacco was easy to understand but hard, backbreaking work. Some farms had apparatuses that the workers rode to harvest the crop. It made the job easier, but it didn't save any time or money, so Will wouldn't purchase one.

After a few rounds, while Rod and Will were busy swapping out trailers, Carla showed Alex where they had put the water jug. Jimmy and Marcus made their way over as well, and after a quick drink, they all headed back to the field.

Alex wiped his brow with his shirtsleeve. "Man, this is hot work." Alex turned to Carla and flashed his Colgate smile. "I don't see how you do it being a girl. I mean, not that girls are weak, but this is tough work." Looking her up and down, he continued. "I still can't believe you lifted those big bags of fertilizer either."

Carla smiled but didn't comment. Before she bent back down, she adjusted her baseball cap. Her hair was stuffed underneath and was always trying to pop out. She would never get the tobacco gum out if it sprang free, making it a constant battle.

A few more rounds and they all headed for water again. Carla and Jimmy got there first and had already filled their cups when Marcus and Alex walked over. Alex bent down and picked up the stack of plastic cups. Noticing that the only red cup was on top, he extended it to Marcus. Before Marcus could grab it, Rod jumped in-between them and grabbed the red cup and began pouring. Laughing over his shoulder as he grabbed the water jug, he yelled, "Snooze, you lose!" Alex had a strange look on his face as he glanced from Marcus to Rod. Marcus gave Rod a wink then started singing, "Nobody knows the trouble I have seen ..."

Everyone swallowed fast and headed back to the field. Rod walked beside Alex, but behind the others. "So did you think the one red cup was for the one black worker?"

Alex shrugged. "Didn't know, being in the South now and all."

Rod looked toward Marcus. "I've known Marcus and his family my whole life. We've grown up together. Don't see or think color when I look at him. Even if other people do, *out here,* all that goes away. Just like in a battlefield. Everybody's working together to get the job done, and everybody helps everybody out like one big team." Rod nodded toward Will, who was now glaring at him. "Now Will, on the other hand, sees dollar signs when he looks at us just standing around, so we better get back to work."

Alex nodded and smiled before he bent down to get to work.

By the time they got to the other end of the field, Edgar and Sadie were there with nabs and sodas. They grabbed their snacks and either plopped down on the ground or sat on the tailgate of Edgar's truck. Carla picked up a handful of dirt and rubbed her hands briskly, letting the sand sift through her fingers and hands. Alex was watching with curiosity, so she explained that the dirt acted like powder to the tobacco gum, although he didn't appear to understand.

They laughed and carried on during the break, talking about how hot it was. It was going to hit one hundred again today, for about the seventh day in a row. Alex said he was not used to the extreme heat, and he took his shirt off during the break. Carla, although enjoying the view of his bare chest, told him he really needed to wear a shirt, even if he couldn't handle long sleeves.

Marcus cut her off. "Let the man go shirtless if he wants to, Car." Standing behind Alex so he couldn't see, Marcus winked. Jimmy, however, didn't take the hint and reiterated that he really needed to wear the long sleeves because the tobacco would make him all gummy. Marcus changed the subject by asking Jimmy how the work was coming on the car Jesse was helping him fix. The diversion worked and Jimmy didn't mention the shirt again.

When they started back to work, Alex left his shirt off and kept it off for the rest of the morning. At noon, they stopped for lunch. Edgar came back out to the field to pick them up and take them back to the house. Will told Alex he could stay and have a sandwich with them, or if he went home to be back at 1:00. Jimmy would stay with them to eat lunch. Marcus was going home for lunch and bringing back Annie Mae to help at the barn.

As Alex handed Rod the shirt that he had borrowed, Marcus

grinned. "Hey, Alex, want to know why you need to wear long sleeves out in the field?"

Alex was standing with a hand on his hip. "Yeah, I guess so. Why?"

Marcus walked over, took the arm on the side that Alex had used to carry the tobacco under, and pressed it against his body, holding it there a couple of seconds. When he released it, he grinned and said, "Raise your arm now."

Alex slowly tried to pull his arm away from his side. His flesh was stuck together by the sticky tobacco gum. It was like pulling off a Band-Aid. He grimaced as he slowly began the torturous act of raising his arm. It pulled at his skin and every tender hair follicle on both his arm and his side. By the time he reached the heavier hair right under his arm, he was sucking in air through gritted teeth.

Marcus slapped his knee, laughing. "Them little hairs hurt, don't it, man!"

Rod and Will joined in the initiation joke by laughing at Alex's misery. Rod adjusted the bill on his cap and winked. "Now you're part of the team, man!"

Jimmy, who never laughed at any person's pain, said softly, "Yeah, you really need to wear a shirt. I hate tobacco gum. I guess it gums up your lungs too. That's why they say you shouldn't smoke, huh?"

Alex gave Jimmy a dismissive look and tried to laugh off the joke, but the truth was he didn't like being the brunt of a joke. He was much better at being the instigator.

Carla gave him a sympathetic smile and reminded him about the sand. "Grab a handful and rub it on the inside of your arm and your side and you won't be sticky." Alex did as he was told, and the trick worked. The sand stuck to the film of sticky tobacco gum and coated his skin like baby powder. He could move freely again.

Will walked over, patted him on the back, and told him to go home and rest but to be back by 1:00. "We're finished in the field for today. When you come back, we'll be putting it in the barn. It's easier work and cooler."

Alex nodded and left. As he drove the three miles home, he was feeling tired and a little humbled. Joke aside, he really liked everyone, and even though the work was hard, he thought it was going to be all right. All his life, he had driven by fields of one crop or the other and never considered how much physical work it took to harvest. Now he was finding out firsthand.

The barn work was much easier. Carla, Jimmy, Annie Mae, and Will got the tobacco from the trailers and put it on the looper. The looper was a big sewing machine-type that strung the tobacco together with a stick in the middle so it could be hung in the barn. Rod and Marcus climbed up in the tier poles of the tobacco barn. Alex's job was to take the tobacco off the looper and hand it up to them. Just like in the field, everybody laughed and cut up constantly but worked hard. The time flew by, and soon the job was done.

Before Alex left, he asked Rod, "So what do you guys do around here for fun? I mean, all this work is just peachy, but you have to have some down time."

Rod laughed. "Yeah, man. Will ain't in charge all the time. Hey, tell ya what. Come over any time you want. We can do some fishing or you can help me with a couple of bird dogs I'm training."

Carla rolled her eyes. "Actually, some of us like to do normal stuff like go to the movies, shop, grab a burger, or just hang out. Not everybody's as big a redneck as Rod here."

Alex laughed. "I don't know anything about fishing or working with bird dogs. Sounds fun. I'll have to come check that out." Then winking at Carla, he said, "And, of course, the normal stuff too."

Alex hung around for a few minutes, talking bird dogs, trotlines, and fishing with Rod. Will told him what days they would be working the rest of the week before Alex left.

Annie Mae gave everyone a hug before she left too. She went on about how much they had grown. She laughed at Will. "I knew one day we'd all be working for you!" The comment made everybody laugh, including Will.

That night, Daniel walked out to the barn with Will and showed him how to fire up the burners. Val had to pry them away for supper. Everyone was talkative that night, telling about their first day of barning. Even Sadie bragged about how she helped Grandpa bring snacks to the field. Daniel and Val exchanged prideful glances, listening to their brood chatter away. The physical work was good for them, making them strong in both body and soul. Many of life's lessons can be learned working in the fields.

Chapter Twenty-Nine
ONE UGLY FIELD

*A*LEX STARTED GOING over at night to hang out. He and
Rod were especially getting along great. Of course, Rod made
friends with everyone. He took Alex coon hunting and fishing and let
him help train one of his bird dogs. It amazed Alex how one could tie a
few bird feathers on a fishing pole, flip it around on the grass, and a dog
would learn to point at it.

Carla went to the movies once with Alex, but it wasn't a date because
Jimmy had tagged along. That's when Carla noticed other girls giving
Alex approving glances. They practically gawked at him, the way boys
ogled over Jackie. Although Alex didn't respond, she knew he was aware
of the attention. This made her not just jealous but self-conscious as well.
Carla saw herself as plain—not ugly, but she didn't stand out in a crowd.
Unfortunately, boys seemed to be attracted first to physical appearances.
She ignored the fact that she was first attracted to Alex for the same
reason.

The field Will rented from Mr. Thomas had not done well, and when they arrived, the weather reflected Will's foul mood over the situation. It was an overcast day and had been drizzling on and off all morning. It was late morning and Will wanted to jump in and get the field done before they broke for lunch. After the first trailer was filled, Will left on the tractor to take it back to the barn, leaving the others in the field.

Alex unloaded his armful of tobacco in the trailer just as Rod walked up with his. "What's up with this field? It looks different."

Rod grimaced. "Well, several things. First, you can't get to it with irrigation, so it didn't grow very well right from the start. I think every shower that came our way missed this field. The only good rain that fell on this field happened right after Will sprayed it, which was when he didn't need it to rain."

Alex asked, "What was he spraying for?"

Carla walked up and unloaded her armful of tobacco, pulling off a huge tobacco worm from her shirtsleeve. She shivered. "Well, tobacco worms for one thing. They're eating this field up! Look at 'em. They're all over the place!" She shivered again. "I hate these things!" Carla flung the worm at the tractor, hitting the exhaust pipe; it sizzled like bacon cooking in a frying pan.

Marcus and Rod both tossed one at the engine as well and soon they had all taken aim and carcasses were clinging to the motor. Growing tired of their target, they eased back into priming, but the game didn't stop. Every time someone found a worm, they would take aim at the next person to stand up in the field. It turned into a big tobacco worm fight with everybody flinging worms and ducking behind tobacco stalks to avoid being hit.

They were already wet from the rain and now they were covered in slimy, green worm guts. The game continued until Rod's keen ears picked up on the sound of Will coming back. They only had minutes to finish filling their trailer before he would reach them, so they hustled back to work.

Will didn't say a word when he arrived and the trailer was only half-full. He also didn't mention the worm guts dangling from the tractor and spattered on his workers' clothes. His expression, however, was enough. They finished out the field in silence, with the exception of a few snickers.

That night when they sat down for supper, Will wasn't there. Val asked where he was and Rod explained he was bringing back an empty trailer from the field and would be home any minute. They said grace and started the meal without him.

Carla and Rod had everyone laughing when they told Jesse about the tobacco worm fight. When they heard the back door open, Daniel gave them a warning look, so they dropped the subject.

Will fixed his plate and took his seat. It was obvious his mood was foul. Conversation continued, but Will was silent and seemed to only play with his food. Daniel gave him a sympathetic look. "Tough luck in Mr. Thomas' field, huh?" Will didn't make eye contact, just mumbled in agreement.

Rod, looking guilty now, said, "Sorry about the worms."

Sadie giggled. "They were sizzling." She raised her arms and wiggled in her chair. This made Will give in and crack a smile, so they all laughed until they cried all over again.

Will quickly resumed his sour mood and finished his meal in silence. The men continued to chat while Val and Carla cleaned off the table. Finally, Will revealed the other reason he was upset. When he had gone back to the field to retrieve his empty trailer, he had run into Mr. Thomas.

They were chatting casually when Mr. Thomas clicked his tongue and said, "I tell ya Will, I hate to say it, but that is one *ugly* field of tobacco." This, of course, was a true statement, but Will had been insulted and overcome with anger. He replied harshly to Mr. Thomas and left abruptly. Now Will was feeling guilty for the outburst and regretted his behavior.

Val was standing at the sink and washing dishes. She looked back over her shoulder sympathetically. "I'm sure he understands, honey. What was it you said that was so bad anyway?"

Uncomfortable, Will squirmed in his seat and rubbed the back of his neck the same way Daniel did when under stress. "Well, ya see," he started. "When he told me I had an ugly crop, I just blurted out the first thing that came to my mind, and I said, 'Well, so's your daughter!'"

Val gasped. "Will! No, you didn't!"

Will nodded and rubbed his face with his hands. He kept them there as he mumbled, "I don't know why I said it. It just popped in my head, and before I knew it, it was coming out of my mouth."

Daniel was rubbing his chin. "Well, not that it matters, but what does his daughter look like?"

Val shot him a disapproving look. "Daniel!"

Daniel shrugged. "Well, I was just thinking that if his daughter is pretty, he really won't be offended. He'll know he was just speaking out of turn." Daniel looked back at Will, waiting for his answer "Well?"

Will shrugged. "Gee, Dad I don't know what she looks like. I haven't seen her in years. They live just over the county line, so she didn't go to school with us. I wouldn't know her if she walked in the room."

Daniel turned to Rod and Jesse. "What about y'all? Seen her lately?" Jesse shook his head "She's a redhead is the only thing I remember."

Daniel grunted and clicked his tongue.

Rod nodded and snapped his fingers. "Yeah, I remember her now. She *is* a redhead, and the last time I saw her, she had braces. The kind with one of those big head gear contraptions wrapped around her head."

Will grunted. "Oh no. She probably is ugly. I'm mud, just pure mud."

Rod and Jesse exchanged glances and looked as though they were trying not to snicker.

Val turned around, dried her hands, and put them on her hips. "Well, Will, you will just have to march right over there and apologize. There is just no way around it, and the sooner the better."

Daniel nodded his head slowly and looked at Will. "Son, she's right.

Might as well go on over there now before it gets bedtime and fix it. You'll be miserable until you do."

Will nodded and slowly pushed himself away from the table. Daniel got up from the table and gave Val a kiss on the cheek. "I think I'll ride over there with him in case he needs backup."

Val shook her finger at him. "Just don't do his work for him. This is his mess. He needs to take care of it."

An hour later, Val was sitting in the den watching *The Waltons* when they got back home. Val looked up as Will hurried past her, making his way to his room. She called after him to ask how things went, but Will kept walking and blurted, "Fine!" Daniel, who was grinning, plopped down in his recliner and picked up the newspaper.

Val looked over at him. "Well? What happened?"

Daniel flipped a corner of the newspaper down so he could see Val's face. "The girl's name is Rachel and she is, indeed, a flaming redhead." And just before he flipped the paper back up, he added, "Will has a date with her on Saturday night."

Val's mouth fell open as she slid up to the edge of her chair. When Daniel didn't offer up any other information, she popped him on his foot. "You can't just leave me hanging. What happened?"

Daniel laughed and put the paper down. "Well, we got there and Mr. Thomas wasn't even at home. Rachel came to the door and knew right away who Will was. In fact, she knew all about what he had said today, so she wormed a date out of Will to make up for it." Daniel shook his head. "She's quite the little actress. She had Will groveling out an apology and squirming like an earthworm."

Val put her hand to her cheek and shook her head as though she was trying to picture the scene. "So ... Not that it matters or anything, like you said earlier, but what *did* she look like? I mean other than the red hair. Is she ... *ugly?*"

Daniel rubbed his chin. "Well, I couldn't see all that good from the

truck, but I'd say she's not bad to look at. Maybe all that dental work paid off."

Everybody picked on Will pretty hard the rest of the week leading up to his big date. It was obvious that it was beginning to get under his skin. He tried to get Rod to come with him and double date, but Rod had other plans. He resorted to asking Alex if he and Carla would tag along. Alex agreed, so plans were made and it was obvious that Will was relieved that he wouldn't have to deal with Rachel alone. There was something about her that made him nervous, or maybe it was just the whole situation; either way, he felt better knowing they wouldn't be alone.

Will and Carla picked up Alex first that night. It was the first time she had been to his house. It was a huge colonial-style home set back in the woods. It wasn't visible from the highway and the Branches didn't know Alex's grandfather and grandmother who lived in the house.

Alex had told them that his grandfather had a stroke last year, which left him paralyzed on one side. That was another reason they had made the move. His grandmother needed help taking care of him, and since the house was definitely large enough to support both families, Alex's mother volunteered.

Alex's father traveled a lot for work and did most of his business over the phone, so he could live virtually anywhere. To hear Alex talk about it, working was all his father did.

The evening started off uncomfortable, but by the end of the meal, everyone was laughing and having a good time. When the evening ended, Will dropped off Alex first. Carla was hoping Alex would try to give her a good-night kiss, but the opportunity didn't present itself, so she was left feeling unfulfilled. He may not have seen it as a date anyway, but she was still holding out hope that he would.

However, when Will dropped Rachel off, he had the perfect opportunity when he walked her to the door. Carla watched from the

car as he stood there on the porch with her for a few minutes, looking uncomfortable as they said their good-byes. She was so proud when Will casually and gently reached for Rachel's hand, pulling her slightly toward him. He gave her a light peck on the cheek and said his final good-bye. Carla sighed and thought it was the sweetest thing she had ever seen.

When he climbed in the car, he had a grin plastered across his face. As he was backing the car up to turn around, Carla smiled. "Well, you got that out of the way. Don't have to worry about seeing her again."

Will turned and glanced back at the house. "Uh yeah, I guess so." He didn't tell Carla, but he had just asked Rachel if he could see her again, and she had said yes. Will would soon find out that sticking his foot in his mouth was the best step he had ever made.

Chapter Thirty
FIRST OF THE LAST

*W*ILL AND RACHEL continued dating for several weeks and it was obvious to everyone that she was going to be the one. As it turned out, she and Will had a lot in common. She had plans to take some business classes at the community college and was working part-time in a local accounting office. Not only was she a perfect match personality wise, but her knack with numbers, for Will, was a definite plus. He didn't share his feelings with anyone, but it was so obvious he didn't have to. Rachel was destined to be his business partner in more ways than one.

Carla continued to moon over Alex as well. They enjoyed each other's company, but they were never alone. When they were not working, Rod was always dragging the boy off somewhere else. They often exchanged quick glances that Carla interpreted as mutual attraction, but that was as far as anything had gone. Now with football practice his priority, Alex missed working completely.

Marcus was also at practice, which left Will short in the field. Val and Daniel helped on Saturdays and sometimes took days off during the week to help. Margaret and Edgar were available to help at the barn or in bringing trailers back and forth to the field. Sadie was in tow, of course, and everyone was getting tired.

Carla was ready for school to begin. Then she would see Alex every day. Rod seemed to also be ready for the first time in twelve years. He told Carla that knowing it was his senior year, and his *last* year, until freedom made it seem bearable. Every day was a *last day* event—last *first* day of school, last *second* day of school—all the way down to the last day of school *forever*!

Jackie plopped down beside Carla on the pew. Carla looked up with a start but relaxed when she saw it was Jackie. Jackie elbowed her and laughed. "What's wrong? Did you think I was Alex?" Carla shrugged but didn't comment.

"I don't know why you keep inviting him. He's obviously not going to show up."

Carla sighed. "You never know."

"What I do know is that you need to take some of your own advice. You keep telling me to get a good church boy, somebody that will be good for me instead of the scum I usually wind up with, and look at you going for the bad boy."

"Alex isn't scum. He comes from a good family. He's not a bad boy either. I don't *think* he is anyway. Maybe he just needs somebody like me to give him a change of heart."

Jackie rolled her eyes and they dropped the subject. They both watched as Ms. Karen and Marty took their usual spot a couple of pews ahead of them.

Carla whispered, "Aren't they sweet? I'm glad Ms. Karen finally found somebody. I hope they get married soon. She's not a spring chicken anymore."

Jackie grunted and Carla shot her a disapproving look. "I don't know why you don't like Marty. He's just a little reserved, probably because of all the stuff he's had to deal with. I mean his uncle dying the way he did, then his divorce and all." Jackie straightened her skirt and mumbled under her breath, "Very reserved, I'd say."

Carla gasped. "That's it, isn't it? Marty never once paid any attention to you, even though you flirted with the poor man constantly, like you do every other man. That's what's eating you, isn't it?"

Jackie crossed her arms. "Oh, you know good and well I wouldn't want anything to do with that old man!"

Carla laughed. "Yeah, but you're not used to being completely ignored either, are you?"

Jackie smirked. "Come on. You've got to admit it's weird how I never caught him once checking out my butt or staring at my cleavage. I mean all men are pigs. It comes natural."

Carla laughed but then looked deep in thought. "What about Rod and Will? Have you ever caught them, you know … sneaking a peek?"

Jackie smiled. "Oh yeah, but they always blush and look the other way like it didn't happen."

Carla swallowed. "What about my dad?"

Jackie sighed and smiled. "Now your dad is one of the few exceptions to the rule. That's the kind of man I want to marry. He honestly doesn't see anybody else in the room but your mom, and it's written all over his face. Your dad looks at me the same way he looks at you, and I like that."

Carla sighed with relief and changed the subject.

The next day was the first day of school and they were discussing what outfits they would wear when Sadie came barreling down the aisle and ran to their pew. She gave Jackie a big hug before finding her usual spot at the far end of the pew. Margaret was not there yet, which was unusual. As she waited, Ms. Thelma stopped to ask where her grandmother was. Sadie told her she should be there any minute so she sat down beside Sadie on the pew, breathing heavily.

She was a heavyset woman and got out of breath easily. She picked up a bulletin and began fanning herself. "I think I'll just sit a minute and wait for her. It's been a long week and I'm tired."

Sadie smiled. "Me too! I've been working hard this week."

Thelma smiled politely, but when Sadie showed her hands as evidence, she gasped.

Ms. Thelma examined Sadie's little hands, rubbing her fingertip over her hard calluses. "Oh my, you have been working hard. How did you get these, sweetie?"

Sadie hung her head and said, "Well, Mama keeps saying I get them when I am playing." But then she jerked her head up. "But Rod knows. He said I got them working hard but not to say anything."

Ms. Thelma put her hand to her chest. "Do you really have to work, honey?"

Sadie nodded. "Oh yes! Will says everybody has to do their part!" Sadie smiled and turned her attention to doodling on the bulletin.

Thelma looked flustered, and by the time Margaret arrived, she said she forgot what she was going to ask her.

Later when Daniel and Punchy had taken their places in back for the offering, they saw Will and Rachel slip in. Punchy whispered to Daniel. "Looks like you might have a bunch of redheaded grandchildren in your future there, Dan!"

Daniel grinned. "Maybe too early to tell just yet."

Punchy nudged him with his elbow and nodded toward Mr. Rollins sitting on the back pew with his daughter. "Good thing he didn't rent that field from Mr. Rollins, huh?" Punchy made a face and exaggerated a shiver, because Mr. Rollins did, indeed, have a homely daughter. Daniel frowned at Punchy, but deep down he was thinking the same thing.

After Sunday lunch, Carla sat on the porch swing playing her guitar while Sadie played in her favorite spot. Carla occasionally laughed at her, because she would say the silliest things when she was in her imaginary world. Will was over at Rachel's and Rod drove off with Jesse, so when she saw Alex coming up the drive, she was thrilled. This would be her chance to have him all to herself.

When he got to the front steps, Sadie ran and jumped in his arms, giving him a good squeeze. She immediately rattled off that Will and Rod were not home.

He looked disappointed. "Ah man, and I was hoping to go fishing." Sadie laughed. "But you can!"

He sat Sadie back down. "I don't know. My daddy said that's a good way to get shot in this neck of the woods. Can't go fishing unless somebody is with you who knows who you are."

Carla laughed knowing that was true. Some didn't take to strangers helping themselves to their fish and were not afraid to run them off with their shotguns.

Alex stuck his hands in his pockets and looked at Carla. "What do you say? Want to go do a little fishing? I reckon I *pert near* know how ta bait a hook."

She laughed at his attempt at a Southern accent. "Sure, let me go put my guitar up and tell Mama." When she came back outside, they went to the barn and grabbed a couple of fishing poles. Rod had rigged an old icebox filled with dirt to keep worms, so he always had bait. His makeshift scoop was a milk jug with the bottom cut off. She scooped a jug full of dirt and worms and dropped it in a coffee can. "Well, do you want to take the pickup or walk?"

Alex shrugged. "Walking is fine with me."

Carla and Alex made their way to the pond, stopping once to peep into one of the tobacco barns. Carla loved the smell of tobacco as it was curing in the barn and Alex seemed fascinated by the golden-yellow color the bright green leaves had turned. When they reached the pond, they walked out onto the pier and got their hooks baited, casting them out into the water.

With their corks floating in the rippling water, they propped their poles up against a makeshift railing and sat down. Carla didn't care much for fishing, but she loved coming to the pond to sit. There was something about being by the water that made the sun seem brighter, the insects sound louder, and the world better. She had never felt that more so than right now, sitting there with Alex.

Rod got back home about fifteen minutes after Carla and Alex left to go fishing. As soon as he walked in, Val told him that he should probably go down to the pond and check on them.

"Check on them? Check on them for what?"

Val shrugged. "Well, you know, check on them."

Then Rod nodded and smiled. "Don't worry, Mom. They're just friends. I don't think Alex thinks of Carla that way. Something tells me from seeing his family he's more into the high-society type."

Val raised her hand. "Well, that may be, but I can assure you that Carla likes *him*, and all it takes is for one person to start doing the liking."

Daniel, who had been nodding off in his chair, yawned and stretched. "How do you even know Carla likes him? She's never acted like it around me."

Val grunted. "Believe me: all the signs are there. She's been smitten with that boy since day one."

Rod and Daniel exchanged looks and shrugged, but Rod promised to go to the pond right after he grabbed a snack. He said he needed to check his trotline anyway, so Val was satisfied.

They fished in silence, but that was the good thing about fishing; silence was okay and even expected as part of the experience. After a while, with no nibbles to speak of, Alex pointed to some milk jugs floating at the far end of the pond. "What's that for?"

"Oh, that's Rod's trot line. He usually just gets turtles though." Alex shook his head. "Never met a family with as many uses for a milk jug, and to think, we just throw ours away."

Carla laughed when she thought about their water jugs and the scoop in the worm box. "Yeah, I guess you're right. I honestly don't think we use then for anything else though."

Another few minutes of silence passed then she asked, "So you ready for your first big day at a new school tomorrow?"

Alex threw a blade of grass into the water. "Yeah, I guess. I know I'm ready to play some football. I think we have a good team. Some of the other players say it's the best team the school has had in a couple of years."

Carla smiled "Good. I look forward to cheering you on."

Alex looked out at the water then back at Carla. Leaning closer, he nudged her with his shoulder teasingly. "So tomorrow are you going to show me around school, or are you going to pretend like you don't even know me?"

Their shoulders were still touching and Carla felt the need to break his intense gaze for a second. She looked out at the pond. "I doubt you'll need me to introduce you around. You'll be the new guy. All the girls will scope you out in the first five minutes." When she dared to look back, Alex was still staring at her intently, and his face was close enough for her to feel his breath.

"Maybe. But I bet there's not a single girl there who can pick up a hundred-pound bag of fertilizer." They both laughed lightly and then Alex reached over with his hand and titled her head up, leaning in closer. Their eyes locked and then automatically closed.

Their lips almost touched, but Rod called out from the shore. Alex opened his eyes, giving Carla an apologetic grin, before he stood. He walked toward them and asked Alex if he wanted to help him check his trotlines.

Alex said, "Sure." He left Carla, disappointed, sitting on the pier.

Rod allowed Alex to walk past him onto the pier. Carla turned around and glared at Rod, who was grinning from ear to ear. He glanced at Alex then back at Carla, then adjusted his ball cap. "Well, well now. I do believe I might be getting some of that twin sixth sense after all. Something tells me you were in trouble, and I got here in the nick of time."

Carla fumed at him as she crossed her arms over her chest and abruptly turned back around.

For the next hour, Rod and Alex checked trotlines, talked, and fished. It was like Carla wasn't even there. When they got back to the house and Alex was getting ready to leave, he called Carla over to his car. "Hey, wait for me out front tomorrow morning if you get there first, all right?"

Carla grinned and nodded. They exchanged good -byes and Carla stood there watching him drive away. As she walked back in the house, she caught herself once again singing "Summer Loving" from the *Grease* soundtrack.

That night, when Carla crawled into bed beside Sadie, she was almost too excited to sleep. They had almost kissed! If it hadn't been for Rod … Oh, well. It was fine, she thought. At least now she knew he felt the same way about her and it would happen eventually. There would be more opportunities for stolen kisses at school.

She finally dozed off to sleep, daydreaming about her senior year and how it was going to, indeed, be her best year ever.

The next morning, Carla was in a mad rush to get ready. Except she couldn't do anything right. She spilled milk on her shirt and had to change it last minute, couldn't find a shoe, and then had to wait for Sadie to get out of the bathroom before she could brush her teeth. Rod kept telling her they had plenty of time, but she wanted to get there early to wait for Alex. Deep down, she realized she didn't trust Alex to wait on her, so she wanted to get there first.

As Rod and Carla were getting in the car, Will came out of the barn and yelled for them to wait up. Carla threw her hands up in exasperation.

"Hey, Rod, listen. Watch out for Jimmy, okay? Some of those kids are pretty rough on him and I won't be there to take care of him."

Rod nodded. "You got it, man!"

Carla immediately felt guilty. She had been thinking of herself and her own little world and hadn't thought once about Jimmy and how he wouldn't have Will there to protect him.

When they pulled into the parking lot, Carla scanned the front of the school, madly looking for Alex. She was about to give up when she saw him standing close to one of the side doors in the courtyard. He waved when he spotted her, and she waved back. She couldn't believe it. He actually waited! She had to hold herself back to keep from running to meet him.

"There's my tour guide!" he said as he reached down to grab her hand and give it a gentle squeeze. Carla melted but kept her composure, pulling him toward the main entrance to the school. Once inside, just as Carla had predicted, all the girls were exchanging giddy looks and pointing toward Alex. A couple of football players walked by calling out greetings to Alex, which she could tell made him feel more at ease and confident.

Then it happened! Darlene Baker eyed Alex from across the school lobby. She looked Alex over approvingly and then started making her way in their direction. *Oh yeah,* Carla thought, *this will be good. Here comes "Miss Can't Use Your Ole Stinking Outhouse" Darlene Baker, interested in my boyfriend.*

When Darlene got there, she said, "Hello, Carla." But the funny thing was that she didn't even look at Carla. She was staring right at Alex, and to Carla's utter shock, Alex was looking at Darlene. He was even giving her his brightest smile. That smile should be reserved for her, not Darlene.

Rod walked up and Carla thought surely he would shoo Darlene off, but he didn't. Rod nodded at Darlene. "Hello, Darlene. You're looking good."

Darlene flipped her hair back with her hand. "Thank you, Rod. Why don't you introduce me to your friend here? I don't believe we've met."

"Oh yeah, sorry. This is Alex. He moved here a couple of months ago. He's a Yankee but he's cool. Helped us all summer in tobacco."

Darlene stuck out her hand. "I'm Darlene." Alex let go of Carla's hand and reached out to shake her extended hand. Darlene didn't shake his hand; however, she just held onto it and turned to Carla saying, "You don't mind if I show Alex around, do you?"

Before Carla could even breathe a protest, Darlene had pulled

Alex away from Carla's side. He allowed her to pull him across the lobby toward her usual entourage of friends. He threw Carla a quick, apologetic look over his shoulder, but she could tell he wasn't sorry at all.

It happened just that quickly; Carla had been inside the school house forty-five seconds at most, and Darlene had stolen him away. Carla was shattered. She should have known this would happen. She should have made a move earlier in the summer. She should have kissed him instead of waiting for him to kiss her! He wasn't her boyfriend at all! They had never been on an official date. They had no understanding. Carla had been fooling herself the whole time. Jackie was right; she was never going to be a match for Alex. Darlene Baker was the type of girl who attracted the Alexes of the world, not her.

Darlene never left his side the whole day, and Alex never once looked Carla's way. Instead of this being her best first day of school, it was her worst. When she got home that day, she wanted to cry into her pillow until the sun went down, but that's what happened in a perfect world. In Carla's world, she would be working in the field or at the barn until it was dark.

It was times like this she was glad Rod couldn't sense her feelings. Sometimes, it was just better to suffer alone.

Chapter Thirty-One
REASON TO HUG

CARLA WAS HAVING a fitful sleep, dreaming about Darlene Baker swooping in and taking Alex away from her. When she awoke in the middle of the night, she sighed heavily, realizing it was not a nightmare but reality. Sadie was squirming in bed as well, and Carla soon realized the reason why. The bed was wet. Carla closed her eyes for a second and mumbled, "Not again." Poor Sadie would feel terrible when she woke her up, but it had to be done.

Carla gently nudged her, calling her name softly. Sadie squirmed and blinked her eyes until she finally opened them wide.

She stared at Carla looking confused, and then her lip rolled out in a pout. "I'm sorry, Carla. I didn't mean to."

Carla gave her a smile. "I know, sweetie. Let's get on up and get all changed so we can go back to sleep. Deal?"

Sadie nodded and slowly began to crawl toward the end of the bed.

Carla slipped down the hall to grab a clean set of sheets. When she returned, she hesitated before flipping on the lights. "Ready for the lights, Sadie?"

Sadie nodded and squinted until her eyes adjusted. Carla began to strip the bed and put on clean sheets. Sadie went to her dresser and pulled out dry pajamas and underpants and began to change.

"I was having a bad dream again. This man was chasing me. I don't know what he wanted, but he scared me."

Carla gave her a sympathetic look. "Well, it was just a nightmare. Try to forget about it when you get back in bed and have happy thoughts." Carla thought it must be nice to have nightmares that weren't real. Her dreams were all too real, and no amount of happy thinking would change anything.

As Carla changed the bed linens, she noticed Sadie watching her. Sadie always felt guilty when this happened.

As Carla finished, she said, "Ya know, Sadie, this is really good practice for me."

Sadie opened her eyes wide. "For what?"

"Well," Carla continued, "when I'm nurse, I'll have to change sheets all the time, for this very same reason. Some nights, I'm sure I will be really tired and sleepy. So by doing this, I'm learning shortcuts on how to do the job as fast as I can, so I can get the sick person back in bed quickly."

Sadie looked relieved. "Really, Carla?"

Carla nodded. "Yes, I'll be an ole pro at this, and I'll show up all the other nurses who haven't had my experience. So thank you. I can officially say I have already begun my nurse training."

She gave Sadie a hug, and with the sheets now changed, they crawled back in bed and Sadie nuzzled up close to Carla. After a few seconds, she sleepily said, "I love you, Carla. I think your sick people will really like you."

Soon her breathing was steady and Carla knew she had gone back to sleep. Maybe she could too, if she followed her own advice and thought happy thoughts.

Ridgewood was having its first home football game. When Carla arrived, the players were running out on the field. Darlene Baker had walked over to the fence separating the field from the stands and waved, calling out something to Alex. He grinned and responded in kind. Carla felt her stomach churn at the exchange. This was supposed to be her night. She was supposed to be yelling encouraging words to Alex, not Darlene. She almost wished now she had just stayed at home.

Jackie came up beside Carla and put her arm around her shoulder. "Hey, hey, cheer up! None of those nasty thoughts I can tell are swirling around that little head of yours." Jackie glanced over where Darlene stood with the other cheerleaders, looking *oh so perfect*. She grunted and looked back at Carla. "She's not worth it, honey, and believe me: neither is he." When Carla didn't say anything, Jackie grabbed Carla's hand and pulled her along. "Come on. I have to go up to the box and let them know the band isn't doing the anthem."

Jackie was one of the pom-pom girls who danced to the music the band played during the half-time show. It was perfect for Jackie. She got to wear a tight sweater and short skirt and shake her booty on the field, in front of an attentive audience at every game. She helped choreograph the dance moves, but they always had to make her tone things down. Jackie's moves were always more Playboy bunny than innocent high school musical.

When they reached the press box, nobody was there except Josh and Robert, two definite geeks who were into technical stuff with the sound system. Jackie sat on one of the rolling chairs and made it roll to the other end where they were concentrating on the knobs and buttons on the control panel. "Hey, boys. I have a message. The band is not going to be ready to do the anthem, so play the tape."

They stared at her but didn't speak. She raised her eyebrows and repeated the message. "Got it?"

Finally, Josh swallowed hard and said, "Why can't the band play?"

Jackie rolled her eyes. "Well, it seems somebody borrowed Mr. Willis' keys this afternoon and didn't give them back, so nobody could get into the band room. They have it under control now. The door is open and they are on the way out to the field, blah, blah, blah … But won't be here in the next five minutes, which is kickoff, so as I said boys … *Backup plan*. Play the tape."

Josh cleared his throat. "Well, umh, Houston, we have a problem." He opened up a drawer and pulled out a mangled cassette tape that was labeled "The National Anthem."

Jackie gasped. "Ooooh, somebody is in trouble."

Josh stammered for a second then explained. "There's just too many people in and out up here. Somebody left it just lying on the floor, and then bam! I rolled over it with my chair. I didn't know it was there! It's not my fault."

Jackie shrugged. "Well, it's not my fault either, but you'd better do something, and it better be quick. She glanced down at the players and coach on the field. "Because it looks like it's show time *now*."

Josh looked panicky, but Robert seemed unmoved. "Well, we'll just have to start the game without it tonight."

Carla couldn't stay quiet any longer. "You can't just skip it. It's the *National Anthem*."

Jackie pointed to the microphone. "I know! Just sing it into the microphone!"

Josh and Robert looked deadpan. "I can't sing and neither can Robert." Josh's voice cracked as if to prove his point. "I mean seriously we can't carry a tune in a bucket."

Robert then chimed in. "Besides, what if we forget the words?"

Carla, now frustrated, rolled her eyes again. "Like I said guys, it's the *National Anthem*. What's the world coming to?"

Robert waved his hand at her. "Well, you sing it then!" He went back to playing with knobs and mumbled, "You sing it or the game goes on without it. Take your pick."

Carla shook her head. "Oh no. This is your problem. I'm not even the messenger, just an innocent bystander."

Jackie rolled her chair back across the room and grabbed the microphone off the counter. "Hey, Carla, let's do it together!" She stood with the microphone in hand and pointed under the counter. "We'll sit under here. No one will even see us. Come on. Let's do it! You need to do something wild and adventurous to get out of this funk you're in." Then she gasped. "Hey, I know. Let's sing it like Annie Mae. Let's give it a little soul and make her proud while we're at it." She grabbed Carla's hand and shook it "Coooome ooooon! Let's do it!"

Just then, Mr. Sweeney, the announcer for the game, burst into the box. "Sorry I'm late, guys. Hear the band isn't ready so act like frogs and hop to it." He took his chair, grabbed the other microphone, and welcomed everybody to tonight's game. "Now if you'll please stand for the National Anthem."

The crowd in the stands rose to their feet and Josh exchanged a desperate look toward Carla and Jackie. Jackie nodded and jerked Carla down to the floor. She covered the microphone with her hand and looked over at Josh, who pointed at her and nodded, giving her the go-ahead.

Jackie looked at Carla and whispered for her to start if off and she would join in. Carla nodded and, closing her eyes, took a deep breath and slowly began. As the words poured out, she got into the rhythm and, with Jackie singing backup, delivered a soulful rendition. It was almost flawless. When they finished, Jackie put the microphone down on the floor and gave Carla a big hug. "Girl! We rocked!" Then raising her head, she peeped out at the stands. "Listen to that! They loved it! Yahoo!"

Mr. Sweeney asked the crowd to give the girls a hand and then gave the girls an approving nod, before he began the usual announcements.

Rod had slipped out on the field to wish Marcus good luck, while the coach ribbed him about not playing. After Marcus heard the girls sing, he said, "That's what I'm talking about! Got some sisters singing to get us going up in here!"

Rod looked up at the box, shaking his head, and said under his breath, "You have no idea."

After the kickoff, the players were set for their first play. The quarterback threw the ball down the right sideline into Marcus's hands. He dodged two players with his fancy footwork and returned the ball all the way down the field for a touchdown. The home stands went wild.

Marcus threw the ball down on the ground and yelled, "How do you like that copper pot, copperhead?" Soon, he was surrounded by teammates celebrating their first touchdown of the season.

The Ridgewood Chargers won the game twenty-eight to seven, without much trouble. Marcus and Alex both played well. Even though Carla enjoyed the anthem stunt with Jackie, the rest of the game was a letdown. She sat with Rod and Jesse and rooted the team to victory, but it was only halfhearted.

After the game, Carla saw Alex walking Darlene to his car. He opened the car door for her to get in and gave her a kiss on the cheek, before closing the door. It was official. They were a couple, and he no longer even knew Carla had existed. Her senior year would be just like all the others. Old feelings of not being quite good enough came creeping in, feelings she hadn't had since the outhouse incident in the first grade.

On Monday, the buzz at school was trying to figure out who the sultry and seductive anthem singers were. Carla made Jackie and Rod promise not to tell, but she knew it was just a matter of time before Josh and Robert blabbed. As it was now, they were still afraid Josh would get into trouble for breaking the cassette tape and were now trying to get it replaced.

At lunch, Carla and Jackie sat with Judy and Robin, their usual foursome. Rod sat with Jimmy every day, but the occupants of the other two seats at his table changed daily. Guys usually ate quickly and then headed outside or to the gym instead of sitting around talking, so their lunch companions were brief encounters. When Rod and Jimmy finished eating, they went to put away their trays. Jimmy was still snacking on a bag of Doritos he had bought, so Rod took his tray up to the counter with his.

Jimmy still walked with his slight slump, just as he had as a child. His mom was always scolding him and telling him to stand up straight. When he was bumped walking past Johnnie Timms, a few chips caught flight and landed right in Johnnie's lap. He jumped up making his chair slide across the room. "Watch it, doofus!"

Johnnie was sitting with Alex and Marcus. Marcus eased back in his chair and held his hands out. "Come on, man. Somebody bumped him. Chill out." Alex, however, was silent and even looked as though he found amusement in the scene.

Jimmy looked upset. "I'm sorry, Johnnie."

But Johnnie was not the type of person to accept apologies. He pointed his finger in Jimmy's face. "Don't let it happen again or I'll bust your nose."

Jimmy apologized again and then simple-minded Jimmy reached out and gave Johnnie a hug.

Everyone who was paying attention to the initial exchange froze. This was going to be bad. Poor Jimmy had done the worst thing he could've done. He would have gotten off easier if he had punched Johnnie. He could have laughed that off with a "Is that all you got?" comment. But a hug? That would require complete redemption of his manhood.

His face turned scarlet as he pushed Jimmy off. "What the—?" Then he drew his fist back. "You just asked for it!"

But before he could release the punch, Rod stepped in, blocking the shot by standing in his path. "Come on, Johnnie. Let it go."

Marcus was on his feet as well and added, "Man, you'd better listen up," and walked over beside Rod.

Alex was still seated. A couple of other boys got on their feet as well. Johnnie was not well liked, but no one ever stood up to him. He was just tolerated.

Rod, who was always grinning, wasn't showing a single tooth. Marcus stood just as stoic by his side. Looking the situation over, Johnnie let his fist drop but kept it clinched it by his side. "I guess your buddies got your back this time."

Rod brought back his usual smile and glanced at Jimmy, then at Johnnie. "I do believe you were right, Jimmy. I think Johnnie could use a hug." He turned to Marcus and the other boys who were now standing. "What do you think, boys?" Marcus nodded, glaring at Johnnie.

Rod was the first to walk over and lay a rib-cracking bear hug on Johnnie. As he did, he whispered in his ear, "Don't touch him again, man." Marcus lined up next and lifted Johnnie off his feet with his hug. Four other boys, all from the football team and Johnnie's teammates, followed suit. Johnnie's face turned red as his breathing was temporarily forced to a halt with each lung-squeezing hug he received.

Rod slapped Jimmy on the back and they walked away, leaving the other boys to handle Johnnie. As they passed a misty-eyed Carla, she gave Rod a smile and mouthed, "Thank you." He just shrugged and winked.

When she glanced back at the crime scene, the other boys had done their job and left. Johnnie was hunched over in his chair, rubbing his ribs and moaning, trying to regain his breath.

Alex, still sitting, laughed. "Are you all right, man?"

Johnnie gave Alex a pained glance. Alex turned his head and laughed harder. That's when Alex saw Carla staring at him. It was the first time their eyes had met since the first day of school, when he had abandoned her for Darlene.

Their eyes locked for only a second, but to Alex, it felt like an eternity. To anyone else in the room, Carla's eyes would not have revealed anything other than a casual second glance. Alex's guilty conscience, however, exposed her true feelings of disappointment, betrayal, and hurt. Not just with his lack of participation in defending Jimmy but of his total disregard of her since that first day at school.

Carla was the first to divert her gaze elsewhere, leaving Alex's gut feeling a pain deeper than the superficial pain Johnnie was experiencing. He wished he could make things right again with Carla or that it could be as easy as walking over and giving her a hug. Maybe it was that simple, but Alex knew, just like in defending Jimmy, he wasn't going to move a muscle.

Chapter Thirty-Two

SUNSHINE ON MY SHOULDER

*D*URING THE FIRST weekend in October, Chatham County always held a Harvest Day celebration. Events took place from noon until midnight. The festival was started by local farmers to celebrate the end of the harvest. Booths lined the park, selling everything from popcorn to pocketbooks, most of which were run by local churches as fundraisers. There were pickup games of softball, and the kids ran wild on the playground equipment. Folks brought blankets to spread on the grass or lawn chairs and hunkered down for the day. Millsville General Store closed shop for the day and had since the start of the event over fifty years earlier.

Will ran an "Out of Season Turkey Shoot" that began right after the fireworks, since most people with little children would have gone home by that time. Rod and Carla always helped out. Rod had to help run the turkey shoot, because if he were a contestant, nobody would pay to shoot. Rod had won every turkey shoot he had ever participated in, since he was five.

The Branch family arrived at the park around 1:00 and set up on the grass in a shady area, with a perfect view down toward the lake. Sadie pulled Val and Daniel away immediately in search of Marty. He was bringing one of his horses for the children to take turns riding. He said it would be a very tame horse, and he would walk with the rider while holding the reins, but Val had still not agreed to the adventure./Rod and Will disappeared immediately and Margaret and Edgar went to pull their shift at the church's booth.

Carla pulled out her guitar and began playing, and Jesse fell right in with his harmonica. They played a little and talked a little, both preoccupied in their thoughts. They both looked up when Alex arrived with his family. Alex's mother had brought his grandparents to the event. When they saw her struggling to get Mr. Cox's wheelchair out of the trunk, they both jumped up to help.

Carla eyed a guitar in the back seat. "Wow, that's an awesome guitar. Whose is it?"

Mrs. Cox answered, bending down close to her husband's ear, "It's yours isn't it, honey?" She stood back up and said, "He's had that thing since he was a little boy. He sure does miss playing it." She bent down again toward him and said, "Maybe you could let Carla play your guitar a little. What do you think?"

Alex looked antsy to get away. "Well, if you're set, I'm going to take off."

His mother dismissed him with a quick nod. He shot one quick glance at Carla before he left, but it was obvious she was trying not to look his way.

Mrs. Maxwell wrapped a blanket around her father's legs and patted his knees. "Daddy, I think I smell apple pie. How about I go round us up a couple of slices?" When she stood up, she asked her mother if they would be okay until she got back.

She nodded. "I think I'll stay right here with these two nice young people until you get back, dear." She and Jesse rolled his chair down to where they had set up and positioned Mr. Cox so he had a nice view of the lake.

Carla was still holding his guitar when Mrs. Cox said, "Why don't you play it, honey?" She put her hand lightly on Carla's arm and lowered her voice. "After his stroke, playing his guitar is what he said he missed the most. He still hopes that one day he'll be able to play again." She shook her head. "It's never going to happen though."

Carla carefully sat down with the guitar and Mrs. Cox gave her a coaxing nod. So she began to strum it softly. "It has a beautiful sound."

Mrs. Cox smiled. "Go ahead, dear, and play us a song."

Carla asked, "What about some John Denver? Does Mr. Cox like him?"

"Why, yes." She turned toward her husband and said, "You know, honey." Then clapping and tapping her foot, she sang, "Thank God I'm a Country Boy!"

Mr. Cox mumbled a few garbled syllables and scrunched his face up, although only one side moved.

Carla started strumming gently. She looked over the lake almost in a trance and began to sing. She didn't chose a peppy song but one that fit the day, and one that in Mr. Cox's mind fit his old friend.

Sunshine on my shoulders makes me happy.

Jesse picked up his harmonica and softly began to play along. It was beautiful, and to Mr. Cox, the whole world seemed to stand still.

Sunshine on the water looks so lovely.

Mr. Cox did not smile, but a smile was in his heart. He closed his eyes and was taking in every note. His left hand was tapping lightly on his armrest, and he was in another world. Time had frozen and he was not in the present, maybe not even in the past but in the future, when he would no longer be in a wheelchair; he would no longer feel old and feeble but alive. By the time Carla finished the song, a tear gently rolled down Mr. Cox's face.

Alex, who had been caught by his mother and asked to take her apple pie back while she rounded up a couple of drinks, had witnessed the last half of the song. Carla had a beautiful voice and the effect it had on his grandfather was evident. Even standing on the side of his paralysis, he could see how much he was enjoying it.

Alex had not done one thing to make his grandfather feel better or give him any amount of pleasure since they had moved there. Now in a matter of minutes, Carla had taken the time to do something simple and give an otherwise ignored old man a moment of joy.

When the song was over, Carla looked up and saw Alex staring at her. Alex didn't say a word but walked over and handed his grandmother the pie. Carla, looking uncomfortable now, stood and gently laid the guitar down beside Mr. Cox and thanked him. She reached down and gave him a hug. Mrs. Cox reached over and returned the hug to Carla. She whispered in her ear, "Thank you, sweetie. You have no idea what that meant to him."

After the emotional exchange, Alex asked, "You're quite the little songbird, aren't you?"

Jesse was now up too and replied for her, "Oh yeah, but only when nobody's watching." Then Alex's face lit up and he snapped his fingers. "You sang the anthem opening night, didn't you?"

Carla blushed and didn't reply but reached down on the ground and grabbed her softball glove and put on her baseball cap. "Well, got to go, fellas. I think there's a pickup game calling my name."

As she took off, Jesse said, "That's another thing she's good at—softball. Girl runs like lightning and has a killer arm."

Alex watched as she disappeared in the crowd and just shook his head.

Later in the day, Alex caught a few minutes of the coed softball game. Jesse was right. Carla was not intimidated playing with the guys. She was just as quick and her throws were dead-on. Jackie was steady on the mound as well and talked the talk to go with it. Darlene, of course, didn't want to sit around watching the silly softball game, so she had him off in other directions before he was ready to leave.

Sadie did manage to get Val over to Marty's horse corral. She let Jimmy hold Sadie up so she could stroke the horse, but she would not let her ride. Her excuse was that you could never tell if the horse might suddenly get spooked with the huge crowd. A balloon could pop and the horse would suddenly go wild. It was too risky.

Daniel consoled her by saying that maybe they could go over to Marty's house one day, where it was a controlled environment, and she could get her ride then. Val didn't say a word. In the back of her mind, that wasn't going to happen either, but there was no point in arguing about it now and spoiling the day.

Jimmy was helping Marty with the horses and seemed to love every minute. He often went over to Marty's at his request to help him with a few things around the stables, especially when he had children over to ride.

When Val and Daniel were distracted by another couple stopping by to chat, Marty walked over and whispered to Sadie, "Maybe Jimmy here will bring you over sometime to ride, and it can just be our little secret." Sadie's eyes lit up and she nodded excitedly. Jimmy beamed. "Yeah, I have my license now.

Will had volunteered to help Rachel with her shift at the Methodist church's booth, which sold drinks and ice cream. They only had to work an hour shift, but to Will it seemed like an eternity. Rachel kept scolding him for trying to hurry the customers up.

"You know, making the kids hurry up and make up their minds is not going to make the time go by any faster. It's not like we are missing anything, anyway." She puffed and added, "If this was your personal booth and the money went in your pocket, you'd have a different attitude."

Will apologized. "You're right. I just have some things to get set up before the turkey shoot tonight, and my mind just isn't on screaming four-year-olds who don't know what flavor of ice cream they want."

She gave him a forgiving smile, which Will returned, and they continued to finish out their shift with him in a better mood.

Surprisingly, when their shift was over, Will didn't want to rush off to the turkey shoot set up but led Rachel down to the lake. They found a secluded spot with plenty of sunshine. Rachel leaned back and tilted her face up toward the sky. The sun was bouncing off her auburn hair, which hung loose behind her.

Will stared and took in the beautiful sight. After a few minutes of silence, Rachel finally opened her eyes sleepily to see Will still staring at her. She gave him a soft smile and asked, "What are you thinking about, William Branch?"

He leaned over and gave her a soft kiss on the lips. Then he whispered, "You actually."

She smiled. "Oh yeah?"

"Yeah." Then he looked down at his side, picking up a little black box. When their eyes met again, he was serious. "You and the rest of my life actually." Rachel sat up straight, putting a hand to her chest. She was already tearing up when she slowly took the box from Will's extended hand and opened the lid. With tears flowing freely down her face, she managed to say, "It's beautiful."

Will took the ring out and put it on her finger and asked again, just for confirmation. "Are you sure it's okay? I mean, we can exchange it for anything you want."

She reached over and hugged him tightly. "Oh, Will. It's perfect. I wouldn't change it for the world."

Then Rachel broke free and gasped. "Oh, Will. I have to go show my mom before anyone else finds out. I want her to be the first to know." As she stood up, she grabbed his hand to pull him up. "That's all right, isn't it?"

Will laughed. "Yeah, yeah. I can see now you're going to be pulling me around the rest of my life, getting your own way." She smiled and, still holding his hand, gave him another soft kiss on the lips.

When they found Mr. and Mrs. Thomas, Rachel ran over and didn't say a word but extended her hand to show her mother the ring. Rachel's mother immediately began crying and they hugged each other. They would hug, stop for a second to look at the ring, and then hug again, crying nonstop. This continued for several minutes. Not a single word was uttered between them.

Mr. Thomas walked over to stand by Will and put his hands down in the pockets of his overalls, and without making eye contact, he said, "Well, I reckon you'll be having a bunch of ugly children now, won't ya', boy?"

Will squirmed and almost began to sweat. "Ah, yes, sir ... I mean no, sir." Will didn't know what to say. He knew the man was still referring to the ugly daughter comment that started this whole thing, so he looked at Mr. Thomas and said, "We're okay about that whole misunderstanding, right? I mean, you're not still holding a grudge or nothing, are you? I really do want to start over on the right foot, especially now that we'll be family."

Mr. Thomas grinned and gave Will a firm slap on the back. "I am more than over it, son, especially now that it looks like you'll be paying for that comment for the rest of your life." They both let out a hearty laugh and turned back toward the women who were still crying and hugging each other.

After Will finally got Rachel to break free from her mother, they went in search of his parents. Luckily, the whole Branch bunch had been brought back together by growling stomachs, in search of Ms. Margaret's famous fried chicken.

Val saw them approaching and punched Daniel in the arm so he would stand up beside her, as though she sensed something was up.

Rachel extended her hand to Val, who gasped and threw her hands up to her cheeks, repeating, "Oh my gosh. Oh my gosh." Val was crying too, of course, but soon got enough composure to give Rachel a hug and turned around to tell the others what was going on.

Daniel walked over to stand by Will while all the chaos took place before their eyes. "That's a mighty big ring there, son. Must have set you back a pretty penny."

Will swallowed hard. "Yeah, that's how I knew she was the one, Dad. I didn't bat an eye spending that kind of money." He put his hands in his back pockets and continued. "Of course, now I got a good deal. You know me. I got them to come way off the price."

Daniel clicked his tongue. "Yeah, I bet you did." He hesitated then whispered, "I don't know that I would tell Rachel that though."

Will shook his head. "Oh no. I know. Just between us men. Got it."

Rod walked over and gave Will a hug. "Congratulations, man! Can't believe you actually found a girl willing to spend the rest of her life with you."

Jesse was next to shake Will's hand. "Congratulations, man! I'm happy for ya."

The men stood back, watching Margaret, Val, and Carla ooh and ah over the ring. Rachel seemed to be loving every minute of it.

Edgar winked at Will. "First time I seen you spend any money on something other than a good business deal, son. I reckon she done stole your heart for sure."

Will nodded and turned his gaze toward Rachel, who looked up in time to catch his gaze. She gave him a smile that melted his heart, and without breaking his gaze said, "Yeah, but Grandpa, I still think it's the best investment I'll ever make."

Rachel stayed to help Will with the turkey shoot but mostly just stared at her ring. She broke down and cried at least a dozen more times that night. When he dropped her off at her house that night, it was hard to tear himself away from her. They had talked the whole way home making plans. No long engagement and no big wedding. Will had found the one person who seemed to be as frugal as him. As Will was driving home, he knew that God definitely knew what he was doing when He threw them together.

When they went to bed, Val and Daniel talked for what seemed like hours that night. Val cried with happiness and kept saying she couldn't believe time had passed so quickly. She had the sudden feeling that all the kids where slipping away. When Carla graduated in the spring, she would be heading off to college and that would just leave Rod and Sadie. Rod didn't have plans, but they couldn't count on him staying around forever either. That just left Sadie.

Val sighed. "Well, she's the baby. She just can't grow up. That's all there is to it. She just has to stay little forever."

Daniel hugged Val close and laughed. "Maybe we should try to make another baby, because I'm pretty sure we can't stop Sadie from growing up."

Val rolled her eyes at Daniel and said, "You know good and well we can't make another baby."

Daniel pulled her close and kissed her. "I just said we'd *try*." Val returned his seductive smile right before she let him envelope her in his arms.

A few miles away, Mrs. Cox was tucking her husband in bed and kissing him good-night. When she turned off the light and lay down by his side, Mr. Cox was at peace. That night he drifted off to sleep with the guitar's melody ringing in his head one last time. The next morning, when his wife woke up, she immediately sensed something was wrong. He was in the exact position she had placed him the night before, except that his face had changed.

His right side, which was usually pinched and strained, was now relaxed. He had a calm and peaceful look, almost smiling. She felt for his pulse, but it was gone. One lone tear slipped down her cheek as she reached over and kissed him softly on his head. He was at peace now, and as sad as she would be living without him, she was glad he was now at rest. Yes, he had dreamed of playing his old guitar one final time, but it seems that all his heart had really needed was just to hear it being played one last time.

Chapter Thirty-Three
CHRISTMAS AS USUAL

WILL AND RACHEL decided on a December wedding because the church would be all decked out with poinsettias and a Christmas tree, so no flowers would be needed. It was a small but beautiful ceremony that took place on a cold, brisk day.

They drove to Sugar Mountain afterward, where Mr. and Mrs. Thomas had rented a cabin for the weekend as a wedding gift. Mr. Thomas had also given Will and Rachel the deed to the ugly field that had started it all, right after they got engaged. His thought was that since it had never been any good at growing anything but grass, it may as well be a yard. Will found a good deal on a beat-up single-wide trailer that would be home, until they could save enough money to build a house.

When everyone had waved the happy couple off, the rest of the family went back in the church to clean the reception area. Jackie followed Carla into the ladies' room while she changed from her bridesmaid's dress. Jackie had brought a change of clothes as well, so she could stay and help the family clean up.

"So do you think Mark would ever ask you to marry him? Or do you even want him to?"

Jackie grunted. "No and no."

Carla came out of the stall, now in jeans and a T-shirt. She hung her dress on a peg on the wall so she could put it back in the plastic bag.

"I don't love Mark. I like him and we get along great, but I'm not going to be hopping straight out of high school and into a marriage." She shrugged. "Besides, Mark would never ask anyway; he feels the same way. He's just in it for the moment. He's getting what he wants and I'm getting what I want."

"But Jackie, why do you do it? I mean, why give yourself so freely to somebody when you know you don't want to spend the rest of your life with them? I just couldn't do that. Besides, it could go really wrong, if you know what I mean."

Jackie nonchalantly examined her nails and said, "Oh no? Well, it's worse in my opinion to pine away over somebody who's dating somebody else and doesn't give you the time of day." Carla's face told her the comment had hurt. She sighed and continued. "Look, all I'm saying is that you need to shake him off for good. He and Darlene are perfect for each other. Everybody says so; it's like on that movie *Memories* with Barbara Streisand and Robert Redford."

Carla interrupted and corrected, "'Memories' is the song. *The Way We Were* is the movie."

Jackie rolled her eyes. "Whatever. You know what I mean. He may have loved her deep down, but Barbara didn't fit in his lifestyle. She was a strong-willed woman who had a lot on the ball and he wanted a pretty but stupid showgirl."

Carla sat to put on her shoes. "I guess."

Jackie sat beside her. "I'm just saying you've got to move on. You're actually wasting your senior year daydreaming over some stupid boy who's not even good enough for you to begin with. You should be excited right now, waiting to find out if you got into UNC or not, which is your lifelong dream in case you have forgotten. Instead, you're acting all goofy.

You'd better hope the admissions board doesn't get wind of this, or you won't get in," she said jokingly as she gave Carla an elbow to her side. This finally brought a smile to Carla's face.

Then her face turned serious again. "But if they're such a good match, why are they constantly breaking up?"

Jackie looked as though she wanted to scream "Because that's just *them*! That's what they *do*. They fight; they get back together. Twenty-five years from now, they'll be doing the same thing." She nudged her and said, "Come on. Let's go get this place cleaned up then we can hit the town and try to find your Romeo!"

Carla knew deep down that Jackie was right and vowed to begin the process of shaking the dust off her feet from Alexville and move on. She was also right about another thing. She should be anxious about UNC. Now all of a sudden, she really was. It would soon be time to hear back, and she definitely could not take one more major disappointment in her life.

Christmas that year was one of their best ever. Will was a married man now, which was exciting, and Sadie was still hanging on to her belief in Santa Claus. Carla was heeding Jackie's advice, going days at a time without one thought of Alex. She was even feeling somewhat festive and decided it was time she learned how to cook. She helped in the kitchen all the time and Val was a great cook, but Carla just followed orders and it wasn't sinking in on how to complete recipes on her own.

Looking through old cookbooks that Margaret had, Carla found a recipe for fruitcake. She wasn't a big fan of fruitcake, but she wanted something traditional other than fig pudding. She didn't see anything else that screamed Christmas like a fruitcake. It was a several-day process and she followed the recipe exactly. On Christmas Eve, it was finally complete. It looked great and smelled like it should, but there was something a little off with the texture. Since she was unsure about it, Carla decided to let Rod try it before presenting it at the big family dinner that night.

Rod took a small spoonful and scrunched up his face. Sadie tried a small bite too but spit it out. Carla herself took a taste and, trying to think objectively, said, "It's hard to say, because I don't like fruitcake, but I don't think it's bad."

Rod asked, "Why did you make it if you don't even like it?"

She shrugged. "I just wanted something different, something that screams *Christmas*." Rod picked Sadie up and sat her on his knee and looked at her, laughing. "Well, it screams all right, doesn't it, Sadie Lou?"

She giggled, and then squirmed down to run off.

The front door opened and in walked Jesse. Carla's eyes lit up. "Jesse, come here and try my fruitcake!" She got a big spoonful, but before she put it in his mouth, she hesitated. "Wait! You do actually like fruitcake, don't you?"

He grinned. "I like anything with cake in the name."

Rod agreed. "If anybody can handle it, it's him. His stomach is a bottomless, rock-solid pit."

Jesse took the bite and swallowed. "Hmm, not bad. Actually, it's pretty good."

Rod slapped him on the back. "Well, help yourself. It's all yours, man. Nobody else is going to be touching that thing." He got up and motioned for his barstool. "Actually, sit down and have a slice. I still need to take a shower before we head into town."

Jesse sat at the bar and Carla gave him a hefty slice, and then she sat opposite him to watch him enjoy the fruitcakes of her labor.

Rod took his shower and disappeared in his room to get dressed. When he came out, Jesse was coming out of the bathroom and the commode was flushing. The overwhelming smell of air freshener hit Rod. "Dude, easy on the spray."

Jesse smiled. "Sorry, man." He rubbed his stomach. "Had to make room for more fruitcake and couldn't hold it."

Rod gave him a look of disgust. "You really do have a cast-iron stomach."

The boys went to town and completed their last-minute shopping, and then Jesse returned home. The Branch family got together that night at Margaret and Edgar's. It was the same routine, except this year, Rachel was there to enjoy it with them. Her family would get together the following day, so Will would now have a new tradition of being away from his family on Christmas.

Edgar read "'Twas the Night before Christmas" and Luke's gospel of the birth of Jesus. Val sat beside Daniel on the couch and leaned her head against his shoulder, looking very content. The same expression was on Rachel's face as well.

After the stories were read, Edgar gave out his usual unwrapped hand-me-down gifts, which everyone still loved to receive. He presented Rachel and Will with the antique clock right off the mantle, where it had always sat. Luckily, he had discussed this with Margaret ahead of time. It was handed down to him by his father for being the first child to learn how to tell time, and he had wanted to pass it down to his first grandchild who got married. Rachel and Will were honored.

That night, when Edgar and Margaret were climbing into bed, she said, "You did good again tonight, Papa. Them young'ins still love your hand-me-down gifts."

He smiled. "I can't believe how time flies. Soon now, I'll have to start digging up stuff for great grandchildren. Never thought I would see the day. My daddy didn't live long enough to barely see his grandchildren, must less great grandchildren." As he got adjusted under the covers and Margaret switched off the light, he added, "Yep, if I had known I would be living this long, I would've rethought this giving stuff away deal. One of these days, we ain't going to have nothing left."

Margaret puffed. "I'll make a deal with you. If we live long enough to give away all the junk you have around this place, I'll chip in for store-bought gifts."

Edgar thought for a minute then turned to Margaret and said, "If I go before you do, keep giving out the gifts for me, okay?"

Margaret rolled over to look at him. "For heaven's sake. Don't talk like that."

Edgar repeated himself. "Just promise me though, if I go first, you'll keep the tradition."

She replied, "But why would you talk like that? Are you feeling poorly?"

Edgar rolled over on his back. "No, actually I feel great, too good almost. Just promise me, old woman, if I go first—"

This time she cut him off. "Oh for heaven's sake. I *promise*." Then she rolled back to her side and mumbled, "Never met a man who would ruin a perfectly good holiday with talks of death."

Edgar smiled and let her stew for a minute then whispered, "Merry Christmas, Margaret. I love you."

She rolled back over, laying her hand on his chest, and replied, "I love you too." With that, nothing else needed to be said, so they both drifted off to sleep. They didn't have to dream of younger days, because the present was pretty good.

Chapter Thirty-Four
PROM NIGHT FAVOR

C ARLA DID HEAR back from UNC, and it was good news. She was once again focused on what was real and what was important. That didn't include Alex. Jackie, for once, was right and Carla had been wasting her time in a fog. If only Jackie would listen to Carla once in a while. She broke up with Mark but didn't slow down. With Jackie, it was one boy after another, and Jackie didn't seem to have very high standards. Every time Carla or anyone else tried to make her wise up and see the dangerous game she was playing, she just blew them off.

Carla was getting more excited about getting out of high school. Since Alex's grandfather had passed away, his family had decided to move back north after he graduated, taking his grandmother with them. Alex was applying to colleges there and, with his dad's backing, was guaranteed to get into any one he wanted. Darlene, of course, would trail behind him. Out-of-state tuition wasn't a problem for her family.

The last big event would be the prom. Carla and Jackie had decided to go stag but were going to extra lengths to look like a million bucks.

After one of their many shopping excursions, Carla dropped Jackie off at the store to work her shift. Carla walked over to the garage to talk to Jesse.

Jesse was under a hood, greasy up to his elbows. His dad was asleep behind the office desk. As soon as he saw her, he started wiping off his hands and leaned against the bumper. He looked like he was ready for any kind of an excuse to take a break. "So what do I owe this honor to?"

Carla smiled. "Well, to be honest, I have a favor to ask."

"Uh, oh. Something tells me I'm not going to like it."

Carla smiled. "Well, not necessarily. Just hear me out; it could be that you wind up liking it a lot."

Jesse crossed his arms over his chest. "Okay, go ahead. Let's hear it and then I'll decide."

Carla sat beside him on the bumper and began to explain. "Well, you know the prom is next week and there is a certain girl that would very much like for you to take her, but she's afraid to ask."

Jesse immediately turned red and looked uncomfortable. He started to speak, but Carla didn't give him a chance.

"Listen. I know dancing is not your thing and that's okay. It's not her thing either. I know you didn't go to your own prom, but honestly, Jesse, I think one day you'll regret not going. This way you can say you attended a prom at your old high school."

Jesse rubbed his jaw. "Before I say no, just for curiosity's sake, who's the girl?"

Carla cringed and in a mousey voice said, "My friend Judy."

Jesse looked confused as though he was trying to put a face to the name. "I barely know her and she barely ..." He paused and shook his finger at Carla. "Oh I get it. She doesn't want me *specifically*. She just wants somebody to take her, and you thought of good ole Jesse."

"Yes, I did, because like I said, one day you'll regret not going to the prom. This will be your last chance to experience an American pastime that ranks in the top ten of most people's nights to remember."

Jesse grunted. "Wasn't that part of the ad campaign for last year's prom?"

Carla got right in front of Jesse, putting her hands together. "Please, Jesse, Take her as a favor to me. She won't go if she doesn't have a date, and she'll regret it for the rest of her life. She has a dress and everything. She bought it before her stupid boyfriend dumped her last minute for somebody else. The only way she can make him eat mud is to show up with an older, handsome, likeable, hardworking—"

Jesse cut her off. "Fake flattery isn't going to help your cause."

She puffed and put her hands on her hips. "I'm not faking. Oh Jesse, *please*. You don't have to get a tux or anything. Your brown suit will be fine. She doesn't have to have a corsage or anything." She leaned up against his chest, just like Sadie would do, and got right in his face. "Pretty please, Jess. I'll owe you."

Jesse, looking extremely vulnerable, eased her off and mumbled something that vaguely sounded like a yes, and that she would definitely be paying him back big time.

The night of the prom, Jackie came over to dress with Carla. "I am so glad we're going stag. I honestly can't think a single boy in the whole school that I want to dance with all night and then have to force myself to kiss good-night."

Jackie laughed and gave her a nudge with her hip. "Not one?" Standing back to take a look at herself in the mirror, she continued. "I intend to dance with my all exes actually."

Jackie helped Carla with her makeup since she never wore any. Carla watched her friend carefully though, so Jackie wouldn't overdo it. Carla's dress was black with a lot of sparkle. It was cut low in the back and high on the sides. It had a modest neckline so her parents would allow it, but that actually made it sexier. Carla was only five foot, three, so she bought the highest heels she thought she could manage, and instead of trying to tame her ringlets, she decided to let them go wild.

Hollywood had never seen two more beautiful starlets walk the red carpet. Jackie definitely had the Marilyn Monroe look down and Carla, although sexy, was softer and aloof. Rod and Jimmy were also going stag, so they decided to ride together. Aunt Sarah brought her camera so she could take group photos.

She kept reminding Jimmy to stand up straight. "You have on a tux; you need to show it off."

Val cried and Herman lectured the boys on being careful on the roads.

When they arrived at the school, the foursome split. Rod had a long list of ladies to hit the dance floor with, so he wanted to get started. Carla and Jackie found a table, which soon filled with other girls in their flock. It seems it was a bad year for couples; there were more people there stag, and they seemed to be the ones having the most fun. Carla danced until her feet ached and soon had to sit down and give them a break. Jackie sat down with her and sent one of the boys off in search of two glasses of punch.

Carla saw Jesse on the dance floor with Judy. It was a slow dance, which was the only kind she knew Jesse would even attempt. She had seen them chatting a few times earlier at their table and they seemed to be having a good time. He had caught her eye once and gave her the sweetest grin and thumbs-up, which she interpreted to mean thank-you.

As she looked on, she nudged Jackie with her elbow. "Hey, look at Jess and Judy."

Jackie found them on the dance floor and rested her chin on her hand. "Aaaah, they look so sweet."

"Yeah, look how he's holding her tight, and that expression on his face. They look so romantic." Jesse was holding Judy and was swaying to the music. His eyes were closed and his expression said they were the only two people in the world.

Carla sighed. "I'm so glad he came. Wouldn't it be funny if they wound up getting married?"

Thirty minutes later, when the punch never made it to their table, Jackie and Carla went in search of refreshments for themselves.

Marcus saw Carla and yelled for her to come over. He gave her a hug. "Carla, you look amazing. We were all just talking about it. I didn't even recognize you. I wish Mama was here to see you tonight. She wouldn't believe it."

Carla smiled, enjoying every compliment she received, and replied, "Why, thank you, Marcus."

Jesse called from behind. "I, however, recognized you right away. I think you're the one who got me into this ordeal, so I'd say you owe me a dance while my date is freshening up in the ladies' room." Jesse stood with his hand extended and slightly bowed.

A slow song had just started to play, so Carla followed Jesse to the dance floor. It felt strange slow dancing with Jesse, so Carla filled the awkwardness by talking. She asked how his night was going and told him how sweet he looked earlier dancing with Judy. "It's like you were in another world."

Jesse grinned. "You girls think you know us guys so well. You always try to read more into things than what is really there."

Carla just smiled. She knew her instincts were right. There was no denying the expression he had on his face, and one day he would thank her.

Carla noticed Alex and Darlene were on the dance floor as well. They looked like Barbie and Ken or the plastic figures off a wedding cake. They were both so perfect, yet they looked exactly like you expected them to. That was the fun thing about the prom. People got all dressed and up and looked completely different in their fancy clothes. Yet Alex and Darlene didn't look different. Sure, they were fabulously dressed, but somehow they looked the same, perfect.

The evening really was one to remember. Even Jimmy had an amazing night. He turned out to be quite the little jitterbug. He walked with such a slow turtle-like manner, yet when he got on the dance floor, he cut loose. People were calling him the Michael Jackson of the event.

That night, when Carla got undressed to go to bed, she went to the bathroom to wash her face. She took one last look at her face all made up and had to admit she didn't look half-bad. She was no Darlene Baker, but she didn't have to be. On second thought, she decided to leave her makeup on. She wanted to go to bed tonight looking like sleeping beauty. Maybe that would guarantee her prince charming would show up in her dreams.

Chapter Thirty-Five

BEARABLE PARABLE

CARLA AND ROD had to stay after choir practice on Wednesday night. The graduates needed to practice for the Sunday morning service. The students would march in with their caps and gowns and the service would be in their honor. Ms. Patsy was teary-eyed while she watched them walk in. She was giving them instructions on how the service would proceed when Margaret and Sadie came into the sanctuary.

"I would really love to have one of you graduates say a few closing words on Sunday. Maybe something you've learned over the years, or just a thank-you to the congregation for their support."

No one made eye contact with her. When no one volunteered, she turned back to the choir to dismiss them with final instructions for Sunday. Rod started making faces behind Ms. Patsy's back to Sadie. He wasn't making fun of Ms. Patsy but just goofing around with Sadie. Margaret saw the exchange and went over to scold him.

"If you have so much showmanship, why don't you give that speech on Sunday?"

Ms. Patsy turned around smiling and clasped her hands together. "Oh, Rod. I would love for you to. Your brother did such a good job."

Rod began squirming. "No, ma'am, I'm not good at speaking like Will is. I would be too nervous."

Sadie ran over. "Do it! Do it! Do it!"

Carla laughed and joined in. "Oh yes, I think you should. It would mean sooooo much to us other graduates."

Margaret looked at Patsy and said, "Well, it's settled then. He'll do it."

Rod protested. "Grandma, I don't want to. I don't have anything to say. I don't know what to say."

Patsy gave him the sweetest look. "Oh Rod, just tell about something you know. You'll do fine. The most uncomfortable speakers sometimes have the most wonderful things to share."

Margaret huffed. "Oh for heaven's sake, son. Half these people in here on Sunday mornings are asleep anyway. You're making more of it than it is." She turned abruptly and walked off.

Rod collapsed on the pew and Sadie crawled up in his lap. Rod looked at Sadie and said, "You know this is all your fault, don't you?"

She giggled. "Are you going to tell one of your hunting stories?"

Rod ran his hand down his face in torment and mumbled, "I don't think that's what she has in mind."

Sadie protested. "But it would be a parable, just like Jesus." Then she hopped down and ran off. The other graduates left snickering. Rod knew they were relieved that he had been the one caught in the trap and not them.

Carla punched him on the arm. "Who's making funny faces now?"

Rod smirked. "Well, don't forget your stomach is going to be churning on Sunday morning too."

She shook her head. "It doesn't work like that, remember? If I'm with you and know what's going on, it doesn't bother me at all. I can sit back and enjoy just like everybody else."

Rod was tormented all week, trying to think of something

inspirational to say, but nothing was coming to mind. That Sunday, after everything in the program was finished and the pastor ended his short sermon directed toward the graduates, he turned the service over to Rod for closing remarks.

Rod walked up to the podium and the pastor sat down to his right in his chair. Rod was noticeably nervous and a light sweat could be seen forming at his hairline. He took a quick glance out across the congregation and caught Sadie's grinning face. She looked so excited and was sitting up tall to see. It actually helped to calm him down, so he tried to imagine that he was just talking to her and not the one hundred plus people in the room.

With that in mind, he decided to take her advice and tell one of his hunting stories. The worst thing that could happen was that everybody would hate it and they would never ask him to speak again. That, he decided, would actually be a good thing.

"A while back, I went on a bear hunting trip in Canada. At the end of the day, one of the other hunters came running in yelling he had shot one but it had taken off. He was at one of the locations close to camp, so I offered to go help him track it down. I knew the feller. He'd been coming up there bear hunting for years.

"When we got out in the woods in the area he was hunting, he led the way shining the flashlight, and I followed behind. I had my gun ready in case we came across any trouble and we were making our way pretty good." Rod calmed down and eased his way into the story, feeling comfortable. The congregation seemed to be listening intently.

"All of a sudden, the hairs stood up on the back of my neck and me and the feller both stopped dead in our tracks. It had gotten pretty dark by this time, so we could only see right where the flashlight was pointed. As we stood there listening, we heard this deep growl coming from our right side."

Seeing the questioning stares he was receiving from a few in the audience, Rod nodded and said, "Yep, you got it, a bear. An angry bear was coming our way. I whispered in the feller's ear that we had to turn back.

He nodded, so I didn't waste time turning tail to run. But it didn't take me long to realize I had to stop because I couldn't see where I was going. Then it dawned on me then that the feller with the flashlight hadn't moved."

Everybody seemed wrapped up in his story, which encouraged him on. "I stopped, listened, and turned around slowly. I heard the bear again, but this time from behind me. He had kept advancing toward the spot where the feller and I had stopped

"The feller got so scared he froze in his tracks." Rod threw his hands up. "Now we were really in a predicament! He's frozen with nothing but a flashlight and no weapon and I'm here with the gun but can't shoot because I can't see and the bear is somewhere between me and this feller, so even if I did start firing toward the sound of the bear, I could just as easily shoot that feller." Rod stopped, rubbed the back of his neck, and shook his head while remembering it all, just like it was yesterday.

"Just that quick, a simple thing had turned into quite a mess." Rod took a deep breath and continued the tale. "But it all worked out. The feller was actually standing so still that the bear just kept on moving, and after about thirty minutes, it had moved on through. It took me a few minutes to bring that feller back to reality though. He was pretty shaken. I don't think he said a word for nearly two hours."

He started to leave the podium but added one last comment, "Oh, we did go back the next morning to get his bear. It was a little one though." Grinning, he continued. "It wasn't even worth all that trouble, actually." Stepping back from the podium, he turned toward the pastor and nodded.

The pastor stood and stared at Rod. "Is that all, Rod? I mean, did you want to expand upon your, your, um, bear story?"

Rod made a few strange body movements that oddly enough resembled those of Barney Fife. He put his hands on his hips and nodded. "It's a parable."

Mr. White continued his blank stare and repeated, "A parable?"
Rod nodded. "Yeah."
Then, realizing he needed to elaborate, he turned back to the

podium and looked out over the congregation. "Well, my grandma is always saying that half the people in this church ain't even saved and just come for show." Everybody's eyes opened wide, and an audible gasp could be heard coming from Margaret herself. Daniel looked like he was struggling to stifle his laughter.

"The way I figure it, those people are like that feller in the woods. He knew what to do. Been hunting for years. He had the flashlight and I was there to protect him with the gun, but he just stood there. I think some people in the church are like that. They come every Sunday and hear the message. They know what to do, and they have the light to guide them, like, you know, our Bibles, but something has frozen them in their pews. They are in a heap of trouble. The bear—or the evil of this world—is heading their way, and it's eventually going to attack. But they just sit there, and if they sit there long enough, the bear is going to wind up being between them and God."

When Rod returned to his seat, Ms. Patsy, who was seated behind his pew, patted him on the shoulder. She was teary-eyed again. Mr. White still looked a little dazed but asked the musicians to play the invitational hymn and the congregation stood to sing.

Surprisingly, Rod's message had connected with several members of the congregation. The members had to sing the song through twice to allow enough time for people to come down. After the second time, the musicians played softly and the congregation stood quietly in prayer while some finished taking care of their spiritual business at the altar.

Mr. Rogers, who was eighty-seven years old, was hit the hardest by Rod's message. The man had tears in his eyes, when he told the pastor he had been frozen on the pew for seventy years and was finally ready to shake free from that bear. It seems Rod's simple bear parable had affected people more than Ray Steven's Mississippi squirrel.

When the service was over, Sadie was the first one to find Rod. She jumped up in his arms and said, "I knew they'd like your bear story."

Even Margaret forgave him for his embarrassing comment and told him it was about time somebody said what needed to be said.

Chapter Thirty-Six

HOLDING HER HAND

MARGARET WALKED INTO Millsville Store with Sadie at her side. She grabbed drinks and nabs for everybody Will had working the field that day.

Mr. Mills eased over to the register to ring up Margaret's purchases. She asked, "Where's Jackie today?"

Mr. Mills sighed and replied that she had called in sick. "I doubt she hangs around here much this summer anyway. She's looking for a job in town. Can't make a living off what I pay her here at the store." Mr. Mills shook his head. "I don't even know that I've made much of a living off this place."

"You've done all right. Ever think about selling? Retiring?"

He nodded. "Yep. I actually got something in the works that I started looking into about a year ago. I know I can't handle all this lake traffic when it gets here. It's about time to sit back and watch the traffic, not be out there in it."

Margaret nodded and grabbed her purchase. "Come on, Sadie. We've got to get these drinks to the field while they're still cool."

As she was putting everything in the truck, Marty drove up. Sadie ran and jumped up on the side of his truck, almost before he had it in park.

Marty winked at Sadie. "So is Jimmy still bringing you over tomorrow to ride horses?"

Sadie nodded and giggled. She started to speak but stopped when Margaret walked over.

"Sadie, you can't take off running like that in a parking lot. That's a good way to get run over."

Sadie frowned. "Sorry, Grandma." Then she hopped off Marty's truck and ran back to theirs. She gave Marty one last wave and smile as she got in the truck with Margaret.

"What were you and Mr. Marty so chatty about?"

Sadie shook her head. "I can't tell you. It's a secret."

Margaret put the truck in gear and slowly headed out of the parking lot. "I don't know about keeping secrets. Does anybody else know about this here secret?"

Sadie nodded. "Jimmy knows too, but he's not going to tell either."

"Oh, I see. Well, if Jimmy knows about it too, it must be okay."

Jimmy was going to pick Sadie up the next day and take her over to ride Marty's horse. He had taken Sadie up to the store a couple of times to buy ice cream, so that was going to be their excuse.

Everybody seemed to be more than ready to take a break when the drinks arrived. The temperature was only in the nineties, but it felt much hotter. Edgar was driving the tractors back and forth for Will from the field. Everybody else was taking turns in the field, pulling the tractor up as they worked and turning it around at the end of the rows. Will didn't have as much help this year, and it was going to be slow-going all season. Today, nobody was available to help, so Val had taken the day off. Leroy and Annie Mae had plans this morning but would be there in the afternoon. Daniel had tried to take the day off but couldn't. He promised to make up for it the rest of the summer.

That afternoon, Edgar had a doctor's appointment. Margaret showed up at the field with Sadie at two o'clock sharp, waving him off the tractor. Everyone finished out their row and went to get water, while Edgar gave over his tractor driving detail to Will.

Margaret looked at Val. "You sure you want Sadie to stay here? I can take her with us to the doctor's office."

Val shook her head as she swallowed a mouthful of water. "No, we're going to finish out these two trailers, which we'll have on this next round. Annie Mae will take my place at the barn, so Ms. Sadie and I will be heading to the house. Besides, if she goes to the doctor's office, she'll probably catch something and get sick."

Sadie looked surprised. "Uh-uh. I'm never sick, Mama."

Val replied, "I know, honey, but the doctor's office is full of sick people."

Sadie looked at Edgar. "Are you sick, Grandpa?"

Edgar looked offended. "I most certainly am not. I'm fit as a fiddle."

She tilted her head to one side and asked, "Then why are you going? You might get sick too."

Edgar looked at Margaret and started to reply but seemed to change his mind. He mumbled under his breath as he walked off.

When they started back to work the field, Val took the tractor row, but instead of working in front of the tractor, she worked from behind. She told Sadie to stay behind her. Sadie nodded and played happily behind Val, trying to catch a butterfly. The only sounds made were that of the tractor engine and the sound of leaves being snapped from the stalks. It had been a hard day. They were all tired and ready for the easier work at the barn.

When they finished out that row and came out at the edge of the woods, Will had a sharp turn to maneuver into the next tractor row. Val was standing at the end of her row, holding Sadie's hand to keep her out of the way. She had her face tilted toward the sun, and her eyes were closed. She had her other hand on the small of her back and was leaning back, getting a good stretch.

The next few seconds are still a mystery, because nobody actually saw what happened. Will had jerked the trailers to and fro and almost had them ready to make the turn. As he jolted the trailers forward for the last time, a tobacco leaf flew out of the first trailer and over the side.

As it floated to the ground, Carla and Val would recall later hearing Sadie yell, "I'll get it!" She stepped forward and stretched to retrieve the fallen leaf, just as the back trailer's tire hit a deep rut on the other side. This caused the trailer to rock back hard in Sadie's direction when it righted itself. Nobody saw the trailer actually hit Sadie on the side of her head, but they all claim to have heard the odd noise that it made. When asked later, nobody wanted to describe the sound.

Then there was the silence. No noise at all. No tractor engine, no insects buzzing, no rustling of tobacco leaves in the wind. Nothing, not even breathing; it was as though God temporarily took sound away from the world. That is, until Val let out a gut-wrenching scream. "No!"

As awful as the scream sounded, the look on Val's face was worse. When Sadie fell to the ground, Val was still holding her hand, so she pulled Val forward. Val was bent over, staring at Sadie's still body. The look on her face was contorted and, along with her stance, gave the appearance of someone who was sick and bracing to throw up. She was holding her daughter's little hand so tightly in hers that her own fingernails dug into her palm. No tears fell from her face, and it was as though she was only breathing in and not exhaling.

Marcus, who had been on the other side of the trailer, appeared right in front of the scene as the trailer passed. Carla looked up at him and somehow had enough composure to mumble for him to run and call for help. Marcus ran off the field with his lightning speed, charged with adrenalin.

Val fell to the ground and started to reach over toward Sadie, but Carla bent down beside her and pulled Val back.

"Mama, we shouldn't move her." Val turned and looked at her like she was an alien.

Carla repeated it, now crying. "Don't move her, Mama. Something …

doesn't look right. I know you want to grab her, but you can't. You might make it worse. You can't *move* her." Carla looked back down at Sadie and continued to cry. Carla started to reach for Sadie's wrist but changed her mind and snatched her hand back to her side.

Edgar and Margaret had not yet left the field, so they had heard Val's anguished scream. They ran toward Sadie and fell to their knees beside her little body. Edgar reached out and laid his hand on Sadie's arm and closed his eyes. He began to softly pray.

Then there, in the little tobacco field, Sadie was surrounded by the same people who had witnessed her miraculous birth. Not another word was uttered until the emergency personnel arrived. No one would have been surprised to learn that it was the same crew who escorted her to the hospital the day she was born.

Sadie's death was as untimely as her arrival had been, and the world was once again changed forever.

It was reported that it took the emergency crew twenty minutes to get to Sadie, but it only seemed like seconds. They had a hard time getting Val to break her grip on Sadie's hand, and when she did, she lay on the hot sand crying inconsolably. The crew took all the appropriate steps and was gentle with Sadie, but it didn't look good. Paramedics said they could follow the ambulance to the hospital, but they would not allow anyone in the vehicle. Marcus stayed behind to call his parents so they could get Daniel.

When Daniel arrived at the hospital, they had placed the family in a small room where a doctor had come to verify what they already knew. They could have gone back home at that point, but nobody wanted to leave. They waited for Daniel, so they could go in together and see Sadie one more time. When Daniel entered the room, he scanned it quickly, each face staring back at him, but no one spoke. They were still in their work clothes, just as they had left the field. Everyone's face was streaked with tears.

When Daniel's eyes met Val's, he ran to her, falling to his knees in front of her. As tears streamed down his face and Val finally spoke, all she could say between sobs was "I was holding her hand."

He reached for her, pulling her toward him, and replied softly in her ear as his hand clutched the back of her head. "I know."

She wrapped her arms around his neck and squeezed him with all her might, as if he were the only thing she had left to hang on to. "Oh, Daniel, I was still holding her hand."

Daniel continued to cry along with her. "I know, honey. I know."

No statistics in the world could prepare Val from having her child snatched away from her own hand. By a mother's side should be the safest place in the world, but sometimes it's not safe enough. A child who came into the world unplanned, born with such fanfare, and caused so much joy, was now gone.

The doctors explained that an inch this way or that, a second forward or back would have had a different outcome. In the end, little separated the accident from a simple bump on the head with a few tears to tears that would last forever.

Chapter Thirty-Seven
SAYING GOOD-BYE

*T*HE NEXT TWO days were a blur for the family. People came and went, delivering casseroles and offering condolences. Sometimes, Val could greet the people at her door and give kind words of appreciation, and other times, she couldn't come out of her locked bedroom to even face family.

Daniel was suffering the most confusion. He was having trouble getting it all to make sense, when actually it just never would. He assumed it was because he was not there when it happened, or the fact that her little body had looked so perfect lying there.

Guilt ran rapid through everyone's mind. Will shouldn't have hooked two trailers up or planted the tobacco so close to the woods, forcing such a sharp turn around. Val should have gone back to the house as soon as Margaret brought Sadie to the field. Margaret should have stayed with Sadie and let Edgar go to his appointment by himself. Edgar should have canceled his appointment, and Daniel … Well, Daniel wasn't even there.

And what happened to Carla's healing touch? She should have known what to do to save her. She hadn't attended a single medical class yet, but if it was her calling, why hadn't she known *something* to do? She didn't even know how to administer CPR correctly. What kind of nurse was she going to be if she didn't even know the basics?

Reality was that Sadie was gone. She was gone the second the trailer landed its fatal blow and nothing anybody did, or didn't do, could have saved her. Her time was up and no one had the authority to extend it except for God, and He had called her home.

Herman, Sarah, and Jimmy stayed with them, helping in any way they could. Sarah told Herman she was glad that Jimmy had not been in the field that day. She didn't think he could have handled it. He was sensitive about another's pain. He couldn't even go hunting with Rod because he didn't like to witness even the life of an animal being taken.

Visitation night at the funeral home was the worst. It was an endless line of friends and family who didn't know what to say. The ones who were truly close friends didn't have to say anything. They just cried and hugged, which was all the family needed. Then there were all the introductions of people. It's an odd thing to lose someone so extremely close and have to endure introductions to strangers at their funeral, people that may never see again. Everyone has a friend of a friend or a coworker who wants to show their respect to someone in the family.

Another oddity of life is that when the death is that of a child, there is the temptation to somehow blame the parents. There always seems to be criticisms, finger-pointing, and of course, gossip.

Pastor White overheard just that as he mingled with his hurting congregation at the visitation. Ms. Thelma was talking to Ms. Peters, stating that it wasn't a good idea to have a child that young working the fields in the first place. "Why, last summer, she showed me the calluses on her hands herself and told me that she had got them from working! Not only that, but she said that Val had tried to make the child think she got them from playing of all things." Ms. Peters looked shocked.

Before the conversation escalated any further, Mr. White interrupted the two ladies. "Pardon me, ladies. I couldn't help but overhear your conversation."

Ms. Thelma's face began to flush.

He directed his attention toward her and continued. "Are you implying there was some form of child abuse or improper child labor issues occurring? I can assure you, if that is the case, the church will not stand for it and will see to it that justice is done. So tell me, Ms. Thelma, should the church be seeking to file some sort of charges here?"

"Well, I'm not saying that anything *irregular* was going on. I was just simply saying."

Mr. White cut her off curtly. "Ms. Thelma, I asked you a question. Does the church need to investigate this matter or not?"

Ms. Thelma shook her head timidly and whispered, "No."

Mr. White continued. "The tongue is the strongest muscle in the body, Ms. Thelma. One must learn to control it. I would hate for Ms. Margaret to have to ever hear the vile remarks you were making."

Ms. Thelma turned white and her hand flew up to her chest. "Oh my, no. Oh no, no. Please."

Mr. White smiled sarcastically and said, "Very well then ladies. Good evening." Marty, who overheard the whole exchange, couldn't help but smile to himself. Those two old biddies got what they deserved. Sadly, it was the only thing funny about the whole evening.

Mr. White helped the family with details for the funeral service. Names were printed on the program, songs were selected, and pallbearers picked. Jesse, Marcus, Leroy, and Punchy were all honored and humbled to serve as pallbearers. When the pastor asked if anyone wanted to participate in the service, Edgar said that as head of the family, he felt as though he should speak. No one else would be able to speak, and the thought of putting his Sadie in the ground without words from her family tore him apart.

Rod said he knew exactly what he wanted to do for the service and asked Carla and Will to help, which they of course agreed to do.

Somehow, the family managed to walk in and take their places. They listened to Mr. White talk of the joys of heaven and the sorrow of losing a child. When Edgar got up to speak, tears rolled down the family's faces before he even opened his mouth. He had not shared what he intended to say, and it didn't matter. The courage to speak with such heavy heart was enough.

Edgar looked out across the sad faces of his friends, then at his own family, and began in his usual slow and even tone. "My family is hurting." He paused for a second and looked down at the podium. Margaret let out a hiccup and Val blew her nose, tears streaming down her face.

"Sadie, however, is not. As a matter of fact, I don't think she hurt a day in her short life. How many of us can say that? She never once had a cold or even a headache." He paused as though thinking. "Many of you asked me how this could happen. I have asked myself that question too, but the fact is there is no explanation. They called it a freak accident. I don't like that term."

He raised his voice slightly. "There is nothing in this world that is not part of God's plan." A few soft amens were said as he softened his tone and continued. "However, I don't *blame* God for taking Sadie away, and I don't want my family to either. I don't want us to blame *God* for anything. I want us to thank him!" He looked at his family and directed the rest of his speech to them. They were the ones hurting most, and they were the ones who needed the message.

"I want us to thank God for giving us a miracle every day she was with us. I want us to thank God for a child who was never sick, a child who was never sad, a child who loved with all her might." He smiled in remembrance. "When she gave you a hug, she hugged hard." His fist pounded on the podium and a tear streaked down his face. "Because she loved hard. She loved with all her might, and when she played, she played hard and had the calluses to prove it!"

Mr. White glanced at Ms. Thelma, who began blubbering.

"I thank God that Sadie came into this world so you could all see the tender side of my Margaret." Her eyes met his as she smiled through her tears. "The side that I knew was there, but that she sometimes keeps hidden from others." Pausing one last time, he continued. "Yes, we'll miss her, but we have so much good to remember. We have a lifetime of good memories, and even though it was short, I can make it last."

Edgar walked to the side of the podium in a more intimate stance. "Once, when Sadie was a toddler, I was walking outside one night with her on my hip. I was watching what caught her eye and repeating the names to her as you do with children. She would look at a tree and I would say, 'Tree.' She would notice a rock and I would pick it up, so she could touch it and say, 'Rock.'

"Then she noticed the moon in the sky, and oh, what a beautiful full moon it was. So I, of course, pointed up toward the sky and said, 'Moon.' Sadie even repeated it back in her baby talk. '*Mooooon.*' Well, a few weeks went by and I found myself walking outside with Sadie once again at night, and the same game began. Except by this time, she was saying and repeating a lot more words and could even string a few together to almost make a sentence. I caught her looking up at the sky again and noticing the moon. I followed her gaze but realized that the moon wasn't full like it was the last time. It was just a crescent moon.

"I didn't know what to do. If I told her that's the moon, was she going to be confused? The last time it was big and round; now it's just a little sliver." Edgar looked down and smiled before he continued. "I finally had to say something, so I said, 'Moon, Sadie. That's the moon.' Do you know what she did?" Tears rolled down his face. "She turned her sweet face to me and said, "'Bout all gone, Grandpa." Tears rolled down his face unashamedly now. "'Bout all gone, Grandpa." He paused. "I tell you this. There is not a night that has gone by since when I haven't looked up at the moon in the sky and thought about that and smiled. There will not *be* a night that goes by from this day forward until the day I die that I won't look at the moon and remember my Sadie, and not a single tear I shed today would I trade for that precious memory."

He wiped his eyes with his handkerchief and looked up toward the sky. Through tears, he softly said, "We love you, Sadie, and we'll see you soon, sweetie." He slowly stepped down off the stage and returned to his seat by Margaret. As he sat, he patted her hand. She smiled at him through her tears.

The service ended, the pallbearers were dismissed, and the casket was rolled away. The sobbing family exited with Val leaning heavily upon Daniel. The congregation followed, walking the short distance to the graveside. There, the pastor said the last short farewell, then Rod, Will, and Carla stood at the final resting place of their precious little sister and sang her favorite hymn: "It Is Well with My Soul."

Not able to bear the image of Sadie's coffin in front of him, Rod kept his eyes closed through the entire song and in his mind imagined he was singing in church with Sadie by his side on the pew. The words to the hymn, with their healing power, helped Carla and Will to get through the song. They sang it for their family, and they sang it for Sadie, because it was the last time they could.

That night, Herman and Sarah stayed late with them, mostly just sitting together in silence. Will had gone home with Rachel and Rod was in his room with Jimmy. Val was sitting on the couch beside Daniel, leaning on his shoulder, while Edgar sat in the recliner with another cup of coffee.

Val looked over at him. "Thank you for speaking today, Edgar. I've never heard you tell that story about Sadie and the moon before."

He smiled and replied, "I've never *told* that story before. It was sort of mine and hers, but I thought it was about time to share it."

Margaret took out her handkerchief, dabbed at her eyes again, and with a shaky voice said, "I've never loved another living soul like I loved that child."

Everybody in the room looked at Margaret in unison and said, "We know!"

They all laughed, even Margaret. "You know what I mean."

They nodded and drifted back into their own thoughts, but the momentary laugh was healing.

Jackie stayed late with Carla as well and they lay on her bed listening to music, but not doing much else. Carla rolled over to face Jackie and said, "You know, you were right about Alex." Jackie raised her eyebrows and Carla continued. "*Seriously* this whole thing with Sadie has made me think about a lot of things. Life is short and people just need to surround themselves with people who care about them and love them. Alex obviously doesn't love me. I don't even know if he loves Darlene as much as he does himself. I want to be with somebody who really loves *me*, someone that loves me as much as we all loved Sadie. Somebody who misses me when I'm not there, who would travel to the ends of the earth just to be with me, or stay put right here in little dinky Millsville forever if that's where I am."

Jackie gave her a sad smile. "You'll find that person, Carla. He's out there now somewhere, just waiting to meet you." She sighed and stared up at the ceiling. "I've been doing some thinking myself, and you're right about a lot of stuff too."

Carla nudged her. "Oh yeah? Finally going to change your ways, huh?" Jackie nodded and a tear rolled down her face. Carla frowned and rose up on her elbow. "Hey, are you okay? I didn't mean—"

Jackie cut her off. "It's nothing; I do sad, about like you do backwards."

Jackie got up. "Look, I've been here long enough. I'm going to take off."

Carla stood and they exchanged a long hug.

Jackie whispered in her ear, "Call if you need me. I love you. I haven't told you that enough, but I do, ya know."

Carla nodded. "I love you too."

When Jackie left, Carla reached under the cover, grabbed Sadie's pillow, and held it to her nose to breathe in her scent. She cut off the light and, hugging the pillow tightly, lay down in the dark, wondering why life had to be so sad sometimes. People needed caution lights to warn them danger is ahead, so people could brace themselves, but then again, what could brace a person for a day like today? Even a boxer knowing the punch is coming can take but only so much before his body has had enough. Today, Carla realized she had more than enough and let sleep take her over.

Chapter Thirty-Eight
COMFORTABLY NUMB

THE DAYS WENT by following Sadie's death and the family went through their good and bad moments. They tried to go back to normal tasks because that's what people do. Val wasn't suffering any more than anyone else in the family, but she was having the hardest time not showing it. She was getting there and trying every day to make progress. Everyone was changed in some way by Sadie's passing. Some showed visible signs, and for others, it was more internal.

Will began to hug Val after every visit, which was a little overkill since sometimes he would be at the house two or three times a day, if he was working the fields.

Margaret baked. She baked all of Sadie's favorite cakes and pies. She told Edgar she had known all along he had put Sadie up to the crazy parade of dessert requests. This was her little way of keeping up the tradition.

Val's change was more internal. She vowed to keep her worrying at bay. She had worried about everything with her children. Keeping Sadie close and physically holding her hand had not protected her, which made her realize she could not control or alter her children's destinies.

The first day that Val helped in the field, everyone was worried she would have trouble, but it turned out that the work didn't make her think of Sadie. Yes, Sadie had died in the field, but the field wasn't Sadie. Sadie was on the carport or porch playing in favorite spots, or sitting on her barstool during meals. Sadie was in her room, lying on the floor and coloring, or sitting by Margaret on the pew at church. That's where she was missed.

When they finished working that first day and were cleaning up at the barn, Val looked out across the backfield and noticed one lone bloom standing tall. Will walked over to her side and she said, "I hate seeing a bloom skipped like that in the field. It's like a sore thumb! I'm going to go snap it off and head on home, okay?"

He nodded and Val slowly made her way down to the edge of the field.

When she reached the row and walked toward the bloom, she reached up to snap it off, but something strange caught her eye. A hummingbird was sitting on one of the flowers. Just sitting there. Not buzzing around. Not trying to feed on the flower's nectar. It was just sitting there.

Suddenly, Val remembered what Sadie had said last summer. "If I were a hummingbird, I would sit still, so people could see how pretty I was." Val knew, of course, that Sadie had not reincarnated into a hummingbird, but to her, it was a sign. It was her own personal message from God that Sadie was okay and that she would be too. She needed to quit blaming herself and get back into life. She stared at the hummingbird for several seconds, and the bird seemed to be looking back at her. Finally, it gently flew away and Val was left feeling calm and more at peace. The event didn't miraculously make all her pain go away, but from that point on, it seemed more bearable.

Days later, Rod was talking to Daniel and wanted to know if he and Jimmy could ride to Carolina Beach to do some fishing. Val walked through the room with a load of laundry, heading for the washer. "I think you should go. You need to get back to doing normal things, fun things you love, instead of working all the time."

Rod and Daniel exchanged surprised looks.

Val added, "Just don't drive all that way, fish for hours, then expect to be able to drive back. That's a long way and you'll need to sleep before you get behind the wheel."

Rod nodded, still surprised she agreed so easily. He rushed to call Jimmy before she changed her mind and quickly made preparations to go.

The plan was to leave after lunch the next day, arriving late afternoon. This part of the plan worked. They ate a big lunch, packed a snack for that night, and made great time driving. Blues were running that night and Jimmy and Rod were pulling them in faster than anybody else on the pier. It seemed that no matter which spot Rod chose, that was the place to be. It wasn't even 9:00 and they had their cooler completely full. Everything was still going according to plan.

When they headed out to the truck with their gear and catch of the day, a man carrying a cooler approached them, looking nervous. He walked over and asked if they had any luck tonight.

Jimmy beamed and opened their cooler. "Yeah! Look!"

The man whistled. "Um, wouldn't want to sell them fish, would ya?"

Rod shook his head. "No, we caught 'em. We plan to eat 'em."

The man ran his hand through his hair. "Well, I appreciate that, but I was sort of hoping you boys could help get me out of a bind. I told my wife I was out all evening fishing. I don't think she will believe me unless I come home with something to show. The fish market is closed, and I ... Well, I'm just trying to avoid hurting her feelings, ya know. I don't want to start a fight."

Jimmy frowned and shook his head. "I don't think you should have lied to your wife. Why did you lie about fishing anyway? Most men go fishing and lie about that, saying they were at work. You sort of did it the other way round."

Rod tried not to snicker. Jimmy really was so naive at times.

Rod cleared his throat. "Well, sorry, man. Wish we could help you out, but we've got a good three-to four-hour drive ahead of us to get back home."

The man started fidgeting then pulled out fifty dollars and said, "Look I'll give you fifty bucks for your fish."

Jimmy's eyes grew big. "Wow! Fifty bucks! They ain't worth that much."

Then looking at Rod, he asked, "Are they?"

The man was getting desperate now and was practically forcing the money in Rod's hands. "They're worth that to me. Look, I'll give you the fifty bucks and you boys can go back out and keep on fishing. Your pier ticket is still good, and it's still early in the evening. You drove all this way—why not enjoy it for a little longer?" He was scooping up fish and putting them in his cooler as he talked. His cooler was smaller and couldn't hold all of their catch, but he took what he could, leaving Jimmy and Rod with the leftovers.

When the man sped away, Rod clicked his tongue and shook his head, staring down at the small amount of fish remaining. "I sure would hate to go home with just this little bit of fish, wouldn't you?"

Jimmy just shrugged his shoulders. "But we got the fifty dollars too."

Rod winked. "That ain't the same as fifty fish. What do you say we do what he said and go back out and fish another couple of hours? The way we're bringing them in, it may not even take that long to fill it back up."

That was when the plan went off course. The boys should have packed up then as planned and made the trip home before it got too late and they got too tired. Instead, they headed back out to fish, and although they were still bringing the fish in better than most on the pier, it took every bit of the two hours to get their cooler close to full again. Rod just couldn't bear to leave without making up for the fish he'd sold.

Now, for the second time, they headed out to the truck and packed to go home. They both bought a Pepsi and candy bars before they took off to get a caffeine jolt to keep them from getting sleepy. At this point though, they were wide-wake and didn't think that would be a problem.

They laughed and talked on the way, and it felt really good. They reminisced about playing at the fort and at the Up and Down when they were kids. They talked about having to go out and find jobs when the tobacco crop was done, and they of course talked about girls.

They found a great rock station and would sometimes sing along. The station was in nighttime mode and wasn't playing many commercials, and the boys loved that. Lynyrd Skynyrd, The Rolling Stones, Eagles. It was a regular rock fest.

Jimmy spoke up, "I like this station. You don't have to worry about getting sleepy if you have some songs like this, do ya?"

Rod laughed, but they were both already getting tired and just didn't know it. Soon, the conversation became less interesting and so did the highway. Then the radio station played "Comfortably Numb" by Pink Floyd, an awesome song, and one of their favorites, but its mesmerizing lyrics and melody made the boys just that: *comfortably numb.*

They both fell asleep before the song was half over. Jimmy's head rolled back, resting on the window. Rod still maintained his upright position but was just as gone. Soon, the road curved slightly, but Rod's steering did not. The truck left the paved road on a path of destruction, guided by no one. The scraping sound of metal against metal and splintering wood jolted the boys back to reality, and then all they could hear was their own screams.

Carla jolted upright in bed, gasping. She sat, paralyzed with fear, clutching her chest for several seconds, before her heartbeat returned to normal. Then she felt a calming sensation and steady breathing also returned. She fluffed her pillow hard, almost punching it, and mumbled, "Stupid Rod." Whatever had happened, it was over and he was okay. She didn't even bother to wake anybody else up, but boy was he going to get an earful from her when he got home.

The crashing noise that jolted them awake was a mailbox they plowed over and sent sailing. They were traveling fast, right through the middle of someone's front yard. The next object in their path of destruction was a dog chained to a tree, also in the middle of the yard. It looked scared to death and had stretched its chain taunt. The truck was moving too fast for Rod to stop and the dog was directly in his path. Had the dog stayed close to the tree instead of trying to run, it would have been safe, but as it was, the collision was unavoidable.

Rod and Jimmy screamed, glanced at each other, screamed again, then turned back to the inescapable scene ahead and screamed again. Rod had no reaction time to work with, and even if he had, his choices were not good. Kill the dog or hit the tree—a very large tree.

The last thing they both saw before making contact was the dog's wide eyes looking in their direction. His front paws were kicking into the air as though he was still trying to pull free of the leash and the tree to get out of the way. They both *heard* and *felt* the dog as it collided with the truck.

Rod slowed down and got the truck under control as quickly as possible. When he put it in park, he turned to Jimmy wide eyed and asked if he was okay. Jimmy nodded.

Rod ran his hand down his face, then without looking over at Jimmy said, "I better get out and see what I've done."

Jimmy again didn't speak, but nodded.

Rod got out and glanced at the front of the truck. He let out a sigh of relief when he saw there wasn't any major damage. The truck was old and a few more dents and scraps wouldn't be noticed anyway.

He walked to the other side of the truck and stood staring back toward the yard they had just plowed through. Jimmy got out too and stood by his side, and then they both made their way toward the dog. The dog, of course, was dead. They had smacked him good with the grill and then run over him. They also left huge ruts in a yard that was otherwise tidy. The mailbox was intact, just dented, but the post was in several splintered pieces.

No lights came on in the house and no vehicle was parked on the carport. Rod knocked on the door but no one came out.

Rod scratched his head. "I don't know what to do. Nobody is at home. I hate to just leave."

Jimmy looked at Rod. "We could write a note and say we're sorry. Maybe give them our names."

Rod sounded hesitant. "Yeah, we could, but …" Rod grabbed Jimmy's arm and pleaded. "Look, Jimmy, I *cannot* let Mama find out about this. Do you understand? I mean after what happened with Sadie, if she knew about this, well, she would go completely over the edge."

Jimmy nodded but looked sad.

"So listen. You've got to promise me right now that you will never tell another living soul about this, okay?"

Jimmy nodded.

"I mean it now, Jimmy. Nobody. If you tell one person, then they tell another person, then they tell somebody, and it will wind up getting to my mom. You understand? You promise?"

Jimmy nodded again. "I promise, Rod."

Rod ran his hands through his hair, looking around at the devastation while deep in thought. "Now how can we make this right?"

After surveying the damages, they decided to move the dog and the mailbox over by the carport, so they would be seen right away when the owners got home. There wasn't much they could do about the yard, so they just stomped down some of the divots of grass and ruts they had made.

When they had done all they could, Rod got a piece of paper out of the truck and wrote simply.

WE ARE SORRY. IT WAS AN ACCIDENT … FELL ASLEEP.

Jimmy frowned. "Ain't you going to sign your name, Rod?"

Rod shook his head. "I can't. If they call, Mama will find out." Then it dawned on him. "I know!" He pulled out the fifty bucks the man paid him for the fish and stuck that in the mailbox with the note. "There. That should pay for fixing the mailbox."

Jimmy gave him a concerned look "But what about the dog, Rod?"

Rod just shrugged as he patted Jimmy on the back. "I'm sorry. That's all we can do, Jim. It will be okay. How about you say a prayer for the family's loss and for the dog?"

Jimmy nodded and they bowed their heads. Jimmy began. "Dear Lord, please be with this family, and please don't let them miss this here dog too much. It was an accident and we're both real sorry. I shouldn't've fallen asleep, and we shouldn't've sold those fish, and we should have gone home early." Rod cleared his throat to hurry Jimmy up. "And please, God, take care of this dog. I'm sure he was good dog and he tried real hard to get out of the way. Amen."

Rod was embarrassed to admit it, but he found a little humor in Jimmy's prayer. He thought back to the look on the dog's face as it tried to get away. He tried to imagine what they must have looked like from the dog's point of view.

When Jimmy finished, he still looked as though he didn't want to tear himself away from the dead dog, but Rod eased him away regardless. After they were back on the road, Jimmy turned around and looked on the scene one last time. "Rod why do you think they had that dog chained to the tree anyway?"

Rod thought about it for a second, then the irony hit him, or maybe it was just the fatigue catching up with him, because all of a sudden, it was extremely funny and he couldn't contain his laughter. He laughed with as much dignity and concern for Jimmy's tender heart as he could muster. "Well, I guess, Jimmy, with them living so close to the highway, they had the dog chained up, so he wouldn't wonder out in the road and get run over."

Jimmy didn't seem to find any humor in the situation. Rod tried to stifle his laughter, but every time he thought about it, he got tickled all over again.

Soon, Rod calmed his laughter and Jimmy fell back to sleep. With

Jimmy snoozing Rod was alone with his thoughts. The dog should have been safe and his owners had taken great care to keep him out of harm's way. Just like Sadie.

Life doesn't come with cocoons for protection, nor does it acknowledge safety nets. Life comes with sadness and tragedies, no matter how hard people try to avoid them. Possessions and people we cherish the most can sometimes still be taken away, even when we securely tie them to tree, and even if we are still holding their hand.

Chapter Thirty-Nine
SECRETS

CARLA CAME OUT of the store and was making her way around back where she had left her bicycle. She had just grabbed the handlebars when she heard someone call her name. She looked up to see Alex waving from his car. He jogged over to where she stood, wearing her standard blue-jean cutoffs and tank top with her hair pulled back into a ponytail. She would never know it, but this was how Alex thought she always looked best.

"Hey, glad I caught you. I actually stopped by your house yesterday, but you were in town." Carla nodded. "Yeah, Will, actually cut me some slack this week to run some errands for school. They said you had stopped to say good-bye. That was nice of you."

"Well, yeah, to say good-bye and thank your family for everything last summer and to see how y'all are doing since, you know, Sadie."

Carla smiled. "Thanks. That was kind of you to check on us." After an uncomfortable pause, she asked, "So when are you heading out?"

"In a couple of days. So what's with the bike?"

Carla smiled and shrugged. "I'm just making sure it still works. I was thinking about taking it to use on campus since I won't have a car."

Alex nodded, looking uncomfortable. "I especially wanted to say good-bye to you, Carla. I feel like I owe you an apology, and I have for a long time. I guess I don't have to tell you, but I'm a big jerk sometimes."

Now Carla was the one feeling uncomfortable. She said, "You don't owe me anything, Alex. You never did."

He interrupted and said, "No, I do." He sighed. "Do you ever think about that day at the pond? I mean, before Rod showed up?"

Carla didn't say anything.

"Well, I do. I did every time Darlene and I had a fight, actually." He smiled and then looked at Carla. "I just wanted you to know that you fascinated me from day one. I wouldn't have made it through last summer without you. I don't know why, but I just wanted you to know all that, and like I said, that I'm sorry. I realize now I hurt your feelings."

Carla thought that was the sweetest thing anyone had ever said to her. "Thanks, and it's okay, really. Things turned out like they were meant to."

Alex nodded. "I guess this is good-bye." Then grinning, he said, "Until our class reunion when we're old and gray, that is." He leaned over and kissed her on the top of her head. He whispered, "You'll be the first one I'll want to see." He turned to walk off and she stared after him, watching him drive away. It was a strange feeling, knowing she might never see him again.

Sundays were the hardest for the family. They were all met with a parade of people at church asking how they were doing.

Val had told Daniel once that she never knew what to say. Nothing fit how she actually felt. She was finding some peace in things but still missed Sadie terribly.

There were many times she would even forget Sadie was gone and expect her to walk in any minute, chatting away about something silly.

But when reality hit, she wanted to crawl into a ball and cry. On several nights, she and Daniel did just that when they went to bed. Neither one would say a word; they would just cry themselves to sleep in each other's arms. Sadie was still the first thing Val thought about when she woke in the morning. It was as though she expected to wake up and realize it was only a bad dream.

Outside, Rod and Jimmy were telling Marty and Punchy how they had applied for a warehouse position in town. One of the questions on the application was to list all machinery that they could operate. Jimmy said he did not want to make a bad impression by misspelling anything, so he used the space provided and drew pictures of the ones that he was unsure about the spelling. It gave the interviewers a good laugh initially, but when they examined his artwork, they realized he had talent. They said he didn't qualify for the position he was applying for, but they would like to contract with him occasionally for artwork. Jimmy had been thrilled.

As the men continued to laugh, Charlotte, a young, single mom, walked by with her little boy, Sam. Marty bent down to talk to Sam, but he turned away, hiding behind his mother's leg. She scolded the boy, saying, "Now don't be bashful, especially after Mr. Marty let you ride his horse all afternoon last week." She looked up to Marty apologetically. "I'm sorry I don't know what's gotten into him lately. He's all of a sudden become bashful."

Jimmy bent down to talk to him and Sam went right to him. Jimmy picked him up and walked off, and they were instantly engaged in conversation. Jimmy always connected with the children, probably because he was so childlike himself. They didn't feel as though they were talking to an adult.

Charlotte apologized again.

Marty shook his head. "No problem. You bring him over again soon." His eyes still followed Jimmy and Sam as he continued. "He seemed to really enjoy himself and took to the horses."

She said her good-byes then headed to her car where Jimmy and Sam were whispering. As Charlotte approached the boys, Marty heard her say something about them sharing secrets. He stared at the two intently, scratching his chin.

When Charlotte backed the car up to leave, Marty ran to grab Jimmy. Wrapping his arm around Jimmy's shoulder, he said, "I changed my mind, Jimmy. I will be needing you this week at my place ..." Marty continued to talk as he watched them disappear down the road. Sam's big, brown eyes were staring out the window in his direction.

Chapter Forty

PROMISES

𝒯HE NEXT MORNING, when Jimmy was helping Marty on his farm tasks, Marty asked questions about Sammy, but Jimmy never said anything of any importance. When they finished for the day, Jimmy said good-bye and headed down the drive in his car. Marty drove the tractor down to the lower pasture to grab his hammer. He had left it earlier that day when they were repairing the fence, so when Jimmy turned around at the highway and headed back up the drive, Marty didn't hear him.

Sam told Jimmy that he didn't want to come back to Marty's, but he hadn't said why. He asked Jimmy if he would get his Matchbox cars that he had left inside Marty's house. He told him what room he had been in when he last remembered playing with them. Jimmy went inside and went to the back of the house into a room that looked like a catch-all/ guest bedroom. There were a small twin bed, a desk, and storage boxes that seemed to contain some of Mr. Cleo's old clothes.

Jimmy looked in all the obvious places and didn't see the cars, so he began to be more aggressive in his search. He looked under the bed and in the closet and then began to dig around in the desk drawers. In one drawer was a box of photos, and since Jimmy was so easily distracted, he began to shuffle through them. To his shock, there was several of Mr. Cleo. One, a shot of him posing by the fireplace, looked just like Jimmy remembered him. The next three shots, however, were of Mr. Cleo's body lying on the floor in front of the fireplace. He was in an unnatural position, and based on what Jimmy had overheard about Mr. Cleo's death, he realized these were of the murder scene.

Jimmy didn't like looking at them and didn't know why Marty would want to keep them. He wanted to throw the photos down and run, but he continued on to the next photos. The next few were photos of a young boy. The boy looked familiar to Jimmy, but he didn't know from where. It wasn't anybody from school or church, yet he felt like he should know him. The little boy was sitting on the bed in this very room. Then the next photo was of the same boy, but he was stripped down to his underwear and looked scared.

Why would somebody take this picture? It didn't look like a happy picture to Jimmy. Actually, now that he thought about it, none of the photos were happy. None of the pictures made Jimmy smile or think happy thoughts. They made him extremely uncomfortable and sad.

Then the last photo was of Sam. Sam was sitting on the bed in this very room, just as the other little boy had been. Sam didn't look happy either. Jimmy noticed in his hands were the Matchbox cars he was supposed to be trying to find.

He was just about to resume his search when Marty walked in. He jerked the photos out of Jimmy's hands. "Looks like somebody's a little too nosy for their own good."

Jimmy put his hands in his pockets. "I was just looking for Sam's Matchbox cars. He said he left them in this room."

Marty slammed the drawer closed. "Is that right? What else did little Sammy say?"

Jimmy shrugged. "Just that he wanted his cars back." After thinking a second, he said, "I don't think he wants to come back. He must not like riding, huh?"

Marty reached up over the desk and pulled a box off the shelf and reached in to retrieve Sam's cars. He handed them over to Jimmy who said thanks and started to take off. Marty put his hand out to stop him. "Whoa, there a minute. You don't just walk into somebody's house and ramble through their personal things, Jimmy."

"I'm sorry, Mr. Marty. I was just getting these cars. I didn't mess anything up." Then Jimmy remembered the photos, and making a confused face, he asked, "Why do you have those pictures of Mr. Cleo, and who's that little boy?"

Marty groaned. "See there, that's why you don't go nosing around people's things, Jimmy. All of that is none of your business or anybody else's." Taking a deep breath, he began to explain. "Now those photos of dear, Uncle Cleo were taken by the police department when they investigated his death. I asked if I could have a couple." Then he pointed his figure at Jimmy to emphasize his point. "And now some people would get in a lot of trouble if they knew I had them and we don't want that, do we, Jimmy?"

Jimmy shook his head. "I just wanted a couple. I don't know why. Maybe I thought if I stared at them long enough, I would find some clue that the police missed. You know they never did find the killer, and I just thought I would try to help. Now that little boy is just a family friend of my ex-wife. It's her picture and it just accidentally ended up in my things when I moved. I just haven't tossed it out yet."

Jimmy seemed satisfied with his explanations. "Oh, okay. Well, I got to go now." Marty held him back once again. "Now, Jimmy, like I said, you shouldn't have gone rummaging through my things. Your mama and daddy wouldn't be too happy about this if they knew. Now I ain't going to tell them, but you need to *promise* me not to tell anybody what you saw in here. Like I said, people could get into trouble, and it would be all your fault. Do you promise?"

Jimmy nodded. "Yes, sir. I won't tell anybody. I promise."

Marty smiled and patted him on the shoulder. "Good boy. That's what I wanted to hear. We don't want to upset your mama. Now you head on home and we'll forget all about this."

Jimmy nodded and headed out the front door. Marty followed him outside and stood on the porch. He smiled and waved as Jimmy took off. When he disappeared down the drive however, Marty's grin disappeared. He walked back in the house, slamming the front door. Running his hands through his hair, he began to mumble to himself. "Stupid kid! Stupid, stupid kid! Nothing is going right lately!"

Marty went into the kitchen and swung his arm across the table, sending the few items on top crashing to the floor. He paced back and forth across the kitchen, running his hand through his hair. He continued to mumble to himself. "Okay, just a little bad luck is all. Just a temporary setback. I just have to be more careful is all. Jimmy won't tell anybody. Heck, the kid don't know nothing. He's d-d-dumb. Besides, he *promised*. Jimmy won't tell another living soul if he promised he wouldn't."

Having calmed down now, he ran his hands through his hair slowly one more time, then pulled out a chair and sat at the table. "Yeah, just a little bad luck is all. Just like little Sadie. I mean, how can you explain that tragic accident any other way?" Then drumming his fingers on the table, his eyes glazed over as if in a trance. "Yeah, no other way to explain it; just bad luck and bad timing." He clicked his tongue. "Such a shame too. The day before she was coming to see me. I do hate we never had our little time together." He slammed his palm down on the table. "That's why I rushed things with little Sammy. I have got to slow down and be more careful." He rubbed his chin and breathed more evenly. "Just bad luck, that's all. Just a little bad luck, and luck always changes."

He began to grin.

Jimmy tossed and turned all night. Something wasn't right. Those pictures bothered him. He didn't like seeing poor Mr. Cleo. He didn't like seeing it, and he didn't like not being able to talk about it. It made him sad. The little boy made him sad too. The little boy actually made him feel the saddest, and he didn't know why. He still felt like he must know the little boy. Why else would he keep popping up in his head? Jimmy didn't like feeling like this. No, he didn't like this feeling at all.

Chapter Forty-One
OUT IN THE OPEN

THE NEXT DAY, Jimmy was still bothered and confused. He pondered things that morning while he ate his cereal.

Sarah frowned at Jimmy's serious expression. "What are you concentrating so hard on this morning?"

Jimmy looked up. "I can't figure out where I have seen somebody before. I know I didn't go to school with them or to church ..." He trailed off, still going over where he had seen the little boy.

Sarah smiled. "Maybe you just saw them where they work. That's what it usually is with me."

Jimmy shook his head. "No, they're not old enough to work."

"Maybe you saw them on TV or with somebody else you know." She sighed. "I've got to go to work. Are you working today in tobacco or over at Marty's?"

Jimmy shook his head, still distracted. "Oh, sorry. No, ma'am. Will's taking loads in today to the market, so we have the day off."

She kissed him on the head. "You're thinking too hard. Usually, it will pop in your head when you're deep in thought about something else, so stop thinking about it, and it will come to you." She grabbed her purse to leave and told Jimmy to have a good day.

Jimmy decided she was right and that he just needed to do something to get his mind off things. He called Rod and they made plans for the day. Rod had set up his bull's-eye target and deer dummy in an empty field back behind the house and was doing some bow and arrow target practice that morning. Jimmy decided that was as good a distraction as anything else, so he decided to join him.

They messed around target shooting and goofed off all morning. Rod was an excellent shot and didn't need any practice, but he said it kept his arm loose. The fall would bring in bow season for deer and he wanted to be ready. Jimmy gave it a try with Rod giving him pointers. He had shot the bow several times in the past with Rod, but he just couldn't master the fine art of the bow. His arms wouldn't stay steady and he found pulling the string back extremely difficult. He never even came close to hitting the bull's-eye, and he couldn't bring himself to even take aim at the fake deer.

Jimmy stayed busy the rest of the day while trying to forget the photos, but they just wouldn't go away. He had more questions and something about it told him it wasn't right. If only he could let his brain stop thinking about it for a few minutes, maybe he would remember where he had seen the little boy. For some reason, he was really concerned about the little boy.

The next day at church, the preacher was delivering his sermon when he mentioned the little Peterson boy who had been murdered a few years back. Jimmy didn't seem to be paying attention to the sermon until the pastor mentioned him, and then it all clicked. He shifted abruptly in the pew, which drew attention from his mom. She must have thought he had dozed off and was jolted awake, so she gave him a stern look.

Unfortunately, Sarah wasn't the only one who noticed Jimmy's behavior. As soon as the Peterson boy was mentioned in the sermon, Marty looked Jimmy's way. When he saw his reaction, he knew that something had clicked in that slow brain of his. Marty's hand was now forced and he was going to have to do something about poor Jimmy. He might not have the full picture yet, but even simple-minded Jimmy was going to piece things together eventually. He would have to act quickly, and there was no need to put it off until tomorrow. He would have to cancel his plans with Karen for the afternoon. That was actually a good thing. He was tired of the charade he had to endure by pretending to enjoy her company anyway. She was about twenty-five years older than what attracted Marty, and sometimes it sickened him to pretend otherwise.

After church, it was lunch as usual at Margaret and Edgar's. Following the meal, Edgar was the first to retire to his recliner. The ladies were just starting to clean up the kitchen and everyone else was disappearing in their own directions one by one.

Jimmy was quiet the whole meal, so Edgar motioned to him. "Son, I can tell something's on your mind. What's got you to thinking so hard today?"

Jimmy looked at him, but just shook his head.

Edgar gave Jimmy a sympathetic smile. "Don't let the sun go down on a problem, son. Best to get it out in the open."

Jimmy shrugged. "But what if you can't? What if you made a promise? You're not supposed to break promises, right? But I mean, what if it's something you think you really need to tell, even if it's a secret?"

Edgar nodded. "Well, son, I don't know what the secret or the promise is, but you're going to have to follow your heart. You give it some thought and God will tell you what to do. God tells us in his Word that we shouldn't make promises and not keep them, but he also said we shouldn't have to make promises period. We should just do what is right and let our actions speak for themselves, without our mouths getting in the way."

Jimmy let what his grandpa said sink in and he slowly got up. He looked back at Edgar. "I think I'm going to go target shooting and do some thinking."

"That sounds like a fine idea. You pray about it, son, and you'll make the right decision."

Marty had been watching the house from the woods ever since the Branches came home from church. He had watched as Will and Rachel left to go home and as Carla walked up the drive to their house. His stomach was growling, but he didn't dare leave; Jimmy had to be taken care of today. There was no other way. Then, Jimmy came out alone. He had a concerned look on his face, as though deep in thought. That was a good sign, Marty thought. The boy might still be trying to figure things out. His luck hadn't run out yet; all he had to do now was follow Jimmy. When he got him alone, he would do what needed to be done to make sure Jimmy never talked again.

Rod peeped in the den. "Where's Jimmy?"

Daniel shook his head.

Edgar, who had almost dozed off, said sleepily, "Said something about going out target shooting again."

Rod grinned. "I don't know why he bothers; he would never actually shoot a deer anyway." Rod puffed out his chest and rubbed it. "He doesn't have that natural-born killer instinct like I do."

Edgar laughed at his joking but then grew serious. "Something's eating that boy today. Something about trying to decide if he should break a promise."

Rod perked up immediately. The dog incident! He's going to tell somebody what they did! He immediately excused himself. He needed to go find Jimmy and talk some sense into that boy right now.

Jimmy only fired one arrow and it didn't get halfway to the target. His fingertips and his arms were sore from the target practice the day before, and his brain was exhausted. He plopped down on a log to think. That was why he had come out there anyway. He knew he had to tell somebody about the pictures. His gut was already telling him that. But what if he had waited too long? What if Marty had destroyed the photos? Nobody would believe him. Something wasn't right about the pictures of Mr. Cleo either, and as he sat there, it came to him.

In the first photo of Mr. Cleo, he was wearing the exact same thing as the crime scene photos. The police couldn't have taken that, so did that mean Marty killed Mr. Cleo? How could that be? Why would he do that? Jimmy broke out in a sweat. He had to go tell someone, and he had to go now. He had to find a way for someone to figure this out.

Jimmy rose to his feet only to look up and see Marty on the other side of the field, coming out of the woods. Jimmy froze. Marty had that stupid grin on his face, as he began making his way toward Jimmy. Jimmy knew he should run, but he couldn't.

Marty called out, "Hey, there Jimmy. Doing a little target practice, I see."

Jimmy, not wanting Marty to advance closer, finally found his voice. "Don't come any closer or—or I'll shoot."

Marty laughed out loud. "Come on, Jimmy. Did you hear that line on a movie? We both know how bad you are with that bow, and more importantly, you couldn't hurt a fly, and we both know it."

Jimmy gripped the bow anyway. Marty slowed his pace but kept advancing. Finally, Jimmy yelled again. "Stop! I mean it this time." He shakily got an arrow ready and held it in the bow but never raised it up to shoot.

Marty sized him up and softly said, "You know, Jimmy, we can work this out. I do have some things on my chest that I need to confess. What do you say? You and I head back to the house and we can sit down with your family and have a little chat?"

Jimmy realized then that Marty held something in his hand. It looked like some sort of steel pipe. He could only assume he meant to use it as a weapon.

When Rod approached the field, he was surprised to see Marty there. He hadn't seen his vehicle at the house and he didn't live within walking distance. Besides that, he still had his church clothes on, minus the jacket and tie. He could see that he and Jimmy were engaged in conversation, but something wasn't right. Marty was standing in the middle of the field, out in the open, and Jimmy looked different somehow. Then it dawned on him. Jimmy must be telling Marty about the dog. He picked up his pace and almost broke into a run. Then, all of a sudden, he stopped. What he saw take place next was too much for his brain to process.

Jimmy had picked up the bow and took aim right at Marty. Jimmy, who always slumped slightly, now stood straight. Jimmy, who shook when trying to pull back the string, pulled the string taunt and motionless, aiming dead ahead. Jimmy, who couldn't hit the broad side of a barn, landed his arrow squarely in Marty's left shoulder.

Marty stumbled back momentarily and then raised his other arm, which held what looked like a pipe. He made one step toward Jimmy, and Jimmy, without even looking down, reached behind him and grabbed another arrow, firing a second shot lower, catching Marty in his upper thigh.

Rod ran as fast as he could toward the scene. He stopped before reaching Marty, who had fallen to the ground and was lying on one side, wincing in pain. At least he wasn't dead, Rod thought. He looked at Jimmy, bewildered, but the Jimmy he saw was foreign to him. He was still staring at Marty with an expression comparable to a mama bear protecting her cubs. Jimmy had a third arrow poised and in the bow ready to take aim. He stared at Marty, as though oblivious to anything or anyone else around him.

Rod slowed and walked toward Jimmy with his hands outstretched in front of him, ready to tackle Jimmy and take the bow if necessary. He had no idea what he was thinking and he was prepared for anything. As he got closer, Jimmy was still standing tall and poised to shoot. Rod was still in shock. The bow and arrow was steady as a rock.

"Jimmy? You okay, man?"

When Jimmy heard Rod's voice, he slowly came out of what looked like a trance. He let the bow drop to his side and his natural slump returned. He turned toward Rod as though nothing had happened and in his usual laidback tone simply said, "Oh, hey, Rod."

Rod stared at him for a second, waiting for an explanation. When Jimmy didn't offer one, Rod nodded toward Marty, who was still squirming on the ground. "Need to tell me something, Jimmy?"

Jimmy glanced back at Marty. "Oh yeah. Rod, can you watch him for me? I need to go call the police."

Rod was still in shock and didn't reply, so Jimmy added, "Or do you want me to stay here while you go call?"

Rod finally came to his senses and, glancing back at Marty, said, "I think Marty here might feel safer if I stayed with him, don't ya think?"

Jimmy nodded and started to leave. Before he took off though, Rod grabbed the bow and arrow from his hand and said, "Maybe I should hang on to this for you."

Jimmy smiled and let him take it then began running across the field toward the house.

Rod glanced back at Marty. "You doing okay, man?"

Marty grunted and mumbled something under his breath.

Rod looked back up toward Jimmy, who was now at the far end of the field but still within earshot. "Hey, Jimmy! Make sure you tell them to send an ambulance too."

Jimmy paused, shook his head, and took off again.

Jimmy only had to stay in jail long enough for authorities to find the pictures in question in Marty's house. Marty had moved them but evidently hadn't been smart enough to destroy them. Sarah was worried the whole time Jimmy was in jail, but when he walked out, it was as though nothing had happened. He talked about how nice everyone was and how they let him play cards with the guards. He got a tour of the place like he was on school trip.

The truth was that, after details began to come out about Marty, Jimmy was a regular hero, especially to Ms. Charlotte. Little Sam told the police about his afternoon with Marty, and though the man never actually violated the child, it had definitely been part of his plan. One more afternoon riding the horses and Sam would have been a changed child.

Officers contacted the police department in Charlotte as well and found out other sick details of Marty's former life. It seems he had never been married for starters. There were also several questionable crimes against children in the area that they were very interested in talking with him about. Marty would definitely be going down for Mr. Cleo's murder, but it would take years and the advancements in DNA testing to reveal all of Marty's other evil acts.

Val and Daniel would also never know that had Sadie lived only one more day, she would have been added to the long list of lives ruined by Marty. Sadie had, in fact, been on Marty's radar for a long time, and he had woven a tight web to get her, Jimmy being part of that plan. He looked for children who were ignored or had low self-esteem, but Sadie was so well protected by her close-knit family that Marty found her to be a tempting challenge. It was a challenge that he couldn't resist, and one which ultimately led to his demise. First, he would have taken her innocence, then her laughter, and then he would have taken Sadie completely away, never to be found.

Val and Daniel, if given the choice, probably could not have freely sacrificed their child to save the lives of other children, or even the world. God himself knows the pain of that kind of decision and he didn't put that burden upon them. He simply took Sadie away as painlessly and swiftly as possible, so she never suffered. Then God stayed close to the family to help them heal.

He was holding their hand the whole time ...

Chapter Forty-Two

THE UP AND DOWN

$\mathcal{T}$HE NEXT DAY, Val helped Carla pack for her big move into the dorm. Carla was excited, but with everything that had happened that summer, she had mixed feelings. She caught Val dabbing at tears several times, and even though she would laugh it off, Carla hated to give her another reason to be sad.

That night, a big meal to send her off was planned by the family. Sarah, Margaret, Val, and Rachel worked together to make all her favorite dishes. They reminisced about old times when Carla played nurse at the fort and the Up and Down.

At the end of the meal, Will stood and tapped on his empty tea glass with his spoon and said, "Not to take away from Carla's celebration, but I have an announcement myself, and since we're all here together, this seems as good a time as any."

Everyone immediately glanced toward Rachel with questioning stares. She shook her head. "Oh no! It's not that. I'm not pregnant."

Will cleared his throat and momentarily looked embarrassed. It obviously never occurred to him how his announcement would sound.

Rod looked as though he was stifling a snicker as he watched his big brother backpedal to get back on topic.

Will cleared his throat and started again. "Well, you're looking at the new owner of Millsville General Store."

Cheers and applause broke out in the room. The family began congratulating Will and asking a dozen questions.

Rod nudged Jesse. "You'd better watch out. He'll be trying to buy up the garage next."

Jesse and Will exchanged looks. "Well, actually that's how I had enough collateral to make an offer to Mr. Mills. Jesse here and I are officially business partners. We plan on turning that intersection into *the* place to stop when you come to Gordan Lake!"

Jackie came after the meal to see Carla off and they talked for an hour outside, just like they had done a 100 times. When she got ready to leave, she gave Carla a hug. "Don't let those snooty UNC students change you. You're better than all of them." They cried and said their good-byes.

As Jackie drove away, Carla looked up at the full moon and thought about Sadie and Edgar's story. She felt restless but didn't know what to do other than head back inside.

Carla gave Val and Daniel a hug as she headed through the den and thanked them for giving her a special night, then went to her room. When she walked in, she immediately noticed a note on her pillow. She picked it up. All it said was "Meet me at the Up and Down." After all the joking at dinner, she figured Rod and Will must be up to some kind of special send-off from their old stomping grounds. She slipped her shoes back on and quietly slipped out the front door.

The Up and Down was just to the right of the house, barely a few feet into the woods. As a child, Carla remembered it as being deep in the woods and the gully itself being huge. The area looked different from a child's perspective. The gully was nothing more than a ditch, and not a very deep one. Carla found the tree still marked with the red cross that served as her nurse's station. Jesse was sitting on the ground beside it. He stood up as soon as he saw her and shook his legs out. "Man, I got stiff sitting out here. I thought Jackie would never leave."

Carla smiled and looked around. "Are you the only one out here?"

Jesse nodded and looked as though he was now a little embarrassed. "Yeah, sorry." He reached into his pants pocket and pulled out a present. "I had a going away gift for you and didn't want to give it to you in front of everyone else."

Carla's eyes lit up when she saw the gift. She reached over and gave him a hug. "You didn't have to do that, Jess. How sweet." After she let go, she took the gift and unwrapped it. It was a beautiful heart-shaped pendant made of white gold.

Carla gasped. "Jesse, it's beautiful. You really didn't have to do this. I don't know what to say."

Looking uncomfortable, he pointed at the necklace as she was taking it out of the box. "I know you don't like yellow gold, so I got the white. The clasp is supposed to be a good one too, ya know, so it won't fall off."

She put it around her neck. "It's perfect, Jess. I love it." She reached over and gave him another hug then played with the necklace, still admiring it as it sparkled in the moonlight.

Then a thought came to her, and with a questioning look, she said, "I really do like it, but it being a heart, people might think …"

Jesse stared down at the ground for second. "Think what, Car? That my feelings for you are not exactly the same as, say, Jimmy's?" He looked back up and met Carla's eyes and she knew.

There was a long pause before Carla finally said, "Jess, I don't know what to say. I mean I've known you *forever,* but I've never thought of you that way. I mean, you know I love you to death. You're just like family."

Jesse took a step forward and interrupted her. "But I'm not family, Car." She glanced away, but Jesse kept his eyes focused on her.

Then Carla asked, "But what about Judy?"

Sounding frustrated, Jesse said, "I haven't talked to Judy since the prom." Then throwing his hands up and letting them rest on the top of his head, he closed his eyes. "I don't like Judy. I never did. That was all in your head." He took his hands down, made a step closer, and looked at Carla. "That day when you came in the garage and asked me to take her, you threw me off because deep down, I was hoping you were getting ready to ask me to take *you*." He glanced down, and when he looked back up again, he continued. "And that night when you said I looked so in love dancing with Judy, it was you I was thinking about, not her."

Carla didn't know what to say. "I ... I just ... I mean, how long have you felt like this, and why haven't you said anything?"

Jesse rubbed eyes. "I never said anything because I was afraid to at first. Afraid that you would respond ... Well, exactly like you're doing now. And then, of course, there was the whole Alex thing going on." He gave her a sideways glance "You know you really are pigheaded too, sometimes."

She gave him a scornful look so he sighed and apologized. "Look, I'm sorry. I know I'm hitting you with this out of nowhere." He stepped closer and was right in front of her now. "You want to know how long I have felt this way?" He glanced up at the sky. "I don't know exactly, but I honestly think it started the day you brought food to me and my dad that day after church, when we wouldn't come over to Margaret's for lunch. Me and my dad, we were dying, Car. He was gradually slipping away from reality and taking me with him. You came in talking ninety miles per hour, force-feeding us, and shocked us back into the real world." He reached for her hand and pulled it up to his chest. "Car, I dearly love your brothers and your family, but I wouldn't have practically lived at your family's house all these years if it weren't for you. You were the reason I kept coming."

Carla felt uncomfortable being so close to Jesse. Other than that day at the pond, she had never been intimately close to a man. She had unconsciously backed away and her back was now against the tree. There was nowhere else to go.

He glanced up and looked at the red cross. "I was terrible at playing war with your brothers, especially Rod, but I would sometimes get wounded on purpose so I could hang out at the hospital with you."

The thought made Carla smile. "I've just never thought of you like that, Jess."

She started to apologize, but Jesse grabbed her other hand. He now held both her hands and was leaning close to her. He looked at her and softly said, "Close your eyes."

Carla looked unsure.

He asked, "You do still trust me, right?"

She nodded.

"Okay, then. Close your eyes."

He leaned in until his forehead touched hers. "Imagine the person standing in front of you is somebody else, a stranger, and all you know about this person is that they care deeply for you. He loves the way you care for people, the way you stick to your guns about things you believe in. He loves sitting around playing the guitar with you, and he knew you had a sultry soulful voice way before you hid to sing the National Anthem.

"He also knew how drop-dead gorgeous you were, even before he saw you in your sexy prom dress." He sighed. "He knows everything about you, Car. Like that you can't back up a pickup to save your life, but you can work just as hard as any man." He turned his head slightly to sniff her hair. "He knows that you wash your hair in Gee Your Hair Smells Terrific and will sometimes, when nobody is looking, open a bottle in the grocery store, just to smell it because it reminds him of you.

"This person, Car, loves you so much that he stood by for a whole year and watched you pine over someone else and didn't get in your way." He chuckled lightly. "This person ate a *whole* fruitcake, which tasted *awful,* just so he wouldn't hurt your feelings."

Carla gasped and looked up. "You said you liked it."

Jesse smiled and shook his head. "I actually threw up after the first slice."

Carla's eyes began to fill and she started to say something, but Jesse squeezed her hands and leaned back toward her, so she closed her eyes again.

Jesse breathed deeply and his voice almost cracked when he spoke. "This person, this *man*, Car, loves you so much that he can't imagine his life without you. This person has seen you at your worst, but still wants you to be a part of his life."

When he paused, Carla opened her eyes and looked at Jesse. "I just don't know if I can think of you that way. I—"

Jesse interrupted her and with pleading in his eyes said, "Then don't *think*, Car." Taking a chance and leaning toward her, he whispered, "Just don't think."

She couldn't break away from Jesse's gaze, and when he leaned down and his lips met hers, she didn't try to break free from his embrace. So there at the Up and Down, Carla received her first real kiss. It was deep and passionate but gentle. Jesse broke away once, just long enough to read Carla's face, then wrapping his arms completely around her, he kissed her again. Carla's arms slowly reached around Jesse as well, and she finally let go and allowed herself not to think.

Val came down the hall and into the den and sat back down in her chair. Rod had just come in and plopped down in the middle of the floor with a bowl of ice cream. As she sat, she asked, "Rod, do you know where Carla is? I thought she was in her room, but she isn't. I could have sworn that's where she went when Jackie left to go home."

Rod nodded and put another big spoonful of ice cream in his mouth. Talking with his mouth full, he said, "She's at the Up and Down kissing Jesse." Rod was always a master of sneaking up on people and he had slipped up on them unnoticed. But he left when he saw the two embracing.

Val looked shocked. "What do you mean? *Kissing!*"

Rod wrapped his arms around toward his back and made smacking sounds. "I mean just that—kissing."

Daniel snickered.

"But Jesse's like family."

Rod and Daniel exchanged glances and laughed. Daniel smiled. "I love that boy like one of my own, but that boy ain't ever thought of Carla as a sister." Rod nodded in agreement.

Val still looked confused. "But Carla, I'm sure, doesn't like Jesse in that way."

Rod laughed. "I hear tell it only takes one person to start to doing the liking."

Val gave him a stern look, realizing he was using her own words against her. Glancing at Daniel, she asked, "How did you figure things out and I didn't, Mr. Smarty Pants?"

Daniel rubbed his stomach. "Well, my dear Watson, it stands to reason that when a young man hangs around a home as much as he did and there is a pretty girl in the picture, after a while, statistics will prove that eventually he's coming for the female companionship and not the male bonding, or the fried chicken."

Rod laughed. "But you still do have the best fried chicken. It's just, you know, man can't live on chicken alone."

Val could not believe she could've been so blind. She sat there trying to wrap her brain around it until tears formed in her eyes.

Her only little girl really was growing up.

The next day, Jesse came over to help Carla load her things. He had volunteered to take her to campus and help her move in. Val wanted to go, but Carla said she didn't want to say her good-byes at school. When it was time for her to leave, Daniel and Val walked her out to the truck. Jesse stayed by the truck while they said their good-byes.

Daniel hugged her first and told her was proud of her, and then Val took her turn. After Val hugged her daughter, she cupped Carla's face in her hands and through her tears said, "You're still my little girl and always will be. I know you may have felt as though I forgot that, but I never did." She hugged her again and told her she loved her.

Carla climbed in the truck beside Jesse and rolled down her window.

"Ya know, I'm only twenty minutes away. It's not like I'm going to the moon, or that I won't be coming home practically every weekend." She waved and then Jesse drove her away.

Val and Daniel stood there until the vehicle was out of sight. Without looking at Daniel, Val said, "I'm glad Jesse is taking her. It would be harder on her with us blubbering in front of her new friends."

Daniel responded without looking at Val as well. "Yep. And her new friends wouldn't have enjoyed those three hundred statistics you rattled off earlier about germs and mishaps on college campuses either." She turned and looked at him with tears in her eyes. He wrapped his arms around her and whispered, "We're going to be all right, Val."

She nodded. "I know. I know."

Epilogue

WILL SAT BEHIND the register and was steadily ringing up customers. Without looking up, he asked, "Will that be all?"

"No, actually. I was hoping you could tell me what happened to the quiet little store that used to be here?"

Will looked up. "Alex, oh my gosh!" He nodded for one of the others to take over the register and walked around to shake Alex's hand. "Man, it's good to see you. How've you been?"

"Can't complain, although I still do." Alex looked around at the store. "You know, I just can't believe this place. I heard you took the place over and that the lake traffic was doing okay, but jeesh. You have your own little city here. They need the change the name to Willsville, not Millsville." Will laughed. "Just giving the people what they want. What brings you around?"

Alex explained that they were visiting Darlene's parents, who had taken the kids out on the lake in their boat. He and Darlene had run up to the store to grab a couple of things for lunch. "Darlene's in here somewhere; place is so big I lost her."

They chatted for a few minutes and Alex asked about the family. "They're all doing well. You just missed Rod. He was in town last week for a few days. I can't keep up with him these days."

"Yeah, I've been seeing his picture plastered on the front of all these hunting and fishing magazines. He's doing pretty good, huh?"

Will laughed. "Yeah, I still can't believe he's made a living out of that. Killing that record bear a few years back made it all happen. Do you know they actually pay him to use certain rods and reels or wear certain boots?" Will snapped his finger. "You should walk over to the shop. I think I just saw Carla pop in over there with Jesse's lunch. She usually brings him something over every Saturday. They'd both love to see ya."

Alex thanked him and shook Will's hand again before heading over to the shop.

When Alex opened the door to the garage, he heard the usual shop noises as men worked in the bays. The shop was triple the size of its former self with several employees. He had only stood there a second or two when he heard a female voice from a back office say, "I'll get it. You go ahead and eat."

Carla stepped out of the office and Alex smiled his Colgate smile. She was just as beautiful as ever and exactly how he pictured she would look. She was dressed in faded jeans, tennis shoes, and a T-shirt. She was still the farm girl from his past.

She ran over and hugged him. "Alex!" He hugged her back, and when he released her, Jesse appeared from the back room. He was holding a half-eaten sandwich. He walked over and reached to shake Alex's hand. "Good to see ya, man."

Alex nodded. "Thanks, man, you too. I like what you've done to the place."

Jesse nodded. "Yeah, Will's about to work us to death. We're doing good, but he's one pushy business partner."

Alex laughed.

They had been there catching up for a few minutes when Marcus came in the front door, so the handshakes began again. He had stopped by to put up his campaign posters in the shop window. He had turned into quite the little politician and had helped Will in the past getting things done in the community.

The three stood there for several minutes catching up, each telling about their kids and their jobs. Alex asked about Jackie and Carla said, "Jackie's doing very well. She lives in Virginia now, but she always stops by when she comes home to visit."

The shop phone rang and Jesse excused himself. He shook Alex's hand again. "Good seeing ya, man. Take care."

Alex nodded, and when Marcus finished putting up his poster, the three walked outside.

Alex looked out at the busy road while shaking his head. "I never thought Highway 46 would be four lanes."

Carla laughed. "Dad says all those years of telling people from Raleigh to go to Millsville Store and turn around were a jinx. Because of the four lanes and median, now that's the only way you can get to them."

Then a little girl about five years old came running out the door yelling, "Mama!" She ran to Carla and grabbed her leg. "Can I go in the store now to get my ice cream? I finished my lunch." She was still chewing and had crumbs around her mouth.

"In just a minute, sweetie." Carla reached down and wiped her daughter's mouth. "And this would be our youngest, Lizzie."

When Carla looked up, she saw the look of surprise on Alex's face. He stared at Carla and she gave him a knowing smile. "I know. She looks just like her. I guess I don't have to tell you how spoiled she is. I don't know who's worse: my parents or Edgar and Margaret."

Then Darlene walked up, looking just as beautiful as ever and just as possessive. She slid her arm through Alex's. "There you are." She looked over at Carla and Marcus. "Well, what do you know? Hello, Marcus, Carla. I see you haven't ventured far from home." She looked around. "The place has changed though. I guess I can see the attraction."

Carla smiled. "Yeah, no place like home." Lizzie kept tugging at her leg, so Carla excused herself to take her back inside, saying her good-byes. Darlene told Alex she would be in the car and left as well.

Marcus pointed back toward the shop. "Don't let Carla fool ya.

She's probably got more stamps on her passport than I have campaign promises."

Alex raised his eyebrows. "Really?"

Marcus leaned against the shop window. "Yeah, she's teamed up with some doctors who go to some of these third-world countries and have free clinics. She goes on about two or three trips a year, and you know Jesse is about as henpecked as they come. He don't let Carla go nowhere that he don't tag along. He can fix anything that has an engine, so they always put him to work on something while he's there too. They're quite the little team, actually. They even do some fundraisers down at the church every year to fund their mission trips. Let me see. What do they call it?" He rubbed his chin and then snapped his fingers. "I know. It's called Sadie's Crescent Moon Ministries. Spreading a little light in a dark world."

Marcus shrugged and reached for Alex's hand. "Well, got to go, man. Good to see ya." He and Alex shook hands and Marcus left. Alex was ready to do the same when Carla came out of the shop, holding Lizzie's hand. The girl had a freshly washed face and his bet was they were heading over to finally get that ice cream. They stood there for a second and Alex said, "Well, I need to be heading off. It was good to see you, Carla. I was hoping I would. You didn't show up for our class reunion."

"Yeah, couldn't make it. I was out of town." Alex smiled, thinking that she was probably even out of the country. He couldn't get over how good she looked, and he thought that he would, indeed, be completely henpecked too.

He looked at her and smiled. "You really do look great, Carla."

She returned his smile. "Thanks. You too."

He started to say something else when he heard a horn blow. He cringed. "That would be Darlene."

They both laughed. He reached over and gave Carla a hug and said good-bye. As he walked away, he hesitated and turned back around to look at her one more time. "Still the most fascinating."

Jesse came out of the shop and rested his hand on Carla's back, rubbing it slightly as they watched Alex get in the car.

"You okay?"

She looked at him and smiled. "Perfect."

"Your heart's not going pitter-patter?"

She turned to face him and put her hand up to his cheek. And before she kissed him, she whispered, "Every single day."

CPSIA information can be obtained at www.ICGtesting.com
Printed in the USA
BVOW01s1804101114

374445BV00001B/2/P